FRONTIER
SOLDIER

FRONTIER SOLDIER

High Meadows Series - Book 3

CONNIE SEIBERT & SANDY MAXWELL

authorHOUSE®

AuthorHouse™
1663 Liberty Drive
Bloomington, IN 47403
www.authorhouse.com
Phone: 1 (800) 839-8640

Published by AuthorHouse 04/06/2015

ISBN: 978-1-5049-0439-1 (sc)
ISBN: 978-1-5049-0440-7 (e)

Print information available on the last page.

To our friend who just turned
ninety-four years young. Your Sweet Spirit has
blessed us more than you know.

Betty Turner

Chapter 1

"**H**EY, JOE, THE DOC wants to see you in his office right away."

Joe McCall looked up from the chart in his hand. "Thanks, Sam." He finished writing on the chart then slid it into a slot at the foot of the bed he was standing by. Looking at the wounded soldier in the bed, he gave him an encouraging smile. "I'm glad you're doing better, Clay. You might be out of here soon."

"What did you do this time to make the doc mad, Joe?" The patient in the next bed grinned up at him.

"He probably didn't sweeten the doc's tea just right this morning," a voice piped up from across the room.

"Tell the doc we need beef steak for supper tonight. This soup fare is getting old."

The good-natured teasing came at Joe from several different beds that were lined up on both sides of a long rectangular building that was part of the De Camp General Hospital on David's Island. The hospital was on the western end of Long Island Sound in New Rochelle, New York. It was set up to care for the hundreds of men who had been wounded during the civil war. Most of the men were in fairly bad shape by the time they arrived from the battle grounds. They lay on their beds, some suffering quietly, some not so quietly. Some didn't make it through the first night of their arrival. Despair seemed to settle around the beds as they struggled to heal, inside and out. Thus, Joe and Dr. Mitchell overlooked a lot of the loud grousing and bawdry jokes that echoed through the ward as a form of entertainment. Or diversion.

Joe grinned easily at the men. "I'll tell him, but it'll probably do as much good as it did to tell him you want pretty nurses to give you baths and tend your wounds."

There was little privacy in the buildings at De Camp Hospital. At the entrance of each building a room was on either side of the door. One was for supplies, the other was an office used by the doctors. Joe knocked on the office door, then quietly slipped inside.

"Come on in, Joe, and have a seat for a minute. I need to finish signing these papers, and then I'll be right with you." Dr. Terrance Mitchell kept writing as Joe took a seat in front of the rickety metal desk where the doctor sat. He finished with the papers then rubbed his eyes and looked up at Joe. "What can I do for you, McCall?"

Joe ducked his head to hide a grin, pretending to rub a smudge off the toe of his shoe then straightened in his chair. "You sent for me, sir?"

"Oh, yes, I did. I remember now. I seem to lose track of what I'm doing these days."

"It's no wonder, with the schedule you keep, sir."

"We all have impossible schedules with all the wounded that have been coming in. The last count was one thousand eight hundred. Everyone keeps saying this cursed war can't last much longer, but I don't see it coming to an end anytime soon." He leaned forward and fixed Joe with a tired stare. "That's what I want to talk to you about."

Joe saw the older man's shoulders slump with fatigue and wondered if he had already missed something in this conversation. He hesitated, then asked, "You want to talk about the end of the war?"

"No." The doctor leaned back in his chair. "I want to talk about the end of your army career."

Joe scratched at his mental reserves, wondering what the doctor was trying to get at. He shrugged. "I don't understand, sir."

"Do you know you technically are not part of the army now?"

Joe thought a moment. "No, I guess I didn't realize my time was up."

"Two weeks ago your tour of duty ended."

"Oh. But of course I want to stay and help. They'll let me stay on and continue working with you, won't they, Dr. Mitchell?"

"They will *beg* you to stay, I have no doubt about that. You're a hard worker and have made a name for yourself here. But..." He leaned forward again, studying Joe's face for a few moments before he announced, "I have other plans for you."

"Sir?" Joe shifted in his chair. He couldn't keep the surprise out of his voice. "I can't imagine what that would be, Dr. Mitchell."

The doctor rose, clasped his hands behind his back and began to pace the short length of space behind his desk. "Where do I start?" he murmured to himself. For a few moments the doctor was lost in thought.

Joe watched the man he had come to know as mentor, father, and friend. He was very much aware of the weight loss, pale features, and dwindling stamina that had plagued the doctor the last few months. But Dr. Mitchell had refused to talk about his own health. When Joe brought up the subject of him taking more time to rest and care for his own needs, the doctor would brush it off saying he didn't have time to lay around and rest.

The doctor stopped pacing and stood behind his desk. "I guess I should apologize first."

"For what, sir? You haven't done anything to apologize for. At least not to my knowledge."

The doctor lowered his chin and peered at Joe over the top of his spectacles. "You may feel differently after you hear what I have to say."

Joe was baffled. Nothing came to mind. No slight, no cross word, nothing. "I guess you better just tell me then."

"Do you remember the day you were brought in with that nasty leg wound? That was one of the best things that has happened to me since this crazy war started. After you started healing, you began helping me with the other wounded men and I knew right away you had something special. You were meant to be a doctor, Joe. There is strength and gentleness in your hands that's needed for surgery. When we had to amputate that man's leg the other day, I know you saw the tremors in my own hands and you offered to take over. I watched you tie off those arteries and stitch him back up and I tell you...it was a work of art."

Joe reddened at the elaborate praise. "Hardly that, sir."

"I tell you, it was! That's why I've arranged for you to train with a doctor in Washington."

Joe stiffened and stared at Dr. Mitchell. He tried to say something but words escaped him. Before he could regain his composure the good doctor continued.

"Do you remember the meeting I went to last week? I was with the doctor who came to teach on new procedures that he's using in surgery. I invited him to stay with me at my house in town. I've never met a more brilliant doctor. I told him about you and how gifted you are and how you've memorized every medical book I could get my hands on for you. Anyway, after a little persuasion I convinced him to take you as a student. His name is Dr. Abraham Kline and he has a teaching program at University Hospital. He takes four young doctors as students for a year. They have to have two years of training or experience before he will even consider them. You don't quite have the two years, but you're close enough. Also, you will be joining his students in the middle of the year.

"The only reason he agreed to my proposal was one of his students dropped out who didn't perform to the doctor's high standards. I'm afraid he'll be rather hard on you until you prove yourself."

It was Joe's turn to stand and pace across the narrow room. He finally voiced his concern. "Why would you put me in such an impossible position, Dr. Mitchell?"

"It's not impossible. I *know* you are up to this challenge. Now tell me you'll do this and make me proud. Surely you know I've come to think of you as a son. I'm already as proud of you as any father could be."

"Thank you, Dr. Mitchell. And you know how much I think of you, but can I have some time to think about this? It's an awfully lot to consider."

"Yes, you can have until six this afternoon." The sage old doctor looked at Joe intently, a half smile on his lips, determination lighting his eyes. "I want you on the ferry that leaves then. You'll stay at the Hotel Benton tonight and leave in the morning on a coach headed for Washington. I have it all arranged. Once you get to Washington you'll need to find a room close to the University Hospital to live in. They can probably direct you to a place close enough for you to walk."

"This is so sudden!" Joe raked his fingers through his hair and shook his head. "I feel like you're trying to get rid of me."

4

"You know better than that, Joe. As a matter of fact, I'll be on that ferry with you. I'm leaving New York. Going to sell my home in town and go west."

"Honestly, sir? What's in the west for you?"

"I have a sister who lives in Pennsylvania. She's all alone now so I'll be going to live with her."

Joe nodded as he studied the doctor for a long time. Finally, he sighed in resignation. "I hope you don't mind my asking, but... I was just wondering . . . if you don't want to answer, I'll understand, but can you tell me what kind of illness you have? You know I've noticed things, symptoms and all."

"Yes, I knew I couldn't keep this from you for very much longer, so you might as well know now. I have a cancer growing in my abdominal region. Another doctor has confirmed it. There's nothing that can be done so don't put too much thought into it. I'll check into the hospital close to my sister when the time comes. They know me there and will take care of me."

"I really hate to hear that, sir."

"Thanks, Joe, but if you'll finish your training with Dr. Kline and pass his tests, I'll feel like I've accomplished something that will continue on when I'm gone. Will you do it, Joe? I like the sound of Dr. Joe McCall."

"I don't know if I can do what you're asking, but I'll do the very best I can to make you proud of me."

"Like I said, I'm already proud of you. You can hang your sign anywhere you want right now, but I really think this next six months will be a great benefit to you in the future."

"It can't help but be so. I need to know the cost of the schooling, since I have limited funds."

"Son, it's all taken care of. You just show up for training in a week and I'll be a happy man."

"Sir! Dr. Mitchell, how can I ever thank you?"

"By being at the ferry tonight at six o'clock. There's another matter I need to discuss with you but it can wait till this evening. Now, go pack your bags and say your goodbyes and I'll see you at the landing."

Late that afternoon Joe and Dr. Mitchell boarded the ferry, making their way to the inner part to get out of the cold air. "Let's sit in those seats away from everyone so we can talk," the doctor said, leading the way. They found it was relatively quiet around them so the doctor got right down to the subject that was on his mind. "Remember the young lady I took in a couple of years ago? Miss Abigail Bedford?"

"Yes, I've met her. She came in all the time looking for her brother. He joined the army at the beginning of the war and now seems to be lost. She's really good with the soldiers, always cheerful, and, I must say, was quite helpful at times. If I remember correctly, you hired her to cook and clean for you at your house in town."

"Yes, you're right, I did hire her. But more to help *her* than anything. She has no one but her brother. She's the other good thing that happened to me when this ridiculous war started and I've grown quite fond of her. When I sell my house and leave for Pennsylvania she'll be out on the streets with no one to look after her." Dr. Mitchell paused and let that information sink in.

"Wait a minute, now." Joe shifted nervously in his seat. "Is this the other matter you wanted to discuss with me? Why do I have an uneasy feeling about this?"

"Because, Joe. I want *you* to look after her."

"Now listen, Dr. Mitchell. You know I can't do that. It would be quite inappropriate for a single man like me to be looking after a young lady."

"Oh, pshaw!" the doctor said, waving off Joe's concern. "I'm not asking you to move in together. I've made arrangements for her to also go to a school in Washington, to train to become a nurse. A woman I know there went to Dorthea Dix's school for nurses but she felt the rules were too rigid and has started a school of her own. Abby would be too young to go to Dorthea Dix's school anyway since she would have to be at least thirty-five. Mrs. Cranston has accepted Abigail and she will live with Mrs. Cranston and the other students at the school. I believe the school is actually Mrs. Cranston's home. All I ask of you is that you check in on her once in a while and see that she is doing all right."

"Well, I guess there wouldn't be any harm in that. I hope you gave her a little more notice of your plans for her life than you did me. I think you enjoy arranging other people's lives," Joe said, giving his mentor a sly grin.

"Just the two most important people in my life, is all. Actually Abby doesn't know yet. I'll talk to her tonight and she'll be on that coach in the morning. I'm afraid she's going to fight me on this but I'll *insist* she go.

And I don't want her to know how sick I am or she'll just try to follow me. She doesn't need to feel obligated to take care of me. I'll have all the help I'll need and probably more than I want." Dr. Mitchell was quiet for a few moments then looked into Joe's face. "Do you understand what I'm asking you to do?"

Joe nodded. "I think I've got a clear picture of it, but do you understand how hard it'll be for me and Miss Bedford to ride out of your life tomorrow? I don't think she'll like it any more than I do."

Dr. Mitchell looked away from the young man he had grown to love and tried to blink back the inevitable tears pooling in his eyes. He failed, for when he looked again at Joe McCall, tears ran down his face. "I know. I really do understand how you must feel, but it's the way I want it, Joe. Please honor me in this."

Joe couldn't respond with words. He was so choked up by his own emotions that he just scooted closer to the old man, put his arm around his shoulder and wept with him.

Chapter 2

"WELL, NOW, AREN'T WE a pair, Dr. McCall?"

Joe McCall was startled to hear Abigail Bedford's voice. She had hardly said a word since they had left the Benton Hotel. Joe and Abigail shared their coach with only one other man who had acknowledged them when he first climbed aboard but had kept to himself for the first leg of their journey. Joe judged him to be a businessman, around thirty years old. He appreciated the man's quiet demeanor for he felt sure his own mental state would keep him from attempting any polite conversation. At least any that would make sense.

Miss Bedford stared at Joe, waiting for his reply. He focused on the scenery out his side window, wondering what had prompted such a comment from a seemingly proper young lady. Finally, he glanced at her. "I'm not sure I understand what you mean, Miss Bedford. *Are* we a pair?"

"We are a pair of noodle brains, as my mother would say." She fidgeted with her reticule for a bit before laying it on the seat beside her.

"Noodle brains?" Joe honestly didn't know what else to say to such a strange combination of words. Maybe he had overestimated the prim Miss Abigail Bedford.

"Yes, *noodle brains*," she went on. "I don't suppose Dr. Mitchell gave you any more warning than he did me about his great plans for our future. He just came in yesterday evening and told me to pack my things. While we ate supper together he told me where I was going. I was so shocked, I just got up, packed my bags, and got on this coach this morning. Just like he told me to." She sighed deeply and stared out the window. "Noodle brain. That's what I am."

"I would think you would be pleased to be taken care of. The doctor is helping you to prepare for your future, not trying to make you into a… noodle…anything."

"That's why you're a noodle brain too, Dr. McCall." She turned in her seat to face him. "Look at me. I'm not a child that needs to be taken care of. I'll be twenty five years old before too long. For a year now I've been traveling alone all over the country searching for my brother in every military hospital I could find. I'm now sure he must be dead." Abigail paused for a moment as the pain of loss flickered in her eyes. "I know if he were alive, I would have heard something from him by now. Nothing would have kept him from finding me. I was in need of money when the doctor offered me the position of housekeeper and cook. I've come to love that silly, old manipulating man as much as I did my own dear father."

"I think he loves you as a daughter, too. That's why he arranged for you to go to nursing school."

"Of course I know that. But it was wrong of him to decide my future without consulting me. I have no desire to be a nurse. I have seen enough devastation of the human body in all the hospitals I've visited to last me a life time. I'm afraid it will haunt me for the rest of my life."

Joe considered her confession with no lack of sympathy. "May I ask then, Miss Bedford, what *do* you want to do with your life? Unless, of course, it's too personal a question, and if so, I would ask that you forgive me."

Miss Abigail Bedford took a calming breath. A mischievous smile spread across her face as she uttered one word and one word only: "Cheese."

"*Cheese?*" Joe repeated, almost in a whisper. He stared hard at her wondering if, at last, she had lost her mind. *Noodle brains, and now cheese. Indeed!*

Their fellow passenger made a rather strange noise. Something between a cough and a laugh. Like he couldn't quite make up his mind which one to do. The sound came out like he'd strangled himself.

"Are you alright, sir?" Joe looked at him, concerned.

"Yes, yes, quite alright," the man assured him. He was red faced, however. "Sorry to have interrupted your conversation. Please...do continue."

Joe watched him for a few moments. *Strange man,* he thought. *As a matter of fact, this whole conversation is strange. My total life has become strange.* Frustration threatened to silence him altogether but he turned his attention back to Abigail wondering if it was worth it to continue. He eyed her skeptically. "Now, did I hear you correctly? Did you say, *cheese?*"

"Yes, you heard me correctly." She crossed her arms defensively. "And don't laugh. I'm very serious."

"No, I wouldn't think of laughing." Joe wanted nothing more than to burst out in a tension-relieving belly roar. Of course he restrained himself. "But really now, would you please explain why you want to make cheese a part of your life? Maybe I'm a noodle brain after all, but for the life of me, it makes no sense as far as I can determine."

"It's really quite simple," she said, relaxing a little. "I was raised on a dairy farm. We had all the milk, cream, and fresh butter a person could want. Oh, and my mother? She made the most wonderful cheese! She learned how from her own mother. We experimented all the time making different kinds of cheese. I guess it got in my system because I still dream of all the cheese I would like to experiment with. We sold our cheese back then but that's as far as we got before my mother and father died and this *stupid* war started! Mother and I never got a chance to do anything about our recipes."

"I'm truly at a loss for words, Miss Bedford. I promised Dr. Mitchell that I'd take the responsibility to see that you are doing all right at the nursing school. I don't think that school is going to help you in your career choice of making cheese, though. Maybe you should change your mind and continue with the plans to be a nurse. I'll help you get settled when we get to Washington. You'll see, it'll work out fine."

Abigail stiffened, looking straight ahead. "I'm not going to Washington."

Joe was stunned. "What are you going to do then? Where will you go?"

"When we get to Philadelphia I'll find a way to get to Lancaster."

"What's at Lancaster? What will you do there?"

"I'll find Dr. Mitchell's sister. Don't look so worried, Dr. McCall. I release you of your promise to Dr. Mitchell. You don't have to worry about me. I'll find my own way. I have been corresponding with Grace Fielding for some time now. That's his sister, you know. She told me all about his diagnosis and that he's dying. I'll go there and help her take care of the doctor until he needs to be put in the hospital. She's in poor health herself and will undoubtedly need a lot of help. I'll write the school and see that the doctor's money is returned, then take care of him and his sister. Somehow, I'll find a way to make my cheese. Don't you worry. I'll figure it out."

"It sounds like you've made up your mind but I don't think the doctor is going to like you changing his plans and showing up at his sister's place."

"He'll fuss and carry on a bit, I'm sure. But I think he'll be happy to see me. I'll just tell him to rub his mad and get glad." Abigail giggled at the thought.

Joe nodded, thinking a while. "Does it make *me* a noodle brain if I still train in Washington like our good doctor planned for me?"

"I suppose not. Actually I think it would break his heart if you didn't go and train with Dr. Kline. Don't you want to work with Dr. Kline?"

"Yes, I really do. I'm extremely nervous about it, but I'm determined to work hard and finish the training."

"You will do wonderful, Dr. McCall, I have no doubt."

"I hope you're right. But, I insist you let me make arrangements to see you safely to Lancaster. I don't know how safe it'll be to travel in that direction now."

For the first time, the other passenger opted to join the conversation. Joe and Abigail both turned toward him as he voiced his unsolicited opinion. "It's not safe at all for a young woman to travel alone in that direction."

Abigail didn't give Joe time to respond. "Who are you and how would you know it's not safe?"

Before he could answer, a shot rang out and the coach lurched, throwing Miss Bedford into the arms of the stranger.

"Are you all right?" he asked while trying to right himself and set Miss Bedford back on her seat as the coach plunged forward.

"I'm so sorry, sir! I hope I didn't hurt you."

"No, not at all. I'm fine. I wonder what that…." He stopped mid-sentence, shocked that Miss Bedford had produced a pistol that looked rather large in her small hand. She sat searching out the window for someone to shoot. No other shots were heard so the coach began to slow to a less neck-breaking speed. The two men then exchanged puzzled looks and the stranger burst out laughing.

"What's so funny about being shot at!" Abigail demanded.

"Nothing, so please forgive me," he managed to say around his laughter. "It struck me funny that here I was telling you it's not safe for you to travel to Lancaster and you're the only one here that was ready to defend yourself. Where did you get that pistol?"

"My brother gave it to me when he left to go in the army. I know how to use it too." She tilted her chin, with an air of importance.

"I have no doubt you could end the war with that pistol," said the stranger. "*If* ladies were allowed to join in this crazy war."

Abigail bristled. "Are you making fun of me, sir?"

"No, I think you're wonderful! As a matter of fact, I think I'm in love with you and the answer to *your* dreams."

"Before you propose don't you think I should know your name," she said with adequate sarcasm.

Joe couldn't believe what he was hearing. "Wait a minute!" he interrupted. "I don't think it's proper for you to be talking to Miss Bedford like that. We don't even know you."

"Hush, Joe," Abigail scolded. "He is the first man to ever declare love for me and I'm anxious to hear why he thinks he loves me and is the answer to my dreams." She looked boldly into the stranger's eyes. "And if he gets out of hand…I'll just shoot him."

The stranger let out another peal of laughter. In-between outbursts, he told Abigail, "You are the most interesting woman I have ever met!"

"But, sir, we have *not* met," she said with cool calculation.

"Let me remedy that right now. I am Timothy Sutton." He extended his hand to her. "And I already know you are Miss Abigail Bedford and your traveling companion is Dr. Joe McCall."

Abigail looked at his hand and guardedly put her own into his. "I'm pleased to meet you, Mr. Sutton." A little smile worked its way onto her lips.

Joe shook hands with the man and was promptly ignored as Mr. Sutton and Miss Abigail turned all their attention on each other.

"Miss Bedford, I have learned this day you are a woman with intelligence, strength, and integrity. All qualities I admire. And if I may say so, a very *pretty* woman with intelligence, strength, and integrity."

Abigail felt heat rise into her cheeks. "You may say so and thank you. Now *why* do you think you are the man of my dreams?"

"Because, Miss Bedford," he paused for effect, "*I am cheese!*"

"Explain yourself, please, Mr. Sutton." Abigail narrowed her eyes, but her smile broadened in anticipation.

"My brother has a large dairy farm out of Harrisburg. I live close by and Frank and his wife have talked me into going into the cheese business with them. We are building our first cheese barn, as we speak, and will be finished before long. I would love for you to share your ideas with me."

Joe felt suspended in time, in a place where he didn't belong as his two traveling companions talked on and on, up until they stopped for the night in a small town. At the boarding house they ate a good supper and slept fairly well, then had breakfast before continuing on to Philadelphia.

The man who rode shotgun on the coach told them at supper that an old duffer in the hills had fired the shot they'd heard. He said they never see him and he never hits anything. They long since decided the old man just doesn't want anyone stopping and fires a warning shot to run off any would-be intruders.

As the stage rumbled along the next morning, Abigail told Joe what her plans were. "Joe, Mr. Sutton has invited us to stay with his aunt in Philadelphia tonight. He told me that Lancaster is indeed under threat of the confederates and they are preparing the town in case of attack. He brought his mother and aunt to Philadelphia to stay with another sister of theirs until the threat is over. I will be staying with them until it's safe to travel. Then Mr. Sutton will take me to Lancaster to find Dr. Mitchell's sister."

Mr. Sutton looked at Joe. "I think it would be a good idea, Dr. McCall, if you spent the night with us too. That way you can see Miss Bedford will be well chaperoned and taken care of. I promise to take good care of her."

"Your aunt may not appreciate you inviting strangers to spend the night."

"You needn't worry about that. My mother and both my aunts will be delighted to have you and Miss Bedford. Aunt Leslie has a large house

13

and she loves to receive company. So what do you say? Will you stay in Philadelphia with us?"

"If you're sure it will be all right, we'll stay. I'll feel better leaving Miss Bedford if I meet the women in your family."

"Good! You both will have a grand time with my mother and aunts. They're all very entertaining. Just don't let Aunt Iris talk you into playing cards with her. She'll take all your money and not have a bit of sympathy for you."

Everything Timothy Sutton said was true. They had a grand time with Mr. Sutton's mother and two aunts. Aunt Leslie, as she insisted on being called, was a wonderful hostess and when Joe left the next morning she invited him to stay with her anytime he was in Philadelphia.

"Thank you, Aunt Leslie. I've certainly enjoyed myself and will look you up if I'm ever in town again. This will probably be the last good time I'll have for a while. I've been told Dr. Kline is a hard task-master, so I'll have my nose to the grindstone for the next six months."

"I'm sure you'll do fine and make a wonderful doctor. We'll take good care of Miss Abigail, so don't you fret over her."

"Thank you for that. It does ease my mind to know I can tell Dr. Mitchell she is in good hands." Joe turned to Abigail. "Miss Bedford, would you walk to the coach with me, please? I would like to speak to you for a moment."

Joe and Abigail walked to the waiting coach. He turned to face her and looked her in the eye. "I need to know that this is what you want to do, Miss Bedford. Are you sure?"

"I am *positive*, Dr. McCall. I'm wondering if God had this planned all along. It seems like a dream come true for me."

"Very well, then. If something happens, wire or send a letter to the University Hospital. I don't know where I'll be staying, so that would be the best way to get in touch with me. I would like to hear from you and know how you're doing."

"I'll write when there is news to tell. Thank you, for being a friend, Dr. McCall. I'll be waiting to hear good news from you too. Goodbye, Joe."

As Joe settled in for the ride to Washington, that feeling of being suspended in time and space returned to him. The coach jostled its way out of town as Joe brooded over his situation. *What have I gotten myself into? I guess there's nothing to do but go forward and find out what's in store for me. God, please help me.*

His thoughts abruptly staggered when he realized that for the first time in a long, long time, he had called out to God for help. It caused him to think back to his father who had dragged him to church when he was growing up. A longing for family took root in his heart and stayed with him throughout the rest of his journey.

Chapter 3

"HEY, JOE, YOU AWAKE?"

"Yeah, I'm awake."

Joe lay in the darkness after he and his roommate had turned in for the night. The weeks and months had seemed to fly by, and here they were practically at the end of their training. They had stayed up late, as usual, studying and comparing notes from the day's activities. He was tired, but sleep hadn't caught up with him yet. He waited for his roommate to continue speaking.

"You know, Joe, I still can't believe how tough Dr. Kline is! I wouldn't have passed that last test if you hadn't helped me study. I just wanted to say thank you."

"You've already thanked me, Harrison. Besides, I wanted to pay you back for all the help you gave me when I first came here."

Harrison snorted softly. "I wouldn't have given you a snowball's chance in hell for those first couple of months. Dr. Kline was so hard on you, it didn't seem fair. Now, if it had been *me*, I'd have told him off and left the school!"

Joe chuckled. "I was warned he might do that. Dr. Mitchell told me he was a brilliant doctor but might be hard on me until I proved myself."

"Well, you've done that! I think you're his favorite student now."

"I don't know about that, but I've learned more from him than I ever dreamed possible. I didn't know anything about women's health issues when I came here. Working in an army hospital doesn't give you any experience with the fairer sex."

"I can imagine that's so. My father says women come in three categories. Those who come to you with the slightest hint of a pain or problem. They love attention. Then those who don't want to see a doctor and will wait until their problems are advanced. They don't want any *man* to touch them, even if he is a doctor. Then there are those who fit into the category of sensible. He doesn't think there are too many in that group."

The room was quiet for a while. Then, "Joe, you still awake?"

"Yes, Harrison. What's really on your mind?"

"I was wondering what you're going to do when we finish our training. You know we've only got two more weeks. Are you going to stay in Washington?"

"That's the one thing I do know for sure. I will *not* stay here in Washington. Someday this place may amount to something, but right now it's not very appealing to me." Joe was thoughtful a few minutes before he continued. "I really don't know what I'm going to do, Harrison. There are times when I feel I don't belong anywhere. I suppose you'll go back to Philadelphia and join your father's practice?"

"Yes, that's the plan. He has a good practice and also has big plans for expanding. He wants to build a clinic that will serve a wide range of people, from the poor to the wealthy. The war has slowed the progress on his plans, but it can't last forever. He wants to take on several other doctors besides me. And that gives me an idea. Why don't you come to Philadelphia with me and meet my father? It'll give you a place to start."

"Thanks, I'll think about it. It's nice of you to ask. Let's get some sleep now. I've got floor duty in a few hours, then a surgery tomorrow morning. I'll be observed and graded on my work. You need to get some sleep too. Don't you have a surgery in the morning?"

"Yes, but I'm not too worried about it. It'll be easy compared to your surgery. Be sure and think about going with me, Joe. I'd be proud to work with you."

"Thanks and goodnight, Harrison."

Joe lay and contemplated the conversation with his roommate. He'd been fortunate to share a room with Harrison Brighten. He had gotten along with most of the other men that Dr. Kline was teaching. Except one, who seemed to resent Joe for coming into the program late and then excelling, only to be admired by the others and Dr. Kline.

I don't guess there's anything I can do about that. Lawrence won't have to put up with me very much longer. I'll be gone. But to where? God help me know what to do with myself.

Loneliness overwhelmed him as he lay looking up at the dark ceiling. He had gotten a letter from Abigail Bedford a few days ago. She wrote that Dr. Mitchell had died. She said the good doctor was proud of Joe and begged for word of his progress. Then he would brag on Joe to anyone who would listen.

Joe got a lump in his throat thinking about his old friend. He had to smile into the darkness, though, when he thought of the news that Abigail and Timothy Sutton were going to be married. *It looks like she's going to get to make her cheese after all.*

The next two weeks passed in a whirlwind of activities and duties. The last day of training arrived, and with it, a special dinner for the men who had completed their study with Dr. Kline. All of the hospital staff that could be spared were invited. Some of the men had family and friends who attended. There was a presentation of certificates that Joe wasn't expecting. When his name was called, he went to the front where Dr. Kline handed him a rolled up paper tied with a blue cord.

"Congratulations, Dr. Joe McCall. I expect to hear great things about you in the future. Dr. Mitchell was right about you. You were born to be a doctor. It is a great gift that God has given you."

"Thank you, Dr. Kline. It has been a privilege to learn from you."

Joe went back to his seat and while they finished giving out the awards, he unrolled the paper. It was a certificate of completion, awarded to Joe McCall for his studies and work at University Hospital. His eyes smarted with unshed tears. *How can I hang this on any wall? It's a big lie!* Harrison interrupted Joe's self deprecating thoughts.

"Joe, congratulations, we did it!"

Joe stood to greet his roommate. "Congratulations to you, too, Harrison."

"My father surprised me this morning. I didn't know he was going to come, but here he is! I'm glad you can meet him now." Harrison turned to the distinguished looking gentleman standing beside him. "Father, this is the man I've been telling you about, Joe McCall. Joe, this is my father, Dr. David Brighten."

The two men shook hands. "I'm glad to finally meet you, Dr. McCall. Harrison has told me good things about you."

"It's nice to meet you too, Dr. Brighten. Wow! How are you two going to handle having *two* Dr. Brightens in the family?"

"We'll figure something out," the elder Dr. Brighten laughed. "What I want to know is, are you going to go to Philadelphia with us tomorrow? I can tell you there is plenty of need there and we can definitely use more doctors."

Joe looked from the older doctor to his son and saw sincerity in the invitation. "Yes, sir, I would love to go back to Philadelphia with you and Harrison. We can talk about your ideas and see what we think might be worked out. Do I need to make arrangements for transportation to Philadelphia?"

Harrison spoke up, "No, it's all taken care of. Father has hired a carriage and driver to get us back home. Now let's get something to eat. There is some mighty tasty looking dishes on the table." The older man was already moving toward the food-laden tables.

Being introduced into the Brighten household was like being thrown into a tornado. Joe was surprised to find out his friend had five sisters! The two youngest girls were not married and were drawn to Joe like bees to honey. The three sons-in-laws tried to keep a number of grandchildren corralled but they ran amok about the house anyway. Everyone accepted Joe like it was the normal course of events. His only reprieve came from being put up in the house next door where Dr. Brighten made his clinic. Harrison proudly showed Joe the house where he would be working with his father. Joe was impressed with how the Brighten family had fixed it up. The main floor had a pleasant waiting room, two examination rooms, and a larger room for surgeries or more complicated procedures. The large kitchen was used for storage and washing instruments.

"We're also going to put a desk in here so that father and I can do any paper work we may have," Harrison explained.

"It looks like this will work just fine for you and your father, but how could you work another doctor into your practice?"

"We'll work it out, Joe. I'm not worried about that. Father has big plans and is quite impressed with you, you know."

"He's a good man and you have a wonderful family."

"Thanks, but I have to warn you about Carolyn and Penny. They think you are about the most handsome man they've ever seen. Especially Carolyn. She's the one that just turned eighteen."

"Penny is quite young to be thinking of beaus, isn't she?" Joe smiled thinking of the pert fourteen year old Penny.

"Don't let her hear you say that. You'll break her heart."

"I promise she won't hear it from me."

"I'll take you upstairs now and show you where you'll be staying. There are four rooms up there. We've fixed a couple of them for families of patients who may need to spend the night." Harrison led Joe into the first room at the top of the stairs. "You should be comfortable in this room," he said.

"Very nice. This will be just fine. I'll go get my things and settle in. Your mother did say supper would be ready in about an hour, right?"

"Yes. You can use the back door to come and go. Don't worry about locking it." Harrison pointed to the bed. "Aha! Penny has been here."

It took Joe a minute to see the clues. He laughed when he spotted an apple and two pieces of candy on the pillow. "How do you know it was Penny?"

"I know because she's my sister and that's exactly the kind of thing she would do. She must have it bad to give you *two* pieces of her favorite candy. I bet you'll find they're peppermint."

On the way down the stairs, Harrison informed Joe that the family would all be going to church in the morning. "We'd like it if you would go with us."

Joe found he liked the idea and readily agreed. "I'll be looking forward to it, but will you wake me in time to get ready?"

"You've got it. I'll be over to get you for breakfast or you can just come on over to the house when you get ready. I'm sure someone will be up and around."

It had been a good while since Joe had been in church, so when Sunday morning dawned bright and beautiful, his spirit soared. He walked with the family the four blocks to a pretty white church with steeple and bells chiming. He relaxed and began thinking maybe he'd found where he belonged.

The congregation was lively. They sang with gusto, prayed with sincerity, and the preacher preached with passion. He spoke on a man's walk of faith, reading from the eleventh chapter of Hebrews. Finishing his sermon, he challenged his people: "Are you a man walking in faith with the Almighty?" He was a small man but when he lifted his voice it echoed throughout the room and through the walls to the world beyond. "But without faith it is impossible to please him, for he that cometh to God must believe that he is, and that he is the rewarder of them that diligently seek him." The room fell silent as he said softly, "Are *you* God's man, walking in honesty, integrity, and faith, no matter the consequences?"

The message had a powerful impact on Joe. He knew he didn't fit the description of a man of faith. *I want to be that kind of man, God,* he prayed during the benediction. *Show me how I can be that kind of man. Only you know what it will cost me to walk with you in honesty, integrity, and faith.*

Joe didn't have time to meditate any further. People swarmed to greet the Brighten family and meet the new doctor. Penny, who had managed to sit next to him while Harrison sat on the other side, took delight in introducing Joe to their friends in the congregation. He was surprised to find Aunt Leslie waiting to greet him.

"I'll have to admit I'm quite put out with you, Dr. McCall," she scolded. "You came back to town and have not been to see me."

"I just got back to town yesterday, Aunt Leslie. I'm a guest of Harrison Brighten and his family. I can assure you I was going to visit you as soon as I could."

"I'll forgive you this time. The Brighten family is wonderful. Does that mean you will be working in Philadelphia?"

"I'll have to wait and see, but, yes, I am considering it."

"Fantastic! I'll be in touch to set up a time for you to come have supper with me. By the way, did you hear about Abigail and Timothy?"

"Yes, I had a letter from Abigail filling me in on all the news."

"It's wonderful to have a young lady of her caliber join our family. She is delightful and our Timothy is so in love with his Abigail, it's just fascinating to watch them together. I must go now. It's good to see you again. I'll be looking forward to visiting more with you."

The Brighten women prepared a wonderful Sunday dinner. As they were finishing up their meal, Mrs. Brighten asked Joe, "Did you sleep well? Is there anything you need in your room?"

"The room is wonderful and I slept better last night than I have in a long time. Especially after eating the nice, juicy apple and those peppermint candies that were left on my pillow."

All eyes turned to Penny, and she blushed prettily. "I'm glad you enjoyed it," she said, ducking her head for a moment.

"Well, thank you, Penny. It was a considerate thing to do," Joe told her.

Mrs. Brighten started clearing the dishes from the table. "Why don't you men go to the living room and talk while we clean up in here."

"Good idea," Mr. Brighten said. "We can discuss what we're going to do in the next few days. I'd like to show Joe around town if we don't have too full a schedule of patients in the morning."

"Aren't you a dreamer," Mrs. Brighten said to her husband. "Mondays are always a busy day and you know it. Remember not to schedule anything for Wednesday evening." She turned to Harrison. "Your father and I are taking the family to dinner at the Golden Palace to celebrate you finishing school. They are having a wonderful art exhibit there. Anyway, I've heard it's quite wonderful. I don't remember his name, but there is a new artist who excels in western art, whatever that is. And, of course, you must go with us, Joe."

"Thank you, Mrs. Brighten. I wouldn't miss it for the world. I'll need to shop for some appropriate clothing, though. I'm afraid I would be out of place in my old worn out things. The Golden Palace sounds like a fancy restaurant. Maybe Harrison can direct me to a good place to shop."

That night when Joe excused himself to retire a little early, he went to his room and stretched out on the bed. There was a bible on the small table beside the bed. He picked it up and searched until he found the book of Hebrews, then read the scripture passage the pastor had used for his sermon that morning. *It would cost me dearly to walk as a man of faith. Honesty? I've lived a lie for several years now. If I did what I should, I could go to prison…or be hanged. Do I have that kind of courage? God, I really want to be a man that pleases you. Help me know what to do.*

Chapter 4

"OH, JOE, YOU LOOK so handsome!"

"Thank you, Carolyn. You look quite beautiful, yourself. Purple definitely looks nice on you." Joe had gone shopping with Harrison and felt presentable for the ritzy Golden Palace where the family was going to dine. Mrs. Brighten was especially excited about seeing the art exhibit on display at the restaurant.

"Are we all here?" Dr. Brighten asked when they had gathered at the front door.

"Except for Mother," said Penny, "but here she comes."

Mr. Brighten turned toward the staircase and beamed as he watched his wife descend the stairs. "I hope you children appreciate the fact you have a beautiful mother."

All eyes were on Mrs. Brighten when she stopped near the bottom of the stairs. She held a black doctor's bag in each hand. "Would you do the honors, David?"

"Of course, my dear. Harrison, Joe, this is a gift from the family." He offered a bag to each of the young doctors.

Harrison was especially animated as he took the bag from his father. "This is great! Thank you, Mother and Father, and you, too, sisters."

"You're welcome, son."

Joe held back. He was surprised at being given a gift and a little embarrassed.

"Don't be bashful, Joe," Dr. Brighten said, extending the shiny black bag in Joe's direction.

Joe tentatively reached for the bag. "I don't know what to say. I wasn't expecting a gift, much less one like this. It looks very expensive. You shouldn't have done this on my account."

"Well, we wanted to do it for you, Dr. Joe McCall *and* Dr. Harrison Brighten." He smiled proudly. "You'll find them stocked with everything a doctor might need in an emergency."

"Thank you very much. I'll treasure this special gift. If you'll wait a minute, I'll run it over to my room."

"Oh, no you don't! A doctor needs to carry his bag with him at all times. You never know when you might need it. Mine is already in the carriage. Now, let's get loaded. We'll have to snuggle up to get us all in, but that just makes it more fun."

While they waited to be seated at the restaurant, Joe looked apprehensively at the elegant, glittering dining room. The chandeliers especially intrigued him. "Harrison," he said quietly as he nudged his friend, "I think I'm out of my element here. I've never been in a place like this."

Harrison smiled. "Don't worry, you'll do fine. We don't do this very often. It's my mother's idea for us to get a bit of polite society once in a while. I've learned it's best to just relax and be myself, so follow my lead and enjoy this night. We might not get a chance to do this again for a long time."

"If you say so. Just don't let me embarrass myself...or your family."

They were seated at one of the bigger tables that had been reserved for them. Joe, again, had that sense of being suspended in a time and place where he didn't belong. But as the meal progressed, he realized he had relaxed and was enjoying himself. The three ladies were delightful and entertaining as they commented on the food, the small orchestra, the elegant décor, and the important people in the room.

Mrs. Brighten asked their server where the art exhibit was located. "There are several large rooms down the hallway that's to your right. You will find the art exhibit in those rooms, ma'am. I found the artist to be quite talented and I'm sure you will enjoy meeting the young man. He is truly fascinating."

Dr. Brighten stood. "I'm going to take Harrison and Joe to the lounge. You ladies go on and we'll join you in a bit."

The men found comfortable chairs around an ornate fireplace in the lounge. They drank coffee from small cups on fancy saucers and David Brighten lit a pipe. A number of men came over and spoke to the Brightens. Harrison was introducing Joe to one of these acquaintances when Penny came rushing into the room.

"Joe, you have to come look…." she began breathlessly, but was gently held at bay by her father.

"Penny, what are you doing in here?" he quietly reprimanded his daughter. "This is not a place for a young lady. Where is your mother?"

"Sorry, Father, but she's the one who sent me to get Joe. She said to bring you and Harrison too."

Harrison apologized to the man he was talking to. "Excuse us, please, Edgar. It seems we have been summoned." He smiled sheepishly. "We have to keep our ladies happy, after all."

"That's quite all right. Maybe we can visit another time, Dr. McCall."

"I'll look forward to it, sir," Joe said.

Penny grabbed Joe's hand and tugged. "Hurry, Joe. You've just got to see this picture."

"What kind of picture is so important that you have to drag us away from our friends?" Dr. Brighten scolded. "And, I must say, *rudely* drag us away."

Penny stopped and stared up at Joe for a moment. "It's a picture of him."

"Penny, who do you mean? Who is *him*?"

"It's a picture of Joe, Father."

Joe chuckled at the concentration on Penny's face. "I don't see how it could be me, since I've never had my picture painted."

She was still studying Joe's face when she seemed to make up her mind. "I'm sure it's you, Joe. It looks just like you."

"Well, take us to it, daughter. Let's find out about this mysterious painting."

Penny led the three men to a room that was decorated in varying shades of blue. Pictures hung on all the walls with a select few displayed on tripod stands in the center of the room. "Over there, by Mother."

Penny led the way and stood by her mother and Carolyn. Mrs. Brighten turned and looked quizzically at Joe then back to the painting.

Harrison was the first to speak up. "Penny's right. That is you, Joe."

The oil painting was titled, Frontier Soldier, and was a perfect image of Joe. The man in the painting wore a soldier's uniform and stood by a river next to his horse. He had short black hair and a thin mustache that traveled down the sides of his mouth to a goatee, just like the one on Joe's face. His hazel eyes seemed to be looking at the sunset on the distant mountains.

Sounding a little breathless, Carolyn said, "You look so...I don't know...*lonely*, Joe."

As they stood staring at the picture, a masculine voice came from behind them. "It seems you all like my picture of the Frontier Soldier."

They turned as one to face the young man with the deep voice. He was tall and muscular, with sandy-brown hair, a captivating smile, and dressed in western cowboy clothes. An audible gasp escaped from Penny as she took in the striking figure. He made eye contact with Joe and an astonished looked passed over his face then quickly changed to a brilliant smile. "Well, I'll be! If it isn't the Frontier Soldier *himself*! I think the name is McCall? Joe McCall, if I remember correctly."

The artist held out his hand and Joe responded by shaking the offered hand. "I don't think I ever heard your name," said Joe.

"My name is Aaron Trinity. You do remember when I made a sketch of you and your horse a few years ago?"

"Yes, I remember that day. It was the day that a rancher decked Major Silcot. The men talked about that for a long time. But how in thunder did you end up here in Philadelphia?"

"It's a long story," Aaron said.

Joe felt a tug on his sleeve. He looked down at a dreamy-eyed Penny. She batted her eyes at him and he knew immediately she wanted to be introduced.

"I want to hear that story, but I need to introduce to you the Brighten family first." He made the introductions and didn't miss the fact that he had lost the attentions of Miss Penny Brighten.

"I love your paintings, Mr. Trinity," she gushed. "I would love to be an artist like you." She flashed a charming smile at Aaron.

He was polite but unaffected. "If I was going to stay in the area I would teach you what I know."

"Are you going to leave?" Penny's face was sudden victim to a frown.

"Yes, I'll be leaving in a couple of days. I've been here for nearly two months and I'm more than ready to head home."

"Where is home?" Mrs. Brighten asked.

"In the Dakota territory, where I painted this picture."

"If I remember it right, you weren't going to do anything with that sketch you made of me," Joe accused amicably.

"I couldn't resist putting you on canvas. I got an invitation from Mr. Princeton, who owns a gallery here in Philadelphia, to do an art show here. He saw some of my paintings at the home of a rancher, Dalton Chandler, and invited me to show off my western art here in the east. He said that other than the war, all people talk about is going west. If you'd like, I'll walk with you and tell you about some of the other paintings."

"Yes, we would like that very much, Mr. Trinity." Joe fought to control his emotions. The name Dalton Chandler evoked terrifying memories and Joe wanted to run from the room. He struggled to remain calm.

"Please call me, Aaron. *Mr. Trinity* makes me feel old."

"All right, Aaron, show us your pictures."

The family was ushered on a tour of the three rooms where his paintings were displayed. They were fascinated by the room filled with wildlife settings of the west. One was a picture of a doe and her two fawns standing in a beautiful spring meadow. "That's right in front of my home," Aaron explained. "This next picture is the lake behind our house. I just happen to be there at the right moment to sketch the geese taking flight. The elk in this next picture were hard to catch. I sat for two days waiting for them to come to the back meadow close to the lake."

The men were impressed with the horse paintings, especially the one titled *Diablo*. "That big, gray stallion belongs to my brother-in-law, Paul. The other is a wild mustang stallion who brought his herd to our back meadows. I've called this next picture, *Victory*."

The group was silent while they studied the two pictures. Finally, Joe said, "You did a wonderful job on these. I can almost feel the heat of the battle between the horses."

"Thank you," Aaron responded. "That's the best compliment I could ever get from anyone."

"You must truly live in a little bit of heaven," Carolyn sighed. She was looking at a picture of a white haired toddler sleeping on a blanket in a meadow covered with colorful wild flowers.

"It's probably the closest thing to heaven on this earth," Aaron told her. "That's Charity Myers. Her mother is Angel Myers. She married a young rancher who lives down the mountain from us."

"Have you been able to sell any of your pictures?" Dr. Brighten asked.

"Yes, quite a few have been sold. Mr. Princeton is going to sell the others for me. I've donated ten to be auctioned off at the fair here in your town this spring. The money will be used to help pay for the military hospital that's being built here."

"That's very generous of you, Aaron," Mrs. Brighten complimented.

The family saw pictures of buffalo, antelope, and a painting of an especially dangerous looking rattlesnake. "Oh, how awful!" Carolyn said while taking a step backward. "It looks so real, like it's going to strike at you any moment."

Aaron laughed. "Actually, it was quite dead when I made a sketch of it. I just made it come alive while painting the picture."

"You certainly did a good job of it," Carolyn said sharply. "I'm ready to go to another room!"

Aaron laughed again and led the way to a room across the hall. "This is my favorite room. It's filled with paintings of the people I've come to know and most of whom I love."

In the center of the room on a tripod, was a large picture of a young woman sitting on a rock watching a flock of sheep. A huge, white dog lay at her feet and a smaller, black and white dog sat close by keeping an eye on his mistress. Blue skies, a prairie stretched out before her, and looming mountains in the distance, made for a tranquil scene.

Penny asked, "Do you know this girl?"

"Yes, absolutely. She's the girl I hope to marry this summer. I haven't seen here in close to two years."

Disappointment was in her voice, but Penny admitted, "She's a very pretty girl."

"Her name is Bonita. Her Indian name is White Flame."

Carolyn was shocked. "Indian name! She has an Indian name?"

"Yes. It's a long story, but the name was given to her because she has a fiery spirit. She's Basque. Her family was sheepherders who came to the area where I live to find pasture for their sheep. Everyone in her family was killed by a Sioux war party. She hated Indians for a while until she met some of our Arapaho friends."

"You actually have Indian friends?" Harrison asked.

"Yes, there are pictures here of some of them. Over there is one I titled, *Indian Maiden*. When I sketched her she was taking care of an old Indian woman who was dying. They called the old woman Grandmother. Willow was sitting in front of the tepee playing a wood flute and making the most beautiful, haunting music I've ever heard."

Mrs. Brighten had wandered to another painting. "Who is this? The title says *White Cloud*. Is that an Indian name, too? She *can't* be Indian, she's way too fair, but she's dressed like one."

"That's Angel Myers, Charity's mother. You saw Charity in the other room. A Ute chief gave Angel the name White Cloud Medicine Woman, because of her white curls and her healing abilities. Her doeskins were given to her by the Cheyenne when she helped a sick girl in their tribe. White Cloud and her friend saved the grandson of a Ute Chief, so the chief named the friend Princess Warrior because of her bravery. The story goes that a couple of bad men beat the chief's grandson and stole his rifle. Princess Warrior shot and wounded one of the men and chased them off. Then stood guard while Angel, White Cloud, patched up the Indian boy."

"Mother," Penny called, "over here is a picture of Princess Warrior. She's beautiful!"

They made their way to the picture of a young woman on a reddish brown horse. She was all western, from her cowboy boots to the top of her black cowboy hat that had an eagle feather in the band. Her long black hair was pulled back from her face showing off a pair of clear blue eyes. "She *does* look like a princess, doesn't she, Mother?"

"Indeed, she does know how to sit on a horse and look royal at the same time. I wonder if she knows how to shoot that rifle she's holding."

"I can vouch for that," Aaron answered. "She saved my father's life by killing a grizzly bear that was after him."

The ever curious Penny asked, "What does the M M on the rifle stand for?"

"Another long story, I'm afraid," said Aaron, "but the shortened version is that it was her brother's rifle. She likes to carry it to remember him. They were very close and it was extremely painful for her when she found out her brother was killed by rustlers. His name was Michael Mayfield and hers is Maxine. She married Paul Miles, so her name is Maxine Miles now, the same initials that are on the rifle."

The family moved on to the last of the paintings. No one noticed that Joe couldn't seem to tear himself away from the image of Princess Warrior. Tides of emotions swept over him as he stared at the beautiful face. Each wave that hit grew stronger and ran deeper as he struggled for control. He felt he was going to drown in the sea of hopelessness that threatened to lay him out flat. He blinked back tears when a hand lightly landed on his shoulder.

"You all right, Joe?"

"I will be in a minute, Aaron. Would you have time to visit with me tomorrow?"

"Sure, I'll have all day. The only thing I have to do is be back here for the evening exhibit. It's the last night for my showing. Then I'll be leaving the next morning."

"Harrison and I are going to visit one of the military hospitals in the morning. Would you like to go with us? I'll help you get ready for the evening exhibit when we get back. What do you say?"

"That would be great. I don't know anyone here except the gallery owner and he's busy all the time. So if I won't be a bother I'd be glad to go with you."

"Good. I'll be looking forward to our visit."

Before Joe turned from the Princess Warrior, he reached out and gently touched the face on the painting.

Chapter 5

ARRISON PULLED THE BUGGY up to the front of a long barracks-type building set quite a distance from the main hospital.

"What are we going to do here, Harrison?" Joe asked.

"This is where the wounded confederates are housed. Most of the doctors have their hands full, so they've asked me to come out and check on the conditions in there. Some complaints have been made and need to be checked out."

Joe turned to Aaron. "It may not be pleasant in there, Aaron. You can stay out here if you'd like."

Aaron nodded but said, "I'll go on in with you. If I can't handle it, I'll come back out."

Unpleasant was not the word to describe the place. *Horrific* was better but even that word was barely adequate. Harrison glanced around and immediately took charge. "Joe, you check the men on that side of the room. Be sure and note anything you see that needs attention. I'll check the beds on this other side. Aaron, you can wait here, or follow one of us. It's up to you."

"I'll be fine. You two go ahead," Aaron answered.

About thirty minutes later there was a commotion at the last bed on Joe's row. Someone was shouting, "I don't want no blasted Yankee doctor taking care of me! I'll take care of myself!"

Joe shook his head in disbelief. The belligerent prisoner could not be more than fourteen years old. Joe went immediately to the last bed where the so-called orderly was berating the young soldier. "What's the problem here?" Joe demanded. He glared at the orderly then at the boy.

"I was just telling this dirty rebel that he better behave himself when you come to check him out. He's been nothing but trouble and if he don't be good I'll send him on to the prison whether he's healed or not."

"I'll take care of this. You can go back to your duties," Joe said with an air of authority.

"Yes, sir," the orderly responded as he turned away.

Joe looked the boy over, noting the dirty face and filthy, ragged clothing. A soiled bandage was wrapped around his left leg. Joe's gaze traveled to the boy's face again and to his unruly red hair. A look of desperate determination lit his eyes, his mouth set in stubborn defiance. "What's your name?" Joe asked softly.

If looks were lethal, Joe would be a dead doctor. The boy gritted his teeth and glared. "What's it to you? You don't care about me none. Why should I tell you my name?"

"I would simply like to know. Are you ashamed of your family name?"

"No, I ain't ashamed!"

"Then tell me your name," Joe prodded the boy.

"It's Trinity. *Rand* Trinity. And my pa was the best man on this earth…until he got killed."

The name Trinity surprised Joe and from the corner of his eye he saw Aaron making his way toward them. "That's quite a coincidence, since my friend here has the same last name."

"What're you talkin' about?" the boy scowled.

"Like I said," Joe answered patiently, "this is Aaron Trinity."

Aaron moved to the opposite side of the bed. "I think I'll finish checking out these other men," Joe said. "Why don't you and Aaron visit a few minutes until I can get back here."

Rand and Aaron took a few moments to size each other up, then Aaron spoke. "You said your last name is Trinity? What was your father's name?"

"You tell me first." Rand jerked his chin up a notch. "My pa never told me about no Aaron Trinity."

"That's because your pa probably didn't know about me. But my father's name is Scott Trinity. Did your pa ever mention a brother named Scott?"

Rand's eyes narrowed to slits, the belligerence firmly in place. "What you going to do about it if he did?"

"I really don't know," Aaron answered truthfully. "My father told me I had an uncle named Randal. I think they called him Randy."

Still suspicious, the boy soldier asked, "What's your pa look like?"

Aaron shifted, stuffed his hands in his pockets. He peered down the length of the barracks thinking about his answer, then looked back at Rand. "He looks somewhat like me, but dad has told me that I look a lot like my uncle Randal and my grandfather."

Rand gave Aaron another scrutinizing look then settled back on his bed. "You favor Grandpa more than my dad."

"You *know* where your grandfather is? I wish I could meet him!"

"That'd be hard to do since he died a while back." Rand closed his eyes against his misery. "I don't have no family now."

Aaron realized all that belligerent behavior was Rand's fear and anxiety lashing out at the slightest provocation. His heart swelled with compassion and he had the strongest urge to hug the younger boy to himself. "You have me and your uncle Scott. We're your family. Sounds rather funny doesn't it? Makes us cousins though."

Rand's eyes came wide open. "You mean you're not ashamed to have a cousin that's a rebel?" he challenged.

"No, I'm not ashamed of you," Aaron smiled at him. "I'd like to help, but I don't know how. Why were you fighting with the confederates? You don't even look old enough to be a soldier."

Rand stared a long time at the end of his bed before he answered. "I wasn't a soldier and I ain't no rebel. No one would listen to me when they captured me."

Aaron sat down on the end of the bed. "Tell me about it, please."

"Not much to tell. Pa and me was on a train trying to get out of Virginia. We had been down there looking for his ma. Pa didn't want to fight for the south so we got on a train headed to Philadelphia. When the train was attacked, Pa told me to run and hide, so I did. When it got quiet I went back to find him. He was dead. I buried him myself, then ran in the direction the train was headed. My stupid mistake was to take a coat off a dead rebel. I was freezing at night and didn't think anything about it until the Yankees found me."

Aaron nodded. "How old are you, Rand?"

"Fourteen. I don't think you can do anything for me. I talked until I didn't have a voice left, but they wouldn't believe me."

Aaron thought a few minutes before he spoke again. "Do you believe in God?"

Joe had come back to the last bed and was grieved to see Rand's eyes filled with grief and sadness as he answered, "I don't know. I used to think I did. I just don't know."

"Well, I do," Aaron said without hesitation. "I'm going to pray for both of us and ask God to show us what we need to do."

"Don't give me no false hope, cousin. I don't think I could handle that."

"He's right, Aaron," Joe offered. "If he had on a rebel coat they're not likely to listen."

"I understand," Aaron answered, "but you see, I *do* believe in God and He *is* a God of miracles. Will you two pray with me? I know your faith is weak right now, Rand, but pray with whatever faith you have. Pray that God will give us a miracle."

Rand shrugged his skinny shoulders. "Sure, why not? Don't know if God will pay any attention to my prayers, but I'll pray if it'll get someone to listen to my story."

"Good. I'll be back, Rand." Aaron squeezed the boy's shoulder. "Joe, I'm going out to the buggy."

Joe watched him leave then turned to the young Rand Trinity. "That man has a lot of faith. I hope he has enough for both of us because I need a miracle too. Now, let me see your leg. It says here you have a leg wound."

Later, Harrison dropped Aaron and Joe off at the Golden Palace. They made their way into the back rooms where the art exhibit was set up. "I want to look at your pictures again after we finish getting ready for tonight," Joe said.

"Go ahead and look around. I need to get some cleaning supplies to dust the tables and frames. It won't take too long then we can talk."

After Aaron finished cleaning, he found Joe standing in front of the Princess Warrior with the same look of longing he had had the night before. Aaron stood quietly a few moments watching the expression on Joe's face. Finally, he had to ask, "Besides her beauty, what is it about this picture that bothers you, Joe?"

"If you only knew," Joe murmured, never taking his eyes away from the image.

"I want to know. After all, I did paint her. I hope you realize you can trust me and that I'm a friend."

Joe looked into the eyes of Aaron Trinity and knew he could trust the young artist. But before he made up his mind to tell Aaron his story, he took another long look at the picture that had kept him awake last night. Hesitantly, he began. "My pa gave *me* that rifle when I was sixteen. He had my initials engraved on the stock, M M."

Joe stood quietly to let Aaron absorb what he had just told him.

The room went deathly still as the two men stood shoulder to shoulder looking at the picture. Realization finally burst into Aaron's mind, his mouth gaped, his eyes opened wide, and he stared at Joe. "You mean... *you* are Michael Mayfield?"

"Yes, that's my real name," Joe nodded solemnly.

"Wow! Let's go to the lounge and talk. This is incredible! My mind's having a very hard time processing this information...and I need to sit down!"

"I've been in an awful state ever since I saw this picture last night. I was so shocked to see my sister looking back at me and holding my rifle. How in the world did she ever get my rifle?"

Aaron shook his head and started walking toward the lounge. "After we sit down I'll answer all your questions, if I can. But you're going to have to answer some of mine too! Talk about being shocked...I *really* need to sit down!"

Aaron actually chuckled after they were seated and served cups of coffee. Holding his cup, he looked at Joe and just shook his head some more. "I can't believe I didn't pick up on the resemblance between you two. But then, at the time I sketched you down by the river, you were supposedly dead! Why didn't you see Maxi at the ranches? She lives right there."

"I stayed at camp on guard duty, remember? I never saw anyone except you, and I didn't know I was supposed to be dead." Joe grinned. "Tell me about my sister. Is she really as well as she looks?"

"She is great! She's my sister too you know." Aaron sipped his coffee, trying to take it all in. "This has been one of the strangest days of my life. I'll tell you about the rifle first. I'm not sure I can answer all your questions because I didn't live there at the time, but this is how I understand it. Maxi and Marty came upon this trouble-maker who was manhandling an Indian girl. They took his rifle away from him and were ready to chase him off the ranch when Maxi noticed the initials on the rifle stock and challenged him. He said he found it under the body of a dead man. His story was confirmed by a hired hand whom they trusted, so Maxi believed you were dead. Obviously, the dead man wasn't you, but they never found out how your rifle ended up with him."

Joe shook his head and sighed. "Not long after I left home and joined a cattle drive to Denver, my rifle was stolen off my horse. Some of us boys were allowed to go into town and blow off a little steam while we got supplies. I looked everywhere I could think of to find the man who stole it, but never found him. It's just *crazy* that Maxi would end up with it! Tell me more about her. Is our pa with her?"

"No. The story is that when they got your letter, inviting them to join you, they packed up and left to go find you. Somewhere in the southern part of the Colorado territory your pa had an accident. His horse fell in a landslide and rolled on him. I'm sorry to tell you this, but he died from his injuries."

"*Pa is dead*?!" Joe looked stricken and dropped his head in his hands. "That's terrible news! I'm so sorry for Maxi." Tears welled in his eyes. "That left her all alone. What did she do? How did she go on by herself? I should've been there for her. I just can't believe it…my pa is dead."

"I'm sorry, man. I hate to be the bearer of bad news." Aaron sipped his coffee and let Joe have a few moments to think and compose himself. He finally looked up, and Aaron asked, "Should I continue now or are you up to it?"

"Yeah, I guess so. Nothing I can do about it now, anyway. As long as Maxi is all right."

"She is. Remember White Cloud, Angel Myers? She joined Maxi and the two made their way to Denver. The sheriff there knew of a cattle drive heading to Fort Laramie and arranged for the girls to go along. He knew the ranchers and trusted the men or he never would have made those arrangements. From Fort Laramie, some of the men were going toward the Wind River where Maxi wanted to search for you. Short of it is, Maxi fell in love with Paul Miles and they were married. They have a little boy now, too. Your nephew. You'll be happy to know they named him after you. Michael Paul Miles. They own a ranch that's called the High Meadows Horse Ranch. That's where I live, the most beautiful place on earth."

Joe's mouth turned up slightly, a sad smile mingled with sorrow. "At least she's not alone now, without Pa. So she's married and has a baby. Well, that's great."

"Yes it is. And now it gets a little complicated. Paul's mother lived with them and when my father came along, he married Carmen, Paul's mother. I happened along after that and now we all live on the High Meadows Ranch. Separate houses, of course. I can fill you in on more details later. But, Michael...."

"No," Joe interrupted him. "It's best if you keep calling me Joe for now. I'm struggling with a life changing decision and what to do from here on. Talk about complicated! You don't know what complicated is until you hear my story."

Aaron leaned in and pinned Joe with an eye to eye stare. "Share it with me, please." But he wasn't prepared for Joe's next mind-blowing statement.

"I'm wanted for murder." Joe decided to tell it like it was and not sugar-coat the truth. "Before you get all disturbed, I want you to know I was *falsely* accused of murdering a man. He was the foreman on the Chandler Ranch. Gordon York was his name. Old man Chandler was determined to run out all the smaller ranchers close to the place he claimed as his own. We had a couple of run-ins with him. I was sure the foreman was stealing from me and my partner. My partner was Ray Jackson. He was a bit of a hot-head, but still a good man. The crazy guy fell in love with Chandler's oldest daughter, Cassandra. Can't blame him, she was pretty and sweet. They had it real bad for each other. The old man threatened to kill Ray if he ever caught him on his land. One evening when I came home from checking our cattle there was a note from Ray. Said he was going to get

Cassie, that's what he called her, and they were leaving the area. I went after him. I had figured out where they were meeting. Felt like I needed to talk some sense into them. When I got to that place, I found Gordon York. He had been shot and was dead. Near as I could tell by the tracks Ray and Cassie had been there. Looked like there had been a fight. I heard a bunch of horses headed my way and got the heck out of there. But someone must have spotted me, because the next thing I knew there were 'wanted' posters out for me. I'm wanted for the murder of Gordon York." Joe sagged in his chair as he drank the last of his coffee.

For a while there was only the crackle of logs burning in the fireplace. Aaron finally asked, "Why didn't you turn yourself in and tell the authorities your story?"

"The only authority anywhere around there was Dalton Chandler's man. They would never have believed me. I just changed my looks, put on an army uniform and stayed as quiet as I could. It was shortly after that we ended up at that ranch where you sketched my picture. You said you didn't plan on doing anything with the sketch, so I didn't even think of it again."

"What do you want to do now, Joe?"

"I want to clear my name! I want to have my life back! I want to see my sister again, but don't know if I have a chance. Recently, I made a decision to live my life with honesty, integrity and faith. When I look on my certificate that says it was awarded to Dr. Joe McCall, it disgusts me to know I'm living a lie. Will you add me to your prayers when you pray for Rand Trinity? It's a lot to put on you, but I need all the help I can get."

Aaron looked into Joe's pleading eyes. "You're right, it's a lot to put on *me*, but it's nothing to a God who knows and sees everything. I've got a few hours before the exhibit starts. I'm going to my hotel room to pray, asking God to show us what to do. The exhibit will be over at nine tonight. Will you come back and let's talk again? I'm sure He'll show us what we need to do."

Joe nodded with a grateful expression. "All right, Aaron. If we both agree its God leading us, I'll do it."

Chapter 6

*L*ATE THAT EVENING, JOE returned to the Golden Palace with a heavy heart and anxious mind. He waited for Aaron to close up his exhibit.

"I'm glad you came back," Aaron said. "Would you like to wait for me in the lounge? I shouldn't be too long."

"Sure, I'll see you there and I hope you have some answers for us."

Joe looked around the lounge and found the quietest corner away from staff and patrons. He ordered coffee and tried to quell his uneasy thoughts and emotions, hoping against hope that Aaron had something good to tell him. Finally, Aaron came in and sat across from Joe, leaning in close so no one could hear their conversation. He knew how anxious Joe was so he got right to the subject.

"First, I want to ask if you think it was your partner, Ray Jackson, who killed the ranch foreman?"

Joe thought about that for a moment. "I don't see how it could be anyone else. Ray was the only one who had been there. There were no other tracks but his, Cassie's, and the foreman's."

"Then he is the only one who can clear your name. We need to find him." Aaron leaned back in his chair as if the conversation was over.

Oh, if it was only that easy. He shook his head at Aaron. "How can we do that? Even if we did find him, and I doubt that we can, he's not going to want to confess to killing the man."

"If it was self-defense," Aaron said quietly, "he wouldn't be blamed for the man's death."

Joe shook his head again. "*If.* That's a mighty big word."

"His wife would surely stand up for him," Aaron reasoned.

"I don't know, Aaron. That's probably what I should do, try to find him and confront him about what happened. Trouble is, I don't know where he went."

"Well, let's think about that. Do you know where he was from?"

"I remember him saying he grew up on a farm in Ohio, but I have no way of knowing that he's still there. His family raised chickens and farmed a few acres. He said he got to where he hated to eat chicken."

"That's a good start," Aaron encouraged. "Do you remember if he ever mentioned the name of a town?"

"Man, you're asking a lot, trying to make me remember stuff from so long ago! But, let me think a minute." Joe gazed at the ceiling trying to shake some memories loose. "There was something about a fair...I think he told me about the first Union County fair he ever went to. He entered a greased pig catching contest."

Aaron nodded. "Keep going," he prodded.

"And a creek... A mill... *Mill Creek.* That's it!"

"And how many chicken farms, close to a Mill Creek, in Union County, Ohio, with the last name of Jackson, could there be?" Aaron smiled smugly.

Joe returned the smile with a sigh of relief. "You just gave me a little hope, Aaron."

"That's good, man, but the *first* thing we need to do is get Rand out of that awful prison hospital."

"No argument there," Joe nodded. "But how in the world are you going to do that?"

"I'm not... *you* are."

"Whoa! Me? I hope God gave you good instructions on how that's going to go down."

Aaron leaned in close again, pinning Joe with a stare but speaking very softly. "You told me yesterday that you committed yourself to walk with the Lord in honesty, integrity, and faith, didn't you?"

"Yes," Joe agreed, "that's what I said."

"Then that's what we'll do." Aaron leaned back again, but didn't release Joe from his gaze.

Joe shook his head for the umpteenth time, puzzlement etched on his features. "Spell it out a little clearer for me, please." He fixed Aaron with his own stare, and waited.

"We'll go to the commanding officer at the hospital. You'll need to be the one to lead on this. You'll simply ask him to release Rand Trinity into your care."

"Wait, I don't think it's going to be that simple, Aaron."

"I was reading in Matthew this afternoon and a verse jumped out at me. Jesus was sending His apostles out and in one place he said not to be anxious about how or what you should speak; for it shall be given you in that hour what you are to speak. I feel that's what we need to do. Have faith that God will tell us what to say when we get there." Aaron shrugged. "What harm would it do to try? The most he can do is send us away."

Joe leaned his head back against his chair and closed his eyes. With all his might he fought to squelch the negative feelings in his heart. He was surprised by the ease with which they faded away when he put them in God's hands. He suddenly felt full of faith and determination, excitement building in his chest. He bolted straight up in his chair, startling Aaron. "All right, I may be crazy, but I'll do it. Just tell me when."

Aaron hurriedly laid out his plans before Joe. "My train leaves at 12:00 tomorrow. I want us to go to the hospital as early as we can, so we'll be there before the commander gets busy. We'll catch him as soon as he gets there. We'll get Rand, then all three of us will be on that train when it pulls out."

"Whew, that's a tall order, but not impossible. God will have to smooth out any details we can't foresee. I can be ready, but that boy is another matter."

Aaron laughed. "He was quite a mess, wasn't he."

"You can say that again. He'll need a good scrubbing, especially that red hair, and some clean clothes. How are we going to handle that?"

"One of us can bring him back to my hotel room and clean him up while the other one goes and buys him new clothes."

"All right, but here's another problem," Joe admitted. "I don't have a lot of money."

"I've got that covered. My family sent me here with plenty to take care of all my needs and also to help others. I'll tell you more about that later, but right now, don't be concerned about money."

Joe nodded slowly. "If you say so. Is this where having faith comes into the picture?"

"Faith is *always* in the picture, my friend," Aaron said. "Let's get going now. I have more to do tonight. See you early in the morning."

Joe went back to his room filled with a sense of anticipation. He planned what he was going to tell his friend Harrison and Dr. Brighten in the morning. *Honesty, integrity, and faith. I'll tell them I have a personal problem I need to straighten out before I can commit myself to partner with anyone. I'll hire a carriage in the morning and go pick up Aaron, get Rand Trinity, and be on that train with Aaron at noon. God help me.* That was the closest thing to prayer he could manage before he climbed into bed.

Dr. Brighten and Harrison Brighten didn't fully understand Joe's explanation, but they were gracious and encouraged Joe to do whatever he needed to do to mend his problem. They told him he was always welcome back to their home and bid him a sad farewell.

I will really miss the Brighten family, Joe thought, *but I'm glad that's over with. One problem down, many more to go.*

He walked a few blocks to rent a carriage and went to pick up Aaron who was ready and waiting in the front of his hotel.

"Good morning, Joe. Are you ready to get this done?"

"I'm more than ready. I had a peaceful night's rest, but my stomach has decided to churn this morning. Nothing but nerves."

"I know what you mean. But I still feel this is what we need to do."

Joe heaved a big sigh. "All right then, let's do it."

They didn't talk much on the way to the military hospital. Traffic was light because of the early hour so they were at the hospital in no time. Joe asked a guard at the gate where the office of the commanding officer was located. Following his directions, Joe halted the carriage in front of a building and set the brake. "Looks like we beat the general here," he said, looking around.

"I was hoping we would. I want to pray before he gets here."

As if it were the most natural thing in the world, Aaron bowed his head and began to pray. Joe was surprised when the young man he was beginning to admire, prayed a prayer that was simple yet earnest. "Heavenly father," he began, "Joe and I commit this day to you. Give us wisdom and the words to say that will help us get Rand into our custody. Soften the heart of the General to look favorably on Joe and his request. In Jesus Christ's name I pray."

They were so engrossed in their prayer that they didn't hear the footsteps of General Andrew Hart as he stopped at the side of the carriage. He cleared his throat, rather loudly. Joe looked up and smiled at him. "We were just praying for you, General." *Why did I say that? He'll probably think I'm crazy.*

"Good," the general responded. "I need all the prayers I can get. I assume you have some business with me this morning?"

"Yes, sir. We'll only take a few minutes of your time if you can talk to us right away."

"Get yourself in my office then," the general ordered as he spun on his heel. "I have a meeting in a few minutes so we need to get on with this." He led the way into the building and into his office, then motioned for them to sit.

"That's all right, sir, we'll stand," Joe said. "We also need to be on our way."

The general nodded. "What can I help you with?"

"I'm Dr. Joe McCall and this is Aaron Trinity," he said firmly.

"McCall," the general interrupted. "I don't think I've ever met you."

"Not likely, sir, as I'm new to this area. I'm a guest of Dr. David Brighten and his son, Dr. Harrison Brighten."

"Now those two I *do* know. Fine men, both of them." He nodded for Joe to go on.

"I want to ask you to grant me custody of a young man who's in the prison hospital. His name is Rand Trinity."

The general looked puzzled, then stern. "Now, why would I want to do that?"

"After hearing his story, sir, I feel it's the right thing to do. I believe him when he told us that after his father was attacked and killed trying to get out of the south, he took a coat off a rebel soldier because he was freezing. When our soldiers found him they assumed he was a rebel."

"He could be lying," the general said.

"I realize that, sir, but Aaron's father is the boy's uncle. He's the only family the boy has. We intend to take him out west to his uncle."

"Is this true, Aaron Trinity?" The general's eyes bored into Aaron's.

"Yes, sir. My father has served in the Union army and is now living on a ranch that is supplying horses and cattle to the army." Aaron's voice never wavered.

The general nodded. "God knows we need them."

A soldier stuck his head in the door. "Sir, all the officers are assembled for the meeting."

"Thank you. I'll be there directly." He walked to the only window in the room and stood staring out with his back to the other two. Without turning, he asked, "How old is this boy?"

"He's fourteen, sir," Joe answered.

Without another word, the general opened a drawer in his desk, took out a piece of paper, wrote a quick note, signed it, then handed it to Joe.

"This will let you take custody of the boy. I think you both are doing what you believe is right. Just know this: There is no prayer that will help you, if I see either one of you or that boy again." He walked out of the office without a backward glance.

"Thank you, Father," Aaron whispered.

"Yes, thank you, Father," Joe echoed. But he didn't take time to think about what had just happened. "We need to go, *now*! The sooner we get out of this place the better I'm going to feel."

"You're right. We don't have time to waste. We have a train to catch!"

They hurried to the barracks that housed the wounded confederate prisoners. Joe handed the paper that General Hart had signed to the orderly that was in charge. He then walked to the last bed where young Rand was laying. Rand opened his eyes, surprised to see Joe standing over him. "Can you walk, Rand?"

"Yeah, I can walk," Rand said pushing himself up on his elbows. "Not very good, but I can walk."

"Get up right now, we're leaving," Joe said quietly.

"What? Where are you taking me?"

"Don't ask questions right now and don't draw attention to yourself. Just trust me and Aaron."

Rand moved rather quickly after hearing that. "My things are in that sack right there by the bed," he said, nodding toward the sack.

"Leave them. You're not going to need them." Joe took his coat off and handed it to Rand. "Put this on and walk right out that door down there. Follow Aaron. I'll be right behind you."

Joe was grateful that Rand obeyed and didn't argue. He knew Rand must be hurting when he limped out of the building and climbed into the carriage, but he never complained.

As they drove away from the hospital, Joe began to chuckle. The chuckle turned to heartfelt laughter and Aaron joined in. "Do you know what a miracle that was?"

Aaron agreed. "I believe that it was a *mighty* big miracle!"

Rand had a scowl on his face as he looked from Joe to Aaron then back again. "What are you two going to do with me?"

Joe just laughed harder. He finally got his breath and said, "We're going to give you a bath and dress you in new clothes. You smell pretty bad, you know, and if you're going with us you need to scrub that smell off."

"When I get all clean can I have something to eat?"

"Yes," Aaron answered. "After you get cleaned up you can eat until you've had your fill."

"All right, then," Rand acquiesced. "I'll go with you."

"Rand, in the days ahead, you better stay real close to me and Aaron or we might *all* be in trouble."

"Oh, you won't have no trouble with me. I'm grateful you got me out of that place. Don't know how you pulled it off, but I'm *thanking* you!"

"You're welcome. I'm becoming a big believer in miracles since I met Aaron, so you better thank the one who *really* got you out of there. God is the only one who could have pulled that one off so easy."

True to his word, Rand caused no trouble at all. Aaron had kept his hotel room for another day so they ordered a hot bath. Joe went shopping for new clothes and then they fed Rand until he could eat no more. And when the train pulled out of the station headed for Ohio...all three were on board.

Chapter 7

*T*HE FIRST DAY ON the train was the hardest for Rand. He shifted and squirmed on the hard seat trying to get comfortable. His leg throbbed.

"Are you hurting, Rand?" Joe asked when he noticed all the squirming.

"Yeah, a little," Rand admitted.

"The seat right behind me is empty. Why don't you sit with your back to the window and stretch your leg out. I've got some powder that'll help with the pain. Aaron, can I have your canteen?"

"Sure," Aaron said, handing it over.

Joe dug in his bag, pulled out a tiny packet, poured a white powder in the lid of the canteen, swirled it around, and handed it to Rand. "This is bitter, so swallow it down fast and chase it with more water."

Rand quickly swallowed the liquid, followed by several big gulps from the canteen. His face scrunched up and he shuddered. "You got that right, it's bitter as all get out!"

Joe chuckled. "It'll be worth it if it helps the pain. Before you move to the other seat, tell me how you got shot in the leg."

Rand looked embarrassed and ducked his head. "It was so crazy, what I did, I hate to admit it."

"We're all entitled to a few crazy things in our life. I know I've had my share," Aaron admitted.

"Well," Rand went on, "I told you I found my pa dead when I went back to the train. There was a lot of dead people. After I got over the shock

I pulled my pa out of the train, found a place and buried him. Mostly, I covered him with rocks. There was plenty of those, and anyhow, I didn't have a shovel." Rand stared at the floor for several moments, then shook his head sadly.

"Do you think it was confederates that raided the train?" Joe asked.

"No, they didn't look like soldiers and none of them had on a uniform that I could see. I have a hunch they was just down-right evil men who liked to steal and kill for the pure meanness of it! Why would the rebels *or* the Yankees kill innocent people like that? They could've just robbed us and run off. There was a couple of women in the car that Pa and me was in. Never saw them again when I went back. Figured the robbers took them. Those no-account scumbags stripped everything of value right off that train and off those people." He paused, shaking his head again. Joe wondered if he had asked too much of Rand to relive those awful memories. But then he continued on with the story.

"Anyway, I tried to stay out of sight and headed in the direction the train was going. The second day was when I found that dead rebel and took his coat. I just about froze the night before. The next day I spotted Union soldiers. I plum forgot I had on that rebel coat and was so hungry I ran out of the trees hollering. One of them shot me in the leg. I was lucky he wasn't a good shot and didn't fill me with lead. Then they wouldn't listen to my explanation and took me to where the prisoners were. I almost wished I had died. The slop they fed us was bad...*real* bad. And it wasn't much better in that hospital prison."

Aaron laid his hand on Rand's shoulder. "I'm sorry you had to go through that. I didn't even think that being on this train might bring you bad memories, but I'm glad they didn't fill you with lead. God must have known we'd need each other. Having a cousin is . . . well, I think it's going to be great."

Rand forced a half-hearted grin. "We'll see cousin, we'll see. I want to ask you a question, though. What is that thing on your back? Looks like some kind of funny back- pack."

"That's exactly what it is, a back-pack. A friend made it for me so I can carry my sketch pads and pencils wherever I go."

"You an artist?" Rand's eyes widened.

Aaron grinned. "Some people think so. I'll show you some of my sketches after you rest your leg awhile. I may even sketch you."

"Maybe. I've never had anyone draw a picture of me. Should be interesting." Slowly, Rand got up and moved to the bench seat behind Joe.

The three men traveled through Pennsylvania by rail. Going into Ohio they switched to stagecoach until they reached Columbus. Along the way they asked questions of the locals and found out the town they were looking for was Marysville. Traveling together for days allowed the three to get to know each other better and become comfortable with one another. They found a hotel in Marysville. Aaron and Rand shared a room and Joe was in the adjoining one.

Getting ready to venture out and find a place to eat, Rand asked, "What are we doing here in this town? You said you needed to find someone. Can I ask who it is we're looking for?"

Joe heard the question from his room and came through the adjoining doorway to answer. "I need to find a friend of mine. We were ranching together when he ran off with his girl. He left a passel of trouble for me and I need to find him and straighten some things out. I don't think it'll take long to find out what I want to know, then we'll be on our way again."

Joe quickly changed the subject. "I think all three of us needs to find a barber before we have to buy ribbons to tie our hair back. Don't you think Rand would look cute with pretty green bows in his dark red hair, Aaron?"

"Yea, we can change his name to Randalena," Aaron teased.

"Well, you two don't look much better," Rand huffed. "I'll call you Josephine and Aaron, I'll call…Aarondona."

They were all laughing when they headed out the door. "Come on you two cousins. Let's go find a barber and a place to eat. We've got plans to make."

They asked the barber about the Jackson farm and he knew right where the farm was. "Even with a slow horse and wagon you should be able to get there in an hour," he told them.

"It's Ray Jackson I'm looking for," Joe said.

"Sorry to tell you, but that'll be a problem. His sweet little wife buried him about a year ago. I'm afraid she's in a rough spot now and her with those two little ones."

Joe was shocked. "How'd he die? Was he fighting with the Union Army?"

"Yep. Ray was a good boy. You didn't hear this from me, but that pa of his was just plain mean to Ray. Didn't blame him one bit when he took off. Why he came back with that sweet Cassie is more than I can understand. Now she's stuck on that farm with a bitter old mother-in-law and a mean father-in-law. People talk, but no one knows what to do to help her. She's kind of independent and wouldn't admit she needed help to begin with. But if *I* was Ray's friend and had a way to get her out of there, I would do everything I could to take care of her." The barber said this while looking straight into Joe's eyes. He winked then went back to snipping hair.

Message received, Joe thought. *But how?* Aaron and Rand didn't say anything but also didn't miss the look of despair that flashed in Joe's eyes.

A short time later the three men were seated in a café that was homey and comfortable. "It sure smells good in here," Rand announced. He glanced around, his eyes filled with anticipation, as if he could already taste the food.

"Aaron, I'd like to know something," Joe said. "Do we need to be careful and order the less expensive meals? What I'm trying to ask is, do we need to be careful with the money situation?"

"We're doing just fine, Joe. Order what you want, both of you. We need to put some meat on my skinny cousin's bones. He looks like I did a few years ago, tall and skinny as a rail."

"That was all Rand needed to hear. "I'm going to have a big steak with all the trimmings, then."

"You just do that," Aaron told him, "but remember, along with a good meal comes hard work to build up those muscles. We'll see if we can find some wood for you to chop. That'll put some muscle on you."

"I ain't afraid of hard work," Rand retorted. "Show me the woodpile and I'll chop it. Just keep the food coming. That first day on the train I thought maybe you intended to starve me."

"Yeah, that was a bad day," Aaron admitted. "I wasn't thinking about food. I was just putting all my energy into getting you away from Philadelphia. But the food you put away for breakfast that morning should have gotten you by for a week!"

Joe enjoyed the easy camaraderie between the two younger men. Rand had been quiet on that first day, but now, Joe could see that he was slowly improving, physically and emotionally. "Hey, Rand, do you think your sore leg is well enough that you could ride a horse now?"

Aaron jumped in before Rand could answer. "What makes you think he can ride a horse? Probably doesn't know one end of a horse from the other."

Rand looked offended. "I can ride! Bet I could outride you any day of the week."

Aaron laughed. "What do you think, Joe? Should we rent horses to go out to that farm in the morning? We'll see if this rebel knows how to ride."

"Don't call me no rebel!" Rand exploded.

"All right, all right. I won't call you that anymore. What do you want me to call you, Randolena?"

Rand smirked. "*Cousin* will do just fine."

After they ordered their meal, Joe settled the cousins into serious conversation. "To answer your question, Aaron, I think it would be a good idea to rent horses and ride out to the Jackson farm. I don't know what we'll find out there but I want to talk to Cassie alone at some point. I'd appreciate it if you two would create a little diversion so that can happen. Will you do that for me?"

They agreed to do what they could. Rand asked, "Are we going to stay out there at the farm?"

"No, we're staying just long enough to be polite then come back here. As far as I'm concerned we can leave that next morning. I'll ask around for the best way to get out of Ohio. Cassie might have some idea about that."

Their food arrived and they dug in with gusto. Rand ordered a big piece of chocolate cake, groaning in satisfaction when he polished it off. "Oh, I'm stuffed! It's awful nice to have a rich cousin feed me the way a man should eat."

Aaron smiled fondly at Rand, affirming what Joe had felt all along about Aaron. *You are one special man, Aaron Trinity. You have depth of character I haven't seen in very many men. You have strength that's admirable, because you show it with love and gentleness. Maybe it'll rub off on Rand. Maybe some of it will rub off on me!*

"Just remember," Aaron said to Rand, "there's work that goes along with being fed a good meal."

Rand grinned impishly. "Sorry, cousin, I'm just too full to work right now."

After breakfast the next morning they rented horses and followed the barber's directions to the country road that would take them to the farm. Around half an hour later, Joe stopped at a lane that was lined with apple trees, just like the barber had described. This lane would lead directly to the farm house.

"Let's ride in nice and easy, boys. I don't have any idea what kind of reception we're going to get."

"You take the lead, Joe. I'll follow Rand," Aaron said.

They rode in silence until they cleared the row of apple trees at the end of the narrow lane. A nice, white house with a covered front porch sat in a large open area, surrounded by various sheds and outbuildings, one of which was a huge barn. A green lawn was bordered by flower beds, some showing the first brave yellow daffodils of spring along with a few crocuses. It was a tranquil scene and almost made Joe forget what he'd been told about the owners. "I'll go knock on the door," he said. "You two stay mounted until I see what kind of situation we have."

Joe dismounted, handed his reins to Aaron and walked toward the front door. A flash of carrot-red hair, with a boy of about five years of age under it, came dashing around the corner of the house almost colliding with Joe. The startled youngster stared up at Joe, mouth gaping, eyes wide.

"I'm looking for Cassie Jackson," Joe said. "Do you know her?"

The little one nodded.

"My name is Joe. What's your name?"

"Daniel," he said with shyness.

"Daniel, is Cassie your mother?"

The boy nodded and started to say something but the front door opened and an older woman stepped out on the porch. "Daniel, get in the back yard, *now*," she growled. Then she glared at Joe. "What do you men want?"

Daniel ran back in the direction he'd come, so Joe turned to the woman on the porch. "I'm looking for Cassie Jackson."

"What do you want with her?" the unfriendly woman demanded.

"I was a friend of Ray's. I knew Ray and Cassie a few years back. Just wanted to say hello to Ray but someone in town told me he'd died. I'm sorry to hear that and would like to pay my respects to Cassie before we move on."

The woman stood unmoving, arms folded across her chest. "She doesn't have time to be standing around talking to strangers. You men just go ahead and get on out of here."

Right then Daniel reappeared with a petite, pretty woman in tow. She wore a faded, threadbare dress covered by a large apron. A handful of clothes pins were in her right hand and a little girl about two was holding her left one. "Daniel said there was someone looking for me, Mother Jackson." She smoothed her sandy-blonde hair away from her face and dropped the clothes pins in her apron pocket, a look of embarrassment shadowing her delicate features. Glancing at the visitors, she focused on Joe. "What do you want me for?"

Joe managed to tear his eyes away from the pretty face and studied the flower bed at the corner of the house. "I was hoping you would remember me, Cassie. Ray and I ranched together and...."

"Oh, yes!" Cassie exclaimed. "I recognize you now. You're...."

"Joe McCall," he finished. Cassie seemed confused by the name but didn't argue the point. "I was hoping we might visit for a few minutes," he said.

"And *I* told him you were too busy to be standing around talking," the old woman spat out. "You need to finish hanging those clothes."

Much to her credit, Cassie didn't back down. "It's all right, Mother Jackson. They can come around to the back and we'll visit while I finish hanging the clothes."

The older women *harrumphed* and went back into the house.

Cassie picked up her little girl and led the way. "Bring the horses on around the house," she said. "There's a water trough by the barn." Aaron and Rand took the horses to the trough while Joe walked with Cassie and the children. "It was nice of you to come all this way to see Ray." She looked uncertainly at Joe. "Or was there something else you wanted?" Her two little ones took off toward the barn, leaving Joe and Cassie alone.

"Well, there is, actually. I'll get right to the point, Cassie. I'd like to clear my name from the mess Ray left me in."

Cassie stiffened. "What do you mean? I don't have any idea what you're talking about."

He faced her and looked into her eyes. "I want to clear my name of the murder of Gordon York, your father's foreman."

She shook her head. "But, *you* didn't kill him."

"No, I didn't, Cassie, but your father thinks I did and I've been running from the law for several years now. There's 'Wanted' posters all over the place with my face on them. I managed to change my looks and joined the army. Before long they sent us back east to fight in the war. Actually, I volunteered just to get out of the area."

"But why did my father think you killed Gordon York?"

"When Ray ran off he left me a note telling me what he was going to do. I knew where you two met and tried to catch him before …before…" Joe hesitated trying to find the right words.

"I know, *before* we did something stupid." Cassie ducked her head looking uncomfortable.

"Well, yes. When I got to the place, I found Gordon York with a bullet in his chest. The only other tracks around were Ray's and yours. It looked to me like Ray and Gordon got into a fight and Ray shot him. While I was figuring all this out, I heard horses headed my way and bolted. A bunch of men from your father's ranch saw me leaving and the next thing I know…I'm a wanted man."

Cassie motioned to a couple of yard chairs. "Let's sit down, Joe." She looked weary and worried all at once and lowered herself into the chair before she continued. "Is that why you changed your name? I didn't catch it at first but I remember your name is Michael."

"Yes, I changed it to Joe McCall, for obvious reasons."

Cassie stared into space a few moments. "I'm so sorry, Michael. We had no idea. I can't tell you how many times I wished I had done things differently. I should have stood up to Father but he's a hard man to stand up to. Ray said the same thing to me several times but we were so in love, it seemed the only thing we could do was leave."

"What really happened, Cassie?"

She took a deep breath and closed her eyes, gathering her thoughts. "Father said he would kill Ray if he ever caught him with me so we decided to elope. Gordon York was after me all the time but I couldn't stand him.

He said he loved me and wanted to marry me but I know all he wanted was what my father had. I told Father that, too, but he didn't believe me. Gordon was cruel! To the ranch hands and the animals too. I saw him beat a kid real bad over something stupid. But Father never saw that side of him. He said a man had to be strong and tough to be a foreman over a bunch of ranch hands.

"Well, Gordon saw me leave that evening and he followed me. He challenged Ray and the two fought." Cassie closed her eyes again and shuddered. "It was ugly! I just knew he was going to kill Ray but Ray held his own. Then Ray knocked Gordon down and jumped on top of him. Gordon grabbed a rock and hit Ray in the head. Knocked him out cold. He pulled his pistol and was going to shoot Ray while he was unconscious… so…I shot Gordon."

Joe's mouth dropped open. Cassie glanced at him then looked away. "I wish I could say I'm sorry, but I'm not. The only thing I'm sorry for now is that I didn't stay and stand up to my father."

Joe stared, astonished. "*You* shot him?"

"Yes, I shot him. He would have killed Ray so I didn't have a choice. It was him or Ray and I wasn't going to let Ray be the one dead on the ground."

"I didn't even think of that," Joe admitted, shaking his head. "I mean, that *you* shot York. I just assumed it was Ray."

They sat silently, watching Aaron and Rand talk with the children by the water trough. Daniel came running to where his mother was sitting. "Mama, can I show them the baby kittens in the barn?"

"Yes, you can do that. But remember not to bother anything in the barn," she warned as he raced back. Cassie looked over at Joe. "What can I do to clear your name? I'll do whatever it takes, Michael."

"Call me Joe for the time being. I need to think about it now that I know the truth." He looked into Cassie's face. "Tell me what it's like for you living here. It must be hard without Ray."

Her eyes glistened with unshed tears, her answer barely above a whisper. "You have no idea."

Chapter 8

"THAT'S WHY I ASKED you, Cassie. I really want to know how you're doing."

She dabbed at her eyes and gave Joe an appraising look. "You've heard talk in town, haven't you?" He opened his mouth to respond but she stopped him. "It's all right. I know people are talking about how things are out here."

"I won't deny it was mentioned that you have...."

"Mama, Mama!"

Cassie looked up and saw Aaron coming toward them carrying a tearful little girl in his arms. She and Joe hurried to meet Aaron. "What's wrong, Katie?" she asked, taking her daughter from Aaron.

"Kitty *scwatch* me!" she cried.

"Oh, no," Cassie soothed her. "And what were you doing to kitty that made him scratch you?"

"Nothin," she whimpered.

"I'll have you know, Miss Katie, I am a very good doctor when it comes to kitty scratches," Joe said, acting very serious. "If your mother will seat herself in the chair over there, I will take a look at your injury."

Little Katie's light blue eyes grew wide then she scowled at Joe. Not sure what to think of this stranger, she only stared.

"I see she has doubts, Aaron," Joe said. "Would you please tell these two ladies I am a fine doctor?"

Aaron grinned, playing along. "Yes, it's true. Dr. Joe McCall is a fine doctor and very good at making kitty scratches feel better."

"Thank you, sir. Now if the mother would please be seated." Joe saw that Katie's eyes were not the only ones that grew large at the title of 'Doctor'.

Cassie sat with Katie on her lap. She asked, "Is it true, Joe? Are you really a doctor?"

Joe kept up his act. "Not only a doctor, ma'am, the *finest* doctor there is for kitty scratches. Now, young lady, where is your injury?"

Katie didn't answer. Just stared.

"Let me see…is it under here?" Joe knelt on one knee in front of mother and daughter. He lightly tickled under Katie's chin and got the desired reaction of a small smile trying to break free. "No, not there. Is it here?" This time he tickled her ribs.

Katie giggled and shook her head.

"Not there? Then it must be here," he said tickling her other side.

She giggled some more.

"No, not there. Well, dear girl, where *is* your injury?"

Katie proudly stuck the back of her pudgy little hand under Joe's nose.

"My, oh, my! I see it now. Aaron, I shall need my doctor bag. Will you please retrieve it for me?"

"Yes, sir," Aaron said with a chuckle. "I shall be right back."

"I can't believe it, Joe," Cassie said. "You really are a doctor!"

Joe just smiled at Cassie as he took the bag from Aaron. He produced a small bottle and asked Katie, "Are you a brave girl? If you will be brave, I might have a surprise in my pocket. But it's only for big, brave girls. Can you be brave?"

Katie frowned again and looked at Joe's pocket. Then she looked up at Joe and slowly nodded her head, mumbling, "Uh, huh."

"Good girl," Joe said, looking pleased. "Here's what we are going to do. I'm going to put this medicine on your injury and we are *all* going to blow on it, just in case it stings a little. Aaron, come down here with me. Mother, you help blow too. Get ready to blow on it, Katie."

Joe dabbed a small amount of the reddish-brown liquid on the scratch. "Blow, everyone, blow!" Katie tried to pull away but Joe held on and kept telling her to blow. All four did a grand job of blowing away the sting. In seconds, her hand relaxed and she looked at the three faces around her.

"Did we blow the sting away?" Joe asked. Katie nodded and looked at his pocket. "You were a very brave girl. Are you ready for your surprise?"

A big grin immediately covered her face. "Yes, I bery bra."

Joe reached into his pocket and came out empty handed. "Were did my surprise go?" He reached into his other pocket. "No, not there. Maybe it's in my bag." This time when his hand came out of his doctor's bag he held two red suckers. He handed one to Katie. She took the sucker then threw herself at Joe, wrapping her arms around his neck.

Cassie felt tears spring to her eyes as she met Joe's. Her emotions ran rampant for a few moments until Joe stood up with Katie in his arms. "While your mother finishes hanging up the clothes why don't you show me the kitty that scratched you. But you need to take this other sucker to your brother."

"Cassie watched as Aaron, Joe, and Katie went into the barn. Then she quickly moved in between two rows of hanging clothes and cried. *God help me! Do I dare hope this is the help I've been praying for? I've waited so long for an answer. I won't ask him to take me and the children with him, so please let it be his idea.*

Cassie wiped her eyes then quickly finished hanging the clothes. She walked quietly to the barn, slipping in the side door, unnoticed. She stood and gazed at the scene before her and felt the urge to weep with joy. In one of the stalls on a pile of hay, Rand and Daniel were stretched out on their sides, playing with a couple of black and white kittens. Aaron casually stood inside the stall petting a pure black one. Joe sat on a bale of hay with Katie on his lap, petting another kitten. He was showing Katie how to hold and pet the soft kitten so it wouldn't scratch her again. Katie's giggle warmed her heart.

The precious time in the barn was quickly snatched away when Cassie's mother-in-law and father-in-law came storming in. "What's going on in here!" the older man bellowed.

Katie cringed and hung onto Joe. He didn't miss that Daniel jumped and turned pale. It took all his effort to stay calm, but Joe replied, "You must be Mr. Jackson. I was friends with your son. We're just admiring the new kittens with your grandchildren."

"I don't care who or what you are," the man growled, "you have no right to be here!"

Cassie tried to step in. "It's okay, Mr. Jackson. I invited them to see the kittens."

He glared at Cassie. "And whose barn is this? Certainly not yours! You have no business inviting anyone on *my* property."

"I'm sorry, sir," Joe said gritting his teeth. "We certainly didn't mean to intrude. We'll be leaving now." He motioned to Aaron and Rand.

"You better believe you're leaving!" The Jacksons stormed back out of the barn.

Joe didn't waste any time. "Cassie, you and the children wait for us outside." She nodded and took her little one's hands, exiting the barn. Then Joe turned to Aaron. "Aaron, I *can't* leave her here."

"Don't say anymore, Joe, I agree, we can't leave them here. We'll work things out so do whatever you think is best."

That was all Joe needed to hear. He met Cassie outside and looked around for the children, spying them by the clothes line. "Cassie, I will *not* leave you here another day! When we leave in the morning you're going with us."

Cassie's heart skipped a beat. Did she dare hope? Was this finally an answer to her prayers? "Are you sure, Joe?" she asked, searching his eyes, his face.

"I've never been more sure of anything in my life. I'll be back this evening, about seven. If you want to leave secretly I'll wait at the end of the lane until dark. If you want to say goodbye to them I'll come to the house and be here for you."

Her eyes glistened and she shook her head. "I don't have anything I want to say to them. I'll be at the end of the road as soon as I can get away after dark."

He studied her face a moment. "Will you be okay until then?"

"Yes, I think so. It's been worse. They go to bed early and sleep sound. But if I'm not there that doesn't mean I don't want to go with you. It's because I've been locked in."

"Don't worry, I'll find you. Take only what you really need, Cassie. It would be good if you could get by with a bag for you and one bag for both children."

"All right," she nodded, trying to force down the knot in her throat. "Thank you, Joe." She looked at Aaron and Rand. "Thank you, all of you. You've shown us the only kindness we've had since Ray left for the war."

The men mounted. "Keep your chin up, Cassie. We'll be back. It won't be very much longer." Joe took one last look into Cassie's face then turned his horse.

It was hard to watch them ride away. Cassie repeated over and over in her mind what Joe had said. *We'll be back. It won't be very much longer. God bless you, Joe.*

The men rode back to Marysville in silence, contemplating the awful circumstances they had just witnessed. Several times, Joe almost turned around to go back, but he was too angry and realized he needed to gain control of his emotions or he might do something he shouldn't. Like *thrash* Mr. Jackson. Maybe Mrs. Jackson, too.

They decided to get a bite to eat before going to the hotel. Rand voiced his feelings first. "How could a man be so mean to his own grandkids? Daniel is a sweet kid. I felt like giving that old man a piece of my mind!"

"I'm glad you didn't, Rand," Joe responded. "It might have made things worse for Cassie and the kids. I felt like doing *more* than giving him a piece of my mind, but that would have been wrong. I just want to hurry and get her out of that place. You do realize we're taking on a mighty big responsibility by taking them with us. I'll need help from both of you. It's a long way to go and I don't even know what I'll do when I get there."

After they ate, mostly in silence, they were soon back at the hotel. They made themselves comfortable in the room Aaron and Rand shared. Aaron picked up his carpet- bag and set it on his bed. "Both of you, come here. I want to show you something." He removed the contents of the bag and placed them on the bed. "I consider both of you family and trust you completely." He paused a moment and looked pointedly at Rand. "I trust you," he repeated. He reached inside the bag and pulled out a false bottom. Then he stepped back so Joe and Rand could see inside.

Rand whistled. "Where'd you get all that?"

Joe just gave Aaron a questioning look.

"It's a long story," Aaron said, "and I won't tell you all of it right now but this belongs to my family. We came into possession of it quite unexpectedly. After prayer and a lot of family discussion we decided to put it away and use it for family emergencies and to help people in need. When I came on this trip they decided I needed to take plenty for my needs and plenty to help others. It seemed a little too much at the time, but now I understand. I believe God wants me to use this to help Cassie and those kids."

Aaron reached in and pulled out a small sack, handing it to Joe. "These are gold nuggets, Joe. I want you to use them for Cassie in any way you think best." Then he took out two coins and handed them to Rand. "Here are two twenty dollar gold pieces, Rand. Put them in your pocket and use them for anything you might need. The rest of what is in there belongs to you, too. You're my family. All I ask is that you don't tell anyone else about it or where you got the money I gave you. Money changes people. Carmen, my step mother, says, 'The *love* of money is what corrupts people'. I don't want anything, especially money, to come between us. I love you both." Aaron put the false bottom back into his bag and replaced the items he had taken out.

"I don't know what to say, other than thank you," Joe finally said. "This means a lot to me, being financially able to help Cassie and her children. Thanks just doesn't seem to be enough."

"Yeah, me, too." Rand shoved the gold pieces into his pocket. He looked a little shaken about what Aaron had said to him. "Thank you for the money, but most of all, thanks for trusting me."

"You're both welcome. Now let's talk about how we're going to get Cassie and those kids on the stagecoach with us in the morning. And by-the-way, Joe, we're going home. That's where we're *all* going….Home!"

That evening found the three men again riding to the Jackson farm, only this time they had an extra horse.

"Joe, I've been wanting to ask you something," Aaron said.

"What is it, Aaron?"

"How did you know to put those suckers in your doctor's bag? That was pretty slick. I think you made a friend for life with just one sucker."

Joe chuckled. "I didn't put them in there. The bag was a gift from my friends, the Brightens. When they gave it to me Dr. Brighten said he put everything I might need in an emergency into the bag. He's been a doctor for a long time so guess he knew that I would need a sucker sometime in the future. Katie's a sweet little thing. I'm glad I had them."

"Hey, you two, there's the road that goes back to the house," Rand reminded them. "We going to wait out here on the road?"

"No, let's find a place out of sight and wait. When it's dark enough that I can't be seen, I'll slip up the road and wait for Cassie. She might have a hard time getting two bags and two little ones up the lane by herself."

"Good idea," Aaron agreed.

They found a place back off the road where they couldn't be seen but could watch the road, then waited for darkness. The night was quiet and still. Only one young man rode by on a horse. Finally, Joe said, "I think it's probably dark enough so I'm going to go now."

"Be careful, Joe. How long should we wait before we come after you?" Aaron asked.

"I hope you won't need to do that. It might take Cassie awhile to get out of the house. If I run into trouble I'll make a big enough commotion that you'll know to come running. I have my pistol, so if you hear a shot be real careful rushing in. I don't think it'll come to that but you never know. You saw how Mr. Jackson can be."

Joe made his way up the lane, staying to the side in the dark of the apple trees that lined the narrow road. Reaching the end of the lane, he squatted beside a bush, hidden by the shadows. The wait wasn't long. After several minutes he saw movement at the corner of the house.

Cassie came into view carrying two bags. She was whispering to Daniel, "Hold your sister's hand, Daniel, and follow me. You are my helper now and we're going to meet our new friends."

"You mean my new friend, Rand?"

"Shh, yes, but we must be very quiet and not wake your grandma and grandpa."

A squeaky little voice whispered, "I tired, Mama."

"I know, sweetie. You can make it to the end of the road, can't you?"

They were close enough then for Joe to make himself known. "Cassie," he quietly called out as he stood up. "It's Joe."

"Oh, you startled me!"

"Sorry. I thought you might need some help."

"Yes, that would be nice, thank you."

Joe quickly lifted Katie up into his arms. "Give me one of the bags so you can hold Daniel's hand and let's get away from here." They reached the end of the lane and found that Aaron and Rand had moved out onto the road with the horses. "You have the rope we brought, Rand?"

"Yeah, it's right here," he answered. "Hey, Daniel. How are ya?" he said softly.

Daniel grinned at Rand. "We're going with you. You're our new friends."

"Yes, indeed," Rand replied. "You are going with us and we are friends."

"You and Aaron take one of these bags and tie them on your horses," Joe said. He squatted down to talk quietly to Daniel. "Daniel, you can ride with your mother. You'll need to stay awake. We don't want you to fall off and get hurt."

Daniel's face turned solemn and he nodded. "I can stay awake."

"Good boy. It won't take very long to get to town. I've got a room waiting for you and your mother and sister."

"All right," he frowned. "But what's in the room?"

Joe smiled at the boy's innocence. "A bed for you to sleep in." He helped Cassie mount then lifted Daniel to ride behind his mother. "Hold onto your mother now. Cassie, are you all right with this or do you want him in front of you?"

"He'll be fine back there. What are you going to do with Katie?"

"I'll hold her. And don't worry, I won't drop her." He smiled up at Cassie.

"I know you won't. I trust you."

He somehow felt comforted by that comment. "Everyone ready to go?"

"Yes, we're all set," Aaron answered.

"When I get in the saddle, Aaron, hand Katie up to me." As they were moving out, Joe felt Katie snuggle against him. Her little round face turned up to his.

"Doc-ter?"

Joe felt his heart melting at the sweet voice of the little girl. "What is it, Katie?"

"Gama said I can't have da sucker. I been a bad girl. She trew it in da gar-bage."

Joe couldn't say anything at first, he was so angry. He thought about it and decided it wasn't too late to go back to that farmhouse and drag those two mean people out of their beds and thrash the living daylights out of them! He even knew of two other hombres riding beside him who would gladly help get the job done. His heart finally calmed down and he held Katie a little tighter. They couldn't hurt her now, not anymore.

"I'm sorry, Katie, but don't worry about it. I'll get you another one. Why, you can even pick out the biggest one you want." He felt her body relax in his arms and he smiled into the darkness.

Chapter 9

*T*HE NEXT MORNING THE group was in a scramble of activity, going in different directions to get ready for the stagecoach in time. Joe had been so busy he hadn't really looked at Cassie until they started to leave the hotel. He stopped her and turned her to face him. She ducked her head, not looking at him.

"Look at me, Cassie," Joe said gently.

"Why, do I have dirt on my face?" she said, embarrassed.

"No, but you do have a big bruise on your cheek."

Cassie's hand went to her cheek and she looked away. "It's nothing, Joe."

He took hold of her shoulders and gazed into her face but he wanted to do more. He wanted to put his arms around her and hold and comfort her, but felt he couldn't. "It is *too* something. He hit you, didn't he? Why didn't you leave that place sooner, Cassie?"

"How was I supposed to do that with two small children and no money? I tried hard to put some away so I could leave but they made that very difficult for me. They controlled all the money even when Ray was working there. Mr. Jackson resented any money we asked for and gave Ray the bare minimum, ignoring our needs."

Joe hung his head. "I'm sorry, Cassie. I should have realized how hard it would have been for a woman with children. It just hurts me to think of anyone hitting you. I should have stayed there and protected you yesterday."

"No, you did the right thing. It was easier on me the way we did it."

"Well, as long as I'm around, no one will ever hit you again."

Her face clouded, a mixture of regret, relief, and something else Joe couldn't determine. "Thanks, Joe," she said softly, then abruptly changed the subject. "We better get our errands done or we'll miss that stagecoach. *Please* don't let that happen!"

Aaron and Rand had gone to the livery to pay their bill for the rented horses. Then Aaron bought passage for the small group and waited for Joe to return with Cassie and the children. They had gone to a dry-goods store to buy blankets for the children, food to snack on, a couple of canteens, and of course, two big red suckers.

They loaded into the stagecoach and were ready to depart when a stranger opened the door of the coach and looked inside. Dismayed, he asked, "Is there room in here for me?"

"We'll scoot over and make room," Joe assured him.

Rand was already feeling the scrunch of the crowded coach and nudged Aaron. "Why don't you and me ask if we can ride up front with the driver. It might be fun."

"Sure, I'll try it," Aaron said. They climbed out and talked to the driver, gaining permission to ride beside him.

The stranger appreciated their gesture. "Thank you, young men. That's mighty nice of you. If I wasn't so old I'd take a turn out there, myself."

"You're welcome, mister." Rand grinned from his perch beside the driver.

As the coach slowly made its way out of town, Cassie settled in for the long trip. She hadn't felt this safe since she'd last been at home on the Chandler ranch. Even when she was with Ray she didn't feel safe, especially from his father and mother. The old man was heavy-handed and the woman was mean-spirited. She thought they might soften when their grandchildren were born, but nothing changed. The atmosphere was always charged with hatred and resentment. Then Ray had to up and go fight in the war, leaving her there to fend for herself. It was tough without him. As soon as he returned, though, she was going to talk him into getting their own place. The day she learned he had died in battle was the worst day of her life. Even *then* his parents had not shown one bit of compassion for her. She started praying for a way out of her situation. Always praying. Always watching. Always vigilant, keeping her children as safe as possible. And then, out of the blue, Joe shows up, bringing hope and rescue. Her thoughts drifted back to this morning when he held her to look at her bruised face. She hadn't been touched by a man since Ray had left, except for his father's hard fist. Her emotions had startled her and her mind had been in turmoil since.

She looked across the coach at Joe holding Katie on his lap. Her precious daughter had, in no time, ripped the paper-wrap off her sucker and was enjoying her sweet surprise. "I'm glad you're holding her," Cassie grinned. "I hope you don't get too sticky."

"We have a canteen of water and a handkerchief that will work just fine to wash the sticky off. We'll just let her enjoy her surprise." Joe smiled and winked at her.

Cassie's heart skipped a beat. He had the nicest smile, and those incredible eyes! She looked away. Probably had a nice, incredible girl waiting for him back home, too. *Don't get too close,* her heart warned. "All right," Cassie said and changed the subject. "That Rand is full of life. He has more energy than I've ever had."

"You can say that again. He has his moments of quiet and seems sad. I think he misses his father at those times but he seems to be a good kid."

"Daniel is quite impressed with him, aren't you, Daniel?"

"What?" Daniel said. He had been looking out the window and not listening to them talk.

"I was saying you really like Rand."

"Yeah, we're cousins," he said, bobbing his head. "He said because we both have red hair we can be cousins. I've never had a cousin before. He says Aaron is our cousin, too."

Cassie and Joe smiled at that bit of information. "That's really nice of him," Cassie said.

The journey to Indianapolis had its ups and downs but nothing of any consequence happened. The other passenger had gotten off at one of the stops so Rand and Aaron decided to ride inside the coach for awhile. Between Indianapolis and Springfield, Illinois, Rand began to get bored and restless. "I'm getting tired of stagecoaches," he admitted. "Are we going to travel by stage all the way home?"

Aaron laughed. "No, we can't travel all the way by coach and I'm getting tired of stagecoaches, too. I've been thinking of something and since we're all inside together I'd like to see what you think." Everyone looked at Aaron, waiting for him to go on. "I was wondering if we might outfit ourselves to travel by horseback." He looked at Cassie. "I just didn't know if you would be able to travel that way. Do you ride or would it be too hard on you? We could even buy a wagon and team if that would be better."

Cassie smiled. "I love to ride. I was raised on a ranch and grew up on horseback. If you all would help take care of Daniel, I could manage Katie. I'll have to work out some way to tie her to me, like a sling of some kind, but it shouldn't be too hard. My biggest problem is I don't have the money to buy a horse and saddle."

"I've got enough to outfit us all with horses, that's not a problem," Aaron told her. He looked at the happy, expectant faces around him. "Shall we do it?" The vote was unanimous. Katie cracked them up, clapping her hands in excitement.

After arriving at Springfield, they checked into a hotel. Rand helped haul their belongings to the upstairs rooms, all the while thinking he would like to go explore a little. He thought he better let Aaron know where he was going. He found Aaron and Joe down in the lobby having a discussion.

"Where do you think we can find out about buying horses?" Aaron asked.

"Anybody local would probably know," Joe answered. "But a livery would be the best place. They usually know about horseflesh and where to find it. The sheriff is another idea."

Aaron nodded. "We have time before it gets dark to go ask about it. Who wants to go with me?"

Joe said he would go. Cassie and the children were going to stay in their room to rest. Rand let them know that he wanted to stretch his legs and look around town for a bit and would meet them back at the hotel for dinner. They all agreed and went their separate ways.

The truth was, Rand had money in his pocket, just burning a hole in there. The last few stops on the stage, he was tempted to spend a little, but either didn't have time to look around or nothing appealed to him. Gosh, he hadn't seen this much money all at one time in his whole life. That Aaron was one generous person that was for sure. Not one twenty dollar gold piece, but two! He did, indeed, feel rich. He passed a barber shop and glanced in through the window. Didn't need anything in there, just had a haircut a couple weeks ago. Was it really that long ago? Maybe not. He couldn't really remember. A glance across the street showed a saloon or lounge, he didn't know for sure. Never had been allowed to go into such a place. His pa made sure they walked the straight and narrow. He watched a man stumble out the door and cross to his side of the street. The man gave him a cursory glance, then continued on up the walkway. Rand was glad the man didn't try to talk to him, he didn't look like a very savory type of person. Not that he was judging, but sometimes you can just tell. Steer clear of them, he had been taught. He passed a few more business establishments, then stopped in front of a mercantile. This might be an interesting place. Pushing open the door, Rand sauntered inside.

The place was full of about everything, clothes, farm supplies, tools, food stuff, and it smelled good, to boot. Bet he could find something in here. He nodded to the man behind the counter then turned toward the shelves of merchandise. Wait, was that the unsavory man in the back? He couldn't tell for sure but decided to stay along the sides of the store, just in case. A number of items caught his eye and he busied himself looking them over. He decided not to buy any of them, and thought he would see if the store had any dried beef strips. That would be something he could share with everyone on the ride home. Home? He didn't have a home right now and the thought tugged hard at his heart. He was anxious about meeting his uncle who he had never seen in his life, and hoped his uncle was going to be a lot like his pa. Maybe Rand could eventually feel at home there. At least Aaron lived there and he already liked Aaron a whole bunch.

Rand spotted the dried beef in a big jar on a shelf behind the counter. The clerk eyed him skeptically.

"Whatcha want?" He had a deep, gruff voice, not friendly at all.

"Could I get some of that dried beef?"

"Don't know. Can you pay?" He looked Rand up and down.

"Sure, I can pay." Rand wondered why he would ask such a question.

The clerk took the jar down. "How many?" He laid two pieces on the counter without waiting for an answer

"Uh, I'll need more than that, please." Rand shoved his hand inside his pocket, feeling the gold pieces, then quickly pulled his hand back out. The coin escaped his grasp and fell to the floor, rolling away. Startled, Rand bent down, chasing the coin, which actually rolled in a curve, right around the corner of a floor shelf. Just as he reached to pick it up, a boot came down on top of it. A big boot. Rand straightened, then felt his stomach clench. It was the man from the saloon. The unsavory one.

"Excuse me, uh…but…that's my money," Rand stammered.

The man didn't move. "What money? You see any money around here, Dewey?" he asked the clerk.

"Nope," answered the gruff voice.

Rand felt frozen in place. A long minute passed. The saloon man stared at him.

Rand tried again. "If you just, uh, move your foot, you'll see my money under it."

"Don't know what you're talkin' about. You better git on home to your mama, boy, before you git into trouble."

"You pay for this dried beef first," the clerk demanded.

Rand felt a slow burn under his skin. He knew he couldn't win this fight. "I don't want it," he said through clenched teeth. He turned toward the door.

Saloon man was quick. He reached out and grabbed Rand by the arm. "Now, that's being a mite disrespectful. You gotta pay for the beef, like the man says."

"I don't want it no more!" Rand was thinking as fast as he could. "Let go of me!"

He tried to pull his arm away but the man had a tight grip. "I don't have any more money, anyway."

The saloon man thrust his hand into Rand's pocket, finding the other gold piece. "Well, look at this!" he crowed, bringing the gold piece out into the open. He waved it at the clerk. "The boy told a lie. He *does* have the money to pay fer the beef after all. Give it to Dewey, boy!" He shoved Rand forward and flipped the coin onto the counter.

Rand saw, from the corner of his eye, the saloon man bending down to pick up the gold piece on the floor. He was livid as he watched the clerk deposit the other coin into a box under the counter, then push the two pieces of dried beef toward him. "I should get change back," Rand said hotly.

The clerk crossed his arms on his chest and looked down at Rand. "Prices are up. Things are expensive."

Rand grabbed the beef strips and slung them to the floor, then rushed out the door before the saloon man could react. He felt heat in his face and hate in his heart as he practically ran toward the hotel. Anger blinded him and he stumbled, almost falling. As he came to the hotel, he suddenly dreaded facing Aaron and Joe. *Where are the gold pieces I gave you, Rand? What do you mean, you lost them? Irresponsible! I can't trust you anymore, Rand!*

He made his way to the back of the hotel and found the back steps a quiet refuge. Sinking down, he dropped his head in his hands and felt a huge sob working its way up his throat. *I will not cry like a baby. I will not cry like a baby. I will not cry....*

"Rand? What're you doing back here?"

Rand jumped at the sound of Joe's voice. "Oh, nothing," he mumbled. "How did you know I was here?"

"I was watching for you to get back so we can have supper. I saw you run around the corner. Are you all right?"

"Yeah."

"Well, come on then. Let's go eat."

"I'm not hungry." Rand still had not looked up. He was afraid to meet Joe's eyes.

"That's a first!" Joe chuckled. "Don't you want to join us, anyway?"

"No."

Joe stood there a minute, puzzled. He sat down beside Rand and put his arm around his shoulders. "You miss your father. Is that it?"

Rand shrugged and was silent. Joe tightened his arm into a hug, then stood. "We'll be inside in the dining room whenever you want to come in." He left Rand sitting on the steps.

The others were already seated when Joe came in. They all chorused," Where's Rand?"

"He's not going to eat tonight," Joe answered. He sat down as if everything was fine. "Are we ready to order?"

The meal was good but the mood was somber. Rand was definitely missed at the supper table.

Aaron knew something wasn't right. Rand was never 'not hungry'. He didn't ask any questions at supper, but afterwards, when Cassie took the kids up to put them to bed, he turned to Joe. "What's wrong with Rand? He never goes without eating."

"I'm not sure, Aaron, he didn't want to talk about it, with me, anyway. I asked him if he misses his father and he just shrugged. Maybe he'll open up to you. He was sitting on the back step when I left him. We better go see if he's alright."

"I'll go by myself, if you don't mind. He might talk if there's only one of us. I'll go find him." Aaron stood and made his way out the front and to the back of the hotel. Rand wasn't sitting on the step and it took Aaron a minute to spot him over by a shed. He coughed and cleared his throat so Rand would know someone was there. Rand looked up.

"Hi, cousin," Aaron said, walking over to the shed. "Can we talk?"

Rand shrugged and studied his boots.

"Why didn't you come and eat? We missed you."

Another shrug. "I wasn't hungry."

"Joe thinks you're missing your pa. Is that it?"

Rand nodded but offered no other explanation.

"Did you miss him last week?"

Rand looked up, curious at that question. "Yeah, of course I did."

"Well you ate last week, so I think something else is bothering you. Rand, I want you to know you can talk to me about anything. I don't always have all the answers to all the questions, but maybe together, we can figure things out. We're family now and I have already grown to love you like a brother. Can't you trust me?"

"That's just it!" Rand exploded and kicked the side of the shed. "*I* can't be trusted! You said you trusted me, but now you won't! Not anymore."

"I don't follow. Why won't I trust you anymore?"

Rand hung his head. "You just won't."

Aaron hurriedly winged a prayer to God, asking for understanding and wisdom. And suddenly a thought came to him. "Can we sit down for awhile? Over on the steps would be fine." Rand reluctantly followed and they sat side by side. "It's about the money, isn't it?"

Rand barely nodded. It was getting quite dark by then and Aaron couldn't see Rand's face very well, but the moon shown and glistened on his unshed tears.

"I don't care about the money, Rand, but will you tell me what happened?"

"I lost it all!" A sob caught in his throat and he angrily swiped at his eyes. "I mean all of it! I lost *all* of it."

Aaron put his arm around Rand, but Rand shook it off. "No! You can't love me now! Not now! I'm not trustworthy, can't you see?"

"Well, I doubt you gambled it away. Did you misplace it, maybe, or are there holes in your pocket? Rand, I don't care about the money. I care about *you*. And if it will make you feel any better you can tell me how you lost it. Maybe getting it out in the open will make you rest easier. What do you think?"

Rand took a deep breath. "I went to the mercantile because I hadn't spent any money yet. I mostly wanted to look around and then I saw the dried beef strips...."

Aaron listened to the whole story. He understood why Rand was so upset and wanted to get up right then and go find those men! They had humiliated Rand, not to mention stealing his gold pieces.

"Rand, I am so sorry that happened to you. There was no call to treat you that way and I wish I had been there with you. But I don't want this to ruin your life. Those gold pieces can be replaced, and they will be. As bad as those men were, I don't want you to hold hate in your heart. That isn't good for *you*. It's like a cancer, eating up your insides. Just give it to God and he will deal with those guys. Besides, one of these days, *you're* going to be the big man and people will think twice before messing with you." He hugged Rand, and mussed his hair a little. "That is, if you eat and put some meat on your bones. Let's go see if the kitchen has any food left."

Rand actually grinned a little. He liked the thought of being the big man that no body messed with. "If I was a lawman...those two would be in jail. Forever!"

⬱

Morning came bright and early. Everyone scrambled to get ready to go look at some horses. They had been directed to the Ferguson ranch, about two miles out of town, that had the reputation for selling good stock. They rode out in a rented wagon, laughing and talking the whole way. Joe was glad to see Rand in a good mood. He hadn't told Aaron yet, but he had been standing at the corner of the hotel and had heard Rand's story. He hadn't meant to eavesdrop but he got there just as Rand was telling it, so stood quietly and listened. It burned him no end at what happened and he wasn't sure yet what he was going to do about it. But he *was* going to do something.

The Ferguson ranch was large and impressive and very well kept. They each got their pick of horses and got to ride them to try them out. Cassie picked a beautiful dapple gray whose name was Sweet Pea. Joe chose a reddish brown gelding, Aaron a black mare and Rand a brown mare. Mr. Ferguson even had saddles to sell them, used, but in good repair. He directed them to a neighboring ranch to purchase a pack animal since he didn't have any for sale.

Everyone left happy. Rand and Aaron rode their horses while Joe, Cassie, and the children drove the wagon with the other two horses tied to the back.

"I think we did good back there," Cassie commented. "I wish I could have ridden Sweet Pea, myself, but Daniel enjoyed riding her with you. Thanks for taking him."

"You're welcome. I wish you could have ridden her, too. Mr. Ferguson said she was the best pick we made."

"I'll need to buy some pants or a riding skirt before we leave."

"There's a lot of things we need to shop for. It'll probably take all of tomorrow to get ready."

They arrived at the neighboring ranch. Cassie and the children stayed in the front yard and visited with the rancher's wife while the men went out to the corrals. They came back with two horses; a sturdy pack horse and a small horse with a child's saddle.

Cassie eyed the small horse, realizing what they intended. She didn't hesitate to voice her concern. "What's the small horse for?" she asked, reaching up to stroke its neck. "I hope it's not for Daniel cause he's too little to ride."

Joe said, "I understand your reluctance, but we won't let him do anything that'll hurt him. We'll take it slow and easy and teach him how to ride and care for his horse."

"Joe, I don't know. I don't think…."

The rancher's wife put her hand on Cassie's arm. "It'll be all right, dear. Patches was our little girl's horse. She may have been a little older but she was about the same size as your boy. Patches loves children and never gave Patricia any trouble. She's more like a pet than anything. Our little girl died about a year ago and it's time to let Patches go."

By this time Cassie didn't have the heart to refuse. Rand and Aaron already had Daniel on the horse and were walking him around the yard. "Mama, look! It's just my size!" he beamed.

When they left, Daniel rode his little horse in-between Aaron and Rand. He seemed to be doing fine. As they got to the edge of town, Aaron lifted Daniel off Patches and put him in front of himself. Then Rand took Patches' reins and they wound their way through the traffic of town. Cassie was grateful for the watchful young men who cared for her son.

"I hope you're not mad at me," Joe said.

"You mean about the horse? No, I'm not mad. It just scared me a little. But when I see how good the boys are with Daniel and how happy he is, I could never be mad at that. I want Daniel to grow up to be strong. He needs to be with good strong men."

Joe glanced down at Katie, sitting between them, just as a tear slid down her pudgy cheek. "Hey, what's the matter with my pretty little girl?"

"I wanna ride, too," she said, her bottom lip quivering.

Cassie laughed at the pitiful face her daughter was making. "You'll get to ride with mommy. As a matter of fact, you'll probably get to ride more than you want to."

Katie clapped her hands like she had been given the world.

Chapter 10

*J*OE WAS RIGHT. IT took all the next day for them to get ready to travel. Cassie got an idea for making a carrier for Katie, which she could tie to her own back. She padded and improvised until she had an adequate way to carry her daughter then demonstrated her creation for Joe. "That looks great, Cassie. I'm impressed. She'll be safe and it'll help keep her warm, too." He met her eyes with a smile. "Good job."

She blushed at his praise. "I'm going to fold our blankets under her so her weight won't be on my shoulders. I haven't ridden horseback in quite a long time and I've really missed it."

"Well, it'll be harder in some ways. We can enjoy the freedom to stop and go when we want and we can travel on our own schedule. It may be more dangerous, though, and that worries me. We're far enough north that I don't think we'll run into any raiding confederates. Indians are out there, but I was told there hasn't been any trouble around here lately."

"Joe, I can shoot, you know. You, Aaron, and Rand all have rifles and you and Aaron are going to wear pistols. I would really like to have a rifle to carry but we've spent so much money already that I just hate to ask Aaron to buy me one. Where does he get all the money?"

"I don't know the whole story and he's asked us not to talk about it, but I can tell you this, his family wants to use their money to help people. I'm hoping someday I'll be able to pay them back."

"Maybe I can, too. Right now, though, I'm just grateful for the help."

"If you really want to get a rifle let's go now and buy one. I think it's a good idea for you to have one in case…well, just in case. Besides…" he pulled his hat low over his eyes and squinted into the distance, jaw set, "I have some unfinished business at the mercantile."

Joe went to find Aaron and Rand. "Come on, you two, we're going to the mercantile. There's still some things we need for our trip." He gave Aaron a knowing glance, having already told him his plan.

Rand stiffened. "No, you guys go. I don't need to go there."

"I want you to come with us, Rand. I need you to help me," Joe urged.

"Yeah, cousin," Daniel said, pulling on Rand's arm. "Come with us."

Rand sent a pleading look to Aaron, but Aaron just nodded. "Come on, cousin, everything will be all right, I promise."

Rand reluctantly followed them to the mercantile. He hesitated at the door but finally entered on Joe's heels, keeping as close to him as possible and never daring a glance toward the counter.

"Let's see," Joe said nonchalantly, looking around the store. "What do we need to take with us?" He nodded at the unfriendly man behind the counter and sauntered over to the shelves. Cassie and the children found something to entertain themselves, and Aaron chose to stand close to the front, watching.

Joe picked up a jacket, that he didn't really need, then found a lantern and inspected it closely. He casually glanced at Rand. "Pick out something, Rand. Anything you like or want. How about a knife? That might come in handy."

Joe put the jacket back then looked the riding gloves over. He noticed Rand checking out a hunting knife, complete with its own sheath and a loop to put a belt through. "If you want it, go put it on the counter." He called Cassie over to try on riding gloves and insisted she get a good pair.

Daniel found a small leather pouch filled with marbles. He looked up at Joe, but never said a word. "I think you better get those marbles, Daniel, they might come in handy some day." He mussed the boy's hair, then turned to Aaron. "You need gloves or anything else?"

Aaron shook his head no, then decided he could use another pair of socks, if Joe could pick out a pair for him. Joe got the socks and decided they all needed a new pair. It was something small and light-weight and easy to pack. He put four adult pair and two pair of children size socks on the counter along with two pair of gloves, the knife, and the pouch of marbles. Rand slipped a harmonica onto the counter then went to stand by Aaron, his back to the counter.

The clerk stood unmoving, arms crossed on his chest. His eyes darted from one person to the other then landed on Joe. "That it?"

"Yeah, except for a couple of peppermint sticks. And some dried beef. Yeah, I'll take some dried beef," Joe answered staring into the man's eyes.

The man turned and took down a jar of peppermint sticks, extracting a couple, then took the jar of dried beef strips and set it on the counter. "How many?"

Joe slowly and deliberately pulled the jar across the counter toward himself. He wrapped his arm around it. "*All* of it."

Hearing this, Rand jerked his head toward the counter, eyes wide, watching Joe.

The two men stared at each other for several moments.

"I need my purchases put into a sack," Joe said steadily.

The man took his time finding a flour sack and stuffing everything in. He held onto the sack. "Twenty dollars," he demanded.

Joe reached across the counter and wrested the sack from the surprised man. "I believe it has already been paid for…day before yesterday…with a *gold* piece!"

Rand glared at the man as they exited the store. He walked beside Joe for a bit, then said, "Thanks, Joe. I didn't want everyone to know what happened. It's kind of embarrassing."

"That man should be the one who's embarrassed. It was shameful the way they treated you. And by-the-way, Aaron wasn't the one who told me, so don't blame him. I only wish that other crook had been there today."

"How did you know, then?"

"Well, I was worried about you and thought I'd go find you and Aaron. I rounded the corner as you were telling Aaron what happened, and I heard enough to get riled about it. I had to think on it and figure out what to do. You know, something that wasn't illegal or criminal." He grinned at Rand. "I think it turned out pretty fair, don't you?"

"Yeah, pretty much. Except for my other gold piece."

"You're right, but guess we'll have to chalk that one up to a loss. Don't think about it anymore, all right? We're going to leave this place in the morning and you can just leave that bad experience here in this town. Come on, it's almost supper time and we still haven't bought Cassie a rifle. I think we'll go to the other store for that."

The group was excited as they left Springfield early the next morning. By the end of the day some of the excitement had worn off. The afternoon of the third day they found themselves on the banks of the Mississippi River.

"Wow, would you look at that! How are we going to get across that big ole river?" Rand asked.

"The last town we went through, we were told to travel north along the river to the town of Quincy and then we'll cross by steamer. I suggest we continue on in that direction and look for a good place to set up camp for the night. Looks like the youngest member of our party could use a nap. Maybe we can rig up some fishing poles and catch our supper."

"Can I fish, too?" Daniel asked, excited about the idea. "*Please*, can I?" he begged.

Rand threw a challenge to the other two men. "Sure, you can fish. I bet you and me can catch more fish than Joe and Aaron. Fish like men with red hair, you know. We better hurry and find a camping place because the fish will be biting any time now."

A few miles upriver the group found just the spot they wanted and began setting up camp. The sandy beach lay alongside a grassy section that looked inviting, with forest beyond that. It was a perfect spot. Over the last few days they had gotten into a routine with everyone having specific jobs to do. Even little Katie had a small bag to pick up sticks to start the fire with.

"Do you want me to set up the tarp for you and the kids to sleep under, Cassie? I'll do it before we go fishing."

"I don't think we'll need it tonight. Just let it go for now. You and Aaron better go on and start catching fish. Katie and I will be just fine."

"All right, keep your rifle handy."

With the men gone, Cassie turned to her daughter. "You want to pick up sticks for the fire, now?"

"I tired, Mama."

"I am too. Let's lay down and take a nap, then we'll get a fire going."

Mother and daughter were soon asleep. For the first time in days, Cassie relaxed and let her worries and fears flit away like the orange and black butterfly she saw right before she closed her eyes. She dreamed of butterflies of all colors. Daniel and Katie were trying to catch them as they flew from one perch to another. Their laughter was a delight to hear. She felt at peace in her dream. A place safe and warm. Sensing there was someone behind her, she turned to find Ray...no...Joe, smiling down at her. Which was it, Ray or Joe? She kept trying to focus and make the face look like Ray's, but then she remembered Ray was dead, killed in the war. She was aware of a child calling....

"Mama! Mama, look what I caught! Mama, wake up, look what I caught."

Daniel's voice brought her back from her dream world. She sat up. "What is it, Daniel?" In front of her face was a fish so big Daniel could hardly hold it up. She quickly moved back. "That's wonderful, Daniel, but move it away from my face, please."

"I caught it all by myself, Mama."

Rand was right behind Daniel. "He sure did. I'm mighty proud of you, cousin. That one's almost big enough to feed us all tonight."

"Will you cook it for us tonight, Mama?"

"I sure will. Katie, look what your brother caught for our supper." Cassie turned to where her daughter had been sleeping but the spot was empty. "Katie!" she called. "Did you two see Katie when you came up here?"

"No, we haven't seen her since we left to go fishing," Rand said.

Cassie jumped up, trying not to panic. "Help me find her, you two. She must have woken up while I was still asleep and wandered off. "Katie!" she hollered again.

Rand and Daniel walked around the immediate area calling for Katie but they didn't see or hear any sign of her. "She couldn't have gone too far, Mrs. Jackson. I better go get Joe and Aaron though. It'll be getting dark before too long. Best if we all look."

"Yes, Rand, do that. Hurry please!"

"I'll go with Rand, Mama."

"No! You stay here with me, Daniel."

"But, Mama...."

"No!" Cassie knew she sounded harsh but couldn't help herself.

Rand patted Daniel on the back. "She's right, cousin. Your mama needs you to stay here and take care of her." He smiled down at Daniel. "Put your fish over on the grass by mine. I'll be right back. I saw them just a little ways downriver."

Daniel stood a little taller. "All right, I'll take care of her real good."

"That's what I like to hear," Rand said as he hurried off.

Cassie watched Rand run down the sandy river's edge then quickly scoured the area for any sign of her daughter. *Katie, where are you? Why would you leave?* Then she remembered the small sack Katie used to gather sticks. She couldn't see it anywhere. *That's what you did, my sweet Katie. You went to find firewood. God, help us find her.*

Joe, Aaron and Rand came running back to camp. "Cassie, what happened?" Joe reached out and grasped Cassie's shoulders, alarmed at the frantic look in her eyes.

"Katie and I laid down to take a nap before we did our jobs. I must have been… oh, it doesn't matter! We've got to find her! We've got to hurry before it gets dark. I think she woke up before I did and decided to go find sticks for the fire. I can't find her sack."

"Stay calm. We'll find her. She couldn't have gone very far. You stay here in case she comes back."

"I *can't*! I've got to help find her!"

"All right, then. You and Daniel walk up and down the beach. She just might find her way to the river. Don't go into the forest. Stay close and keep an eye on the horses and our things. Carry your rifle and be careful. Aaron, you go north. Rand, you go south and I'll go east. Do a zigzag pattern and look for any tracks or signs she might have left. If you see anything that looks like she's been there, fire one shot. Wait about ten minutes and fire another shot. We'll come to you. When it gets too dark to see, come straight back here. We'll make a new plan. Let's don't waste any more time. Move out!"

Time seemed to drag for Cassie as she roamed up and down the river's edge. Daniel was being diligent to look for any small foot prints in the sand. She kept trying to pray but her mind was a messy quagmire of thoughts. "Let's go back to the camp now, Daniel. The sun is starting to set and we need to build up a big fire. Maybe that will guide Katie and the men back to camp."

"Did you hear that, Mama?"

"Yes, it was a gun shot. Which direction did it come from?"

"That way." Daniel pointed north.

"That's what I thought too. That would be Aaron. Maybe he found our Katie! Hurry, honey, let's get the fire going."

Minutes later Rand came running from the forest then Joe hurried from the east to meet them at the fire.

"Was that shot from the north?" Joe asked.

"Yes, it would be Aaron," Cassie said, anxiously.

A second shot was heard sending Rand and Joe quickly in that direction. It seemed like an eternity to Cassie as she watched and waited. Complete darkness had fallen when she heard the men coming back through the trees. They broke into the light of the campfire and she frantically searched for Katie in their arms or walking beside the three men. "Where is she? Didn't you find her?" Cassie rushed to Joe, grasping his shirt sleeve. "Please, Joe! Tell me, what did you find?"

Joe realized she was on the verge of hysteria and grabbed her by her shoulders to hold her still. "Calm down, Cassie. I'm going to tell you."

"Is she dead?" Cassie nearly collapsed at the thought spoken aloud.

"No! No, of course not. We didn't find *her* but we found where she had been. Aaron found her shoe print on a game trail a ways into the trees. That little tyke covered more ground than I thought she could. We searched the area thoroughly but didn't find anymore signs. I think...."

"We *have* to go back and try again!" Cassie demanded.

"We wouldn't be able to see anything. It's pitch black in the heavy forest. Besides, she's not there...."

"Make sense, please!" Cassie interrupted again. "I don't understand. Where could she have gone? She'll be terrified out in the dark all alone."

"That's just it, Cassie, she's *not* alone. Someone else found her."

"*What*? *Who* found her?"

"I don't know, but it was clear from the tracks that someone found her and carried her north. It was too dark to follow them. Whoever it was didn't stay on the trail where he found her."

"*He*? You think a *man* found her. What if...." She abruptly fell silent. The desperation in her eyes and the tears now streaming down her face was more than Joe could take.

"Cassie, don't even think like that now." He pulled her into an embrace. "We have to think that it's a *good* thing that someone has her. Now, they'll try to find us."

Joe held her until her tears slowed. "I hope you're right. Do we just sit here and wait? I don't think I can do that."

"No, we're just regrouping. We're going to grab something to eat and ride north toward that town of Quincy to see if we can see anymore camps. If we ride along the river bank we'll be able to see a little bit with the moon shinning on the white sand. Might even find a house or farm where we can ask if anyone has been by with a lost girl."

Cassie wiped the tears off her cheeks. "I'll slice some of the bread and cheese real quick. You can eat on that for now. Then, I'll cook those fish up for you when you get back."

"That's the way," he encouraged her. "We'll have her back before you know it."

Joe and Rand scrambled to saddle horses and get ready. Aaron would stay at camp with Cassie and Daniel. When they were ready to leave, Aaron said, "I think we should pray before you two ride off."

"Good idea," Joe told him. "Please, Aaron, would you pray for us?"

They gathered in a little knot as Aaron started praying, "Heavenly Father, we come to you asking for help. Little Katie is out there with someone we don't know. I pray, Father, that you would be with Katie and whoever it was that found her. I pray that they would take good care of her and bring her safely…." Aaron stopped suddenly.

Night sounds seemed to fade away as the small group stood in a circle with their heads bowed. Someone was singing! No one made a sound as they raised their heads and peered through the darkness, listening.

The gospel train is coming,
I hear just at hand, the male voice sang, distant, at first.
I hear cart wheels moving,
And rumbling thro' the land. He was getting closer.
Get on board, children,
Get on board children, sounded like it came from the river.
Get on board children,
There's room for many a more.

The song changed, and it was very close now.
Swing low, sweet chariot, coming for to carry me home.
Swing low, sweet....

Abruptly the singing stopped. The three men picked up their rifles. A man singing gospel songs probably wasn't dangerous, but just in case, they were ready. A faint padding of feet on sand came toward them. "Hello, the camp!" came a voice. "I'm friendly. Need to talk to you folks!"

"Come on in if you're friendly," Joe answered.

Out of the darkness, a young Negro man appeared at the edge of the firelight. He seemed to be in his early twenties, slightly built. He stood for a few moments eyeing the three men with rifles then grinned. "You all goin' to shoot me?"

"No, no. Come on in to the fire," Joe told him, putting his rifle down.

As he moved closer, Cassie noticed he had a bundle over his shoulder with an old tattered coat draped over it. At the bottom of the bundle were two little feet that she instantly recognized.

"Katie!" she yelled and rushed toward the young man.

The bundle moved and a sleepy voice said, "Mama?"

"Oh, Katie! Yes, it's your mama!" Cassie reached to take her.

Katie threw herself at her mother, her arms going around her mother's neck in a big hug. She finally pulled back, put her pudgy little hands on her mother's cheeks and with a questioning look asked, "Where you go, Mama? I not fin' you."

Cassie started crying again and hugged her daughter. "I was right here, honey."

The relief was palpable, everyone was happy. Aaron approached the young man who had brought Katie back to them. "My name is Aaron Trinity. Thank you for bringing her to us."

"I'm Gabriel. Glad I could be of help."

"Come on over and sit down, Gabriel. Tell us how you found our Katie."

"First, let me give this sack to Katie." He untied the sack he had hanging off a rope belt and handed it to the little girl who was still hanging on to her mother. "Here's your sack."

Katie smiled at him and held the sack for her mother to take. "I get sticks for da fire, Mama."

"That's good, Katie, thank you. But next time wait for mama to go with you."

Gabriel turned back to Aaron who was sitting on the ground with Rand and Joe. "The truth is, I didn't find her, she found me. I was laying real quiet watching a snare I put out to catch me a rabbit for my supper. When she walked up beside me real quiet-like, I about jumped outta my skin! Couldn't understand all her words, but she let me know she couldn't find her mama. Most white children are afraid of black men like me, but she didn't seem to be afraid. We made friends right off like. I'd seen some other people headed to that town they say is Quincy. I thought maybe she belonged to them, so I picked her up to head north. She raised a ruckus about that old sack of sticks she was carrying. She wouldn't leave it behind. Said it was for to build a fire. Ran into people who told me about seeing men fishing along the river back here, so I came back this way."

Cassie had put Katie down on a blanket. "If I can get someone to clean that mess of fish it won't take long to cook them. I know you all are hungry."

Gabriel was the first to jump up. "I'd be right proud to clean them if you might let me eat some. That is, if you have plenty. I'm mighty hungry."

"We have plenty of food, Gabriel, and I insist you stay and eat with us," Cassie replied. "That's the least we can do after what you did for us."

Gabriel didn't have to clean the fish by himself. Aaron, Rand, and Daniel all helped. After everyone was full, the group sat around talking until Cassie handed Gabriel a blanket. "Here, Gabriel, you should stay here tonight. It's too late to find your things and your campsite."

"Thank you, ma'am. I don't got no campsite. All I got is what I have with me."

"All the more reason to stay here with us. I'll fix pancakes in the morning."

"I shore won't turn that down. Thank you, ma'am."

The next morning when everyone was filled with pancakes, horses were saddled and loaded, a problem arose between Aaron and Gabriel.

Chapter 11

"*I* CAN'T DO THAT!"

"What do you mean, you *can't*?"

Everyone was in their saddles ready to start toward the town of Quincy. Aaron had suggested that Gabriel ride behind him since he was going to Quincy too. He was holding his hand down to help Gabriel up behind him, but Gabriel was shaking his head.

"It just ain't fittin' for me to do such a thing."

"I guess I don't understand, Gabriel. What do you mean, it isn't fitting? Are you embarrassed to ride with me?"

"A Negro like me just don't ride with no white man. Besides, people will call you names. You folks been too good to me for that to happen. I'll jus' walk myself to town."

Aaron looked perplexed. Then an idea came to him. He dismounted and led his horse a few feet down the river bank. "Well, come on, Gabe. If you're going to walk, then I'll walk with you."

Rand had a silly grin on his face when he made his move to dismount. "If you two are going to walk then I will too. How about you, Daniel? You going to walk with your cousins?" He winked at Daniel.

Daniel, who figured it out and wanted to play along, smiled and answered, "If my cousins are walking, then I will too."

Rand helped Daniel down from his horse and handed him the reins so he could lead Patches.

In a few moments, Joe had dismounted and joined the walkers, leading his horse and the packhorse. Cassie smiled and called out, "Would one of you help me with Katie? If we're going to walk to Quincy I need someone to help her down when I untie these straps."

Gabriel looked at all of them and shook his head again. "You all jus' being crazy. Ain't no need to do that. I been walking for weeks now and I don't mind walkin'. Just get on dem horses and ride like you should."

Aaron was determined to make his point. "No, we consider you a friend now, so if you can't ride with a white man, then we'll walk with you. Besides, I think God brought us all together for a purpose and I want you to go to Quincy with us."

Gabriel stopped and stared at Aaron. "You jus' trying to make me do what you want. I'm a free man now, and can do whatever I please."

"I know you can, Gabriel. I guess I just want you to know that I don't care what other people think. I want us all to be friends. Even if you were green or pink I'd still want to be your friend. Come on and ride with me, at least to Quincy. I wish you would at least go that far with us."

Gabriel looked down at his ragged clothes and his worn out shoes, held together with strips of leather. He seemed unsure what to do. Finally, he looked at Aaron and nodded. "All right, since ya'll is being so stubborn, someone has to make good sense. Let's ride dem horses."

Aaron smiled to himself as Gabriel got on behind him and they headed toward Quincy. They rode along in silence, climbing the small hills along the river. Finally, Gabriel asked, "Why you being so good to me?"

"Do you believe in God, Gabriel?"

"Sure, I believe in God. Don't understand a lot of things he lets happen in the world but I know there's a God."

"Well, the best way I know to answer your question is that I feel like God wants me to try and be like Jesus. He has blessed me in many ways and I think he wants me to help others as I go along in this life. Can I ask what you're going to do in Quincy?"

"I don't rightly know. I reckon I'll look around and see if I can find me some jobs to do. I figure if I can feed myself and make a little money here and there, maybe I can travel around and see what's out there in this world."

"Have you ever thought about going west?"

"Maybe. I hear talk about that place they call Cal-ee-forn-ya. Is it a long ways from here?"

"Yes, it's a long ways. I've never been that far west. You know, Gabriel, if you're wanting to travel and see different places why don't you go with us? I can outfit you and you'll get to see a lot of country. The place where I live has got to be some of the most beautiful country there is."

"What I do when we get to where you live?"

"You can do whatever you want. You might like to work at one of the ranches or maybe just ride on to the next place."

"When you say you gonna *outfit* me, what's that mean?"

"I'll buy what you need to travel with us. Like a horse, couple a changes of clothes, a warm coat, some new boots, and a bedroll. Can you handle a horse, other than sitting behind me, I mean?"

"Sure can. That's what I did on the plantation I was sold to when they took me away from my mama. I was small for my age so they didn't think I would make a good field hand. They put me to taking care of the animals. I didn't get to ride dem horses unless I was exercising 'em. But I know all about horses. Had to help the house servants too, but that wasn't too bad."

"That's good to know. Can you shoot?"

Gabriel chuckled. "You don't know much, do ya? No white man would ever let a black man have a gun of any kind."

"Oh." Aaron thought for a couple of minutes. "Would you be interested in learning to shoot? Where we're going, you need to know how to protect yourself and learning to shoot is pretty important for survival. *And* to put meat on the table."

"How you know you can trust this black boy with a gun?"

"I don't think you're going to hurt any of us, Gabriel. You took care of Katie and found us. Then you were concerned about people calling us names because you were riding with me. That doesn't sound like someone who would do harm to the people he's with. Think about it and let me know by the time we get to Quincy."

"What if I can't pay you back?"

"I don't want you to pay me back. Just think of it as a gift from God."

"You shore is different than any man I ever knowd. All right, I'll think on it."

Gabriel was quiet the rest of the way to Quincy. The day was a bit blustery but the sun shone on them all morning. Except for the wind it was a pleasant ride into town. They got a few stares as they made their way down the main street, but mostly it seemed the town people were used to seeing all sorts coming and going.

They found a place to eat but Gabriel was told he would have to eat in the back room by the kitchen. He took it in stride but Aaron had other ideas. "He's a friend of ours and I'd appreciate it if you would let him sit with us."

"Sorry, I don't make the rules," the waitress said. "The Negros can eat here but they have to go to the back room."

Aaron wasn't going to drop it. "Can a white man eat in the back room?"

"I don't know why you'd want to but there isn't any rules against it."

"All right, then I'll go to the back room with my friend, here." Aaron turned to Joe. "You all can eat out here but I'm going with Gabriel."

Rand wasn't going to be left out. "If you and Gabe are eating in the back room then that's where I'm going."

Cassie smiled at the waitress. "Is there room for all of us in that back room?"

The waitress looked perplexed, but said, "I think we can fit all of you back there, if that's what you want to do."

"That's what we want to do," Cassie answered. "You just lead the way."

Gabriel shook his head all the way to the back room. When they were seated, he was still shaking his head. "Ya'll is as crazy as a chicken shed full of hungry coons. Maybe I'm as crazy as you all, cause I'm going to let Aaron here *outfit* me and I'll go with you as long as you all agree to have me."

"Let's vote," Joe suggested. "All in favor of Gabriel going with us, raise your hand."

Of course, it was unanimous. Katie threw both of her hands into the air and yelled, "Yea!" which brought a huge grin to Gabriel's face.

The mood turned somewhat serious when Daniel asked Gabriel a question while they were waiting for their food to arrive. "Why did they take you away from your mama?"

A silence fell over the room. Even the waitress stopped and waited for Gabriel's answer. Cassie saw the surprise in Gabriel's face at the question and started to smooth it over but he stopped her. "It's alright. It be a good question. I only wish I knew how to answer it." He looked at Daniel. "I don't rightly know. That's just the way things were. Negro people belonged to the white man and the white man was his master. Master could buy and sell me to whoever he wanted."

Daniel's eyes glistened. "I don't think that was very nice. I wouldn't like it if someone took me away from *my* mama."

"I'm glad you feel that way, Daniel, but don't cry over it now. That's what the war is all about. Negroes is gonna be free now. Abraham Lincoln done said we's gonna be *free!*"

Their stay in Quincy went about the same as it did in the café. But at the hotel, the owner changed his mind and allowed Gabriel to stay in a room with the boys, realizing he was going to lose money when they all turned to leave. Gabriel went shopping with Aaron and Rand while Joe and Cassie shopped to replenish supplies. Early the next morning they were ready to board the steamer that would take them across the Mississippi river. It was an adventure for all of them, especially the younger ones.

The horses were restless and nervous when they were led off the steam ship, but the crew kept everything under control and they were soon ready to ride again. "Come on, Gabe," Aaron said as he waited for Gabriel to get on behind him. "That farm we were told about isn't too far from here. We'll see if they'll sell us a horse."

They found the farm and half a dozen good looking horses in a pasture behind the barn. The farmer seemed eager to sell and let them look the horses over. All the men checked out the choices Gabriel made. "Which one do you like, Gabe?" Aaron asked.

"There's two that are right nice. I'm partial to black though, so I think the black gelding would suit me fine. Do you think I might try him out?"

"I wouldn't want to buy him unless you did. Mr. Castle said he's a six year old and his name is Dancer."

Joe had been talking to the farmer and talked him out of an old saddle. Gabriel saddled the horse himself and made a grand show as he gave the horse a short workout while they all watched. Aaron was pleased when the man didn't seem to mind that Gabriel was black and even complemented Gabriel on his choice of horses.

"You've got a good eye for horseflesh, young man. Take good care of Dancer. He's been a favorite of mine and I wouldn't sell him if I didn't need the money for getting my crops in this year."

❧❧❧

It was an unusual group that left the farm that day. The young men traded off riding beside Daniel, who was improving all the time on his horsemanship. Cassie and Joe followed behind with the pack horse. They had fallen back a ways so they couldn't be heard as they visited.

"We've got quite a collection of different young men with us, Joe. They're good boys, aren't they?"

"Yes, they are. I'm glad Aaron got Gabriel to come with us. Look at him in his new clothes riding with the others. I didn't think Aaron and Rand were going to talk him into that cowboy hat."

"I'm glad they did. He looks nice in it. I'll have to admit it stands out on his black head. I was surprised when he picked out that light gray color but I don't guess he cares that it doesn't match the brown coat he chose."

"No, I doubt it matters at all to him. He's probably never had a new suit of clothes in his life. Aaron's the one that amazes me. He has a good heart and his faith in God shames me, somewhat. I'd like to know more about all of the boys. Maybe we can get them talking about their lives when we make camp at night. Nothing like campfire talk."

"That's a good idea. We'll work on it. Did you see the harmonica Rand bought? We may even have a little music around the fire. I heard him tell Aaron that he and his father played music together. His harmonica was stolen when his father was killed. We probably shouldn't push him to play it until he's ready. It's bound to bring up sad memories."

Joe smiled at Cassie. "That's thoughtful of you. And of course, you're right." She looked up at Joe and their eyes met. He couldn't pull himself away from her pretty hazel eyes for a moment. Something passed between them that was new and strange to Joe. *Uh, Oh! I'm in trouble.* He turned away from Cassie to hide what must have been evident on his face. *I think I'm falling for her. Well, why not? She's a remarkable woman. A bit too pretty for her own good, but she'd make a wonderful wife.*

"I'd give a pretty penny to know what just went through your mind. You had a very strange look on your face," she told him.

He turned his attention back to Cassie but only grinned a crooked little grin. "Someday, maybe, I'll tell you."

Usually when a group of people travel a long distance together they fall into a routine, just like this bunch did. But there was always something interesting going on. Their personalities were so unique there was never a dull moment. Ohio was a good state for them to travel through and find out about each other. The Civil War had not touched Ohio in that no major battles were fought there but many had volunteered and were fighting for the Union. Indians had been driven out except for the northwest corner of Ohio. The further they traveled from the Mississippi river the sparser the vegetation became. Farm land eventually turned into grasslands. Trees and willows grew along the rivers so they looked for streams of water to camp near.

On one of these particularly inviting places, Cassie pulled Joe aside. "This is a good place, Joe. Can we stay here tomorrow, too? I think Katie and I need a day of rest."

"Is something wrong?" Joe asked, concern in his voice. "Are you feeling bad?"

"Oh, I'm fine. There are just days when a woman needs to have a little rest and privacy. Katie and I will hang out around camp. Do you think you can keep the boys occupied tomorrow?"

"I understand and don't worry about the boys. They occupy themselves and Rand keeps everyone entertained. We can hunt for some fresh game, fish, and maybe swim if it's warm enough. It's a good idea to let the horses rest a day, too. You know, we're headed into the hardest and most dangerous part of the trip. I hope we're ready for anything that happens."

Chapter 12

*J*OE HAD THE BOYS up and eager for the day. They had been delighted when he told them they were taking a day to hunt and fish. They fixed their own breakfast and were gone in no time. Cassie had been a little worried about Daniel but they had assured her they would take good care of him. Cassie stayed in her blankets and pretended to be asleep until they were gone. At times, she could hear them in the distance. She heard shooting, but wasn't alarmed because she knew they were target practicing with Gabriel. Katie was content most of the morning to play with her doll she had brought along. The boys came in about noon with a mess of fish, enough for everyone, and roasted them over the fire. Gabriel caught the most fish but they managed to still argue about who was the best fisherman, who was the best shot, and who was the best wrestler. Joe showed them how to box, but they quickly gave him first place in that activity.

"What are we going to do now?" Rand wanted to know after they devoured all the fish.

"It's plenty warm and I thought we might go swimming. It wouldn't hurt for you smelly boys to take a bar of soap with you. That hole Daniel and I were fishing in this morning is deep enough to get us all clean. This evening, you three can walk up the creek and see if you can bring back some fresh meat. That is, if you can keep from shooting each other."

"It's a good thing we fished this morning. With Rand getting in the water all the fish would have turned belly-up and died," Gabriel teased.

"When we finish swimming, I'll show you how to write your name, like I told you I would," Aaron said to Daniel.

"Think you might teach me too," Gabriel cautiously asked. "I always wanted to write my own name. Negros wasn't allowed no learning, thought we was too stupid to learn things."

"I don't think you're stupid, Gabriel," Daniel said. "Aaron will teach us. He's real smart."

"Thank you, Daniel," Aaron said. "I'd be glad to teach you, Gabe. What's your last name?"

"Don't reckon I have one. If I did, I never knowed what it was."

"I didn't have a last name either, until I found my dad. Then I decided on what name I wanted. I asked to be called Aaron Moses Trinity. Why don't you pick a last name. You can think about it while we swim."

"That's right nice of you, Aaron. I'll think on it."

"Well, let's go while the sun is the warmest," Joe said. "We don't have towels so we'll have to let the sun dry us off." Joe got up and went to get his change of clothes. "Don't you yahoos forget your soap."

As they walked toward the stream, someone announced an armpit smelling contest. They unanimously declared Joe the winner. He was washed and the first one back to camp. Mother and daughter were napping so he sat quietly until Cassie stirred. She saw him watching her and smiled. "How long have you been there?"

"Not long. Are you doing alright? Is there anything you need?"

His concern touched a tender spot in her heart. No one had cared for her in such a long time. "I'm just fine. It's been nice to have a quiet day, although it hasn't been that quiet for you, has it?"

"No, but I've enjoyed myself. It's been a very special day. When I was in the army I never relaxed and got to know the men around me. Guess I was afraid they might find out who I was and turn me in for the reward money. So I pretty much stayed to myself."

"There was a reward for you?"

"Yes, your father put up five hundred dollars for me, dead or alive."

"I'm so sorry, Joe," she said, anguish twisting her heart.

"Don't worry about it. It won't be much longer and we'll hopefully get it straightened out."

93

Katie woke up, sleepily crawling into her mother's lap and whispered in her ear. "We're going to go over behind those rocks for a few minutes," she told Joe.

"Take your rifle, Cassie."

The boys could be heard coming back to camp with a new contest underway, about which one smelled the best. Each of them declared their own special scent. Aaron said he smelled as sweet as a fresh cut bouquet of flowers. Rand knew he smelled as manly as a pine forest. Gabriel said he must smell like fresh baked apple pie, because that's the best smell on the earth.

They didn't decide on a winner but went straight to writing lessons. Aaron gave each one a piece of paper from his sketch pad and showed Daniel how to spell his first and last name. While Daniel practiced, Aaron turned his attention to Gabriel. "What did you decide you want your name to be, Gabe?"

"I done decided I want to be called Gabriel Freeman, cause that's what I am, a free man."

"That's a good name. Let me show you how to write it."

Rand told them he knew how to write his own name so he sat next to Daniel and helped him. Aaron did what he loved most and something he hadn't done in a while. He began to draw. The sun was quickly moving to the western horizon when Aaron put his sketch pad away. "If we're going to hunt we better leave now," he told Rand and Gabriel.

"Can I go, too, Mama?"

Daniel's pleading eyes made it hard for Cassie to say no. "I think we better let the boys go by themselves, Daniel."

"Please, Mama?"

Cassie was a little surprised when Joe took the matter in hand. "Daniel, don't argue with your mother. She knows what's best. Besides, I need you to stay here and help me take care of her and Katie. We've got to take the horses to water and keep the camp safe."

"Oh." Daniel was obviously disappointed but didn't argue.

After the boys left, Katie picked up her sack. "I get sticks."

"You're right, Katie. It's starting to cool off and we need to get some more wood for the fire tonight."

"Cassie?"

"Yes, Joe. What is it?"

"Don't go far, and…."

She waited. "And, what?"

"Would you call me Michael from now on? I want you to know me for who I really am and call me by my real name, Michael Mayfield. I'm going to ask the boys tonight to use my real name from now on."

"I would like that very much. And, Michael, I think I already know who you really are."

"And who is that, Cassie? Who am I, really?"

"You're a man who has a comforting strength about you that makes me feel secure. You're gentle and kind in your dealings with everyone which I appreciate more than I can say. Ray was good to me and the children but he did have a fierce temper, although he never took his anger out us. There were times when I thought he would stand up to his father but it's probably best he didn't. He might have killed the old tyrant if he ever let himself go. The love-hate relationship between them was hard for me to understand." She looked into Michael's eyes. "I will forever be grateful to you for taking me away from the Jackson farm."

They stood silently for several moments studying each other's face and trying to read each other's thoughts. Then Cassie spoke again. "You're a handsome man, Michael. Any woman would be proud to have you by her side."

Michael wanted to say many things to Cassie but little Katie interrupted their special moment. "Mama, go!" she insisted, tugging on her mother's hand.

The hunters didn't bring back a deer but did shoot several plump prairie chickens. And Gabriel, without anyone knowing, had set snares up and down the stream and managed to catch a couple of rabbits. The meat roasted over the fire while Cassie made corn cakes, surprising them all by producing a jar of strawberry jam.

"Where'd you get that?" Rand asked, voicing what they all were wondering.

"The last farm we stopped at. I tried to buy it from the farmer's wife, but she insisted I take it as a gift. I've been saving it for a special day and *this* has been a special day!"

Everyone agreed, as they enjoyed their time around the campfire. For the first time since traveling together, Rand pulled out his harmonica and played a few songs. He talked about his father and told how his mother had deserted them. "Pa said she was real pretty and had beautiful red hair like mine. He said she had a restless spirit." The memories seemed to overshadow Rand and he grew unusually quiet after that.

Daniel and Katie fell asleep and while Cassie put them to bed, Michael got the attention of the boys. "I need to talk to you three before we leave in the morning. First of all, I want you to start calling me by my real name, which is Michael Mayfield." Aaron knew the story but Rand and Gabriel didn't, so he told them what had happened, how he was accused of killing a man. "I didn't kill him but there was no way I could prove otherwise. So I changed my looks, my name, and hid in the army. It was while I was in the army that I discovered what I wanted to do with my life...be a doctor. Because of Aaron, I now know where my sister is and I want to be a part of her life but I *have* to clear my name first. It was Cassie's father who posted a reward for me when he found his foreman had been shot and killed. Cassie and I are going to confront him with the truth. That's really all you need to know about that.

"I want to tell you that I'm proud to ride with you. We've had a lot of fun getting to know each other and I feel we've become like family. You've done a good job taking care of Daniel, teaching him to ride and take care of his horse and all. That's great! I can see the little guy changing into a young man already.

"I'm going to be honest with you now, because I need all three of you to become *men* on this next leg of our journey. It's a dangerous country we're getting ready to cross and we need to take it seriously. The land is mostly prairie with very little timber. There's hardly any law in the territories and rough gangs have moved in, doing their ugly business. We might encounter several tribes of Indians, like Sioux, Cheyenne, Pawnee, and maybe Shoshone. The Indians come to hunt buffalo and try to live in peace but a lot of them are angry now that the white man is taking over their land and killing the buffalo, which they depend on for their survival. They raid homesteads, steal, and kill any white man that stands in their way. I've heard they are getting bolder because the war has taken most of the army back east to fight.

"In a week or so we'll be on the main trail that goes west. We might encounter some early wagon trains but for the most part we'll be on our own out there. You've taken the lead so far, but I want Cassie and Katie to take the lead now and I'll stay close to them. You three ride behind us with Daniel. If we run into trouble and have to make a run for it, the closest one to Daniel should grab him and let Patches and the pack horse go. Hopefully, they'll stay up with us but it would be better to lose them than get killed ourselves. If someone comes at us with hostility, you need to shoot to kill. I hope it never comes to that, but if it's necessary, don't hesitate. I promise that they won't think twice about putting a bullet or arrow in you."

Michel paused to consider what else to tell them. "Also, I'm going to push us harder to cover more ground. It'll be hard on Cassie and the children but its best that we get across Nebraska territory as quickly as possible."

Michael looked at each one sitting around the fire beside him. "Any questions?" He waited and when no one spoke up, he said, "Stay *alert* men! Our lives depend on it."

Chapter 13

*I*T WAS A SOBER group that left to cross the Nebraska territory the next morning. Cassie had heard everything that Michael said the night before. Without being told, she took the lead with Katie tied behind her in the pack she'd made. They talked very little to each other for Michael did what he said he would and pushed them to travel faster than they had been. He still stopped to let the children have a break but the stops were shorter than usual. For three days they made good time and saw no one. On that third day they saw a small herd of buffalo which was exciting for them all. Michael shot one and took enough of the meat to last for a couple of days. That night at camp, everyone was worn out. They'd found a pool that had been created by a spring seeping out of the rocks at the base of some low lying hills. Willows in the immediate area of the pool made an inviting spot to camp. At twilight, the aroma of roasting buffalo steaks filled the air, making their stomachs rumble and their mouths water.

Daniel climbed into Michael's lap as he sat on the ground by the fire. He sat very still for a short time then in a whisper, he said to Michael, "There's an Indian watching us."

Michael was instantly alert. "Are you sure, Daniel?"

"Yes."

Keeping his eyes on Daniel, he asked, "Where is he?"

"Just standing by the horses."

"Are we in danger?"

Daniel frowned in thought as he peered in the direction of the horses. "I don't think so. I think he's hungry."

"Let's invite him to supper then." Michael stood while holding Daniel's hand. He called out, "If you're a friend, come in to the fire!"

The others grabbed for their rifles but Michael calmed them. "Easy, men. Stay alert but don't do anything to threaten him."

Without a speck of fear showing, the Indian stepped into the firelight and stood in front of the fire. Without ceremony he nodded to Michael first then the rest of the men. He seemed pretty young, about Michael's age, but wasn't as tall. He was draped in a buffalo robe which fell down to his well-worn moccasins, making it hard to tell much more about him. He had no paint or decoration anywhere that could be seen. Looking at Michael, he said, "What are you called?"

"My name is Michael. What are you called?"

"I am called Talks a Lot by my people. The white man calls me Talker. I travel alone and take news and messages to different tribes of The People. I am Cheyenne. My heart is happy you invited me to your fire. I have not eaten today. Buffalo smells good."

"We're glad to share our food with you," Michael assured him.

The group sat around the fire eating, but talking little. Cassie sat close to Michael with a wide eyed Katie staring at their guest, but he ignored the females. When they were finished eating, Talker told Michael, "I bring news to you."

"What news do you bring to us?" Michael asked.

"There is danger not far away. Three Sioux will soon find you. They look for me, but they would come to you first to steal your horses. I killed one of theirs after they shot my horse. With arrow in him my horse ran a long ways until he died. He was a good horse but that is the way of things." Talker looked at Daniel and spoke about him. "The little one would make good Cheyenne warrior. He knew I was in the dark before he saw me."

Michael looked at Daniel and grinned. "Is that right, Daniel? Did you know he was out there before you saw him?"

"I don't know. I guess I thought there was *someone* out there."

"Ha!" Talker exclaimed. "It is so. He felt my presence. Come to me, little warrior."

Daniel hesitated, looking at Michael. "Can I?"

"Yes, it'll be all right," Michael answered.

Daniel went and stood in front of Talker. "Stand tall, little one. Be proud of who you are." Daniel straightened up as tall as he could get. "You have the spirit of the fox and the heart of a warrior. Your hair is the color of the fox. Talker will call you Little Fox."

Daniel didn't seem to be afraid of the Indian but spoke right up. "I already have a name. It's Daniel."

"That is a good name but your Cheyenne name will be Little Fox. You will be smart like the fox. Would Little Fox like to be brother to Talker of the Cheyenne?"

Daniel shrugged. "I guess so."

"Answer yes or no, Little Fox."

"Yes," Daniel told him.

"Good. Now we have ceremony."

Cassie grabbed Michael's arm when Talker pulled out a crude looking hunting knife but Michael placed his hand over hers. "It's all right, Cassie," he whispered. He felt her relax but she didn't let go of him nor of Katie who was wrapped tightly in her other arm.

Talker made a tiny cut on his thumb. "Give me your hand," he said to Daniel. Daniel frowned but held his hand out. "Warrior not afraid of pain," he said, then quickly made a tiny prick on Daniel's thumb. As a drop of blood appeared, Talker placed their thumbs together and tied them with a strip of leather he pulled out of his long black hair. "You are now my brother, Little Fox, our blood has mixed together. Talker is now your brother. You are part of the Cheyenne people now. You must be brave and give yourself to protect and care for your family, both Cheyenne and white. It is something big for so small a warrior. Will you do what I say, Little Fox?"

"Yes, I will be brave but what about my cousins?"

"I do not know the word *cousins*."

Daniel pointed to Rand then Aaron and Gabriel. "They are my cousins. Tell him what cousins mean, Rand."

Rand was, for a brief moment, surprised at the sudden attention turned toward him, but rose to the occasion as he usually did. "It means we are family, that we belong together."

Talker smiled. "Oh, I understand now. You will tell all people you are blood brother to Talker of the Cheyenne. Your tribe will be called the Cousins. We must give each one a name."

Daniel was quick to get into the spirit of naming the others. "Rand has red hair like me. Should he be a fox, too?"

"I think your cousin with the red hair has the spirit of the coyote. We will call him Red Coyote, yes?"

Daniel was excited, nodding enthusiastically. "Yes, I like that!"

"You must go and tell him his name."

Daniel walked tall and proud to Rand and looked at him very seriously. "Rand, you will now be called Red Coyote of the Cousins tribe."

"Good," Talker continued. "Now, your tall cousin."

"I already have an Indian name," Aaron told them. The Arapaho call me Tall Shadow. My father is Tall Man and they said I was the shadow of Tall Man."

"That is good name but you must have Cheyenne name given by Little Fox. What do you want to call him, Little Fox? When you look at him what do you think?"

"Teacher. He's teaching me and Gabriel to write our names."

"A wise one, huh! Wise Teacher is a good name."

"Daniel went to stand in front of Aaron and declared, "You will be called Wise Teacher of the Cousins tribe."

"Now, your cousin that is the color of the buffalo. We have one like him in one of the Cheyenne tribes. He is called Black Buffalo."

"I've heard of him," Aaron said.

"How do you hear of such a one?" Talker asked.

"My friend, Angel, told me about him. She is called White Cloud."

"Ah, you are friends of the great White Cloud, medicine woman, and the one who protects her, Princess Warrior. This is good. I have seen picture of Princess Warrior at the Fort Laramie."

"Yes, I'm the one who painted the picture," Aaron said, "and Michael, here, is her brother."

"I see I have made good friends this night, but we must finish ceremony. Have you chosen a name for the last cousin, Little Fox?"

"Well, I don't think he looks like a buffalo but he is dark like the night. And I think he is smart and brave." Daniel made up his mind and stood before Gabriel. "You will be called Night Warrior of the Cousins tribe."

Talker then addressed the three young men. "Do you take the names you have been given by Little Fox?"

They all agreed, then Talker told them, "Little Fox and I will exchange gifts and all the men must dance together to finish the ceremony."

Talker pulled out the same hunting knife he used to prick their thumbs and held it out in both of his hands toward Daniel. "I give you this gift to remember your brother, Talker, of the Cheyenne." Cassie was on the verge of protesting but she held her tongue when Talker told Daniel, "You must let your mother keep it until you learn to use it in the right way. Take it to her now."

Daniel solemnly did as he was told then turned a questioning face to Talker. "What do I do now?"

"You must give your new brother a gift."

Daniel put his hand in the pocket of his pants and fingered something. Cassie held her breath. She was the only one who knew the struggle her son was having. When Daniel's father left for the war he gave a small pocketknife to Daniel. Cassie had let him put it in his pocket when they left the farm. Relieved, she saw a hint of inspiration light his eyes and he ran to his saddle bag. He pulled out a small leather pouch and brought it over to Talker. "These are mine and I want to give them to you."

Talker spilled the contents out of the pouch into his hand. "What have we here? Many colors of smooth rocks."

"They're marbles!" Excitedly, Daniel drew a circle in the dirt and put all the marbles inside the circle, keeping out the largest one which was red. He explained that the red marble was called a taw and was used to shoot at the other marbles inside the circle. He showed Talker how to shoot with the taw. "If you shoot one out of the circle, you get to keep it."

"Aha! A very fine gift. I will always think of you when I play your game. Now we must dance."

They improvised a pan for a drum and Katie and Cassie beat out a rhythm with wooden spoons. It was quite a spectacle to watch as the men tried to dance like Talker. When he stopped, he told Daniel, "Talker will come to see you some day. Where do you take your tribe?"

"I don't know. Mama, where are we going?"

Cassie explained where her father's ranch was. "There's a big white ranch house on a hill. You can't miss it."

"I know this place," Talker said. "They fed me well for two days."

Cassie couldn't believe what she was hearing. "You mean my father gave you one of his precious cows?"

"Yes, it is so," Talker said, then laughed. "He did not know it but he gave me a cow. I will talk to my people wherever I go and they will not hurt your people as long as Little Fox is there. Now, Little Fox, you must go with your mother and do as she tells you." He turned to Michael and said, "Bring your warriors and come with me."

For some strange reason Michael trusted Talker and felt like they needed to listen to him. While Cassie put Daniel and Katie to bed, the men walked a distance away from the fire. "Three Sioux warriors will come before the sun shows itself. We must be ready. They will come for the horses and the water. This is the only water for a day's travel. You must be careful where you camp. Get water and move away to sleep. Two will come for the horses and one will try to confuse us with big noise. Wise Teacher, Red Coyote, and Night Warrior, do not let the noise trouble you. They will use knives because it is too dark to shoot arrows."

Rand asked, "How do we fight them if they have knives? I don't know how to fight with knives."

"You fight wise. If you can see a knife you know a person is there. Watch for a glint of moon on metal. Shoot them with your rifle but you must be quick. Do not wait for him to attack. I will show you where to wait. You must be very quiet and listen. Do not move or come to us unless you are called."

Talker placed the three youngest men where they would not be shooting toward each other and could cover a good area around the spring. He told each one to rest until he woke them. "I will wake you when it is time. Do not shoot your friend Talker."

Michael walked to the horses with Talker expressing his concerns. "They don't have any experience with things like this. I'm worried about them."

"You are right, they are young. But this night, if we are all to live, they must learn quickly."

"You could have gone on and not helped us. Why did you decide to stay with us?"

"I liked the little one. I have a son just a little older than him and I need many friends on my travels. Maybe someday I will bring my son to meet Little Fox."

Cassie was waiting for Michael by the fire. "What's going on, Michael?"

"I've got to be honest with you, Cassie. Talker says the three Sioux will strike before the sun comes up. They'll come to steal our horses and to get water. If you can, try and get some sleep while it's quiet. One of us will wake you when we need to be alert. Let the fire burn down and stay with the children, keep them quiet. Talker and I will be close to you and the horses but keep your rifle close." He took Cassie's hand and led her a short distance into the darkness, drawing her into an embrace. "Cassie, I don't know what's going to happen tonight but I want to tell you that I love you. It may be silly to tell you this now, but, well…."

"I'm glad you told me, Michael. I love you, too. I hope Aaron is out there praying. I want both of us to live long enough so I can show you how much I've come to love you."

"God can hear our prayers too, Cassie." And right there, while holding Cassie in a firm embrace, Michael prayed. "God, I ask you to protect all that I've come to love this night and not let any harm come to us. Thank you for sending Talker to warn us and help us. Keep all the Cousins tribe safe. Thank you and Amen."

"We've had quite a night, haven't we?" Cassie sighed.

"You can say that again. I hate to let go of you but you should try and rest while you can."

"Hold me just a little longer, Michael."

Chapter 14

ARON EXPERIENCED THE FIRST heart-racing rush of the enemy. He hadn't slept a wink and was bone weary. All of a sudden he was aware of rustling in the tall grass, way too close. He froze, searching the darkness. A hand, like someone crawling, came into focus, then a body followed the hand. Aaron realized whoever it was didn't know he was there and was almost on top of him. He had no time to think. A shriek, that could stop a person's heart, tore through the quiet night. The Indian sprang, just as Aaron fired, hitting the man in the chest. With quick reflexes Aaron twisted away from the knife but not before the blade tore into his shoulder. Aaron's quick reaction saved his own life. He felt the final shudder of life leave the man then quickly pushed him to the ground.

Gabriel heard the scream, the shot, and the impact of a body falling. He knew he was suppose to stay put but the thought that Aaron might be in trouble was too strong to make him stay in place. He made a quick decision to find Aaron. It was an effort to move quietly, but he made his way in the direction where Aaron was supposed to be. Thinking he was close, he whispered as loudly as he dared, "Aaron, you all right?"

"I don't know for sure, Gabe, but I'm bleeding!"

"I'm comin'!" Gabriel found Aaron in seconds. "Where you bleedin'?"

"It's my shoulder."

"Can't see real good but you might be bleedin' pretty bad."

"See if you can find something to wrap around it, Gabe."

Cassie drifted into a light sleep a couple of times but startled awake at the least little noise. Then the terrifying scream rent the air and she bolted upright and grabbed for the children. Katie whimpered in her sleep when the gun blasted but didn't come fully awake. She snuggled up to her mother. Cassie reached for Daniel but the spot where he had been sleeping was empty. While she was distracted trying to find her son, a dark figure ran from the bushes toward her. Another shot rang out and the figure, in a strange, slow motion, fell backward to the ground. Panic started to rise in Cassie's chest as she struggled with what to do about Daniel. She wanted to run and find him, but where? She didn't have time to contemplate any further, for Talker stepped out of the darkness and came close to the barely visible fire.

"It is over, mother of Little Fox." He then called out into the darkness, "Come to the fire, warriors, our enemy is no more!"

"Daniel is gone!" Cassie screamed at him. "We've got to find Daniel!"

"I'm right here, Mama." Daniel walked up from behind Talker. He didn't have time to explain himself for Gabriel's voice drifted in from the dark.

"Aaron's hurt and bleedin'. I sure could use some help!"

Michael appeared from the willows, grabbed his doctor's bag and headed back out into the darkness. "Where are you, Gabriel? Say something so I can find you."

"Over here. We're right over here."

In short time all the Cousins tribe was at the fire which Cassie had fanned back to life.

"Cassie, please heat a pan of water," Michael said. "I need to clean this cut on Aaron's shoulder to see what kind of damage there is."

The first fingers of light were slowly appearing on the eastern horizon when everyone realized they had come out of the fracas with only one injury. Rand and Gabriel dragged the body of the dead Indian out of sight. All the while, Rand could be heard complaining that he'd missed all the excitement.

"What happened where you were, Talker?" Rand asked.

"Little Fox saved my life."

"Little Fox? How did he do that?"

"He alerted me to the Sioux warrior that was behind me." Talker looked curiously at Daniel. "Why did you come to me, Little Fox?"

"When you shook me, I thought you wanted me to follow you," Daniel explained. "It was dark but I tried to go where you went. I was lost for a minute but then I saw you on the ground and there was someone behind you with a knife. So I took out my pocket knife and threw it at him."

Rand, caught up in the story, blurted out, "Did it stick in him?"

Daniel was sober-faced. "Yes, a little, then it fell on the ground. It didn't kill him. Talker fought with him and killed him."

"Yes, Talker killed the enemy but you were brave by throwing the little knife. That warned me he was there. That is what saved my life."

Cassie had worked up a mother's ire listening to the details. Angrily, she turned on Talker. "Why did you wake Daniel and have him follow you? It was dangerous out there! I can't believe you would do that to a small boy!"

Talker looked at the curious faces that were staring at him. "Whoever it was that shook and woke Little Fox, I do not know. It was not Talker."

Everyone shook their heads saying they didn't wake him. "What did he look like, Daniel?" Michael asked.

"It was real dark but I think he looked like Talker, only...maybe, older."

Everyone was silent as each one pondered the strange event. Without a word, Cassie stomped off into the willows. She could be heard fussing to herself, "If it wasn't Talker, and it wasn't any of us, then *who* in thunder was it?"

"Hold this tight against Aaron's shoulder, Gabriel. I need to make sure Cassie is all right. When I get back I'll put a few stitches in your shoulder."

Aaron groaned.

Michael located Cassie as she stood looking out at the sunrise. He slipped his arm around her shoulder. "You okay?"

"I'm fine. What just happened, Michael? I don't understand it. Scared me to death when Daniel wasn't with me."

"I can't explain it and we'll probably never know for sure. The Indians believe in spirits but I don't know what to think. Maybe it was an angel."

Cassie was quiet for a few minutes. She sighed deeply, saying, "You saved my life, you know. I was so stunned when Daniel was gone that I wouldn't have had time to shoot the Indian who came at me." She looked up into his face. "Thank you."

"You're my first real love, Cassie. I couldn't let anything take you away from me now."

Cassie wrapped her arms around Michael's waist. "Just hold me a minute, then I need to get back to Katie. I suppose everyone will be hungry pretty soon. How is Aaron's shoulder?"

"His coat kept the knife from going real deep but it's a pretty nasty gash. It's probably light enough now that I can stitch it up. I'm afraid it's going to cause him trouble for a few days."

"Will we be able to move away from this place?"

"We'll have to. It won't be safe to stay here. If I remember right we'll be close to the Platte River sometime today. If Aaron can make it that far we'll plan on camping at the river tonight."

"That means we're only a few days away from the ranch!" Cassie exclaimed.

"That's what I figure too."

"What are we going to do, Michael? Have you thought about it?"

"Yes, that's all I've thought about in the last few days. I have so much I want to say to you. I want us to make plans for our future but until we face your father with the truth and I can give you my name with no shame attached to it…well…I…."

"I understand. You don't need to say anymore."

Michael held Cassie a little tighter. "We'll make our plans, my sweet Cassie, but let's get that other business behind us first."

"Oh, dear, I smell bacon. We better get back. If Rand is cooking he'll need some help."

Michael had Aaron stitched up in no time with only a little complaining from his patient. It was Katie who eased the tension from the night's events with her cute antics. When Michael put the same red medicine on Aaron's wound that he had put on her kitty scratch, she sympathetically patted Aaron's cheek and told him, "I blow it for you. Daniel, come blow Aaron's sore so he be brae." She batted her little hazel eyes at Aaron and whispered, "If you *brae,* we get *sucker!*"

Cassie laughed along with the others. "Now you're in trouble, doctor. I hope you've got more suckers in that doctor's bag."

"I have just enough for this time. No one else can get hurt though, because there's only three left."

While they were getting ready to leave, Talker left camp in search of the dead Sioux's horses. He came back with both horses and to say goodbye. "Talker must leave his friends now. I have long journey to make." He offered one of the Sioux horses but Michael told him to take them both. Talker got down on one knee in front of Daniel. "I must go little brother. Remember my words, be brave, take care of your family. Talker will tell all the Cheyenne about Little Fox, his new brother of the Cousins tribe, that he saved my life. Perhaps our paths will come together again." In one swift move Talker mounted one of the horses and rode off to the west, never looking back.

Gabriel was the first one to speak. "I don't know about ya'll but I'm ready to leave dis here place."

"Well, let's leave then," Michael agreed. "Daniel, I want you to ride with me for awhile. I need Gabe and Rand to watch Aaron."

"I'm all right, Joe...I mean, *Michael*."

"I know you're all right but I don't want you using your arm any more than you have to. You've lost a good bit of blood and I don't want it to start bleeding again. Besides, you're still pale. It won't hurt for Gabe and Rand to be handy in case you need some help."

"All right, whatever you say. You're the doctor."

As they were ready to mount, Michael noticed that Daniel was quiet and seemed on the verge of tears. "What's wrong, Daniel, you look upset. Are you sad your new friend left?"

"No, I'm sad I lost my daddy's knife."

"Oh, I see. Well we won't leave until we find it. Do you want to go with me to help find it?"

"No, that dead Indian is there. I don't want to see him again."

"All right, that's fine. You don't have to go. I'll have Rand help me find it."

Relieved, Daniel waited patiently for Rand and Michael to return. He had a big grin on his face when Michael handed him his knife. "Thank you for finding it," he said, putting it in his pocket.

"You're welcome. I'm glad we didn't leave without it. It's special to have your father's knife. Take good care of it."

When they rode away, Cassie and Katie were in the lead. Michael sat Daniel in front of him, and led Patches. Gabe, Rand, and Aaron followed with the pack horse. "I want you to know, Daniel, your father would be proud of you. I know I am. What you did last night and what you saw is scary for grown-up men so I know it must have been scary for you too."

Michael waited for Daniel to respond. When he did, it was with a question. "Were you scared?"

"Yes, I was scared. There's nothing wrong with being scared. You just have to learn to control it when you feel afraid and do what you have to do to protect your friends and family. You did the right thing, Daniel."

"I didn't want to hurt that Indian but I knew he was going to hurt Talker."

"Yes, I know. I didn't want to hurt the Indian I shot either but he was going after your mother and Katie. So I did what I had to."

"I'm glad you did. When my knife stuck in that Indian he looked right at me! I thought he was gonna kill me!"

"Wow, that *is* scary! But you're all right now, thanks to Talker. Let's try and not think about it today."

"All right."

Michael felt Daniel relax against his body and soon heard his soft, rhythmic breathing. He felt a deep love for the little guy that he had never experienced before. *God, thank you for keeping us all safe last night. Thank you for sending Talker to help us. I don't even want to think about what might have happened if he hadn't come along. Help Aaron's shoulder heal and please stay with us as we travel today. Help me to be the man I need to be for Cassie and the children.*

Before they reached the Platte River, storm clouds were heading their way. One of the boys spotted an old abandoned sod house where someone had made an attempt at farming. They decided to take refuge there before the storm was on top of them. The earth house had one room that was small and another that was smaller. When it became obvious they needed to stay for the night, they piled all the saddles and other belongings in the smallest room and laid out their beds in the other one. They found enough wood for a fire and made a pot of coffee. After eating, they stretched out on their beds but weren't ready to sleep yet. They talked about numerous things and when they finally settled down for serious sleep the worst part of the storm had passed and a steady, slow rain pattered on the roof.

There wasn't any room for privacy but Cassie picked a spot a few feet away from the men. "Come here, Katie, and leave Daniel alone. Snuggle up to Mama."

Katie obeyed and climbed under the blanket with her mother. The whole atmosphere of that little sod house changed when Katie said out loud, "Mama, *stink*. You need bath."

Rand was the first to snicker, then Gabe joined in, saying, "Don't laugh, Rand, you don't smell like no purty flower neither!"

Michael couldn't help but laugh out loud. "If we had an armpit smelling contest it would be a toss-up who would win but I'd put my money on Daniel." He reached over to Daniel and tickled him. "You would win for sure," he said, then tickled him again.

It was quite a while before calm was restored.

Chapter 15

"O WE HAVE TO cross this river right here?"

"No, not now, Rand," Michael answered. "We'll travel along beside it looking for a place to cross, then find a camp spot on the other side to spend the night. Cassie got enough vegetables from that homesteader's wife to make us a nice meal tonight."

"She wouldn't let me pay for the vegetables, either," Cassie said, "but the cookies and fresh loaf of bread, she didn't hesitate to let me pay for."

"I can hardly wait." Michael turned his horse. "Let's cover some ground, men. I can taste that bread and those cookies already."

Cassie motioned for the boys to go ahead without her. "I'll stay behind a ways so you can shoot some fresh meat to go in the stew."

Aaron and Daniel stayed with Cassie. "I couldn't shoot a rifle now if I wanted to," Aaron lamented.

Cassie asked, "Is your arm giving you a lot of trouble?"

"It's plenty sore, but when Michael changed the bandage this morning he said it looked all right."

"I'm sorry you had to get hurt, Aaron, and while we're together I want to say something else to you."

"What's that?"

"Thank you. I know you're the one paying for everything and I am grateful for your help. Maybe someday I can pay you back for your kindness."

"That's not necessary, Cassie. It wasn't a loan. It was a gift from God. He's the one who provided the money. You just thank *Him*."

"I have, many times since we left my in-laws farm. Is Katie asleep?"

"Yes, she's asleep. She's the prettiest little thing."

Cassie smiled. "Thank you. I was a little afraid of how she might do on this trip, but she's done just fine."

"She must take after her mother."

The report of a rifle woke Katie and made their horses dance a little. "Mama, I can't see," Katie complained.

Aaron reached over and patted Katie on the back. "It's all right, honey. I think Michael just got us some venison to go in that stew your mama is going to make."

"I hungry, Mama."

"I know, sweetie. Aaron, since they're going to have to take care of whatever it is they shot, we might as well take a break. If you and Daniel can find the sack of cookies on the pack horse we'll have a little snack."

Two days later, as Cassie rode beside Michael, she commented, "I'm starting to recognize the country side. We should be at the ranch this afternoon. How are we going to do this, Michael?"

"We're going to ride up to the ranch house and knock on the door. I don't know after that. It'll depend on who answers the door and what kind of reception we get. Tell me a little about your family."

"I have two brothers. Brian is the oldest. I'm next, then Jeff is the other brother. Margaret is the youngest and my father's favorite little girl. She loves ranch life and is almost like one of the hands."

"What about your mother?"

"Mother is sweet. What you would call a real southern lady. I've missed her so much and can't wait to see her. Her name is Cherry. I think she finally forgave her mother for naming her Cherry Blossom. She hated it when she was a young girl."

"I think it's kind of pretty. Do you look like her?"

"People say I do but I'm not sure. I think I have more of her personality than her looks. Actually, Margaret looks like her and has father's temperament. My father is a hard man but somewhere in there I think he really loves his family."

"How do you think he'll react to you coming back home?"

"He'll probably rant and rave at me for a while then hopefully, calm down enough to listen to what we have to say. Do you think I should confront him alone first?"

"No, we'll do this together, Cassie."

Later that afternoon as they were riding at a good pace, they suddenly brought their horses to a halt. Rand gave a low whistle, then said, "Wooee! Would you look at that! Cassie, is that your place?"

"I don't know if you could call it *my* place, but it's where my family lives. I didn't live there very long before I left to marry Ray."

"It's a *grand* place!" Rand said.

"Oh, yes, my father always has to have the biggest and best."

"It looks kind of lonely to me," Michael said, as they all looked at the large, white, two story house sitting on a hill. There was a huge barn and any number of other out-buildings scattered around. White fences outlined two fair sized pastures with horses grazing in both. Cattle grazed everywhere they looked.

"All right, men, I'm not sure what to expect here," Michael told them. "If I say we're leaving, don't ask questions. I'll explain later. Hopefully, everything will go all right and we'll be welcomed."

Aaron assured Michael, "Don't you worry about us. We'll be fine."

Michael gazed lovingly at Cassie. His eyes told her volumes as she read the concern and love that shone from them. "You ready?" he asked softly.

"Yes, I'm ready. Let's get it over with."

The Cousins tribe rode up to the Chandler ranch with pride and purpose. They tied their horses to the hitching rail at the front of the house then all stepped up on the large front porch. Aaron looked at Michael. "Why don't Gabe, Rand, and I wait out here on the porch while you and Cassie go in and see how things are?"

Michael looked at the comfortable porch-swing and nice wicker chairs scattered around the porch. "That might be a good idea, Aaron."

"Mama, I want to stay on the porch, too. Can I?" Daniel asked.

"All right, but be good and do as you're told," Cassie answered.

"I will," he promised.

Michael gave Cassie an encouraging smile and knocked on the door. A black women opened it and stood looking at Michael. "What can I...." Her eyes fell on Cassie and she let out a little gasp. "Lord, have mercy!

Cassie, my baby, you are a sight for these old eyes!" She grabbed Cassie into a bone crushing hug.

"It's good to see you, too, Millie. Where's mother and father?"

"Your mother is upstairs with Margaret and your father is out yonder checking on some of his cows." Millie looked around at the strange faces. "I know that nice young man, Aaron Trinity, but who might all these other people be?"

Cassie started with the one standing closest to her. "This is Michael and he's holding my daughter, Katie. The two over by the porch rails are Rand and Gabriel. The boy on the swing is Daniel, my son. These men have seen me safely here to the ranch. They've been really good to me, Millie, so treat them *nice*."

"You know I will. Well, come on in this house and I'll go fetch your mother."

Aaron said, "The three of us are going to sit out here on the porch for awhile, Millie."

"That will be just fine. I'll be bringing you out some cold tea and maybe there'll be chocolate cake left over from last night. How does that sound?" They all smiled their approval saying it sounded real good.

Millie's attention turned to Katie. "You sure is a pretty little thing. Would you like to go with Millie and help me look for that chocolate cake or maybe some cookies? Do you know I took care of your mama when she was just a little girl like you?" All the while she was talking, Millie was reaching out to take Katie. Katie looked at her mother and when she got a smile and nod she reached her little hands out to Millie.

Michael and Cassie followed Millie into the large, richly furnished front room which was immaculate. Michael immediately felt out of place. "I think maybe I should wait out on the porch too. I feel too dirty to be in this nice, clean house."

"Rubbish!" Millie scolded. "You two just make yourself comfortable. I'm going to take Katie with me to the kitchen. CeCe is working on some things for supper but I'll send her up to get your mother. My, oh, my, is she ever goin' to be surprised!"

Michael had just asked Cassie who CeCe was when they heard a squeal from the top of the stairs. "Cassie! I can't believe it! Is it really *you*?"

Michael was fascinated as a young version of Cassie flew down the stairs and into Cassie's arms. "It's me, all right," Cassie said. "Maggie, you've sure grown into a woman since I last saw you." She looked over at Michael. "Michael, this is my sister, Margaret."

Michael offered his hand. "I'm pleased to meet you, Margaret."

She took his hand but looked confused. Eyeing Cassie she questioned, "This isn't your husband, is it? Wasn't his name Ray?"

"Yes, his name was Ray. He died in the war over a year ago. Michael and some other friends brought me safely here to the ranch."

"Oh, I'm so sorry, Cassie. You were so crazy in love with him. I didn't blame you for running off with him."

During this exchange between sisters, Michael was aware of a beautiful, frail looking woman make her way down the stairs. She quietly stood at the bottom until Margaret and Cassie became aware of her presence. Cassie only paused a moment then flew into the arms of her mother. They both wept and held each other. "CeCe said we had company but I never would have imagined it to be you. Oh, Cassie, it's so good to see you! You look wonderful. Is this your husband?"

"No, Mother, this is Michael. Ray, my husband, died in the war a little over a year ago."

"Ray, yes, that was his name. I remember now. I'm so very sorry, dear. The things I hear about the war are just dreadful. I need to sit down for a while. I'm afraid the shock of seeing you again has made my knees weak. I want you to tell me all about what has been going on in your life."

While Michael and the women were finding chairs in the front room, a young black girl calmly walked through with a large tray of tea and chocolate cake, heading toward the front door. "Where are you taking that tray, CeCe?" Margaret asked, sounding agitated. "Can't you see the company is here in this room?"

"I be taking this tray to where my mama told me. She said to take it out to the company on the *front porch*."

"We have company on the porch? Who is it?"

"I don't know, Miss Margaret. Mama said that nice Aaron Trinity is here with some other young men."

"Aaron is *here?* Why didn't someone tell me?" Margaret quickly excused herself. "Here, let me open the door for you, CeCe. You should have told me *sooner* that Aaron was here!"

"How could I, Miss Margaret, when I just found out myself?"

Michael was distracted for a moment when the front door closed and he got a mental picture of Gabriel's face when the pretty black girl walked out onto the porch. *Wish I could see that...*he chuckled to himself.

His attention was brought back to the living room when Katie dashed in with chocolate all over her face. A smiling Millie was right behind her. "Mama! I eat chockel cake and *milk*. Mmm, good! Milwee give me more!"

"Who is this?" Cherry Chandler gave her daughter a questioning look. "Cassie, is this my grandchild? Why didn't you say something sooner?"

"Yes, Mother, this is your granddaughter, Katie."

"Oh, she's beautiful," Mrs. Chandler laughed. "Especially decorated with *chockel* frosting, she's beautiful!"

"Katie, this is your Grandmother Chandler. Say hello to her."

Katie managed a shy hello before Millie intervened. "Come with Millie now, Katie. We need to wash your face. Then maybe you can help Millie in the kitchen."

Katie seemed happy enough to go with Millie and escape the adults.

For a while there was friendly conversation out on the porch and inside the house with the reunion of mother and daughter. Aaron was used to Margaret's flirtation with him and didn't think anything of it when she greeted him with a hug in front of the others. He introduced her to Rand, Gabriel and Daniel but looked perturbed when she paid so little attention to her nephew. It was plain to see that Rand was clearly fascinated with the charming Margaret.

But Gabriel? Who could know the emotional turmoil going on inside that boy over the black girl who kept her eyes down and wouldn't look at him. She just served each one their cake and tea but he watched her. What he saw, he liked. Gabriel was not a large man himself and this girl was petite, with a fine figure and pretty features. He guessed her to be about eighteen or nineteen. He wanted desperately for her to look at him so he could see into her eyes, but she wouldn't. Her long lashes fluttered with each toss of her head as she served the adults. Gabe was pleased by the way she knelt down and spoke to Daniel, who didn't get any cake or tea.

"Don't look so sad, little one. My mama thought you might like to come to the kitchen with your sister and have a *big* piece of cake and a glass of milk. Does that sound good? If you want me to bring it out here, I'll do that for you. But, if you go to the kitchen with your sister, I'll take you out to the barn and show you the new puppies. They was just born about a week ago."

Daniel didn't hesitate. "I'll go with you! Can we go see the puppies first?"

"We could, but my mama would want us to come eat our cake first."

"All right, let's hurry though!"

CeCe giggled, took Daniel's hand and led him off the porch and around to the back of the house.

A deep disappointment thudded in Gabe's chest. *I sure wish she'd have invited me to go with her. She wouldn't even look at me though. Maybe she's already a married woman or has been spoken for.* He tried to put the matter out of his mind, but failed miserably. *I wish she would've at least looked at me…and smiled.*

Gabriel didn't have time to dwell on the matter any longer because a bunch of cowboys came riding into the ranch yard heading to the barn. One of them stopped at the porch and handed his horse over to a young ranch hand. As he scanned the group on the porch he recognized Aaron and a big grin spread over his face. "Well, Aaron, what brings you here? You come to see my Margaret?" Dalton Chandler laughed. "You've got to get my approval before you start thinking of my daughter."

"Oh, Father, Aaron and I are just friends," Margaret gushed. "Believe me, I've tried to change his mind about that funny little girl he thinks he's in love with but it hasn't worked yet." She batted her eyes at Aaron. "If you have any ideas just tell me what they are."

"Well, if he's not here to see my daughter what are these young men here for?"

"They brought Cassie home, Father."

"*Cassie?* You mean Cassie is *here?*"

"Yes, she's inside with Mother."

"I can't believe that girl would have the *gumption* to show up here after running off with that no-good scoundrel! *Cowards* is what those two were."

"Father, be nice to her," Margaret encouraged.

"Don't tell me what to do, young lady. I'll go and see for myself what this is all about." He looked at Aaron. "I'll talk to you later, Aaron, and meet your friends then."

Gabriel didn't like the man. But he had the good sense to keep his thoughts to himself. *I wonder how he treats that pretty girl who served us.*

Chapter 16

HEN DALTON CHANDLER STEPPED into the house a hush descended on the room, as if everyone was holding their breath. He found his prey and struck the first blow. "So, it's true! You've come back like a whipped pup with its tail between its legs! I can't believe you found the courage to face me after what you did."

Cassie stood and squared off with her father. "You're wrong, Father. I didn't come back here like a whipped pup. I came back to straighten things out between us."

"And how do you think you're going to do that? The facts are the facts and you can't change that."

"The problem is, you don't *know* all the facts."

"Oh? And I suppose you think you do?" Mr. Chandler's face was getting red.   Michael was proud of how Cassie hadn't backed down, was strong and composed. He decided it was time he stood beside her. He got up and took the few steps to her side. "Mr. Chandler, if we could sit and talk calmly, I think we could clear things up in no time."

"Don't you even speak to me, you *coward*! Running off with my daughter like you did!"

"Father, this is *not* Ray. My husband died in the war over a year ago."

"Well, who in thunder is he then? And what's he got to do with anything?" For the first time, Dalton truly looked at Michael. "I know you. We've met somewhere. I'm just not sure where."

Michael saw in the old rancher's face the exact moment of recognition. "Yes, we met some years ago. I'm Michael Mayfield. I had a small ranch I was trying to make a go of when you moved in and decided you wanted my little valley for yourself."

"Why you…you…brazen *murderer*! You dare to come *here*! Of all the gall…."

What happened next took everyone by surprise, especially Mr. Chandler. Daniel marched into the room, looked up at his grandfather, and ordered, "Don't you yell at my mama!"

Dalton sputtered a few moments as he looked down at the small boy. "Your mama?!"

"Yes, my *mama*! You shouldn't yell at her cause she's real nice and I'm going to take care of her."

Mr. Chandler seemed at a loss for words. He finally found his tongue and asked, "What's your name, boy?"

"My name is Daniel Dalton Jackson and this is my mama, Cassie Jackson."

Michael could see that Mr. Dalton was trying to look tough, but if you really paid attention you could tell he was starting to soften at the sight of his grandson. What really cooked his goose, though, was when little Katie came running into the room.

"Mama, see the puppies! I hole one. CeCe let me hole one." Katie tugged on her mother's hand. "Hurry, Mama!"

"Katie, you're interrupting our conversation. I can't go now. I need to talk to your grandpa." Katie's eyes got big and she looked up at the strange man.

Another distraction came when Margaret bustled in the front door with Aaron, Gabriel, and Rand. "Mother, I'm going to take Aaron and his friends to the west pasture to see the new colt. I'll come back and help Millie and CeCe with supper preparations."

"Of course, that would be…." Cherry Chandler gasped softly and clutched her chest. Michael turned to see her pale, a pained look on her face. "I can't…breathe."

"Aaron, go get my bag!" Michael said, as he easily scooped the small woman up into his arms. "Someone show me where her bed is."

Mr. Chandler stepped in front of Michael. "You take your hands off my wife!"

"Get out of the way, Father!" Cassie shouted. "Michael is a doctor, let him help Mother."

CeCe was the only one who seemed to be thinking clearly. "Follow me, doctor." She quickly led the way up the stairs and opened the door into a lovely bedroom. She quickly turned the covers back. "Lay her right here."

"Thank you, CeCe. I need you to loosen her clothing." Michael turned and saw Cassie and Mr. Chandler anxiously waiting at the door. He didn't hesitate to take control of the situation. "Please wait downstairs. I need a few minutes to check her over. CeCe will be here to help me."

"Come on, Father," Cassie said, pulling on her father's arm. "She's in good hands. Let's do what he says."

Margaret came into the room and handed Michael his bag. "May I stay?"

"No, it would be best if you wait with the others. I'll be down in a few minutes to talk to all of you." When Margaret left, he asked CeCe to close the door then turned to his patient. "How are you feeling now?"

"It's starting to ease up a little."

"Have you had these attacks before?"

"From time to time, but not this bad."

"Does anyone else in the family know you have a weak heart?'

"No, just Millie."

Michael had taken out his stethoscope. "I'm going to listen to your heart so be very still."

CeCe stood quietly waiting for Michael to give her instructions. He finally straightened from listening to Cherry's heart. "I'm going to have CeCe help you get into a nightgown. I want you to be as still as you can and let her do all the work." Then he told CeCe, "Get a basin of warm water and sponge her face before you put her gown on. Prop her up with pillows. She'll breathe easier that way. She is not to do *anything*. Do you understand?"

"Yes, sir, I'll do jest as you tell me to."

"Good girl. I'm going down to talk to the family. I'll be right back."

When Michael got to the bottom of the stairs the room went quiet. Mr. Chandler, Cassie, and Margaret stood to their feet. Cassie hurried to Michael. "How is she?"

Michael put his arm around Cassie and walked to where the others could hear. "She's all right for right now. CeCe is helping her get comfortable."

"What do you mean, for *right now*?" Mr. Chandler had calmed down but his voice was still rather demanding.

"Mr. Chandler, your wife has probably had a weak heart for some time and as she gets older it may weaken still. She's had other light attacks and I'm sure she has kept this to herself because she has not wanted to worry anyone. I'll monitor her through the night but I think she'll be fine. There was just a little too much excitement for her. The family can go up one at a time and sit with her but you must stay calm and not excite her. Let her rest as much as she can. Do you all understand what I'm telling you?"

Cassie answered, "Yes, Michael, we understand," as the others only nodded.

Michael went back upstairs with Mr. Chandler. Nothing was said between them as they climbed the stairs and went into the room. Mrs. Chandler was lying peacefully on a mound of pillows. CeCe had pulled a comfortable looking armchair close to the bed and was sitting quietly. She stood and made room for Michael. "Well, now your color is already starting to return. I'd like to listen to your heart again then your husband would like to sit with you for awhile." When Michael finished listening to her heart he told her, "Nice and steady. I'll be back every once in a while to check on you." He turned to leave. "CeCe, let's give these two some privacy but I want you to check on her often to see if she needs anything."

"I will, doctor."

As the two went down the stairs, Michael said, "You did a good job, CeCe. If I ever set up a practice anywhere around here, you would make a good nurse. Have you ever thought of anything like that?"

"No, sir, I never thought of no such thing, but thank you, maybe I will start thinkin' on it."

The house was quiet and CeCe headed for the kitchen. Michael found Cassie alone in the front room, crying. "Hey, what's going on? Don't you know your mother has the best doctor around?"

"Yes, I know that much, but it was all my fault."

"Whoa, that's nonsense, Cassie." Michael sat down with her and put his arm around her shoulders. "This wasn't your fault. It just happened. Did you know your mother had a weak heart?

"No, she always seemed frail, but I didn't give it much thought. If we had known, we would have done things differently, but we didn't know."

"Where did everyone go?"

"I talked Margaret into going ahead and showing everyone the new colt and puppies. I'm not sure what to do now."

Millie walked into the room. "I know exactly what you are going to do." I've already checked at the bunkhouse and the men said there's plenty of room for your friends. Your room is right where you left it and *exactly* like you left it. Your mama wouldn't let us change a thing. There's that nice little guest room for your doctor friend. I'm working on a big supper for tonight so after you go see your mama, you and Margaret can come help me get supper on the table for everyone."

"Thank you, Millie. I guess I'd forgotten how efficient you are."

"I don't know nothing about that ee-fish...whatever you said. I *do* know how to feed and take care of my people though."

Millie had told the truth. She indeed knew how to feed a large group of people. There was a little stir after everyone was seated at the supper table. CeCe had helped Millie put the food on the table then left to go to the kitchen to eat. Gabriel abruptly stood up, saying, "I be going in da kitchen to eat with her." He nodded toward the door that led to the kitchen.

"Wait for me, Gabe," Aaron said as he stood to go with Gabriel.

"Me too," Rand said, standing up and clutching his plate.

As Daniel got up to go with his cousins, that was the last straw. Margaret lost it! "What in thunder are you all doing? Why are you leaving, Aaron?"

Aaron said calmly, "Gabriel is a friend of mine and if he isn't comfortable eating at the table with us, I'll just go where we can both be comfortable. You all go ahead and eat."

"Oh, for heaven's sake, sit down, Aaron." Margaret got up, went to the door of the kitchen and said loudly, so everyone could hear, "CeCe, would you please bring your plate and eat in here with the rest of us. Seems everyone had rather have your company than mine." She glared at Aaron.

Chapter 17

"**Y**ou, Cassie? You killed Gordon?" Dalton asked.

"Yes, it was me."

"But…why?"

Cassie sat in the chair next to Michael. "You didn't know the real Gordon York, Father."

Dalton was quiet for a few moments. "Explain to me what you mean."

Cassie took a deep breath. "He was a mean, selfish, horrible man. I saw him kick Bandit so hard the poor little dog crawled under the porch and I couldn't get him to come out for two days. There wasn't any reason other than Bandit didn't move out of his way fast enough. When I did finally get him to come out for food and water he could barely move for another day. I don't think he was ever the same after that." Cassie paused, gathering her thoughts. "Do you remember the young man that Gordon told you he had to let go because he couldn't stay on a horse and fell off, breaking his arm? He lied to you, Father, and I know you hate a liar. I saw Gordon beating one of the horses. That young man, I think his name was Joseph, tried to stop him and Gordon turned on Joseph. Gordon quit beating him when he saw me coming. I asked him what had happened and he said the kid picked a fight and he was just defending himself."

"Why didn't you tell me?"

"I tried, but you wouldn't listen. You always made excuses for him. One time you told me I didn't know what I was talking about. Another time you told me Gordon had to be tough to keep a bunch of men in line and working. The last straw for me was when he followed me into the barn and tried to kiss me and force me to…the only way I escaped that day was another hand came in and asked what was going on. Gordon told him it was none of his business, to go away. He was the hand who Gordon told you just up and left. We never saw him again. I've always wondered what really happened to that man. I couldn't stand to be around Gordon or have him touch me. He *scared* me!"

"I didn't see that in the man," Dalton admitted.

"I know. He *hid* it from you. He didn't want you to see that side of him because he knew you wouldn't tolerate anyone mistreating the animals or the men. You're a hard man, but Gordon York was cruel. He only wanted to have his way with me so he could take control of this ranch."

"Why do you say that? He couldn't take control of this ranch even if he wanted to. When I die, Brian will own this place."

"Think about it. Out in this wild country it wouldn't be too hard to get rid of Brian. Jeffery doesn't want the ranch and is off to school. If Gordon was married to *me*, well, it would be all his to control."

"That's a hard thing to say without any proof, Cassie," Dalton challenged.

"Maybe, but that's what he said when he followed me that day I slipped out and met Ray. He must have been watching me because he showed up right after Ray and I got together. He got hold of my horse and tried to force me to go with him. He said no one was going to take me and mess up his chance to have the ranch. Ray and Gordon got in a fight. I was so afraid he was going to kill Ray. When Ray had him down, Gordon got hold of a rock and hit Ray in the head. Knocked him out. Gordon shoved him away and pulled his pistol. He was going to kill Ray! Kill him in cold blood while he was unconscious! I wasn't about to let him kill the man I loved and the father of my baby…so I shot him." Cassie was quiet long enough to let it all sink in. "You said you would kill Ray if he ever came on this property or tried to see me again. So I made my decision and we ran away. I'm not sorry I married Ray. I'm sorry I didn't stay and stand up to you."

The room was so quiet the only thing that could be heard was regret as Mr. Chandler exhaled. "I guess I was a fool."

"As far as I'm concerned, Father, it's in the past. I just want us to forgive and clear Michael's name. He was coming to try and stop me and Ray from running off. He found Gordon dead when you and the hands saw him."

Michael finally said, "I've tried a thousand times to think of what I could have done besides run away. There was no way I could prove that I hadn't killed your foreman. Remember that day I came to your ranch and told you I thought your hands were stealing my cattle? You told me to never come on your land again without proof or you would shoot me yourself, that none of your boys would ever steal cattle. I've wondered that with very little law in this area, if you would have hung me right then and there." Michael reached for Cassie's hand under the table and waited.

Dalton Chandler pushed his chair back and stood up. "I'm not afraid to admit when I'm wrong. I don't like it much, but it looks like I've wronged both of you." He reached across the table offering his hand to Michael. "I'm sorry and I'll send telegrams as soon as I can to straighten things out."

Michael stood and shook Dalton's hand. "There is one other thing I want to tell you."

"What's that?"

"I love Cassie. Now that this is straightened out I'm going to ask her to marry me."

"How does she feel about you?"

"I love him, Father, and when he does ask me I will say yes."

"That's good enough for me. Now, I've got some thinking to do, so I'll go check on Cherry. Doc, do you think it would be all right if I laid down beside her for awhile? I won't bother her."

"Yes, I think it would be comforting to her. If either of you need me, you know where I am."

Dalton slowly left the room and could be heard climbing the stairs. Michael and Cassie stayed in the kitchen long enough for Michael to ask Cassie to marry him...and steal a few kisses.

XXXXX

"Is that you, Dalton?"

"Now who else would be laying down on the bed with you?"

"There's been so many people in here I wasn't sure. I thought maybe one of the girls had come in and laid down beside me."

"No, it's just your stubborn, foolish old husband."

"You may be stubborn, but you're not a fool."

"I don't know, after talking to Cassie just now, I just might be."

"Did you get things right between the two of you?"

"Yes, and I chewed some mighty tough crow."

"Did Cassie tell you I was the one who told her to run away with Ray and find happiness with the man she loved?"

"Nope, not a word. She kept your secret."

"Well, I'm glad it's all out in the open now. She's in love with that nice young doctor, you know."

"I found out about five minutes ago and he's probably in the kitchen right now asking her to marry him."

"I'm happy for her."

"I am too, but right now you need to go back to sleep. You about scared me to death when you had that attack. Don't do that to me again. I love you and need you too much to lose you now."

"You're not going to lose me any time soon. I've got to live long enough to get to know my grandchildren. They are so precious."

"The little girl is precious, but Daniel Dalton Chandler is *special*. Did you see the way he stood up to me and told me not to holler at his mama? I like the little fellow. He's got *grit*."

"Like his grandfather. Now, snuggle up and go to sleep."

"It'll be my pleasure."

As Dalton held his wife he did something he hadn't done in a long time. He prayed. *God, thank you for not taking Cherry from me, and please help this old fool to be a better man.*

No one saw or heard CeCe climb the stairs and peek in the door to check on Mrs. Chandler. Surprised to see Mr. Chandler in bed with her, she quickly and quietly closed the door and went back to her room.

The Chandler ranch had a whole different atmosphere the next morning. Millie and CeCe loaded the sideboard with breakfast foods and people came in and out all morning, serving themselves. When Michael came in for his breakfast it was quite early. He thought maybe he would have a quiet breakfast, but that notion was quickly dispelled. A man Michael hadn't met came in the door and approached him. "I'm Brian Chandler. Are you the doctor?"

"Yes, I'm Michael Mayfield and I'm a doctor. Is there something wrong?"

"Last evening just as we were getting ready to brand the last cow for the day, one of the men got hurt. He slipped, the cow got loose, and stepped on him. I think his leg is broken. We were really late getting him home last night. When your friends found out what had happened they told me you were here. Think you could come out and help him? He's in a lot of pain. I'd have come and got you last night but didn't know we had a doctor around."

"Sure, I'll be glad to see if I can help him out. I'll just grab my bag and be right with you."

Millie came in just as they were going out the back door. "Does that bag in your hand mean someone is in need of a doctor?"

Brian Chandler answered her. "Yes, Millie, Chet got stepped on by one of the cows we were branding and might have a broken leg. Will you tell Father as soon as you see him?"

"I shore will and if you need me or CeCe for anything let us know."

As Brian and Michael walked to the bunkhouse Brian talked like he had known Michael for a long time. "It was nice of your men to offer to help with the branding this morning."

"I'm not sure how much help they'll be. I don't know if they've done any branding before."

"Rand said he has and the black man seemed eager to learn. Aaron said he'd watch the little boy and keep him out of the way since he couldn't do much with the shape his arm is in."

"You mean Daniel went with them?"

"Yeah, is that his name? Seems like a nice kid."

"Do you know who that *nice kid* is?"

"I just figured he was one of yours. I didn't have time to find out who the young men were or what you all are doing here. Chet is a good hand and I've been worried about him."

Michael laughed. "Well, Brian, that nice kid is your nephew."

Brian halted and stared at Michael a minute. "Did you say my *nephew*?"

"Yes, he's Cassie's boy and you have a sweet little niece, too."

"You don't say. Are you telling me Cassie is *here*?"

"Yes, she is. The men who slept in the bunkhouse helped me bring Cassie back home. Did you know her husband, Ray?"

"I met him once."

"Ray was a friend of mine. He died in the war a little over a year ago. I was looking for Ray and found your sister in a bad situation, so we brought her back here."

"If that don't beat all! I'll be glad to see her again." Brian opened the bunkhouse door. "But let's get this man taken care of first."

Dalton Chandler joined them in the bunkhouse a short time later. "Is his leg broken?"

"Yes, it's a nasty break. I've got it set and I'm almost finished stabilizing the leg. I gave him something for the pain. It'll knock him out but that's the best thing for him right now. He's going to have to stay off that leg for a while. In a few weeks you can fashion some kind of crutch for him to get around on. It would be a good idea for someone to stay and watch over him today."

"Who's going to do that?" Brian asked his father. "Dale went to Ft. Laramie and won't be back till late tonight or tomorrow and I have to go back out with the men." Brian explained to Michael that Dale was the cook for the ranch hands.

"CeCe helped me with your wife, Mr. Chandler. She seems quite capable. I can give her instructions on what to do."

"You mean she would be in the bunkhouse with one of the men here? I don't allow that kind of thing," Dalton huffed.

"I understand, but what would it really hurt? He's not going to be able to do anything to her. He probably won't wake up for a good while. It's a nice day and she could sit out here with the door open and do some handwork or whatever. As long as she can see and hear him if he wakes up or starts moving around. I'll come check on him often."

"Yeah," Dalton conceded. "That would work all right."

"Wait a minute!" Brian interrupted. "What did you mean by CeCe helping with Mother? Is something wrong with her?"

"She's fine now," Dalton told his son. "She had a spell with her heart last evening. Scared me pretty bad but she's all right now. Doc here says we need to keep things calm around her, so don't worry her with ranch matters."

"If you and Brian want to go get some breakfast, could you send CeCe out and I'll tell her what to watch for and what she needs to do. Then I'll join the two of you."

"Sure, we'll send her right out."

CeCe was a little unsure of herself but when Michael explained what she needed to do, she seemed pleased to be the doctor's helper. She hurried back to the house and returned with a basket full of clothing. "I'll just sit right here inside the door and do all this mending."

"Good, now remember, at the first sign of him waking up send someone to get me or you run to the house yourself."

"I won't be forgettin'," CeCe nodded.

Michael left CeCe to her work, went through the back porch and into the kitchen. Cassie, Margaret, Brian, and Mr. Chandler were already seated with full plates in front of them. "Smells good in here," Michael commented, going for the food on the sideboard.

"Fill up a plate and sit down. Millie's bringing us a fresh pot of coffee," Dalton said. "I appreciate you taking care of Chet. He's one of my best men."

"Glad to help," Michael said. He was soon seated at the table beside Cassie. He took one bite of his food then noticed Margaret was frowning and looked ready to explode. "Are you all right, Margaret?"

"No, I'm *not* okay," she huffed. "I just found out all the men left without me. I was looking forward to spending the day with Aaron. They even took Daniel. They could have at least asked if I wanted to go."

"Now, Sis, there wasn't time for that. We were shorthanded and your friends offered to pitch in and help," Brian explained.

"I could go help too," Margaret pouted.

"Sis, you're *not* helping when you get out there with the men. They're so distracted by a pretty girl I'm afraid we'd have more broken bones… or worse. When they're not doing dangerous work you can distract them all you want."

Dalton laughed. "See how it is to have pretty daughters, Doc? You have to keep them hidden or we'd never get any work done around here."

Everyone but Margaret laughed.

"But, just to make my baby happy, I've been thinking that since tomorrow is Sunday, we're going to have a barbecue. We don't do any work on Sunday except the everyday chores. So we'll have church or something of the sort, then in the afternoon we'll have a barbecue and dance. Margaret, I'll put you in charge. You just plan and make it a grand time. We need to celebrate our Cassie coming home!"

"Oh, Father, what a wonderful idea! I'll take care of everything," Margaret gushed as she began to perk up.

"I have no doubt you're up to the task," Dalton said, a grin on his face.

Margaret's mind was already working. "Michael, will you give the sermon for us?"

"I'm not a preacher, Margaret, but I have an idea who you might ask. Maybe he won't preach but I've heard some of his story and Aaron is a real man of faith. I truly envy his walk with God."

"Perfect!" Margaret jumped up and hurried out of the room mumbling to herself, "I've got to get busy...."

Cassie smiled as her sister disappeared down the hallway. "I hope you realize what you just did, Father."

"Yeah, I just made my little girl happy. She doesn't get many chances for social activities, so why not?"

Chapter 18

SUNDAY MORNING WAS A wonderful display of what seemed to be God's blessing on the celebration at the Chandler ranch. Sunlight spilled brilliantly and spread the warmth of spring. Not a cloud in the sky was present to cast a shadow over the day. The prairie was alive with spring grass and wild flowers, displaying their vibrant colors for anyone who took the time to enjoy them. Margaret had everyone involved in one way or another in the day's activities.

By ten o'clock the Chandler family and the ranch hands, along with the Cousins tribe were sitting in chairs or on benches facing the front porch. They had even managed to haul the wounded Chet on a stretcher out to the front yard. He sat in one chair with his leg propped up on another. Even though his pain was still evident, he seemed happy to be out in the sunshine with the others.

Margaret wore an attractive green dress, her hair tied back with a yellow ribbon. She looked as pretty as the spring flowers. But it was Cassie, who Michael couldn't drag his eyes from. She was dressed in a modest, but charming, dress of various shades of blue. Even Cherry Chandler joined them and sat in one of the comfortable wicker chairs on the porch. Nothing could dissuade her from attending what everyone called *church*. At last, Margaret got up to start things moving.

Michael leaned over and whispered to Cassie, "You are the most beautiful thing anywhere in this territory. Wild flowers should be ashamed to show their faces with you around." Cassie shushed him, but had a pleased smile on her face.

"We're going to sing a few hymns," Margaret announced. "Charlie knows a couple of hymns and has agreed to play them on his guitar. Jump in and sing if you know the songs."

Charlie did a fine job playing and getting the hymns started and soon voices blended with his. Before they finished the second song they sounded like they had been singing together for years. Everyone was pleasantly surprised when Cassie and Margaret sang, *O For a Thousand Tongues to Sing*. Margaret carried the melody and Cassie harmonized in a mellow alto, their voices blending perfectly.

Then Margaret announced before sitting down, "I've asked Aaron to speak to us this morning."

Aaron stood in front of the group and looked around at the mixture of people. "I'm so happy to be here with all of you this morning. I want you to know right off that I'm not a preacher, but I told Margaret I would tell you my story."

Aaron began by telling a shortened version of the young boy in the Bible whose name was Samuel and that he was dedicated to the Lord as a little boy. One night he heard someone call his name. Thinking it was the priest, Eli, Samuel went to the old priest just to be told he did not call him. This happened three times. Then Eli realized it must be the Lord calling Samuel and told him what to do. Samuel laid down again and heard his name called again, so he answered, "Speak, Lord, for thy servant hears."

Aaron paused a moment as he looked at the faces waiting intently. "That's what happened to me. God called my name." He continued by telling them of how he was left in a basket at the backdoor of a convent; how the nuns called him little Moses; that he was raised by a woman who lived in a small house on the convent grounds. He didn't go into a lot of detail except to be sure that his listeners understood that he never knew his mother or who his father was.

When he turned sixteen, a letter arrived from his dying mother, mentioning his father's name. "She told me in the letter that she named me Aaron when I was born and my father's name was Scott Trinity. She didn't know where he was but said he was from Mississippi and talked about going to California or joining the army. After months of looking for my father I almost quit because I was so discouraged but had one more lead I wanted to follow. That lead took me to the High Meadows Horse Ranch…and my father. I was thrown into a world of men. Wonderful, tough men, and I wanted to be just like them. My biggest problem was stuttering. Not just a little but I stuttered badly. I hated the look of pity on people's faces when I talked. Then one day, I heard my step-brother telling my father that he thought I was a sissy-boy and it was hard to stand and wait for me to talk. Well, his words hurt me terribly. But when I heard my father agree with him, I was crushed so badly, I just walked away."

Aaron paused and scanned the faces before him. "Well, to make a long story short, I ended up on top of a mountain in the wilderness waiting to die. That's when God called me. I heard him call me by the name I had chosen: Aaron Moses Trinity."

One of the cowboys asked, "You heard the real voice of God?"

Aaron smiled. "It wasn't a voice like you and I have but I've learned since that God is spirit and His voice was in the air around me. He called my name several times until I answered. He asked me if I believed in Him, then asked if I trusted Him. After some soul searching I told Him yes, and I gave my life to Him. I really expected Him to take me to heaven right then. I don't know how long I wept, but it seemed as if I couldn't stop. When I finally did, the most wonderful peace I have ever known settled over me. I still expected to die, but God had other plans and I ended up back with my family."

"Wait a minute," said the same cowboy who had spoken before. "You don't stutter now. What happened?"

"I can't explain it but since that day I haven't stuttered. But that's not the important thing. What's important is that voice that called my name…."

Aaron got very emotional and struggled for control. He finally was able to go on. "That voice now speaks to me in here, inside of me." He placed his hand over his heart. "My step-mother told me the Spirit of God comes to dwell in you when you give your life to God. Today I want to encourage you to listen for God to call your name. When He does call, open your heart to Him and give Him your life. You won't be sorry."

Aaron then took his seat by the Cousins tribe.

The curious cowboy couldn't seem to help himself as he asked another question. "How could you go back to your family knowing they thought you were a sissy? I don't think I could do that."

Aaron chuckled as he stood and answered the question. "My father told me that I only heard part of what was said. My step-brother, Paul, was telling him that when he first met me he thought I was a sissy, but that he had changed his mind and really admired me...Well, he said a lot of nice things. Paul and I are great brothers now."

Margaret stood to take over. "Thank you, Aaron. I'd never heard your story and I think it's wonderful how it turned out." She addressed the others, "We need to get ready for our party this afternoon, so those of you who said you would help set up things in the back yard, be there in about an hour."

"Shouldn't we have a prayer before we go?" someone asked.

Margaret looked a little flustered. "All right, sure, who would like to say a prayer?"

To everyone's surprise Chet offered to pray. It was simple and heartfelt. "God, thank you for what you did for our new friend, Aaron. Thank you, for not letting me get killed. Thank you for the doctor who helped me out and, God, I want to hear your voice. Help me to hear you when you call my name. Amen."

Several amens were heard throughout the group. Reluctant to leave the special services, some stood around in little knots visiting and encouraging each other before scattering in different directions.

The barbecue was a hit with everyone. Millie put on a big spread in spite of the short time she had to get it together. What with CeCe looking after Chet in the bunkhouse all day, Cherry being on bed rest, and Margaret flitting everywhere trying to make all her plans, only Cassie had been left to help Millie in the kitchen. Cassie and whoever else Millie could grab for a few minutes. Half a beef had roasted on a spit in the backyard pit since early morning with potatoes buried in the hot coals around the edge of the fire. Millie baked a whole ham in the oven and boiled a large pot of beans flavored with onions, garlic, molasses and other *secret* ingredients. Somehow she had managed to bake a few delectable desserts along with everything else. The men were not bashful about eating and showed great appreciation for the good food, thanking the ladies over and over again.

Aaron organized a horse-shoe game for the men while the ladies either watched or helped clean up the tables and put the food away. Everyone seemed to thoroughly enjoy the party atmosphere.

Except for Margaret. Her expectations of the day fell flat when the sun went down and lanterns were set out for music and dancing. The big problem was, none of the men knew how to dance. It turned out to be a dance-lesson-session instead of a real dance like Margaret had hoped. The men were eager to learn some dance steps but that's not what Margaret had in mind. Charlie, the guitar player, did a fine job of playing dance numbers and Rand even played his harmonica for a few of the songs.

But then Rand noticed how frustrated Margaret was getting with the clumsy cowboys. He calmly stuck his harmonica in his back pocket and tapped Margaret on the shoulder. "May I have this dance, Miss Margaret?" he said with a bow.

Margaret stared in surprise for a few seconds, then with a curtsey she responded, "Of course, Mr. Trinity, I would be delighted."

Very smoothly and gracefully, Rand took Margaret in his arms and danced around the yard to a waltz.

Aaron had been in the kitchen talking to Michael and when they came out the back door he watched Rand for a few moments as he danced with Margaret. "Look at that show-off!" Envy was written on all the faces of the men as they watched. "Sure don't want him to get too big a head," he said with a mischievous grin. Aaron walked over to Cassie. "May I have this dance?" He took Cassie's hand then called to Charlie, "Play it again, Charlie!" Skillfully, he twirled Cassie around the yard ending with a stunning flourish and received a big applause from the group of spectators.

Brian Chandler brought a reluctant end to the day. "All right, we've got a big day ahead of us tomorrow so I suggest we head to the bunkhouse, men." There was good natured grumbling but they slowly vacated the backyard.

Margaret headed straight for Aaron with fire in her eyes. "Aaron Trinity! Why didn't you tell me you could dance like that? Why didn't you ask *me* to dance with you?"

"Why, I couldn't get anywhere near you. All the boys wanted you to teach them to dance. Besides, I needed to talk with Michael."

A petulant look appeared on Margaret's face and she snapped, "Why couldn't you have fallen in love with *me* instead of that silly little girl, *Bonita*?"

That irritated Aaron…fast! The rude remark rang in his ears and he didn't hold back his retort. "Margaret Chandler! I could never love a woman as selfish and self-centered as you are! You are one *spoiled* girl. Besides, I think you're just using me to make that cowboy, Dillon, jealous. He's crazy about you. Don't you see how you're hurting him by flirting with any man around? I like Dillon and I won't be a part of you hurting him. I really want to be friends with you, but you need to grow up. Besides, my Bonita is not a silly little girl. She's everything I want my wife to be and I'm going to go get her as soon as I take Michael to our ranch."

Margaret looked stunned. "Oh! Oh…how can you say those terrible things to me?" She whirled around and rushed toward the backdoor.

Aaron hated the hurt on Margaret's face but had a hard time feeling repentant about his outburst. Instead he turned his attention to what he and Michael had talked about. He rounded up Rand and Gabriel and took them over to where Michael was standing.

"Is something wrong?" Rand asked.

"No, nothing's wrong," Michael told them. "I just want to tell you what the plans are. I've talked with Cassie and she is going to stay here with the kids. She wants to be with her mother a little longer and let her parents get to know Daniel and Katie better. The four of us," he looked at Gabriel, "if you want to, are going to go on to the High Meadows Ranch."

"You mean you're going to leave Cassie and the kids here?" Rand questioned.

"Not for long, Rand. After I spend a little time with my sister I'm coming back here and Cassie and I are getting married. Then I'll take her and the kids back to the High Meadows. After that I'm not sure."

"I be going with you," Gabriel said without hesitation. "Got to keep my cousins out of trouble."

Rand jabbed Gabe in the ribs. "You sure you want to leave that CeCe girl?"

Michael and Aaron chuckled at Gabriel's embarrassment. "I ain't sure of nothing' when it comes to women, but she sure caught my eye. She may not want nothing' to do with me though."

"You better find out soon," Rand said. "Ask her if she wants you to come back and see her." He talked like he had all the experience in the world with women.

"I jes might do that," Gabriel agreed.

"If you're going to talk to her you need to hurry, because we're leaving in the morning," Michael told him. "We're going light, and moving fast. I'm not taking the pack horse this time. Mr. Chandler says if we ride at a steady pace we can be there in two days. Let's turn in early and I'll see you first thing in the morning."

Michael turned to go back into the house and found Gabriel on his heels. He heard Gabriel speak to Millie who was finishing something in the kitchen. "Miss Millie, would you mind fetchin' CeCe. I'd like to talk to her for a short time."

Millie sighed heavily. "I'll go get her." Michael was sure he heard Millie mumble, "Lord have mercy, that cupid done flung his arrow."

Leaving was a lot harder than anyone expected. Millie made them a wonderful breakfast and packed enough food to last the two days. The cousins brought the horses to the front of the house where the family had gathered. Cassie and Michael were trying not to get too emotional because Daniel and Katie were watching, looking bewildered. Their efforts weren't successful, however. Cassie hugged Rand, Gabriel, and Aaron, and by the time she hugged Michael, tears were streaming down her face.

Daniel broke down and ran to Rand throwing his arms around the waist of his red-headed cousin as he cried his heart out. Rand got down on one knee and held the little guy while they both cried. "I don't want you to go without me," Daniel sputtered through his tears.

Katie started crying and Michael picked her up trying to console both mother and daughter. Katie looked pathetically at Michael and placed her two chubby little hands on his cheeks. "We go too. We go?"

That was Michael's undoing. His burning eyes couldn't hold the tears any longer and they slipped down his face. He looked around at the turmoil and saw Gabriel and Aaron swiping at their eyes. "All right, I want the Cousins tribe to have a council meeting, right here, right now." Michael sat down on the ground, pulling Cassie close with Katie on his lap. He motioned for the others to sit with them. When they made a circle all eyes turned to Michael. "This is the hardest thing I think I've ever done.

I'm sorry we didn't do this last night. I just didn't know how hard it would be. Daniel, I am coming back in two weeks. That is fourteen days. Hold up your fingers." When Daniel held up his fingers Michael asked, "Do you know how many fingers you have there?"

"Ten."

"That's right. Now show me four of them. Good, that's how many days I'll be gone. Then I'm coming back here and your mother and I are going to get married. Do you know what that means?"

"I think so. You're going to be my new daddy."

"That's right. I don't want you to ever forget your real dad. He was a good man and he loved you. You can be proud of him. But, I will try and be a good daddy too. Would you like that?"

"Yes," Daniel sniveled, "but I still don't want you to go."

"I don't want to go without you either, but sometimes we have to do things that are hard. Remember the other day when you told your grandfather you were going to take care of your mama?"

"Yes." Daniel nodded solemnly.

"Well, that's what I need you to do while I'm gone. You'll need to help your grandfather take care of your mama and her family here. After your mama and I are married we'll be a family and will always be together."

"What about my cousins?" Daniel asked, his eyes sliding over to Rand.

"I am going to take you and Katie and your mother to the High Meadows Ranch where Aaron and Rand are going to live. We will stay there for a while then we'll have another council meeting and decide what we'll do. How does that sound?"

"All right, I guess."

"That's my little man. You count the days on your fingers while I'm gone, then you start watching for me."

"You promise?"

"Yes, Daniel, I promise. If it's at all possible I will be here in fourteen days." He looked at Cassie. "I don't care how or what, but you be ready to marry me when I get back. I can't go through this ordeal again." He gave Cassie another hug then quickly mounted his horse. "Mount up, men. We need to cover some ground!"

Chapter 19

*T*HE MEN TALKED VERY little as they rode northwest toward the High Meadows. The sun was high when Michael called a stop to rest the horses. "If I remember right the North Platte isn't too far ahead. We'll water the horses and have a bite to eat there."

"I'm ready," Rand admitted. "Maybe we'll find some trees along the river to stop under. This sun is brutal today."

"What was brutal was leaving Cassie and the kids this morning." Michael shook his head and looked out in the distance as if wishing he could get a glimpse of the ones he'd grown to love.

The horses finally began to grow restless so they moved on until they found the shade that Rand wanted. They ate and let the horses rest and have their fill of the river. Later, they crossed the Platte without difficulty and continued their journey until both men and horses were too tired to go further. The decision was made to have a cold camp, so after eating, they rolled up in their blankets and tried to quickly settle down.

It seemed that Rand always had something to say before he went to sleep and even though he was tired to the bone his curiosity couldn't keep him quiet. "Tell us about that High Meadow of yours, Aaron. Maybe I can dream about how nice it's going to be."

"I don't really have words to explain how beautiful it is, Rand. The house sits at the back of a large meadow with two big pastures, one on each side of the road that goes up to the house. Of course, there's a barn and other outbuildings.

"Aspen trees are mixed in with different evergreens that border the meadow. This time of the year the meadow will be full of colorful spring flowers. There's a lake a short distance behind the house. You've never felt such cold water! Have you ever fished for trout, Rand?"

Silence.

"Rand?"

Aaron smiled and drifted off to sleep with visions of a cabin in his special place. Bonita was standing at the door, smiling and waiting for him.

The men were awake early and took time to build a small fire and make coffee. Rand dug through what was left of the food sack. "Shall we finish off these biscuits? They would go real good with the coffee."

As they drank coffee and ate, Aaron brought up the subject of what to do when they reached the High Meadows. "Michael, I'm worried about bringing you to the house and saying to Maxi, 'hi, here's your brother you thought was dead'. It will be a shock to her no matter what we do, but have you thought about it at all?"

"Sure, I've thought about it. It just doesn't seem real that after all this time we're going to be reunited. My problem is I don't remember my sister ever being weak or delicate in any way."

"No, you couldn't say she's either of those things. She's a strong woman. Well, if you think of anything to soften the blow let me know."

"Sure, we'll think of something."

"It better come to us quick," Aaron said, nodding to the north. "Those distant mountains is where home is."

Gabriel threw the grounds of the coffee on the fire and kicked dirt on top of the coals. "Let's go on home, cousins."

Late that day, Aaron brought his horse to a stop and let the others move closer. "Michael, I think I've come up with a plan that will break it slow and easy to Maxi."

"Tell me about it," Michael said. "I'm for anything you think will help."

"I have the sketch on my pad that I painted the picture of Frontier Soldier from. It's a good likeness of you. Maxi has never seen the picture or the sketch since I painted it after I got to Philadelphia. So here's the plan. I'll show her the sketch and maybe she'll see the resemblance then I can somehow bring it out that it's you."

Michael thought for a few moments. "That just might work, Aaron."

"All right, men, up this mountain road is *home*! Before we get to the meadow you three give me a little time to go on alone. Maybe twenty or thirty minutes. Then come on up to the house. I'll prepare her as much as I can."

"Sounds good," Michael agreed. "Let's get it done. I can't wait to see her!"

They made their way up the wagon road until Aaron brought his horse to a halt. "Just beyond this stand of trees is the road to the house. Wait here and come on up when you think it's been about thirty minutes."

Aaron left his three friends standing with their horses and rode away. *God, please prepare Maxi for what is about to happen. Thank you for bringing me safely home. I've heard people say there's no place like home and now I know what that means.*

When he broke through the trees, he took a deep breath, and urged his horse to a gallop. Before he even crossed the stream that flows through the two pastures he could see Carmen and Maxi peering out the front window. Prince set about barking to let them know someone was around. He didn't see Paul or his father, so he rode right up to the front of the house. He was met with squeals and laughter as Maxi and Carmen burst through the door and smothered him with hugs and kisses.

"Aaron, it's so good to see you! I was wondering if you had decided to stay back east," Carmen said.

"No chance of that. I've never been so happy in my life to be home."

Carmen hugged him again. "Come on in and I'll fix you something to drink then you can tell us about your trip."

"Where's Paul and Dad?"

"They rode down to the Double S to see Marty and Seth. They should be back any time now."

"How have things been since I've been gone? Seems like I've been gone for *years*." He wrapped his arms around the women's shoulders as they went into the house together.

"Everything has been good, and now that you're back, they'll be better," Maxi said. "Did your art exhibit go well?"

"Yes, it was wonderful! The owner of the gallery did an excellent job. I couldn't believe all the interest there was for anything western. Mr.

Chandler was right about a lot of people moving out west. I think the war is luring people to think about venturing out here or Oregon and California. One of my pictures got a *lot* of attention. I don't believe either one of you saw my sketch. Remember that day the soldiers came to the Swanson ranch and Mr. Swanson slugged that officer?"

"Yes, we remember it well," Carmen said

"How could we forget *that*!" Maxi shook her head.

"When I was down at the river at their camp, I made a sketch of one of the soldiers. Then when I got to Philadelphia the gallery owner told me he had room for a couple more pictures, so I painted that soldier."

"Oh? What was so interesting about him?" Maxi asked.

"I'm not sure what it was other than he is a very handsome man. I have it in my pack here. Let me show you." Aaron had taken the pack off and leaned it against the chair he was sitting in at the table. "Maybe you can tell me why people liked it." He flipped the pages on his sketch pad. "Here it is," he said, laying the sketch out for them to look at. What do you think?" His mind was racing to figure out what to do or say next.

Carmen gazed at the image without comment. Maxi stared at it, then glanced at Aaron, then back at the sketch. "That looks like my brother, Michael."

"It does?" Aaron tried to sound mildly surprised.

"Yes, it looks *exactly* like Michael. Did you find out his name?"

"He said his name was Joe McCall. I ran into him at the art show the day before the show closed. He was fascinated with *your* picture, the one I titled Princess Warrior."

Maxi frowned. "Why did he like that one?"

"He seemed to think the girl in the picture looked a lot like his sister."

Prince started barking again and Carmen went to look out the front window.

"Aaron, will you please make sense!" Maxi said with more than a little frustration. "Are you trying to tell me something? This is all very strange."

Carmen called from the front room, "Aaron, there are three men coming up the road. Will you go out with me?"

"It's all right, Mama," Aaron answered. "They're friends I made on the trip home and I brought them with me." He looked at Maxi. "One of them is the man in this sketch, Maxi. Come on out and meet him."

Maxi's hands flew to cover her face, which had drained of all color. "Aaron!" she whispered frantically. "Is it Michael? Do you know if it's Michael? Please. Tell me!"

"Yes, Maxi, it *is* Michael. We didn't know how to...."

He didn't get to finish his sentence. Maxi almost bowled him over as she raced from the room toward the front porch. She whipped past Carmen and threw open the door with a strangled-like shriek. "Michael!" she screamed. With one leap she bounded off the porch steps and flew toward the men coming up the road. "Michael!" she screamed again. Michael quickly dismounted in time to catch the flying woman in his arms, who, by then, had begun to sob.

"Yeah, it's me. Hi, Sis," he said as he held her tightly. "Don't cry, Sis. I didn't mean to make you cry."

Which just made her cry harder.

She finally pulled back and looked up into his face. "It's *really you*! I thought you were dead. Everything added up to you being dead, but I just didn't want to believe it."

"Yeah, that's what Aaron told me. Guess you can't get rid of me that easily." He hugged her to himself again. "I hate that you had to go through all that, Sis."

"Let's give them a few minutes," Aaron suggested. "Rand, you and Gabriel come with me and bring the horses. We'll get them taken care of then see if Mama can find us something to eat." As they walked to the barn, Aaron introduced Gabriel and Rand to Carmen.

"It's good to have you here with Aaron," Carmen told them. "How did you find Maxi's brother, Aaron?"

"I've got quite a story to tell about that. Actually, he found me, but I'll tell all that later, because I see Dad and Paul coming up the road. I've got to give Dad some bad news along with some good."

"Oh? What is it about, Aaron?" Carmen asked.

"I found out that Dad's brother and father are dead."

"Oh, no, that is sad news. He was hoping one day to see his brother again."

"I know. He's talked to me about it. But the *good* news is that Rand is his brother's son; Dad's nephew and my cousin."

"You don't say!" Carmen smiled as she watched Rand and Gabriel taking care of the horses inside the barn. "My goodness. Yes, I can see he is a Trinity." Then she looked at Aaron again. "But, Aaron, how did you find them?"

"I'd love to tell you now, but Mama, it's a long story and God definitely had his hand in it. I think I should take Dad aside and tell him privately about his father and brother, don't you?"

"Yes, Aaron, I think so too. You're such a good son and I'm so glad you're home." She hugged him, then turned her attention to the riders coming up the road.

They watched as Paul stopped beside Maxi, who still had hold of Michael's arm. "You better have a good explanation, Maxine Miles! I don't like coming home and finding my wife hanging on the arm of another good looking man."

Everyone laughed at his bravado, then Scott spotted Aaron standing at the barn door. "Hey, you're back!" He rode straight to Aaron, dismounted, and gave his son a big bear hug. "I sure have missed you! Glad you're home."

"I'm glad too, Dad. I missed you and everyone else around here."

"Who did you bring with you?" Scott said, glancing into the barn.

"I'll introduce you in a minute, but Dad, I really need to talk to you privately, first."

Just then, Maxi called to Carmen, "Mama, the babies are awake. Rosa and Maria are at the front door."

"Goodness, with all the excitement I forgot about the babies." Carmen said sternly to everyone as she turned to go into the house, "No more talking until we *all* get to the kitchen! I won't be left out of any of these conversations. Maxi, that means you and your brother, too."

"Her *brother*?!" Scott exclaimed.

"Yes, her *brother*. We're going to have a good long family time tonight and find out how all this happened."

"We've got to take care of the horses and do chores first, Sweetheart," Scott reminded her.

"That can wait for a little while, all right? After Aaron explains some of these mysteries, all you men can come out and get chores done in no time. Then later at family time we'll get all the details."

"All right, you're the boss...*this* time. Hey, everyone, let's get to the kitchen!"

Aaron grabbed hold of Scott's arm and tugged him to the side of the barn while everyone else started making their way into the house. "Dad, I have some bad news to tell you."

"Well, all right, Son. You talk and I'll listen."

"I found out on this trip that your father and your brother are both dead. I didn't want to tell you in front of everyone else. I hate having to tell you at all."

Scott stood very still looking at Aaron. Finally he asked, "How did you find out, Aaron? Are you sure about this?"

"Yes, Dad, I'm sure. I brought Randall's son home with me. You saw him in the barn. He doesn't have anyone else but us, now, so I brought him home. And I found him in a hospital, Dad! A *filthy* military hospital. He was a prisoner and he's only fourteen! I knew you would want him. I've really gotten attached to him, myself. He's a great kid."

"Of course, I want him! I'm really sad to hear about Randall, though. I was hoping to see him again. How in the world did the boy end up in the military at his age?"

"Well, it was all a big mistake, but I think he should tell you the story. When you're ready, we'll go in and you can meet him. Mama's probably anxious for us to get in there."

"You're probably right. I'm ready to go in now. And Aaron, thank you for telling me in private. That was very thoughtful of you. You are the best son I could ever have." He hugged Aaron again and together they walked to the back door.

Inside the crowded kitchen everyone had already introduced themselves and were gabbing like old friends. Scott immediately went to Rand and folded him into his arms. "So, you're my nephew, huh? You look like a Trinity, so guess I'll keep you," he teased. "I'm your Uncle Scott and you are welcome to live here as long as you want."

"Thank you, sir, I appreciate that a lot."

"I hope you'll call me Uncle Scott and not sir."

"All right, I will, sir...er, Uncle Scott."

"Sometime soon, I want to hear what happened to your pa. But we'll wait for another time." He turned to Gabriel. "And now, who is this young man?"

"Dad, I'd like you to meet Gabriel Freeman," Aaron said. "We met him on our trip and he was a big help to us. Of course, we wanted him to come home with us."

"Welcome, Gabriel." Scott said, shaking Gabriel's hand. "I'll look forward to getting acquainted with you." Scott then stood in front of Michael. "You must be Maxi's long lost brother. I can't tell you how happy I am that you are alive and well. I know this girl, here, is probably beside herself. I'm Scott Trinity and I'm glad to meet you."

"Thank you. And yes, I'm Michael Mayfield. I had no idea that Maxi was going through such a terrible time. I feel bad about that. But I'm so glad I ran into Aaron again in Philadelphia, or I might have never found my sister."

"Papa, up!" One of the twins was trying to climb up Scott's leg.

Paul was holding the other one and she couldn't take her eyes off Gabriel. He looked apologetically at Gabriel. "Sorry, I guess she hasn't ever seen a black man before."

"That's all right, I don't blame her. She's a mighty pretty little thing with all her black hair and brown eyes. How do you know one from da other?"

Scott answered the question. "At times it's hard, but after you get to know them there are little things that help. Rosa's eyes have little specks of black in them and Maria has a funny little mole on the back of her neck. But, personality wise they are quite different. Maria is sweet and quiet most of the time. She likes to play mother with her doll. Rosa is more adventurous and wants to be outside playing with Prince or picking the flowers."

Maxi held baby Michael over her shoulder trying to get a burp out of him. "When this little pig burps for me, I'll introduce you to your nephew, Michael." Her eyes started tearing up. "I can't believe I'm sitting here talking to you after thinking for so long that you were dead."

"I know. It's hard for me to believe too," Michael said. "What's really hard to believe is that I was so close to you when I was in the army and we stopped at the ranch down below. I think it was the Double S Ranch. We were so close…But, then things would have turned out differently if we'd discovered each other then."

Scott stood up and pushed his chair back. "When we have family time right after supper you need to explain what you mean by that, Michael. Right now, we need to go take care of the horses and do chores. Whatever my sweet wife is cooking smells *good* and it's making my stomach growl."

"You can go now," Carmen smiled at him, "but if you tell anything important you'll just have to repeat it later."

Michael started to get up and go with the men when Maxi reached over and stopped him. "Stay here with me, Michael. I'm not ready to let you out of my sight, yet." The baby let out a big burp and started jumping up and down in Maxi's lap. "Here, Michael, meet Michael." She sat the baby in her brother's lap. "I'll help Mama with supper while you hold him. Just stay here in the kitchen with us."

The two Michaels eyed each other for a minute, then baby Michael reached up to his uncle's beard and shrieked his pleasure when he managed to get enough to pull.

"Michael, how did that man get your rifle? I know you would never give it away or sell it?"

"You're right about that. After I left our farm in Texas, Stan and I joined up with a cattle drive going north. I went with one of the other guys to get supplies after we'd been on the trail for a few weeks. Someone stole that rifle right off my horse while I was inside! I about tore that little excuse for a town apart trying to figure out who had taken it. Never did find it. It was a hard thing for me to lose."

"I'm sure it was. You were thrilled when Pa gave it to you."

"I can't believe you ended up with it."

"I'm having a hard time believing you're sitting here talking to me. I have so much to tell you and a million questions to ask."

"I feel the same way. I want to know what happened to Pa. We'll have a couple of weeks to visit and get all our questions answered, then I have to go get Cassie and the kids."

"What? Who is Cassie? Are you married and have children? Where are they?"

Chapter 20

AMILY TIME LASTED LATE into the evening. Michael and Aaron did most of the talking about Michael's life of running from the law, joining the army, volunteering to go back east to fight in the war, and how he became a doctor. Aaron told how they found each other, then how they rescued Rand from the Union hospital.

It was clear when Michael talked about Cassie and the children that he had deeper feelings for them than just being a friend. "They were in an awful situation, so we helped them by sneaking them out of the house and leaving town with them the next morning."

Maxi laughed. "I can tell it didn't hurt your feelings any to rescue the damsel in distress."

A sheepish grin spread across Michael's face. "Not even a tiny little bit."

In the next few days more and more of the stories were told around the table and at family time in the evenings. They enjoyed the time so much it was hard to call it a night until it was so late everyone had a hard time staying awake.

Friday, before Carmen called them to supper, Aaron found his father and asked to talk to him. "Sure, Aaron. Let's go sit on the porch. Is something wrong?"

"No, nothing's wrong. I just want to tell you what I'm going to do before I tell everyone else."

Scott grinned. "You probably don't even need to tell me because I think I already know. When we were down at the Paradise to get the tent for you boys, I saw you looking at the western mountains. You had the look of a man in love, fixing to go find his sweetheart. Am I right?"

"Yeah, you guessed right. It's been long enough and I want her here with me. I've only heard from her once. Every time I read her letter, it makes me smile. In my mind I can see her sitting at our kitchen table practicing her letters. She told me she would leave me clues as to where I could find her. I've made enough money from selling my pictures to take care of Bonita until I can sell more of them. The gallery owner told me to ship as many as I could back to him and he would sell them. Dad, I couldn't believe the price he put on the pictures. Would you believe the one of Diablo sold for one hundred dollars! Of course, Mr. Princeton takes his cut, but it adds up quickly. I feel really blessed."

"Yes, I believe you are blessed. But I still want you to take that one sack of gold with you just in case. You might find someone who needs help."

"All right, thanks, Dad. It's amazing how God has already used that gold for people who really needed a helping hand."

"When are you going to leave?"

"Monday morning."

"That quick, huh."

"Yes, I want to be back to help with the work around here and finish my cabin. I'm hoping to be back by the fourth of July. Wouldn't want to miss that. I have a special surprise for our celebration."

"Oh, and what would that be?"

"It's a surprise. You'll have to wait like the rest of them."

"All right, but I sure hate to see you leave so soon. You don't plan on going alone, do you?"

"Probably not, but I haven't said anything to Rand or Gabriel. I want that to be their decision. Especially Gabriel. Now that he's a free man he has a bit of an independent streak. He wants to see the world, so I think he'll probably want to go with me. I have a feeling that where we go, Rand will want to go. He has an adventurous spirit. We've grown real close these past weeks of being together on the trail. What do you think about Rand going with me and Gabe?"

"It'll probably be all right. He's still pretty young, but he's a smart kid. I can see my brother in him in so many ways. Personally, I'd feel better if the three of you went together. While you were gone someone brought up the scripture that says something like, a threefold cord is not quickly broken."

"Where's that? I'd like to read it."

"I don't know right off but I'll find it for you. It's my turn to read scripture tonight so I'll read that passage for everyone."

"I wish Michael could go with us. He was our anchor on the trip home, but he promised Daniel and Cassie that he'd be back in two weeks. Can't blame him for wanting to go get Cassie and the kids. She's a wonderful lady, Dad. We all got real attached to her and those sweet kids."

"I guess you'll just have to let God be your anchor on this next journey. You know we'll be praying for you and whoever goes with you."

"Yes, I know. There were times on my trip back east that I could feel your prayers for me. When I look back on all that happened, it was as if God had it planned all along. I know He doesn't plan for bad things to happen, but if we let Him, He'll make good things come from the bad. Is that how you see it?"

"Yeah, when you look back you can see how it all worked out, but at the time you're going through some turmoil, it's hard to see beyond the pain of what's happening." Scott stood and stretched. "There's the dinner bell, Son. Let's head in before they start without us and Rand eats everything! He eats almost as much as you did when you first came here. Gabe isn't any slacker when it comes to food, either."

"I hope it's not too hard on Mama."

"I know she gets pretty tired chasing the two girls, but she loves having Gabriel and Rand here. You three have been a great help the last couple of days. I hope when you get back you'll settle in and stay a while."

"If it's left up to me, I won't ever leave again," Aaron said.

When Aaron shared at family time that he was going to leave Monday, he got some disappointed looks. All the family knew, however, that it was only a matter of time before he left to go get Bonita.

Maxi was the one who was vocal about his leaving. "You just got home and now you're going to go running off again?"

"I know, but the sooner I go get Bonita the sooner I'll be able to come back and *stay*."

"I hope you don't think you're going to run off without me," Rand challenged. "I'll have to go so I can take care of you."

Gabriel wouldn't be left behind either. "When we first met, you insisted on me riding with you to dat town, but dis time, I be insisting you take me with you."

"I'd be pleased to have both of you come with me. You sure you don't want to come with us, Michael?" Aaron teased.

"You know, if I didn't have another important appointment I would be going with you. But, you know how it is…." Michael shrugged innocently.

"That I do, brother. That I do."

"I'm glad you two will be going with Aaron," Scott said. "It means a lot to all of us. I'm going to read some scripture now from Ecclesiastes the fourth chapter." Everyone quieted down as Scott opened his bible and began to read. When he got to the twelfth verse, he read it slowly and with emphasis:

"And if one prevails against him, two shall withstand him; and a threefold cord is not quickly broken."

"That's what I'm going to pray for you three," Scott said. "That you will be like a strong threefold cord, watching out for each other, taking care of each other."

Saturday was spent getting ready for Sunday and Aaron's departure on Monday. Church services were at the Double S Ranch. Michael, Rand, and Gabriel got to meet most of the people on both ranches, making for a long day, because everyone wanted to know all about them, especially Michael and his story.

The weather started out rather cloudy and windy, but by early afternoon the sun found its way out of the clouds and it warmed enough for people to sit around outside and swap tales. The men shared with Aaron and his friends what they knew about the country they would be traveling through and gave them advice and encouragement.

Baby Michael delighted everyone when he took his first steps to reach his papa. Paul grabbed him before he fell on his behind and playfully tossed him in the air, eliciting a squeal of delight. Charity Myers and Maria Trinity were content to play with their dolls but the happy squeal from baby Michael brought Rosa Trinity over to Paul so she could be tossed in the air too. Fawn and Marty's little boy, Martin Black Hawk Swanson, was content to sit in his Grandpa Swanson's lap and watch everything that was going on.

Finally, Scott stood. "I hate to break this up but we need to get home."

"Yeah, we need to get to evening chores too." Mr. Swanson stood with everyone else as they prepared to leave. "It was good to meet you, Rand, and you too, Gabriel. When you get through riding the trails with Aaron, I'll put one of you to work. Between the three ranches, I'm sure there will be enough work for everyone."

Gabriel responded to the offer. "Thank you, sir, I jes might be the one needin' to work."

Aaron, Rand, and Gabriel sat in their tent that night talking about their upcoming trip. The plan was to leave before anyone else got up, since they agreed that they hated goodbyes. But it didn't work. Scott and Carmen, each carrying a sleepy-eyed girl, came walking from their cabin, following the smell of bacon and coffee that was wafting from the main house.

Scott teased the boys who were getting their horses ready. "Thought you might sneak out on us, huh?"

"We just hated to say goodbye," Aaron admitted. "I should have known Maxi and Mama would have to feed us before we left."

"Yes, you should have," Carmen agreed. "Just get yourselves in the house. Maxi and I want you to leave with your stomachs full and a sack of food to eat on for a couple of days."

"You talked me into it," Rand said, rubbing his stomach as he headed for the back door.

The women were teary-eyed when they said their goodbyes. Even though he didn't show it, Scott was struggling with seeing his son ride down the road away from him. Carmen sensed his anxiety and reached over and took his hand. "He will come back to us. We will pray him home just like we have the other times he left us."

"Yes, we'll pray, but it's still hard to watch your son become a man and head out on his own."

Michael broke the spell of sadness when he reached over to take baby Michael from Maxi's lap. "Hey, little guy, come and see your uncle." The baby dove for Michael and tried to get a hold of his beard.

"Paul, I'm going to take my girls back to the cabin," Scott said. "I'll be back in a few minutes to help with chores and work with the horses. Michael, you enjoy your sister and don't feel like you have to help, unless you really want to come out and join us. I know you two still have a lot to talk about so make good use of the next week or so. What are your plans after you go back and marry this girl of yours?"

"What I'd really like to do is come back here for a while. I want Cassie and Maxi to get to know each other and I want to spend more time with Maxi, myself. But I don't want to be a burden to anyone. I'd work and help around here for the summer. Think about it. I'll understand if it's too much to expect."

"I don't have to think about it," Scott answered. "We'd love to have you and we'll work things out. I've been thinking that we need to build a bunkhouse even though the Swanson's said we could use the tent as long as we need it. A cabin at the back of the property could be used as a bunkhouse or for visitors. Do you plan on spending the winter up here too?"

"Probably not," Michael answered. "In my mind, I've been working on a plan for me and Cassie to make a home in that little place east of Fort Laramie. It's on the main route to the west. The telegraph is already there. Sounds like it will be right where the railroad will come through. Mr. Chandler has already built a large general store and is working on getting someone reputable to run it. He seems to think it will be a thriving town someday. With the ranches, Fort Laramie, and the beginnings of a town it would probably be a good place for a doctor to set up his practice. I hope to get someone to build a home close to the town this summer. This fall I'll move my family down there, that is if I can get it all worked out. I'll have to find a suitable piece of land to build the house on. Next spring I'll build an office in the town."

"You've got big plans in that mind of yours. I for one hope you succeed in all of them. We're going to need good men out here to help this country grow into a safe respectable place to raise families."

"Of course I've got to talk all this over with Cassie before I do anything. I don't know what she wants to do, but I think it'll please her to be close to her mother. And, I won't be so far away that I can't see Maxi once in a while."

Baby Michael grew restless and started to squirm. Maxi took him and went into the house. Scott and Carmen left with the twins and Michael followed Maxi into the house and found her nursing the baby in the front room. "You've been mighty quiet for a while. Are you upset about the plans I talked about?"

"No, I'm not upset," Maxi said. "That's the wrong word. You're going to think I'm being very childish…but I'm *jealous*."

"Jealous? Why would you be jealous?"

"That's just it. I don't know why I'm feeling this way. I guess I wanted you all to myself. At least for a while. Saying it out loud sounds even worse than childish."

"Nah, don't feel that way. For more than a year your body has gone through a lot of changes with having a baby. Then your long lost brother comes riding in and brings a whole set of new circumstances to your door. I'm sure you were attached to Aaron and have missed him and now he leaves again."

"Yeah, I've been tired and moody for a while. Carmen says sometimes women go through depression after having a baby. Do you suppose that's what it's about?"

"Very easily could be…or you're pregnant again."

Maxi's head flew up from looking under the blanket at her nursing baby. Her eyes were wide with something akin to terror in them. "Why, I don't know! Could I be pregnant again, so *soon*?"

Michael laughed out loud. "I don't know, you tell me. Could you be pregnant again? And don't look so terrified. It happens all the time."

Maxi threw a couch pillow at Michael. "Having babies is something to be terrified of, Dr. Michael Mayfield!" Maxi looked serious. "Calling you doctor sounds very strange to me, but I'm so very proud of you."

"Thanks, Sis."

Maxi stood. "Give me just a minute to lay the baby down and I'll be back."

Maxi had a wonderful day with her brother. Carmen offered to take care of the baby, so in the afternoon, Maxi and Michael went for a ride to the back meadows. They rigged up some fishing poles and fished for a while, talked about their childhood and laughed at the silly things they'd done. It was a mighty good thing she took advantage of the day and spent as much time with Michael as she could, for early the next morning, a horse and rider galloped up the road and halted at the house before anyone was awake. There was the noise of someone tromping on the porch then banging on the front door, sending Prince into a barking tirade.

Paul jumped out of bed, pulled on his pants, and grabbed his rifle. By the time he got to the front door, Michael was right behind him. A man stood on the porch but it was too dark to tell who it was.

"Who are you and what do you want?" Paul demanded.

"I'm Brian Chandler and I need the doctor. Is he here?"

"Yeah, I'm here, Brian," Michael answered. "Let him in, Paul. He's Cassie's brother. What's wrong, Brian?" Maxi lit one of the lanterns and saw that it was Michael's turn to have a terrified look on his face. "Tell me what's wrong!? Is it Cassie? Is something wrong with Cassie?"

"No, it's Daniel. He's been sick and is getting worse. Cassie thought it was just a stomach ache at first, but when she questioned him she found out he was hurting down here." Brian put his hand on the lower right side of his abdomen. "He's running a fever and has been throwing up. Can't keep any food down him. Cassie is worried sick about it. She sent me to get you."

Michael turned toward the bedroom he was sleeping in. "I've got to go, *right* now!"

"What can we do to help," Paul asked.

"You can saddle my horse." Michael stopped at the bedroom door and turned to Paul. "I may need to borrow another horse, so I can switch back and forth."

Brian assured him he wouldn't need but one horse. "Father sent four men out with a fresh mount for you. When you hit the end of the wagon road, go straight toward our ranch. Along the way, there will be men stationed with a fresh horse so you can ride straight through. They'll be watching for you and you'll need to watch for them."

"That was smart thinking," Paul said as he headed out the door. "I'll get your horse saddled."

"What can I do?" Maxi wanted to know.

"Pack me food that I can eat while riding. If it's what I think it is, I've got the ride of my life ahead of me. Minutes will count if I'm going to save little Daniel's life."

Minutes later, Maxi watched as Michael rode down the lane and into the trees. She started crying. Paul took her in his arms and held her. "It'll be all right, baby. He'll be all right."

"I hope so. I can't bear the thought of losing him so soon after I just found him . . . and…and…."

"And, what?"

"I might be pregnant again!"

Chapter 21

ETTING DOWN THE WAGON road to the bottom of the hill was agonizingly slow for Michael. There was a faint glow on the eastern horizon that promised light, but not soon enough for him. Paul's final words kept coming to his mind, 'You won't do that little boy any good if you push this horse so hard he has a fall that could kill you and him. God go with you.' *God go with me, that's what I need. God....* He wanted to pray but the words got stuck in his throat. *I wish I had Aaron's faith. Who am I to ask God for anything?*

The sun finally peeked over the horizon defining the prairie ahead. Michael kicked his horse and the strong animal seemed to sense the urgency of the situation and pushed ahead to a full gallop. Michael lost track of time as the wind rushed into his face, making his eyes burn and his mouth go dry. But he didn't stop to check his pocket watch, or quench his thirst, or rest. *I've got to keep pushing on. God ...*he tried praying again. *God....*The right words just wouldn't come.

"Ask, Michael, just ask."

Those words spoke to his heart and gave him courage.

"Help me make it in time to save Daniel's life. Please don't let him die. I love the little guy more than I could say. Cassie and Katie are so precious to me. I want to be a good husband and father to them.

A floodgate burst open once he started to pray. *I remember when I was young I gave my life to You but I don't know what happened. I just seemed to drift away. Please forgive me for that. I'll really try to do better. Thank you for keeping Maxi safe and helping her find a nice family....*

Lost in his prayer, Michael was startled when he heard a gunshot. Looking around for its source, he didn't see anything at first. Then a second shot rang out and he located a horse and rider coming toward him, leading a second horse. Michael recognized the rider approaching as a cowboy from the Chandler ranch.

"Hi, Doc! You're making good time, but you're off some," the ranch hand greeted Michael. "You need to head a little more southeast. I'll switch the saddles for you."

"Thanks! I need a long drink of water. Sure wish I'd had coffee before I left this morning."

"Sorry, but I can't help you with that. Drank all mine a long time ago."

The water tasted good and Michael used a little to wash his eyes out." You'll take good care of my horse, won't you?"

"You bet I will. I'll cool him off and come on behind you. The next place to watch for your fresh mount is on this side of the Platte River. You'll need a fresh horse to get you across. Hurry, Doc, they need you real bad at the ranch! We've all fallen in love with that little guy. Sure hate to see him so bad off."

"I know what you mean, I feel the same way," Michael said, mounting the fresh horse. "Thanks again, I'll see you at the ranch."

The new mount was rested and eager to go. Michael fell into rhythm with the movement of the horse which dulled his thinking after a couple of hours. Finally, he thought, *I need to eat something. I haven't had any food since last night.* He reached back for the food sack and grabbed the first thing that his hand could get hold of. He brought out a hand-full of cookies. *Oatmeal cookies, my favorite! I'll have to thank Sis for remembering they're my favorite.* A short time later, Michael could see the cottonwood trees along the river. He began searching along the banks for his next ride. The ranch hand wasn't hard to spot since he was waving a red neck scarf over his head.

"Glad to see you, Dr. Mayfield. Have you had any trouble so far?"

"No, no trouble. Say, is that coffee on your fire?" Michael asked, dismounting.

"Sure is. There's some left if you want it."

"If you'll change my saddle for me maybe I can get a few swigs down." Michael dug down in his food sack and found a steak sandwich wrapped in a cloth. "Just what the doctor ordered." He took several long gulps of the lukewarm coffee and climbed back in the saddle.

The ranch hand told him, "You be careful now, but when Don gets here, we'll be right behind you, in case you do have trouble."

"Thanks," was all Michael said as he kicked his horse and headed into the river. He had a hard time juggling his sandwich when he realized his doctor's bag might get water in it and quickly grabbed it holding it up so it wouldn't get wet. He saved both the sandwich and his bag then hurriedly ate the sandwich as his horse raced on. By the time Michael reached the next fresh horse he was weary to the bone. The cowboy that was waiting looked familiar. "Your name is Dillon, isn't it?" Michael asked.

"That's me. You look tired, Doc."

"It's been a long day and yes, I'm tired."

"You really are doing good, Doc. You made it quicker than I thought you would. Is there anything you need?"

"No, just a drink of water. My mouth is as dry as the Arizona desert."

While he was drinking from his canteen, Dillon got his attention. "You see those hills straight ahead? See the one that's a little more pointed than the others? Us boys call it the witch's hat. Anyway, head straight for that hill and you'll be right on course and at the ranch in no time."

Michael mounted his fresh horse. "Thanks, Dillon, see you later."

He was anxious to be with Cassie and the kids and the ride seem to take forever. His horse ran on and on while the dark shadows of evening began to fall. He could feel the horse slowing down but kept urging him on. At last he saw the ranch house in the distance and his heart raced. He refused to think about what might be ahead of him, but he knew whatever it was, he would trust God to see them through.

CeCe sat by Daniel's bed, looking at his little feverish face. She dabbed a cool, wet cloth across his forehead and reddened cheeks. He moaned and rolled his head from side to side.

"Poor baby," CeCe crooned softly. "Jes rest, child. See if you can rest."

"Where's Mama?" Daniel asked. "I want Mama."

"She'll be right back directly, honey. She took a little break to go downstairs for jes a little bit. Shh...jes rest, now. CeCe be here with you now."

Daniel quit tossing and laid very still, closing his eyes.

Well, good. Maybe he'll be able to sleep awhile. My, My, but Miss Cassie has been beside herself all day. Won't leave this child's bed for nary a minute. But ole CeCe here, I done told her to go take a break. Jes a little break and I won't take my eyes off him, neither. No sirree, not even for a minute.

CeCe sat back in her chair watching Daniel carefully. He appeared to be sleeping but his little face was red with fever and his hairline damp with sweat. She closed her eyes and turned her face toward the heavens, laying her head back against the chair. A sigh escaped her lips but her heart was full of concern for young Daniel. A feather soft breeze caressed her face and she startled, sat up straight and looked around the room.

Oh, my heavens, CeCe! Did you fall asleep, ole girl? Surely not! I jes closed my eyes for a second, I swear, jes for a second.

She startled again when she realized Daniel was staring at her. Leaning toward him, she felt his forehead and stroked his cheek. "How are you feeling, now, honey?"

"Not good, CeCe. My tummy hurts some more."

She dabbed his face with the wet cloth. "I am truly sorry bout that, child."

He looked ready to cry, his eyes full of misery. "But CeCe, why didn't you wake me up when my friend Talker came?"

"Shh, honey. No friend came in here." *My goodness, I think he's talking strange things cause of the fever in him. What's that called, hullucins...or something.*

"Yes, he did," Daniel whimpered. "He's my blood brother and he was here. He gave me a gift. It's on the table, but I didn't get to see him... Oww...My tummy hurts! Where's Mama?" He tossed his head from side to side.

CeCe took the damp rag and dabbed his face. Then something caught her eye and she turned to the bedside table. A red marble sat at the edge. *Lawdy! Where did that come from? That wasn't there a minute ago...Was it?* "Shh, little one, I think I hear your mama coming right now." CeCe started for the door just as Cassie and Michael rushed through. "Oh, thank heavens, you're here! He is talking out of his head now. Having friends that ain't here, and talking 'bout brothers and blood gifts and such. Scared me a little."

"Thanks, CeCe, for watching him," Cassie said. "You can go now and see if Millie needs any help."

Michael was already at Daniel's bedside, leaning over the sick boy. "Hey, Daniel. Can you tell me where it hurts?"

Daniel pushed the covers down with his fist and pointed to his side with his other hand. "Are you going to be my doctor now? I sure want my tummy to quit hurting."

"I certainly am going to try and make you better." Michael gently pressed on Daniel's side, but immediately stopped when Daniel winced in pain.

"I don't know what to think," Cassie said. "When he told me his tummy hurt I just thought he ate something that didn't agree with him. Then when he got a fever, I was concerned. He showed me where he hurt but it didn't seem right for just a stomach ache."

"What have you done for him?" Michael asked.

"CeCe and I have been bathing him with cider vinegar and water to keep him cooled off."

"Has he eaten anything lately?"

"Just a little broth at lunch time, but he threw it up later. He doesn't seem interested in food. Can you do anything, Michael?"

Michael turned away from Daniel and spoke softly. "Yes, I'm going to operate on him, with your permission, of course. I'm sure it's his appendix. I need to take it out and I need to do it right away."

"Can't it get better on its own?"

"Possibly, but not likely. The problem is, if his appendix ruptures before I can take it out, I'm not sure I could save his life. All the infection would spill out into the rest of his body."

"Can he live without the ap-appen...."

"Appendix. Yes, he won't even know it's gone. Will you trust me to do the surgery, Cassie?"

"Of course, if it will save his life. You do whatever needs to be done. What can I do to help?"

"You and Millie can prepare the kitchen for me. I can smell supper cooking, but it'll need to be taken outside or put on hold. I'll need two pans of hot water and if you and Millie can find some soft cotton to make little pads about four inches by four inches that will help. I'll need a stack of them. I'm going to use the kitchen table so find something clean to cover it with. While you go do that, I'll talk to Daniel." Cassie turned to leave. "Oh, and will you send CeCe back up here, please."

"Yes, I'll send her up right away."

Michael turned back to Daniel. "Are you going to fix my tummy ache?" He still had his fist clenched but Michael thought it was because of his pain.

"Yes, you have a tiny little organ in your tummy called an appendix. Yours is sick and I need to take it out."

"Will it hurt?"

"No, I'm going to put you to sleep and you won't even know when I take it out. When you wake up your tummy will be a little sore for a few days and then you'll be just like you were before you got sick. You'll be running and riding Patches before you know it."

Daniel's response was simply, "All right, I miss Patches."

"As soon as CeCe gets here, I'm going downstairs to make sure everything is ready. I'll be back pretty quick to carry you down."

Michael turned and saw CeCe standing in the doorway. "You wanted to speak to me, Doctor?"

"Did you hear my conversation with Daniel?"

"Yes, I heard it."

"I want to talk to you about assisting me with the surgery."

CeCe's eyes grew big. "You want me to help you do what you said, to take something out of Daniel?"

Margaret appeared in the doorway right then, asking how Daniel was. Michael asked if she would stay with Daniel while he went down and set up the surgery. "I need to take CeCe and show her what to do, since she will be assisting me." Michael followed CeCe down the stairs. When they got to the living room, he talked openly with her. "Are you squeamish at the sight of blood? If you are, I'll need to ask someone else to help. Maybe Millie."

"Not, Millie! She sends me out to wring the chicken's necks all the time. I have to clean them too. After I do that she plucks and cooks 'em.

She just don't like the blood. What is it that I have to do with the blood?" CeCe had a frown on her dark face.

"When I make a small incision or cut on Daniel's stomach it's going to seep blood. I need you to soak it away so I can see what I'm doing."

"If it'll help you make Daniel better, I can do that. What else do I have to do?"

"When I get it all set up I'll show you. While I'm doing that will you find Mr. Chandler and tell him I need to talk to him?"

"I'll do that right now," CeCe said, heading for the back door.

Michael went into the kitchen and found Millie and Cassie folding the cotton cloth pads. "How are things going in here?"

"We covered the table and the water is hot," Cassie told him. "How many of these pads do you need?"

"Just to be sure I have enough, make a few more. I'm going to drop my instruments in this one pan of hot water to make sure they're clean."

Mr. Chandler came in the back door. "CeCe said you need to talk to me."

"Yes, I'm going to need one of the men to help me. He needs to be able to assist me and not get upset with…well…he can't have a weak stomach." Cassie was in the room and Michael didn't want to say anything to scare her."

"It's all right, Michael," she said. "Dad, how about Skinny? Isn't he the one who saved that calf by cutting the dead mother open and delivering the calf that way?"

"Yeah. He has stitched up the horses a few times when they got gashes."

"He sounds good. Send him in, will you, Mr. Chandler?"

When Michael was satisfied everything was ready, and his assistants were present, he sent everyone else out to the living room. "Mr. Chandler, I don't want anyone coming in and distracting me. If I need help, I'll call you. Close the door on your way out, please."

Just CeCe and Skinny were in the room now. He gave some final instructions. "CeCe, I have my instruments laid out in the order I'll need them. You don't need to know the names of them for now. I'll just say 'next' and you hand the next one to me. My hands may be slippery with blood, so make sure I have hold of it before you let go. When the blood seeps around the wound, soak it up with the pads. Do you understand?"

"Yes, I understand," she said.

"Good. Skinny, you stay right there where Daniel's head will be. I'm going to administer the chloroform the first time. It will put him to sleep pretty fast. Then I want to work quickly to take the appendix out. Skinny, you must watch Daniel carefully and if he looks like he might be waking up you'll need to put this strainer with the cloth over his face and let him breathe a little more of the anesthesia. It's quite powerful and we can't let him get too much. If I tell you to put a drop on the cloth, be *sure* it is only a drop. Do you understand?"

"Sure, I understand."

"All right, good. I'm going to go get Daniel now. Stay calm and don't scare him. While I'm gone I want both of you to wash your hands with hot soapy water."

Michael left the room and went upstairs. Daniel seemed calm enough but still had his fist clenched against the pain. He panicked a little when Michael laid him on the table. "Where's my mama?"

Skinny calmly talked to Daniel while Michael washed up. "She's in the other room. You remember me, don't you?"

"Sure, I know you. I helped you with that calf the other day."

"Yep, you did a right good job, too. You're going to make one fine cowboy. You remember my name?"

"It's Skinny. Mama says your name means you're not fat."

Michael was grateful to Skinny for the diversion and took his place beside Daniel. Taking a small strainer, he placed some of the soft cotton cloth over the strainer and put a small amount of chloroform on it.

"Daniel, I'm going to place this over your mouth and nose. I want you to just breathe like you usually do. This is going to help you go to sleep. Close your eyes and think about how many marbles you gave to Talker."

CeCe immediately looked up at Michael. *Talker? That was what Daniel said when he was out of his head. Talker....*

"Count them for me," Michael continued. "Keep your eyes closed and count slowly. Start with one."

"That's easy. One, two, three...four...five...."

"Are you two ready?" Michael asked.

As Daniel relaxed into a deep sleep, his fist finally unclenched. A red marble fell out and rolled to the floor.

Chapter 22

MICHAEL FACED A ROOM full of anxious faces when he walked into the Chandler's living room. He found the one face that brightened his life and smiled. "It's all over and I'm glad to say that it went well. Daniel's appendix had not ruptured and I expect he'll be wanting to ride Patches in a few days. I've been monitoring his breathing and heartbeat the last little while, and he's doing great."

"Can I go see him, Michael?" Cassie asked.

"In a few minutes, Cassie. He'll be coming out of the anesthesia pretty soon and I want to move him upstairs to your bed before that. You can stay with him as long as you want then."

"I'll go get the bed ready right now." Cassie turned to her mother and Margaret who had a sleeping Katie stretched out between them. "Margaret, will you let Katie sleep with you for a few nights?"

"Of course. We've become best friends these last few days."

"I appreciate it, Sis. You've been a big help watching out for her."

Mr. Chandler offered to carry Katie upstairs. "I'll take Katie if you'll help your mother upstairs, Margaret."

"I'm not ready to go up, Dalton. I'm hungry and I'm sure everyone else is too. Millie, let's go see what we can find to feed everyone now that all the excitement is over."

"I know 'zactly what I'm going to fix for everyone, so don't you fret none about it, Mrs. Chandler. Someone needs to go tell them cowboys on the back porch about how Daniel is. They been sitting out there for a long time now."

"I'll do that, Millie, after I get this sleeping doll up to bed." Mr. Chandler gathered Katie in his arms and kissed her pink cheek. "You know, she looks a lot like you, Cherry."

Mrs. Chandler beamed. "Do you really think so?"

"I sure do, but where did she get these pretty, red curls?"

"My mother had hair that color when she was young. As she got older it changed to strawberry blonde. Don't you remember?"

"I guess not. I was too busy looking at you."

"Oh, go on now! I'll be in the kitchen with Millie and CeCe. I'll see that they take a tray up to Cassie."

Michael carried Daniel upstairs and found Cassie waiting for him. He gently laid Daniel where the covers were pulled back. "He looks so peaceful now," Cassie said softly. "Thank you, Michael."

"I'm just glad I made it here when I did. Daniel may not feel real good when he wakes up, but if he feels like it, you can let him sip on a little water. Do you want me to stay with you for a while?"

"Would you? I don't want to let you out of my sight. I'll have Millie bring you up something to eat."

"You don't need to tell me what my family needs, "Millie said, as she came into the room with a tray of food. CeCe followed her with a second tray. "I already thought about you two. You just relax and eat dis here food while it be hot."

Mille sat a tray with a bowl of stew, bread and butter, and a piece of pie in Cassie's lap. "I can't eat all this, Millie!"

"Don't worry, it won't go to waste," Michael said. "What she doesn't eat, I will. This really smells good, and I'm starved. Thank you, Millie."

Millie beamed at the praise from Michael. "Now you two jes tell me what yo want to drink. I got coffee, tea, or milk."

"A tall glass of milk sounds wonderful," Michael said before he took another bite of stew."

"I think a cup of tea sounds good to me," Cassie said.

"CeCe be bringing it up to you shortly."

A short time later, Michael looked over at Cassie's tray. "I thought you said you couldn't eat all your food."

She laughed. "I guess I was hungrier than I thought. I'll go get you more if you want me to."

"No, I'm just fine." Michael sat his tray on the floor beside his chair and watched Cassie smooth back Daniel's hair. He didn't say anything, just took in the sight of her smooth complexion, delicate features, and her pretty shaped lips.

Cassie looked up and saw he was watching her. "What are you staring at me for?"

"I'm trying to memorize how beautiful you are."

"I'm certainly not beautiful right now. I don't think I've combed my hair since this morning, my clothes are all rumpled, and my eyes are sticky."

"I think you're beautiful just like you are, but your eyes do look tired. You've got dark circles under them that I've never seen before."

"I haven't slept very well for several nights now."

"Why don't you lay down on the bed right there by Daniel? We can talk for a while."

"I think I will." Cassie made herself comfortable next to Daniel.

They didn't get to talk because Cassie fell asleep almost as soon as her head hit the pillow. Michael took a blanket off the chest at the foot of the bed and covered her. Then he noticed Daniel was watching him. "Hey, buddy! How are you feeling?" Michael whispered.

"All right, I guess. Did you get my sick 'pendix out?"

"I sure did, and you're going to be feeling great in a few days."

Daniel gave him a little smile. "Good, I miss Patches."

"I'm sure Patches misses you too. Do you feel like you could take a little sip of water?"

"I guess so. My mouth tastes funny."

"Yeah, I'll bet it does. But that'll go away."

"Should I stay here in Mama's bed tonight?"

"Yes, you just go back to sleep. I'll stay here with you for a little longer, all right?

"All right, but where's my marble? Talker gave it to me and I don't want to lose it."

Michael gave him a sip of water, then studied his face for a few moments. "Did Talker come here, Daniel?"

"I guess so. I didn't see him but he left me the red marble cause I was so sick. CeCe said no one came, but it was right on the table by my bed."

"It could have been one you already had. Do you have other marbles?"

"No, I gave all mine to Talker, remember?"

"I'm not sure where it is right now but I'll find it later. Maybe you should rest now." Michael held Daniel's hand until he fell back to sleep. He was so weary, himself, he laid his head on the bed and knew nothing else until he felt someone shaking him.

"Doctor, your bed is ready downstairs. You need to get some good sleep. Don't worry none about Daniel. I'll stay here with him and Miss Cassie."

"Thank you, CeCe. Come get me if I'm needed."

"I will. You go on now."

It was late morning when Michael stumbled into the kitchen. He headed straight for the coffee pot. No one was around so he searched for a cup and helped himself. He could hear CeCe coming down the stairs, calling back up to someone. "I'll see if the doctor is up yet, and if he can have something to eat."

"I'm in the kitchen, CeCe."

"Good morning, Doctor," she said cheerfully. "Your patient says he's hungry. I expect that's a good sign?"

"Yes, it is. Don't fix anything real heavy this morning, though. Maybe some warm milk and toast to start off with."

"I'll get that ready right now."

"CeCe, do you know anything about Daniel's red marble? He said his friend Talker brought it to him. Was someone here? A young Indian man?"

"No, sirree, Doctor. Nary a soul was in that room but me and little Daniel. There ain't never been any marbles in this house, and I know, cause I do the cleaning."

Michael was silent as he thought this over. "Do you know where it went to? Daniel asked me to find it for him."

"I saw it roll to the floor last night but I ain't seen it since."

"All right, CeCe. You did a wonderful job last night. I want you to know I appreciate your help. You have a way about you that creates a calming atmosphere that helps when you're dealing with people in difficult circumstances. And, you're a fast learner."

"Thank you," she said, almost shyly. "I have to admit I almost ran when you made that first cut and the blood oozed out. It wasn't the same as a dead chicken. It was a real live boy, and I wasn't sure I could do what you wanted. But when you started talking to me and explaining what you were doing, I liked learning. It was something mighty wonderful, what you did."

"You were mighty wonderful yourself. If I ever set up a practice around here, I am still thinking I might need a nurse."

"Do you reckon I really could be a nurse? A *real* nurse?"

"Yes, I do. I would be glad to train you but right now I'm not sure what Cassie and I are going to do. I have some ideas that I need to talk over with her."

"What ideas do you need to talk over with me?" Cassie asked, coming into the kitchen. She found a cup and started making tea.

"Good morning, beautiful," Michael greeted her,

"Good morning, yourself," she smiled at Michael. "Now what do we need to talk over?"

"We're not talking anything over until I've had breakfast and a bath. Then I want to find a quiet corner and tell you what ideas I have."

"I'll fix you some breakfast then," CeCe said, heading toward the stove.

"Wait, CeCe," Cassie said. "I want to fix Michael's breakfast this morning. Daniel is waiting for something to eat if you would take a tray up to him, please."

CeCe giggled. "You sure could use the practice, Miss Cassie." She giggled again, quickly leaving the kitchen with Daniel's breakfast.

"Don't listen to her, Michael. I'm a good cook when I have a real stove with an oven."

"I'm glad to hear that. Actually, you didn't do too bad over an open campfire."

"Thank you, kind sir. Wait until you taste …in fact, you *did* eat something I made. Remember that chocolate cream pie at the barbecue that you ate two pieces of?"

Michael's eyes widened. "You mean *you* made that?"

"Uh, huh," she said with a coy little smile.

"Oh, life is going to be sweet with my new wife!"

"You mean you're marrying me for my cooking ability?"

"Ha! You know better than that. I fell in love with you before I tasted your pie or your sweet lips." Michael enjoyed sipping his coffee and especially enjoyed watching Cassie move around the kitchen fixing his breakfast.

"Dig into this." She placed a plate of ham, eggs, and tender light brown pancakes in front of him.

Before he could finish eating, Mr. and Mrs. Chandler, along with Margaret and Katie, came into the kitchen. "Smells good in here. Do you have any more of those pancakes left over?" Mr. Chandler wanted to know.

"I've got some batter left over," Cassie answered. "I'll cook it up."

Mr. Chandler looked thoughtfully at Michael. "I want to thank you for what you did for Daniel, Dr. Mayfield."

"You don't need to thank me, but you're welcome. And please, everyone, just call me Michael."

"As far as I'm concerned you've earned the title of Doctor," Mr. Chandler said. "And you need to feel honored when people use that title."

"Thank you. I'll try to remember that. It's just hard to get used to. I want to tell you it was a brilliant idea you had about setting up a relay of horses for me to get here. It worked beautifully."

"I'd like to take the credit, but it was Dillon, one of the hands, who came up with the idea. He picked the horses and the men."

Margaret looked surprised. "You mean *Dillon* arranged it all?"

"Yes and I've been impressed with that boy," said Mr. Chandler. "He's a hard worker, not afraid of responsibility and the men seem to respect him. He knows horses and cattle and seems to know what he's doing."

"I'll have to thank him, but right now I have a problem," Michael said.

Cassie looked worried. "What problem do you have?"

"I need a bath and I didn't even take time to bring an extra change of clothes."

"That's a problem easily solved," said Mrs. Chandler. "We have enough men around here that I'm sure we can find something that will do. Millie is doing laundry now so we can get your dirty clothes washed today."

"Just tell me where the buckets are and I'll start bringing water in. But first, I have to go up and check on Daniel."

Later that day Cassie and Michael finally found time to be together. "Do you want to take a walk or sit on the porch swing?" Cassie asked.

"Let's walk. If we get away from the house maybe we won't be disturbed while we talk."

"I know just the place."

Hand in hand the two love birds walked out behind the barn and up a hill behind the house to a stand of trees. They waited to talk until they were quite a ways from the house. Cassie finally said, "Daniel is up and slowly moving around. CeCe is keeping an eye on him for me."

"I know, I've already talked to her about how much he should do. Last time I checked the incision and bandage, it looked good."

"Here's the place," Cassie said. "We can sit on that log. I used to come here when I needed to be alone."

"It's nice. I can understand why you would come here," Michael said, sitting and pulling Cassie down beside him.

"Now, what ideas do you want to discuss with me? I've waited long enough."

"All right, but first, I want to ask if you know anything about Daniel's red marble?

Cassie had a blank look on her face. "No, I guess not. He gave his marbles to Talker, didn't he? What about the red one?"

"Well, I don't know, myself, but Daniel is insisting that Talker was here and left the red marble for him because he was so sick. CeCe said no one has been in Daniel's room but you and her, and maybe Millie. So right before the surgery, when I put him to sleep, his hand fell open and a red marble fell out. I haven't seen it since, but he's asking for it."

"That's strange. Remember when someone woke him up when we were waiting for the Sioux to attack, and no one, and I mean *no one*, said it was them. What do you think about it, Michael?"

"I think it's another unexplainable incident and we will never know." They sat silent for several moments, until Michael stirred. "Well, let's get on to other things. I need to know what plans you've made for us getting married."

"I have it all under control. When you left you said you would be back in fourteen days, so I planned our wedding the next day. That will be May twenty fifth. There's no preacher anywhere in these parts so I've asked my father to officiate the service. He wasn't real crazy about the idea but said he would do it if we would write our own vows to say to each other. That's the main things you need to know."

"Can't we go ahead and get married sooner?" Michael asked, nuzzling her ear, her neck, and burying his face in her hair.

"No, silly, there's too many things involved. You're just going to have to wait. Besides, that's not very far away."

"All right I guess I'll be happy with that. What are we going to do for a honeymoon?"

"That's a surprise." Her eyes lit with mischief as she snuggled closer to him. "You'll just have to be patient, but I promise, you'll *like* it."

"I'll like it as long as I'm with you. My plan is that after we're married, I want us to go back to the High Meadows Ranch and spend the summer with my sister. I want you to get to know her. I'd like to find a place somewhere around that store your father built and have a house built for us while we're gone. In the fall, we'll come back and fix up our own home. Next summer, maybe I'll have a place built to set up a practice." He looked into her face and brushed her lips with his. "How am I doing so far?"

"I like it. Do you think we can find someone to build a house?"

"I don't know why not. Your father found someone to build the store. I'll talk to him about it. You'll need to draw me any ideas you might have for the house."

"That's exciting! We won't be too far from family that way. Father expects this place to become quite a town since it's on the main route to the west. There's a telegraph office in the store already, and from what he says, the railroad will run right through this area."

"I'd still like to run some cattle. I know it's premature, but if Gabriel comes back and talks CeCe into marrying him, I was thinking it would be nice to have them close to us. That way he could partner with me on the cattle and I'd have a nurse to help me in my practice."

"Oh, Michael! Is Gabriel really interested in CeCe?"

"He's not very confident but I can assure you, he's interested."

"Wouldn't that be something? I would love to have CeCe close. She's like family to me. In some ways, you could say she grew up with me and Margaret. She was our maid, but she learned to read and write with us. We have never considered her and Millie slaves or servants and Father pays them a monthly salary. It's not a lot, but they seem to be happy. I think we're their family, too. I don't know what Mother would do without Millie."

They spent the rest of the afternoon sharing their ideas, dreams, and stealing kisses. "I can't wait for my surprise honeymoon," Michael said. He stood and pulled Cassie to her feet and into an embrace. "I love you, Cassie. Oh, how I love you!"

Chapter 23

"**Y**OU ARE BANISHED TO the bunkhouse tonight," Margaret informed Michael, on the evening before the big wedding.

"I am?" He feigned shock and surprise.

"Yes, it's bad luck for you to see the bride the day of the wedding and it looks like we probably won't be able to have the ceremony outside. There's a wicked looking storm brewing and headed this way."

"The storm could blow itself out overnight."

"I suppose, but it would still be really wet and muddy if it rains. Oh, yes, I'm supposed to tell you that Millie took your suit over to the bunkhouse. She wants you to try it on and if it needs altered any more to let her know."

"Thanks, I hope your brother doesn't mind me taking over his closet."

"Jeff won't even know it, by the time he gets out of that school. He'll be some fancy lawyer wearing fancy suits. You're just lucky you're about the same size as he is."

"Well, I better get over there and see how that suit fits."

Michael started out the back door as Margaret called to him, "Better watch out over at the bunkhouse tonight. They're planning a big party for you. Millie baked a lot of goodies and I think they might be up to some mischief."

"Oh great!" Michael mumbled as he went out the back door.

In spite of his misgivings, the evening turned out to be a lot of fun. The bunkhouse cook fried up some thick, juicy steaks. Thankfully, the men were too tired to cause a lot of trouble, but they teased Michael and gave him advice on married life, even though none of the men had been married before except for one. That cowboy didn't offer any advice, just laid on his bunk with a smile on his face. Brian Chandler had a room at the back of the bunkhouse and when he got up to go to bed, he warned the men, "Don't you yahoos stay up too late. You have the morning off except for chores right here. You've all been invited to the house at eleven for the ceremony. You'll get your lunch after the ceremony and then it's back to work."

Daniel, having recovered from his surgery, got permission to sleep in the bunkhouse since Michael was going to be sleeping there for the night. Michael took notice of Daniel's mischievous behavior, when Daniel would glance at Dillon then snicker. But it wasn't until Michael crawled into his bed that night that he knew right away what the snickers were about. Someone had put sand, sugar, or salt in his bed. He decided to ignore it but then he stretched out and something moved around his feet. He froze, but quickly figured out what it was. Daniel was in the bunk over Michael's, and kept peeking over the edge of the bed waiting for a reaction. *Guess I might as well let him enjoy his little prank.* Michael let out a yelp, jumped out of bed, and did a little dance. "There's something in my bed! It's alive! Help! Help!"

This sent Daniel into gales of laughter. The men couldn't keep themselves from laughing either, just listening to Daniel's joyful outburst. The rumpus finally subsided and Michael howled, "Who put a frog in my bed?"

Daniel put his hand over his mouth and giggled. "I can't tell, it's a secret."

"All right then, since you won't tell, I'll just have to sleep in your bunk with you. I'm not going to sleep in a gritty bed with a frog."

"There's *two* frogs!" Daniel announced. "Dillon caught one and I caught one at the pond over the hill."

"So, *you're* the one who put the frog in my bed! You'll have to pay for it now." Michael took his pillow and hit Daniel with it.

Someone yelled, "Pillow fight! Get your pillow, Daniel! Defend yourself."

Daniel was laughing so hard he could hardly swing, but he landed a couple of blows before Michael could crawl up on the top bunk with him. "Now I've got you," he said as he wrapped his arms around Daniel and held him. "You give up?"

"Yes, I gotta go to the outhouse. Will you go with me?"

"I'll go if you'll go to sleep when we get back."

"All right, I will. That was fun. Can I call you Daddy, yet? Do I have to wait until tomorrow?"

The men in the bunkhouse grew quiet. "Daniel, I don't want you to forget what a fine father you had, but I don't mind if you call me Daddy right now. As a matter of fact, I think it would make your father happy. We were good friends."

"I know, my mama told me."

Michael and Daniel pulled on their boots and left the bunkhouse. The cowboy who had been married, remarked, "That is one fine kid and Dr. Michael Mayfield is one lucky man."

Another commented, "Cassie and the kids are pretty lucky, too."

The next morning, Margaret stood surveying the soggy outdoors. "Just like I thought," she said to no one in particular, "that storm left mud all over the place. I'll need to make sure there are extra rugs at the doors or it'll be tracked into the house. I still have a million things to do, plus get myself ready!"

The bunkhouse was busy with all the men doing extra grooming so they could look good and clean for the wedding ceremony.

"Daddy?"

Michael was lost in thought and took a few moments to realize Daniel was trying to get his attention. "What do you want, Daniel?"

Daniel's face was quite serious as he asked, "What time is it now?"

Michael took out his pocket watch for the umpteenth time. "It's nine o'clock. You can go on over to the big house now. I can't go for a while yet. They said I had to stay here until the ceremony."

"Why?"

"I don't know for sure. They just tell me that I'm not supposed to see your mother until the ceremony begins. It's what they call a *tradition*."

"Oh." Daniel frowned, trying to understand. "I think you should get to see her," he finally announced. "She looks real pretty in her dress."

"She does?"

"Yes, Katie looks real pretty, too."

"Well, you better get on over there and get your bath so you'll look pretty, too."

"Guys don't look *pretty*. Mama says they look *handsome*."

"We're both going to look real handsome. Remember, you're supposed to stand by me and when it's time for the ring, you hand it to me."

"I remember. I'll do it good."

"I know you will. Go on now and I'll see you later."

Margaret stood in the middle of the parlor and turned slowly in a circle, surveying the decorations of ribbons, bows, and flowers. "This room looks beautiful," she said to herself, "just like it should for a wedding." The back door opened and closed and Charlie came in carrying his guitar.

"Where do you want me to sit, Miss Margaret?"

"Wherever you are comfortable, Charlie. Why don't you play softly while people are coming in and getting seated. That'll help set the mood, don't you think?"

"Why, I could do that. I'm pretty sure the men are on their way over, now."

"In that case, I'd better get upstairs." She hurried up the stairs just as the back door opened again and men's voices filled the house with laughter and good natured bantering. They quieted down when they entered the parlor and heard Charlie's music.

Mr. Chandler came down the stairs with Mrs. Chandler on his arm and Daniel close behind. After seating her in a wingback chair he took his place in front of the hearth and waited while others were coming in and finding a place to sit. Millie and CeCe sat on the couch that was beside Mrs. Chandler, the ranch hands filled the benches and extra chairs. Michael and Daniel stood to the side of Mr. Chandler, who then nodded to Charlie that everything was ready.

As he strummed a prearranged song, Margaret appeared on the staircase, smiling and descending slowly. She looked alluring in blue satin with matching ribbons woven through her hair. As she walked to her place beside her father, she couldn't help but glance shyly at the bench that held a certain cowboy.

Katie was delightful as she came down the stairs, wearing a green dress with little green bows in her hair and carrying a small basket filled with rose petals. With every step she took, she reached in her basket and dropped a few petals on the floor. So intent was she on her job, she didn't pay much attention to the smiles on everyone's faces. She made her way to the side of her grandfather, looked up at him and beamed. "I did good, didn't I, Gampa?"

Everyone chuckled. "Yes, you did, sweetheart. You look really pretty, too."

As Charlie's music swelled into some sort of bridal march, Cassie carefully made her way down the stairs. She looked gorgeous in a pastel-pink dress, the bodice covered in lace that extended down the sleeves to her wrists. Her headpiece was made of pink netting that fell just below her eyes. Her blond, wavy hair was pinned back at the sides, and cascaded half way down her back. She carried a bouquet of wild flowers tied together with a huge pink bow. Reaching the last stair step, she stopped and gazed across the room at her groom. As their eyes met, her smile turned Michael's knees to jelly and sent his heart to racing. *Thank you, Lord, she's the most beautiful creature you ever put on this earth! What did I ever do to deserve her?*

And all of a sudden…she was there…right beside him. He was so spellbound that he forgot there were others in the room, until Mr. Chandler spoke.

"Well, take her hand and look at me. We need to get you two married." Chuckles sounded around the room. Michael felt foolish in his nervous state but took Cassie's hand and turned to face Mr. Chandler.

"When Cassie asked me to officiate this wedding I wasn't very enthused about it. But sometimes, out here on the range, we have to do the best we can. I've heard that the captain of a ship can marry people when they're out to sea. I guess we're out here in a sea of grass and I'm the captain of this place, so here we are, doing the best with what we have. Before we go any further, I think we need to ask God to be here and bless Michael and Cassie."

To everyone's surprise, Dalton Chandler bowed his head and said a simple prayer. "God, these people are here to witness Michael and Cassie commit their lives to each other. I ask you to be here too. Listen to the vows they say to each other, and throughout the years of their life together remind them of the promises they're making today. Amen.

"I don't have a lot to say. To me, marriage is a serious commitment. A man should keep his promises and mean what he says, even when life gets hard. Now, I told my girl here that I would do this if they would write and say their own vows. So, Cassie, you start and tell Michael what you want to say to him."

Cassie turned to look up at Michael. "Michael, I want you to know I love you with all my heart. I promise you that I will do my very best to be a good wife to you. I trust you enough to follow you anywhere you want to go and even enough to obey you when you give me advice or direction, because I know you will have my best interests at heart. Michael Mayfield, I love you. You are my hero."

Michael was dumb-struck by Cassie's words. He could only stare at her, his heart pulsing with love and admiration. He knew he would die, if need be, to take care of Cassie and the kids. The enormity of this commitment was heavy but his love for her outweighed anything else. Finally, Mr. Chandler cleared his throat noisily, nodding to Michael. "Go ahead, son," he prompted. "It's your turn."

Michael took a deep breath. "Cassie, I love you, Daniel, and Katie, more than I thought possible to love anyone. I promise you that I will do the very best I can to be a good husband and father to *all* our children." He paused and smiled at the woman who, in moments, would be his wife. "I want our marriage to be a partnership, where we share in decisions, in the joys that come to us, and in the sorrows that happen in life. I want to be a Godly man and will need your help and prayers to accomplish that. Cassie, I love you and will cherish every day God allows us to have here on this earth."

Cherry Chandler dabbed the tears from her eyes. The room was immersed in the solemn importance of the commitment that was taking place in front of all of them, as witnesses. Mr. Chandler looked down at Daniel. "Well, does anyone here have a ring?"

"I got one!" Daniel spoke up. He dug around in his pocket and finally pulled out a ring. "Here it is, Grandpa," he said, holding the ring up to Mr. Chandler, who took it and handed it to Michael.

Cassie didn't know about the ring. When Michael slid it onto her finger, she recognized it as being one of her mother's rings that she had always admired. She turned to her mother. "Thank you, Mother," she said softly. Cherry Chandler was too emotional to speak, she just smiled and nodded her pleasure as she wiped another tear from her face.

"There's only one thing left I need to do and that is to tell you, Michael and Cassie, I pronounce you husband and wife. You can go ahead and kiss her, she's yours now."

Michael bent to give Cassie a chaste, token kiss, but Cassie wrapped her arms around his neck and as their lips touched, she held him in a kiss that promised joys in the years to follow. The room erupted in hoots and clapping until she finally released her hold on him. "You're going to get many more of those. That's my final promise to you, husband."

Michael grinned. "Bring it on, wife! I can take anything you dish out."

While everyone crowded around the couple saying their congratulations, Millie and CeCe quickly set out a buffet table of food that was enough to feed an army.

A short time later, Cassie and Michael cut their wedding cake, then Cassie pulled Michael aside. "We both need to change into casual clothes. We're going for a ride. When you get changed, come on up to get me."

"Where are we riding to?"

"That's a surprise," she said with a cunning smile.

"All right, it'll take me a few minutes. Do I need to saddle our horses?"

"No, Margaret and Dillon are going to have them ready for us. I'm not sure what to think of my sister. She's been acting so different lately."

"I think I might have a clue. I'll tell you about it later. See you in a few minutes."

The newlyweds came out the back door to see Margaret and Dillon holding two saddled horses. Everyone had gathered there to shower them with rice as they rode off to the hills behind the house.

"Where are they going?" Mr. Chandler asked his wife as they watched the two riders.

"You know that cabin the men use once in a while when working up in the hills, the one by that mountain lake?"

"Of course I know about it."

"That's where they're going. Margaret and Cassie cleaned and fixed it up for a honeymoon spot while you and Michael were in Cheyenne doing your business."

"They went up there by themselves?"

"No, Dillon took them up. And speaking of Dillon, I hope you're getting ready for another wedding."

Dalton Chandler followed his wife's gaze in time to see Margaret and Dillon walk off hand in hand. He groaned, feigning annoyance but didn't have time to dwell on his youngest daughter. Some little person was tugging at his sleeve. "Grandfather, can I go with the men?" Daniel asked.

"Give me a few minutes and we'll both go check on the men," Dalton answered.

"I go, Gampa, too?" Katie asked.

"No, you're going to stay with me and CeCe," Cherry said. "You're going to help me make cookies for a tea party we're going to have after your nap."

Chapter 24

"MAMA, MAMA!" KATIE SQUEALED in delight, seeing her mother ride up to the front porch. She was swinging on the porch swing with her Aunt Margaret.

Cassie quickly dismounted and greeted her daughter with a big hug and kiss. "Hi, baby, I sure missed you!"

"Miss you, too, Mama."

Michael squatted down beside Katie. "Do I get a hug and kiss, too?" She was more than eager to oblige Michael, throwing her arms around his neck.

Margaret smiled at her sister when she came up onto the porch. "Welcome back, you two. Did you have a good time?"

"We had a *wonderful* time, Sis! Thanks for watching Daniel and Katie for us."

"Yes, thanks," Michael said. "And I hear you helped fix up that cabin for our honeymoon. That was nice of you."

"You're welcome. It was a lot of fun. Cassie and I haven't done anything like that in a long, long time."

"Where's Daniel?" Cassie asked.

"He's off with Father. Those two have become inseparable while you've been gone. Mother will be anxious to see you, Cassie. She's out back working in that little kitchen garden that Millie and her planted."

"She isn't overdoing it, is she?"

"Ha! Millie watches over her like a mother hen. Between Millie and Father, she's lucky she even gets out of the house."

"You go on and visit with your mother, Cassie. I'll take care of the horses," Michael said.

Margaret, and Cassie, holding Katie's hand, walked around to the back of the house. "Well, look who's done come home!" Millie crowed. She was at the clothes line taking off the dry things.

"Hi, Millie. Yes, we're back now. Where's Mother?"

"She jes went in da house. You all go on in, I'll be in directly to fix us something to drink."

Cassie found her mother washing her hands in the kitchen sink. "Hi, Mother, I'm back."

"So I see! It's good to have you home. Did you and Michael have a good trip?"

"Yes, it was perfect. Except for a visit from a mother raccoon and her two babies the first night. She seemed to think we were invading her space."

"Maybe you were. The hands don't use that old cabin very often."

"What's *coon*, Mama?"

Cassie picked up Katie and gave her another hug. "*Raccoon*, and it's a funny little animal that likes to snoop into things."

Millie came in the back door with a basket of dry laundry. "I'll be puttin' these things away and be right back. CeCe is getting da tea or would you all want coffee?"

"Tea sounds fine, Millie," Cassie answered. "Mother, I need to talk to you. Sit with me for a few minutes."

"Do you want me to leave?" Margaret asked.

"No, you can stay. I just want to let Mother know what Michael and I are going to do."

"I can probably guess what you're going to do," Cherry said. "I'm not going to like it, but I really do understand. Michael had to cut his visit short with his sister to come help Daniel and you are going back there to… what do they call it?"

"The High Meadows Horse Ranch," Cassie said.

"Yes, I remember Aaron calling his home the High Meadows."

"Well, you're right. We're going to spend the summer there and come back in the fall. The house Michael is having built for us should be done by then, and we can fix up the house for the winter. Father told Michael he would check on the progress and make sure it all gets done right."

"Your father told me about the land and the house. I'm so glad for you, Cassie. Your Michael seems like a fine man."

"He is, Mother. I love him so much. I know I loved Ray, but the love I have for Michael is so much…I don't know how to describe it."

"Maybe you mean it's a more *mature* love. You're older and wiser than you were when you fell in love with Ray."

"Perhaps that's it. Anyway, I'm very lucky and happy to have Michael in my life."

"When are you leaving?" Cherry asked.

"I'll take all day tomorrow to get ready to go, then we'll leave the next morning."

"I'm going to miss my little Katie, but it's comforting to know you'll be back and not live too far away."

"If I can do anything to help, Sis, let me know," Margaret offered.

"Thanks, I'll do that."

The departure from the Chandler ranch had a little hitch that wasn't expected.

"Don't argue with me, Cassie," Mr. Chandler scolded. "I insist these men go with you, at least part way. Then you'll only have one day to travel alone. We haven't seen any Indians around for awhile, but with spring here, I know they'll be hunting and stirring up trouble. Michael and I have already talked about it and he agreed it would be safer for you and the children to have a few of the men travel this first day with you. They can spend the night and head back here in the morning."

"If Michael thinks it would be best, then I wouldn't dream of arguing," Cassie said.

Dalton Chandler laughed. "You might make a good wife yet. Just keep thinking that way."

Michael looked lovingly at his new wife. "She *already is* a good wife!"

After hugs and kisses, the men waited for Michael to help get Katie into the back pack and attached to her mother and settled for the ride. Daniel was mounted on Patches, waiting close to Dillon. Everyone was surprised when Margaret came leading her horse around the house to join the others.

"What do you think you're doing, young lady?" her father wanted to know.

"I'm going with them," Margaret said.

"We haven't discussed you going," Dalton huffed.

"Well, is there any reason why I can't travel with them? My sister will be there tonight when we camp and I'll be safe with Dillon and the other men to protect me tomorrow."

Mr. Chandler looked hard at Margaret then Dillon. "I don't know...."

"I'll take good care of her, sir," Dillon promised.

"I hope to shout you better! I'll hold all three of you men responsible for her safety. Do you understand?"

"Yes, sir," they all agreed.

"Well, get going then, before I change my mind," Dalton grumbled.

The group found it was an easy ride, warm and pleasant. They saw a herd of antelope, rabbits here and there, and a rattlesnake that had come out to warm in the sun. Michael took the opportunity to educate Daniel and Katie about the dangerous snake, after one of the men trapped the large rattler and cut its head off.

"These snakes are very poisonous," he told the children. "If you ever hear it rattle its tail or if you even see one, don't go close to it, get away as quick as you can."

Daniel listened carefully but Katie, even though she didn't get the full meaning of what Michael was telling them, scowled at the snake.

After crossing the Platte River, evening was upon them and they decided to set up camp along the river. There was an easy camaraderie between the men but they all understood Dillon and Margaret were courting. They respected this and turned their attention to Daniel and Katie. Katie didn't last long into the evening. She was tired and soon asleep as the men visited and played cards around the fire before turning in.

Daniel had his own bedroll and laid it out between the ranch hands. As Michael and Cassie made their bed with a sleeping Katie tucked in beside her mother, Michael whispered in Cassie's ear, "Our honeymoon was too short."

"I know," she whispered. "Be patient, husband."

A short time later, Michael heard one of the men ask Daniel, "Where are you going?"

"I need to go to the bushes a minute," he answered.

"You want me to go with you?" the man asked.

"No, I won't go far and I'll be right back."

Michael was on the verge of falling asleep when he heard the men quietly talking. "He's been gone a while. Maybe one of us should go check on him, Charlie."

Michael slipped out from under his blankets. "That's all right, Charlie, I'll go check on him. Which way did he go?"

"Right out that-a-way beyond those bushes."

"Thanks." Michael made his way through the darkness walking around the wild brush and scrubs. "Daniel?" he called softly. No answer. He took a few more steps and called again.

"I'm over here," Daniel's voice sounded quietly through the night.

Michael followed the sound of the voice, finally locating Daniel. "Why did you go this far away from camp? Are you all right?"

"Yes," Daniel answered.

Michael suddenly realized that Daniel was not alone. Alarmed, he automatically reached for his pistol then relaxed. "*Talker*! What are you doing here? I almost shot you!"

"I came to see my brother, Little Fox."

"Why didn't you come into camp?"

"It is best the others did not see me, and I must leave soon."

"Is something wrong?" Michael asked.

"For you there is nothing wrong. The way you go is safe. Many Cheyenne warriors and a few women are camped a ways from here. We have found a herd of Buffalo and will hunt tomorrow. Our winter food is almost gone and we need the buffalo to feed our people. Talker is the one to make sure warriors are safe for the night. I have found a group of Shoshone sneaking close to our camp. I must go warn my people. I think they mean us harm. Perhaps I am wrong, and they will only hunt the buffalo and not my people. We must prepare in case I am right."

"Where are your people, Talker, I haven't seen any buffalo or Indians?"

"The way of the sun in the morning. Talker and warriors see Little Fox and his people today. I tell my people no harm should come to you."

"Thank you," Michael said. "In the morning some of our people will be going back to the ranch. Will they be in danger tomorrow?"

"Not from the Cheyenne. They would be wise to watch for the Shoshone. They are not many and have no guns, but you should warn your people. The Shoshone do not like the white man."

A movement caught Michael's eye and he suddenly realized Daniel had something in his arms. "What is that, Daniel?"

"Talker brought it to me. It's a puppy!"

"A *puppy*? Where in the world did you get a puppy, Talker?"

"It is a wolf pup. Talker found it this morning. She is very young but I did not see its mother and she will die unless someone takes care of her. Talker wishes he could take the pup to his own son but it is too far away. Maybe it was meant to be that Little Fox should have the pup."

"I can keep it, can't I?" Daniel asked.

Michael couldn't see the expression on Daniel's face but he could certainly hear the anxious pleading in his voice.

"I guess it'll be all right, Daniel. I don't know what your mother will say but we can give it a try. There will have to be some rules though, you understand."

"Yes, I understand," Daniel agreed, burying his face in the soft fur.

"I must go now," Talker told them. "Remember, Little Fox, you must keep the pup with you all the time until she learns to know and obey you. Feed her with your own hand for a time and she will become your friend."

Michael and Talker were squatted on the ground and before they could stand, Daniel released the pup and threw his arms around Talker's neck. "Thank you, Talker! I'm glad I got to see you this time. I was asleep when you came to see me when I was so sick and you left the red marble for me."

"I do not know what you speak of, Little Fox. Talker did not come to see you. How were you sick? I see you are well now."

"I had an operation. My new daddy did it! He made me better. Who gave me the marble?"

"Talker does not know. Who is the new one you speak of?"

Michael told him that he was now married to Daniel's mother. When Daniel got sick Michael performed an operation to save his life.

"Ah, now I see. You are medicine-man for your people."

"Well, I guess you could say that." Michael couldn't see how Talker reacted to Daniel's display of affection, but somehow he knew it must have pleased the man. When Daniel moved back and picked up the small bundle of fur, Talker was gone.

Fortunately, the little critter didn't cause a fuss in the night. It was early morning when a yelp came from one of the men who was sleeping close to Daniel. "What in tar-nation is this *wolf* doing here?!"

"It's mine," Daniel said, jumping up to retrieve the pup. "A friend gave him to me last night."

Everyone but Michael stared at Daniel as if he had lost his mind. Margaret was the one who questioned him. "What do you mean, a *friend?*"

"My friend, Talker, was here last night and gave me the puppy. He needs me to take care of her cause she lost her mother."

"Who is *Talker?*" Margaret asked, seemingly frustrated.

"Wait a minute, everyone," Michael intervened for Daniel. "We did have a visitor last night who gave Daniel the pup. He is a Cheyenne and a friend. Didn't we tell you the story of the Indian who helped us on our way to your ranch, Margaret?"

"Oh, yes, I remember. Was that who was here?"

"Yes, and he gave me some information that will be important for you, while you are traveling back to the ranch."

"What did he tell you?" Dillon asked, looking worried.

"There's a group of Cheyenne camped east of here. They're hunting a herd of buffalo in the morning. You won't have any trouble from them because of Daniel. They consider you his people and Daniel and Talker are blood-brothers."

Charlie whistled and tousled Daniel's red hair. "I didn't know we had such an important person with us. But what is so important about them being close by if they're not going to bother us?"

"Talker told me a small band of Shoshone are sneaking around. He wasn't sure but thinks they might be going to give the Cheyenne some trouble. Anyway, he said you need to watch out for them, that they hate the white man. These Shoshone don't have rifles, but arrows can kill."

Dillon didn't waste any time. "I'm glad we were warned. We need to get Margaret back to the ranch so let's get moving, men! Maybe we can get far enough away from here while they're fighting each other that we'll be out of danger."

"Good idea. I think we should get out of here too." Michael turned to Cassie as he said this and found she looked upset. "What's wrong?"

"What are we going to do with *that*?" She pointed at the pup who was making funny little noises while chewing on Daniel's sleeve.

"We're going to take her with us," Michael answered.

"*How*?" she challenged.

"The same way you carry Katie. Talker left Daniel a leather pouch that he carried her in. Daniel will just have to strap it on his back and be responsible for his pet."

"Do I have a say in this?" she asked.

"Of course you have a say. What is it you want to say?"

Cassie looked at the smirk on Michael's face and the bundle of fur in Daniel's arms. But when she looked into the pleading eyes of her son, she said, "I say we better eat and get out of here!"

Late that evening a weary family made their way up the road that led to the main house of the High Meadows Ranch. Prince barked his warning and an excited Maxi ran out of the house with baby Michael in her arms. "It's Michael! He's back!"

Scott and Paul came out of the barn. Carmen, Rosa, and Maria waited on the porch until the horses calmed. Prince's barking had caused Patches to dance around, which in turn, unsettled the other three horses. "Keep her under control, Daniel."

"Quiet, Prince!" Maxi ordered as she took hold of Daniel's horse. "Hey, you're quite a cowboy, little guy."

"My name's Daniel."

"My name is Maxi, and I'm pleased to meet you."

"Is that your baby?"

"Yes, this is Little Michael. Let's get your horses taken care of out back, then we can all go into the house and get to know each other."

Chapter 25

ON THE FIRST DAY after Aaron, Rand, and Gabriel left the High Meadows, their journey went without a hitch. The weather was fair and they felt they had traveled a good distance. They looked for a stream at the base of the Rocky Mountains to camp by on that first night. After supper, Aaron played around with different tunes on the guitar he had brought along.

Rand voiced his surprise. "How come you haven't played the guitar for us before now?"

Aaron shrugged. "I can't play very good," he admitted. "Carmen taught me to play last winter. She and Paul both play. I really hated to ask if I could bring the guitar with me, but the one I ordered and had freighted back to Fort Laramie probably wouldn't be there by now. I hope it's there when they go pick up supplies. I had it crated for shipment with all my art supplies I'm going to need this next year."

"Why'd you bring it along this time?" Rand wondered.

"Because I'm going to play a song for Bonita when I find her."

"What song are you going to play for her, you romantic son-of-a-gun!"

"It's one I wrote just for her."

"Woooeee! Sing it for us."

"No way. The first time I sing it will be just for her."

"Aww, come on," Rand goaded.

"No, I told myself I would sing it the first time for my girl."

"Well, you don't have to sing it then, just play the tune for us."

"All right. It's the one I've been playing just now but I'll play it again. I need to practice so I'll be able to play while singing to her. I don't want to make any mistakes." He adjusted the strings until he was satisfied then quietly hummed along as he played.

Gabriel liked what he heard. "It's really purty, Aaron. I like it a lot."

"Thanks, Gabe."

Always playful, Rand started teasing Gabriel. "You going to sing to that girl, CeCe, Gabe?"

"I don't reckon I'll be singin' to no one," he chuckled. "I got me other talents to make CeCe look my way."

"Oh, yeah? Just what are those talents?" Rand wanted to know.

"That be *my* secret, but after the night when me and CeCe talked out on the porch swing, she was a beggin' me to come back to see her." Gabe ducked his head to hide a grin.

"*Are* you going to go back and see her?"

"I ain't rightly made up my mind, but I'm a thinking I just might."

Rand was thoughtful for a minute. "I'm not ready to find a girl. I want to be free to come and go when I want. When you get mixed up with a girl and get married you're kinda *stuck* with taking care of her and any kids you might have. No, I'll stick with the free life!"

"It's a good thing you feel that way," Aaron chuckled. "There aren't many girls out here in this country. Well, maybe I should take that back. Bonita popped up out of nowhere."

"I shore didn't think I'd find no purty colored girl like CeCe out here, but there she was, and she wouldn't even *look* at me!"

Rand grimaced. "Can't blame the girl. It *is* rather painful to look at your ugly mug! The poor girl must be desperate to ask you to come calling on her."

Gabriel laughed at the teasing. "I don't know 'bout that but she did ask me to come back to see her. How old do you think CeCe is, Aaron?"

"I don't know, Gabe. Probably about our age. How old are you?"

"No way to tell. I never knowd my family to tell me when I was born, but I figure I'm about as old as you."

"You're both a couple of old men fixing to get tangled up with some woman and settle down. You two will be tied to your families, and me? I'll be free as the breeze to roam or stay put, or do whatever I feel like doing."

Aaron yawned. "This old man is going to get some sleep. Do you two think we should take turns keeping watch?"

After a quick discussion, the consensus was that they would all be alert to danger but not take turns staying awake.

Weather plagued them the next day as they climbed higher into the mountains. A cold wind blew over the snowcapped mountains and toward evening, moisture in the form of sleet, pelted them. They were cold and weary but finally found a thicket of trees that could be used to build a shelter and start a fire.

"Rand, will you and Gabe set up a shelter? I'll search for all the dry wood I can find so we can keep a fire going all night. I think it's going to be a *cold* one!"

"Sure, I'm freezing! Let's get it done."

Aaron returned shortly, dragging part of a dead tree that was relatively dry. He praised Rand and Gabriel's shelter. "Hey, that looks good. You two did a great job. Gabe, I found a spot where there's plenty of dry stuff in a protected place. If you'll help me carry some of it, Rand can start a fire."

"Let's go get it," Gabe said, shivering. "I don't think I ever been so cold in my whole life!"

The three young men worked quickly to set up their camp and take care of the horses. They scrounged up enough food to eat, made hot coffee, and sat inside their crude shelter while trying to get warm. Gabe was the one who checked the food supplies. "We gonna need to shoot us some meat tomorrow. That big slab of bacon will feed us for several more morning's, but the rest of the food Miss Carmen sent is about gone."

"That shouldn't be a problem," Aaron said. "We've seen plenty of game." He knew better than to ask, but he asked anyway, "Do either one of you know how to make biscuits or pancakes?"

Gabriel shook his head, but Rand answered, "Tomorrow at evening camp, I'll take a stab at making some biscuits. I've done it a few times when me and Pa were traveling around. Won't promise how good they'll be, but I'll try."

"That'll be great, Rand. I expect we'll be glad for anything you make. We aren't going to starve, though. We've got a lot of dried beef and there's plenty of game. How about you, Gabe, you ever done any cooking?"

"The only cookin' I knowd about is roastin' a rabbit or chicken over an open fire."

"One of us should have taken cooking lessons," Rand grumbled. "Maybe we'll find us a cook to take with us the next time we travel."

Aaron was thoughtful before he commented, "When I get back home from this trip, I'm hoping to stay put for a while."

"Who knows, maybe I'll be tired of traveling by then and I'll stay home and make sure you treat your Bonita right," Rand said.

"You won't need to worry about that. You just take care of yourself and *I'll* worry about Bonita."

Night settled in and the three finally built the fire up and wrapped in everything they had to stay warm and fell asleep. Sometime in the night the wind died down and a tranquil calm took its place. When Aaron woke he peeked out from under his blanket that was pulled over his head. What he saw alarmed him for a moment. Gabriel was sitting up, his coat collar pulled tight against his neck, and his blanket wrapped around his head. The strange thing was there were tears running down his face. "What's wrong, Gabriel, you all right?"

"I'm about as right as any man can be. I never did see such a beautiful thing. It be like God did it just for me, but you didn't tell me right."

Aaron was still laying down with his blankets wrapped tight around his head. "Tell me what you're talking about. What did I say that was wrong?"

"I *heard* Him, Aaron."

"Who, Gabe? Who did you hear?"

"He called my name! I heard it just as plain as could be."

Aaron's face broke out into a wide grin. "That's wonderful, Gabe. Tell me what happened."

"I was just laying here when I heard, 'Gabriel Freeman.' He knew my name, so that makes it official. I be Gabriel Freeman from now on cause God done called me by that name." Quietly, Gabriel continued, "I remembered your words and I told God, 'I'm here.' He asked me if I'd trust Him and give my life to Him. I just up and told Him I'd trust Him and he could have me if that's what he wanted." A big smile spread across Gabriel's black face. "I think I heard Him laugh. Would God laugh, Aaron?"

"I don't know why not. The Bible talks about laughter being good for you. What else happened?"

"God, told me He wanted me and that He would be my father. I ain't ever had a father, Aaron." Another tear slid down Gabriel's cheeks. "Look what he did, just for me."

Gabriel had made a sweeping motion beyond their shelter.

Aaron, curious, sat up and looked out into the dim morning light. There was a light layer of white snow that had blanketed the area during the night. The branches of the trees were decorated in a shimmering white as the sun reached through the branches and caused the effect of diamonds on the neck of a beautiful young women decked out in finery for a ball. "It is beautiful, isn't it?"

"It be the most beautiful thing I ever seen," Gabriel said reverently.

The two men sat for a while just taking in the glorious sight until Aaron questioned, "You said I didn't tell you right, Gabe. What did you mean?"

"I don't got no peace. You said you had a most wonderful peace when God called your name."

"You don't?"

"No, sirree, I don't."

"What do you feel?"

"You won't laugh at me if I tell you?"

"I don't think so, why would I laugh?"

"I don't know. I never in my life felt quite like dis. It's kinda hard to explain."

"Tell me. Do the best you can."

"All right, I be telling you that there is dis feeling of something inside me trying to get out. Don't know what do with it."

"What's it like?"

"Somthin' like a bubble when you gots to burp, only I think it is...I think it is...I just got to let it go."

"Let *what* go, Gabriel?"

Gabriel started to chuckle. "I gots to...." He threw off his blankets and stepped out of their shelter. "I got happy feelings inside me that I...." Gabriel didn't bother with any other explanations. He just danced around the fire jumping and laughing. "God be good to me dis mornin!"

198

Aaron couldn't help but laugh with Gabriel. Finally, Rand sat up with his red hair flying in all directions. "Am I going to act like that when God calls my name?"

"I don't know, Rand. I don't know."

Gabriel scooped up a hand full of snow and threw it in the air, making Rand laugh. "You know, I bet he's never seen snow before. I've only been in the snow once in the mountains when we were in California."

"Well, let him enjoy it. I'm going to build up the fire and get some coffee going."

The warm sun soon melted the snow and turned the trail into mud. The wheels of wagon trains, over the years, had worn the earth down to dirt making a muddy mess. The three friends veered off the trail and traveled on the spring grass that was coming up. They hadn't seen any human for the two and a half days they'd been gone. That soon changed when they saw a herd of elk on the side of a hill. They halted their horses and watched the beautiful creatures grazing.

"Did you see that?" Rand said, interrupting the quiet.

"See what?" Aaron stiffened, and became alert.

"There's someone down there stalking those elk."

"No, I don't see anyone."

"Wait just a minute. *There*, did you see him?"

"Yes, it's an Indian. Be still and watch. Let's not draw any attention to ourselves. Maybe he hasn't seen us so when he gets busy we'll slip on by."

"I think he done seen us but wants the elk more than us," Gabriel said.

"You're probably right. He's only got a bow."

The Indian must have sensed his time was running out because he stood and let his arrow fly.

"Aw, he *missed*. It just barely skimmed over the top of that elk," Rand said.

"There's a couple of cows that stopped and looked back. Think you can shoot one for him, Rand?"

"You sure you want me to try?"

"Yes, hurry."

Rand put his rifle to his shoulder, took a breath, let it out, then fired. The big cow staggered forward a few steps and fell to the ground.

"Good shot, Rand!"

"Now, what do we do?" Gabriel wanted to know.

"We go down there in a friendly way and help him dress it out."

Gabriel and Rand both gave Aaron a questioning look. "I don't know about that," Rand said. "He may not speak our language."

"Everyone can understand the language of a friendly smile. Besides, there's only one of him and three of us."

Aaron nudged his horse in the direction of the fallen elk with Rand and Gabriel following, leading the pack horse. The Indian man had already reached the kill and watched as they approached. When they were close, the Indian called out, "Hey, you white men ruined my shot!"

Chapter 26

"ITTLE WARRIOR, IS THAT you?" Aaron asked in amazement.

"It is Little Warrior. How is my friend, Tall Shadow?"

"I'm doing good. I want you to meet my cousin, Rand, and our friend, Gabriel."

The men nodded their acknowledgement of each other. "What brings Tall Shadow here?"

"I'm on my way to find Bonita. Rand and Gabriel came along to keep me company."

"Ah, *White Flame*. I think of her many times. Will you take her to be your wife? Maybe she has found another man."

"I hope she hasn't. When I find her, I'll ask her to marry me. She knows I'm coming for her so I don't think she'll marry someone else." Aaron was thoughtful a moment. "I suppose it's possible though. I'll take my chances, anyway."

Little Warrior looked at the large cow elk lying a few feet away. "This is Tall Shadow's kill. Will you take all the meat?"

"No, I wasn't going to take any of it. Rand shot it when you missed with your arrow. We just wanted to help. I hope that was all right."

"It is good. My people will be very happy. Our food is almost gone. It has been a hard winter."

"How far away is your camp?"

"With horse we could be there very soon. Little Warrior and Fox have no horse. It will take one more day to take what we can carry back to our people."

"Where are your horses, Little Warrior?"

"Shoshone stole most of horses. With bad winter our people had to let others go or they starve. We will catch them again, soon."

"Let us help you. We can cut the elk in large pieces and each one of us can carry some to your camp."

"This would be good. Black Feather and Story Teller will be glad to see Tall Shadow."

"Story Teller? Who is that?" Aaron asked.

"It is your friend Mack. He has told us stories from the black book all winter. The Children call him story teller."

"Mack McCallister! I'd like to see him too. I forgot he married Willow and went with your people. Is he doing good?"

"You come, he will tell you all."

"All right." Aaron turned to Rand and Gabriel. "Is that all right with you two?"

"Sure, Aaron, we're with you. If you want to go and help your friends, it's all right with me," Rand answered.

Gabriel didn't say anything, just smiled. Aaron had been watching Gabriel off and on all day and had noticed the smile he'd had that morning hadn't yet left his face.

"Let's get this animal cleaned and quartered, then," Aaron said, dismounting.

Little Warrior made a hand motion and in a moment, his brother, Fox, came walking out of the trees. Rand and Gabriel eyed the new arrival curiously. After Aaron waved a greeting to Fox, he quickly explained, "This is Little Warrior's brother, Fox. He's deaf so they communicate with hand signs."

The three studied each other, sizing each other up, before nodding a greeting.

There was little conversation as the men went to work on the elk. They were ready to load the pieces of meat on the horses, when Aaron realized they were waiting for him to say how to carry out the task. "We need to distribute the weight so it won't be too hard on any one horse."

Gabriel suggested, "Why don't I ride with Rand, and your friends can ride my horse. We can put one big piece of meat on the pack horse."

"That'll work," Aaron agreed. "The pack horse can probably carry some of the lighter pieces too." When they were ready to go, Aaron told Little Warrior, "Lead the way, we'll follow you."

The evening sun was fading fast when they rode into an open area with a number of tepees clustered together. Wood smoke filled the air. A young girl popped her head out of a tepee which quickly led to a series of yelps and cries as people began coming out to greet Little Warrior and Fox. Aaron didn't recognize any of the Indians, many with gaunt, hungry faces. The winter had, indeed, been hard on these people. Then he spotted Black Feather coming toward them along with Mack McCallister. They dismounted, and received a warm welcome.

"It is good to see you, Tall Shadow. We welcome you," said Black Feather.

"It's good to see you too, Black Feather." Aaron shook hands with him then turned to Mack McCallister. "Hey, Mack, it sure is great to see you again!"

"I feel the same way, Aaron. I'm anxious to hear all the news you have. And who are these two young men you have with you?"

Aaron introduced Rand and Gabriel, who had dismounted and were helping to unload the meat. He was aware of the diminished number of the tribe as they milled around the area. "Where are all your people, Black Feather?"

"There is much to tell. Come, we will smoke and talk while the women prepare the food that has been brought." He called to Little Warrior. "When you finish, come talk with us."

Black Feather and Mack led the visitors toward one of the tepees. He motioned for them to sit on buffalo robes that were laid around a small fire burning in the middle of the tepee. Then he went to go get his pipe. While he was gone, Mack quietly told them how bad it was in their camp. "I know it's customary to smoke and talk, but Black Feather has very little tobacco left, maybe none at all. Our people have been close to starving. We have very few rifles and no bullets."

"I understand, Mack. We'll decline to smoke, then. I've never smoked before, anyway. Have you Rand?"

"Sure, I tried it once, but didn't like it. How about you, Gabe?"

"No, never did get a chance to try."

Black Feather came back with Little Warrior following him. "Little Warrior tells me your friend shot the elk that you brought to us. We are thankful for your gift. Will you and your friends smoke with me?"

"I don't think so, Black Feather," Aaron said. "None of us smoke and it would probably make us sick. Could we just talk for a while? Where is your father? I didn't see him when we came in."

"My father has gone to the spirit world, what you call heaven. He died from a wound by a Shoshone warrior."

"I'm sorry to hear that," Aaron said.

"Black Feather is the chief now," Mack told them.

"That is the way of things," Black Feather continued. "Many of our people died the first winter after we left our old home. The sickness was bad that winter. When the snow melted, the Shoshone would not leave us alone. They have raided and killed many of our young men. Our women cannot go far from camp for the Shoshone steal them and make slaves of them."

"Is Willow safe, I hope? And your wife, too?" Aaron asked.

"Yes. They help Story Teller keep the women and small children safe after we realized what our enemy was doing. Story Teller will be a father in the fall. You will see Willow and Sky Flower when they bring us the food they cook."

"That's good news. Congratulations, Mack!"

"Thanks, Aaron. And now, can I ask you a question?"

"Of course, you can ask me anything you want."

"Do you have enough salt that you might share with us? It's okay if you can't, but that would be a big help. I miss the taste of salt and the women will be drying some of the elk meat you brought. They can salt the meat and it will last longer."

"Yes, I'll go get it. We have plenty to share."

Aaron started to get up but Gabriel stopped him. "Let me go. I know right where it is."

The stories that were told were difficult to hear. Between sicknesses and the Shoshone attacks, there were very few of the Arapaho tribe of Black Bird, which Black Feather now found himself the leader. After the meal was brought to them by Willow and Sky Flower, Aaron asked Black Feather a question. "What are you going to do now that the snow is almost gone? Will you stay here?"

"Story Teller and I have been praying for an answer. We cannot stay here or our enemy, the Shoshone, will kill us all. I think often of our old camp close to my brother, Justin Myers. I wish my father had never moved us from the mountains there. How are things now? Is the military strong?"

"No, there are very few soldiers now. Have you heard of the war between the white men that is far away to the east?"

"Yes, we know a little. Is the battle over?"

"Not that I know of. When I left the east they were still fighting. Most of the soldiers were called back east to fight in the war there. There are very few soldiers now. In some ways that would be good for you, but in other ways it will be bad. There will be many more white men move out here to get away from the fighting."

"Will they ever stop coming to take the land and kill the buffalo?"

"I'm afraid not, Black Feather. Your father had the right idea. The only way to survive is to learn the ways of the white man and live in peace with them."

"What you say may be true but it is a very hard thing to do. My father made me promise before he died that I would not let the people forget the old ways."

It was quiet for a while as the men contemplated all that had been discussed. Finally, Aaron broke the silence. "May I talk to you and Mack alone, Black Feather?"

"If you wish. Little Warrior, take our friends with you. They will sleep with the young braves. Take care of our friends." Without another word the three men left, leaving Aaron alone with Black Feather and Mack. "What is it Tall Shadow wishes to say?"

Aaron took a deep breath and winged a prayer toward heaven. "I have an idea I'd like to share. You could set up a cattle ranch and build a ranch house in the foothills down below your old village. Maybe something like the Swanson ranch house, with two wings, one for each of your families. Then you could build a bunkhouse for the young men and a large barn; find a secluded place not too far away for your older people who want to live in the old ways. The young boys can take turns coming and staying in the bunkhouse and learn to be ranch hands. They can go back to the village to live for a period of time to learn from the old ones.

"I'm sorry to have to say this, but *outwardly* it would have to be Mack's ranch. He would have to be the one to do business with other white men, but you all would know it belongs to the Arapaho people."

Black Feather and Mack just stared at Aaron, for what seemed a long time. "Well," Aaron said cautiously, "what do you think?"

"What you said sounds really nice, Aaron," Mack answered, "but how in the world would we ever have the money to do any of that?"

"You've been praying for God to show you what to do," said Aaron. "What if a cattle ranch is what He wants? How do you feel about it, Black Feather?"

He shook his head sadly. "Why talk about what cannot be."

"Maybe there's a way," Aaron said. "Would you like to own a cattle ranch, *if* it were possible?"

"It is a good plan," Black Feather said. "But He Who Preaches speaks the truth. There is no way for us to do such a thing."

Aaron nodded as he carefully looked at each man. "If you both think it is a good plan then I know a way for you to do it. *But*, I must ask you both to never tell anyone about what I am going to do."

Mack glanced at Black Feather. "Now, I'm curious, Aaron. How can you help us start a ranch?"

"God provided a way for my family to help those in need. I feel strongly that the Arapaho people are the ones we should be helping now, but we prefer to keep our name anonymous. Please just tell people, if they ask, that *God* provided for you because that's how my family feels. God is allowing us to give gold to the ones we find who could use help."

"Gold!" Mack exclaimed. "You have enough gold to get us started? Where did you find gold?"

"Yes, I have enough, but our family decided that we would not talk about it to anyone. We would just give it away to help people."

"But, shouldn't we try to pay it back?" Mack asked.

"No, it's a *gift*. I think it's the answer to the prayers you and Black Feather have been asking God about. I wouldn't turn down a gift from God. Would you?"

Mack shook his head. "That would not be wise. What do you think, Black Feather?"

Black Feather didn't answer right away. The weight of responsibility for his people seemed to be heavy on his mind. When he did make his decision, Aaron could tell it had eased his friend's mind. "Black Feather is not a fool. If God has provided a way for my people to live a good life, then I will take what He gives."

"Good, I'm glad. I'll get the gold for you in the morning."

"Give it to Story Teller," Black Feather said. "I trust him. He has proved his love for my people in many ways. Let us talk more about this cattle ranch. Do you know about cattle, Story Teller?"

"I know a lot about cattle and I'm sure Justin and his friends would help us with what we don't know."

The three men talked until Sky Flower came in with the two children. "Ahh, it is long past time for children to be asleep. We will talk more in the morning. You may sleep here, Tall Shadow."

"If it's all right with you, I would like for Aaron to sleep in my tepee," Mack said.

"That will be good. Tall Shadow will not have to wake in the night with the crying of babies."

For three days, Aaron, Rand, and Gabriel stayed with the Arapaho. They hunted one day and brought back enough game to feed the people for a number of days. Rand and Fox hit it off and became good friends. This seemed to please Little Warrior. "Your cousin is a good man, Tall Shadow. Fox likes him and he doesn't make friends quick. It was when the two climbed a tree that Rand spotted the horses in the valley below. Now we go tomorrow to catch the horses. Will you go?"

"I would rather stay here with Mack and visit more with him. I can help protect the women if there's any trouble. Of course I'll go if you need me."

"There are enough who want to go but it would help if we could use your horse."

"Sure you can. I trust you to take good care of her."

"Thank you. You are a good man too. I am proud to call you friend."

"I feel the same way, Little Warrior. I am also glad we're friends."

"Would we still be friends if I go with you to find White Flame? Maybe she will want me for a husband and not Tall Shadow."

The gleam in Little Warrior's eyes said he was teasing, but Aaron wasn't one hundred percent sure. "Are you really thinking of going with me?"

"Would it please Tall Shadow to have Little Warrior and Fox go with you?"

"I would be glad to have you along, but won't Black Feather need you here?"

"He will give me his decision tonight. We have talked. My brother and I know how the Shoshone are raiding the wagon trains and white people who build their homes on the way. Black Feather wishes you to return with your scalp. He thinks the Shoshone would like the red hair of your cousin on their lances."

"Whatever Black Feather decides is fine with me, but don't try to steal my girl!"

Chapter 27

*T*HE NEXT FEW DAYS were what some young men only get to dream about. Little Warrior and Fox did go with Aaron, Rand, and Gabriel. The two Indian brothers didn't follow the regular route that all the wagon trains traveled but took their new friends into wild pristine country that left them in awe of the enormity and beauty of God's creation. Gabriel was especially affected. They traveled on mountain game trails so steep it could stop a man's heart. They crossed so many cold mountain streams they couldn't count them all. Spring was everywhere and the display of flowers and new life inspired Aaron to draw. He only had a small tablet, but took every opportunity to sketch his surroundings. The five young men became closer with each day that passed. Rand learned to communicate with Fox and learned a lot about tracking and other survival techniques from him. Fox had to rely on his other senses, especially sight and smell, because of his deafness. He would occasionally stop the group and have them wait while he climbed a tree and gazed into the surrounding area. Little Warrior never questioned Fox. He seemed to trust his younger brother's ability to sense trouble. Several times, Fox would change their direction and take them around what he thought was danger. One time, he quickly came down a tree and hurried them in a different direction. They rode a long time before Fox stopped. He communicated to Little Warrior that he saw a large group of Shoshone warriors that were probably hunting, but he didn't want to cross paths with so many of the enemy.

"Fox thinks it will be best if we travel until dark, then we should be safe," Little Warrior told them.

"What ever you think is best," said Aaron. "I'm doing all right. Gabriel, are you and Rand doing all right?"

"Sure, but I'll sleep better bein' away from dem Indians Fox saw."

"I'm all right too," Rand said as he dug in his saddlebag for a piece of dried beef.

Then the group moved out toward the west. The landscape began to change with more open spaces and was not as mountainous. As they rode out of a stand of Aspen trees that had leafed out in their vibrant spring colors, they were surprised to find themselves on the banks of a large lake.

"Wow! That's a mighty big lake," Rand said. "Are we going to camp here tonight?"

"We'll see," said Aaron. "Fox and Little Warrior will scout around and make sure it's safe. It'll be a good place if there's no other people close by. Let's stay close to the trees until they return."

Little Warrior returned and was satisfied with the spot they had chosen. "We will stay in the trees a ways so our fire cannot be seen. There is a big wagon train across the lake. They make big fires and much noise. They will not even know we are here."

"Where's Fox?" Rand asked.

"He will be here soon. Fox watches a little longer. Maybe you and Gabriel catch fish to eat."

"Sure, that sounds like fun. Come on, Gabe, let's make fishing poles and find a spot to fish."

Aaron and Little Warrior took care of the horses and set up camp. Aaron built a fire and made a pot of coffee. As darkness closed in, Aaron idly fed the fire small pieces of wood as he sipped a cup of coffee. "What's ahead of us, Little Warrior? I've noticed the land is changing."

"I was very young when I was here before. I remember not too far away are many springs of water that come out of the ground like water on a hot fire."

"Oh, yes, Seth Swanson told us about them. He said some say they are healing waters. Have you heard that?"

"I hear about the healing waters, but I do not know if the story is true."

"We must be close to Fort Hall then. We need to stock up on supplies there if we can. I heard there are freighters who bring wagons up from the Salt Lake area."

"It must be so. That would be the best place to get supplies at the Fort, but we may find at the springs that there are places to buy supplies. From here you must take the lead. We will be seeing more white settlers now. It must not look like Little Warrior and Fox are dangerous. We must look like we are…how do you say…*simple*. Is that the word?"

"Yes, I think I understand. But you and Fox are far from simple."

"Do not let others know you think so. I will understand if you treat us like we work for you."

"We'll see. It's sad to say, but you're probably right."

"Not everyone feels the same way as you, my friend. You do not see the way other white men do."

"I just think we're all the same in God's eyes."

"That is what Mack tells us. You and Mack are the same. You see like your God does."

"I wish everyone could see like God does." The two men sat quietly for a while, then Aaron asked, "What will it be like after Fort Hall?"

"The land is more open. It will be more dangerous, but we will be able to travel faster. There are many Shoshone and some Bannock tribes in the land around the Fort. We must be wise and travel carefully."

Gabriel was the first to come back to camp. "Hey, we sure did catch a mess of fish."

"Good for you. Where's Rand?"

"Fox came along and the two of dem is cleanin the rest of the fish."

"Well, let's get started cooking them," Aaron said, getting to his feet. "Should we roast them or fry them?"

"If you get out that big skillet and a few pieces of bacon. I'll roll them in some cornmeal and fry them in the bacon fat. Mm-mm, that sure sounds good."

"Yes, it does, but we're almost out of bacon *and* cornmeal." Aaron thought a minute. "Go ahead and use it all, Gabe. We'll probably be able to get some more pretty soon at the Fort."

"All right, if you say so. The fish that Rand and Fox bring in, we can roast. I think I hear them coming now."

After they had their fill of fish, Rand requested that Aaron play his guitar. "You haven't played for a while. It's a nice night for listening to music and counting the stars."

"I will, if you'll play along with me on your harmonica. Do you think they will hear it across the lake, Little Warrior?"

"No, we are too far away and they make much noise of their own. I would be pleased to hear your music."

Just as Little Warrior had said, they saw several homesteads the next day. Aaron was able to buy a slab of bacon and a small bag of cornmeal from one of the settlers. The woman was happy to sell them two loaves of bread, but she wouldn't part with the small amount of coffee she had. She kept eyeing Fox and Little Warrior who sat passively on their horses. "They tame Indians?" the woman asked.

"Yes, they're harmless, ma'am," Aaron answered.

"I don't know. They look young and strong to me. I wouldn't be trusting them if I were you."

"I'll keep it in mind. I sure do thank you for letting me buy a few things from you. You have a good day, ma'am."

"You're welcome, but you remember what I said and keep an eye on those two Indians or you might die in your sleep without your hair."

After visiting the tiny community that was building up around what were called Soda Springs, Aaron and his group followed the main trail toward Fort Hall. Several hours after they were on the trail they were surprised when they came over a hill and found a man in the middle of the roadway. He was riding a large mule and pulled another mule loaded with supplies. Dressed in buckskins, he had long hair under a fur hat, and a short beard that covered his lower face. Aaron decided he was a mountain man. Anyway, he looked like what Aaron always thought a mountain man should look like. The alarming part was the long rifle he carried was pointed right at Aaron.

"Hold up there," the man growled. "Let me look at you varmints a minute."

Aaron didn't argue, just motioned for his group to stop. He waited while the man gave them a good looking-over before moving his rifle away from Aaron. "What are you looking for?" Aaron asked. "We're not hurting anyone or causing trouble."

"Thought you might be that gang of cut-throat thieves they're warning people about at Fort Hall. But, ya'll don't fit the description they gave me." He spat a stream of tobacco juice on the ground, then wiped his mouth on his sleeve.

"What are they saying about them?" Aaron asked.

"Well, there's about six of them, but they're all white men and older than you young whipper-snappers. They're a *mean* bunch, robbing and killing any poor soul that gets in their way. You best watch out for them." He stared at the group a little longer. "You got a strange collection of friends, young man. You always travel with Indians, Negroes, and red-headed white men?"

Aaron looked back at the group behind him then turned to the mountain man again, smiling. "I would travel with these men anytime and anyplace that I got a chance to. A man couldn't find more honest, faithful friends than these right here."

"Then you better be counting your blessings. A good friend is hard to find. Had me a good friend once, but some nasty grizzly tore him up so bad he died after suffering for a week. Wouldn't wish that on anyone."

"Sorry to hear that. A grizzly almost killed my father some years back. I've never been close to one."

"Well, you best keep it that way. Where you men headed?"

"Over around the Fort Boise area."

"News from there says they're building a new Fort close to the Boise River. Have you heard yet that Abe Lincoln declared this here land we're on as Idaho Territory, a few months back?"

"No, I hadn't heard that," Aaron answered.

"This country is changing fast. Look at this wild country and enjoy it while you can. It'll never be like it was with so many coming out here to claim the land."

Aaron nodded. "If you don't mind me asking, where are you headed?"

"Don't mind at all. I'm headed over toward Fort Laramie then down to Colorado Territory. Jim Baker is my name."

"That's close to where I'm from. My name is Aaron Trinity and if you get to the mountains north of Fort Laramie, stop at the cattle ranches of Justin Myers and Seth Swanson. My father lives with family above those ranches at the High Meadows Horse Ranch. They'll treat you good and tell them you ran into me and my friends. They'll be glad to hear we're all right."

"I just might do that, young man. You just make sure you and your friends take care of yourselves and stay all right."

"We will, sir. You take care, too."

"I do the best I can. So-long, men."

When Jim Baker came along-side of Fox and Little Warrior, he stopped and signed to them. With a laugh, he rode his mule over the hill and disappeared.

"What did he say to you?" Aaron asked. He was the curious one this time, instead of Rand.

Little Warrior had a big smile on his face. "He told me and Fox to quit looking like we were stupid. To hold our heads up like a true Arapaho. He has known and respected many Arapaho."

"How did he know you were Arapaho?" Rand asked.

"The way we dress. Tribes have their own certain way to make and decorate the clothes we wear."

"Well, no one's going to fool that old man," Rand chuckled.

"You're probably right about that," Aaron said. "When we get to Fort Hall we need to find a place to clean up. I hadn't taken a good look at us until now and we're starting to look *mangy*. Especially you and me, Rand."

"Speak for yourself, cousin," Rand huffed.

Three days later, they crossed the Snake River and rode out into the sagebrush. Aaron found excitement building up in his chest. *I'm almost there, Bonita. Stay safe and wait for me.*

Chapter 28

OT LONG DAYS, MILE upon mile of sage brush, and mounds of lava, accompanied the travelers after leaving Fort Hall. All five men let out a sigh of relief when they saw a river bordered with inviting green trees.

"Do you suppose that's the Boise River, Aaron?" Rand sounded hopeful.

"I'm thinking it must be. We need to get closer and look around. Maybe we can find someone to ask about the Basque boarding house."

"We finally made it, cousin," Rand crowed. "You excited to see your girl?"

"I don't have enough words to tell you how *nervous* and excited I am!"

"Don't worry, Tall shadow," said Little Warrior. "White Flame will be happy to see you. If not, she is not worthy of a man like you who keeps his word and comes so far to find her."

"I hope you're right, Little Warrior. Let's hurry and find her!"

It wasn't long until the sound of bleating sheep could be heard. "Up on that hill, Tall shadow," Little Warrior pointed.

A large flock of sheep covered a green, grassy hill a short distance away. At the bottom of the hill, two men on horseback were watching Aaron and his friends.

"Let's ride on over. I think that might be Bonita's uncle and cousin," Aaron said. "If not, I'm sure they can tell us where the boarding house is."

As they approached the two sheepherders, Aaron realized it was indeed Bonita's uncle, Nicholas Berriochoa, and his son, Bernardo. They didn't seem to recognize Aaron at first and acted nervous at their approach. As soon as he thought they could hear him, Aaron called out, "Hello, Mr. Berriochoa!"

As he got closer, recognition registered on Mr. Berriochoa's face. "Aha! Now I see you clearly. Is it true? Are you Aaron?"

"Yes, it's me. How are you doing?"

"I am fine. We have just brought the sheep up from the south and will be taking them north for the summer. And, how is your family?"

"When I left home everyone was fine. I want to introduce my friends to you and Bernardo. This is my cousin, Rand, and our very good friend, Gabriel Freeman. My two Arapaho friends are Little Warrior and Fox."

"It is good you have such friends to keep you company on such a long journey."

"I won't argue with that. I am blessed to have them as friends."

"This foolish old man must ask a silly question," said Mr. Berriochoa, scratching his head. "What are you doing here, Aaron? What are your plans?"

Aaron hesitated, apprehensive. But then, quickly decided that the truth was best. "I've come to find Bonita. Is she married to someone else, Mr. Berriochoa? Please tell me now, so I don't make a fool of myself."

"You worry unnecessarily. She is not married to another even though others have asked her, but she refused them all. She says, 'I will wait for my Aaron, the great artist. He will come for me. He said he would and he will.' Most of the women at the house tease her and says she only dreams of this great artist."

"I don't know how great I am but I'm glad she waited for me. I'm anxious to see her. Where is the boarding house?"

"Just over the next hill not far from the river."

"I would like to surprise her. Will she be at the house this time of day?"

"She will be there. Most of the women will be preparing for our evening meal. "How can I help you with your surprise?"

"I'm not sure…." Aaron began.

"Sing your song for her, Aaron," Rand suggested.

"You are going to serenade Bonita?" Mr. Berriochoa asked. "What do you think of that, Bernardo?"

A huge smile showed off Bernardo's slightly crooked white teeth. "I think all the girls will be jealous and they will be sorry they have teased my cousin so much. All the time they tell her she only dreamed up this famous artist who is so tall and handsome. If I had not seen you myself I too would have thought you were someone she made up in her dreams."

"Bosh!" Mr. Berriochoa said waving his hand. "Bonita is not a girl to make up silly notions. She is a good, sensible girl and I am glad you have finally come for her. I, Nicholas Berriochoa, *knows* about romance and I may have a way for you to surprise Bonita and sing your song for her."

"That's great! Tell me your plan."

"Your friends can stay here with Bernardo while you walk up to the tree line and make your way to the river through the trees. You will see a path along the river that we use all the time. Find a place to watch for her along that path. I will think of some reason to send her up that way. And then…the rest is up to you, my friend."

"All right! Sounds good, Mr. Berriochoa. Thanks for that suggestion."

"You are welcome. But you must leave now. I will give you time to get to the river before I ride to the house. When your friends hear the bell to come to dinner they can come to the house. I will take care of them."

Aaron untied the guitar from the pack horse and took it out of its case, telling his friends he would see them at the house. Then began his walk up the hill to the tree line, leaving his horse with the others. Excitement stirred his heart with each step he took. *I'll soon be singing to my girl!* His spirit soared remembering Mr. Berriochoa's words about Bonita's faithfulness and her trust that he would come for her. *I don't know what I did to deserve such a wonderful girl, but I'm glad she's soon going to be my wife.*

He found the path then looked for a hidden spot where he could still see through the brush. A fallen log made a good place to sit and he quietly tuned the guitar and strummed a few chords. Then he waited, thinking: *Maybe I shouldn't hide. I sure don't want to scare her. I think I'll just sit by the path so she can see me. Then I'll sing to her.*

He shoved the log to the side of the path in full view of anyone walking that way. *That's better. Sure wish she would hurry, I'm so anxious!*

And then, finally, he heard a voice.

"Sheba, where are you?"

Bonita!

"You are very naughty for running away from Uncle Nicholas! Come, Sheba, where are you?" After a pause, she called again, "Sheba! What has gotten into you? It is not like you to hide from me."

Aaron realized she was getting closer and a moment later he saw her down the path. She had stopped and turned, like she might be deciding to go back. Aaron began playing, softly. She whirled around, peering up the path. And before she could bolt, he started singing:

Lovely Bonita, Please say you'll be mine,
I'll love you forever, My heart will be thine . . . .

Bonita gasped. And for just a few seconds she stood staring. "Aaron?" It is you! You came for me!"

He barely had time to lay the guitar aside before she launched herself into his arms. He stood and held her close, feeling genuine relief and joy unspeakable. This was who he came for, who he wanted. She finally pulled back and looked up at him.

"I can't believe it! You are finally here. Oh, Aaron. I am so happy!"

"I'm happy too, my lovely Bonita. How are you doing?"

"I am fine, now that you are here. You were playing the guitar? I didn't know you played."

"Mama Carmen taught me to play last winter. I'm not very good but it has been fun learning. I wrote a song just for you."

"Just for me? Please, sing it for me. I already love it."

Aaron sat back down on the log and picked up the guitar. "Should I start at the beginning again?"

"Yes, please. I would like that." She sat on the ground and drew her legs to her side, smoothing her dress around her. Then she looked up at him and smiled sweetly. "You can start now."

He instantly thought back to the first time he had met Bonita, high on the mountain, when she insisted he eat her lunch, and she informed him that she would not let him die, and that cute little nose in the air, her feisty, sassy self. Oh, how he loved this girl! He cleared his throat and began to sing.

Lovely Bonita, please say you'll be mine,
I'll love you forever, my heart will be thine.
Come to my arms now, give me your heart,
I'll stay with you always, and we'll never part.
Come, eat at my table…Come, sit by my side,
And say that you love me…For all of time.
Let my love complete you…With me you'll abide,
Lovely Bonita…Will you be my bride?

He paused a moment to gauge her reaction. She had tears in her eyes and said, "Yes, oh yes, Aaron, I will be your bride." She wiped her tears away. "That is all? Is the song over?"

"No, not yet. I'm so glad you'll be my bride. Bonita, will you marry me? Will you go home with me? I'm building a cabin for us. Will you live with me on the High Meadows?"

She got up quickly and threw her arms around Aaron. "Yes, of course, silly. If I say I will be your bride, that means I will marry you. Sing the rest of the song, Aaron. It is so lovely, I love the song." She sat back down and looked up at him expectantly. He had a hard time getting his emotions under control, but continued the song:

I promise to love you, my heart will be true,
There's nothing on this earth, I won't do for you,
I'll give you my riches, and all that I own,
Give me your hand now, and I'll take you home.
Come eat at my table…Come sit by my side,
And say that you love me…For all of time,
Let my love complete you…With me you'll abide,
Lovely Bonita…You'll be my bride.

"Just one more verse, if you can stand it," Aaron said, grinning. Bonita nodded, wiping more tears from her eyes.

Through life's bitter winters, and stormy days too,
Let my love embrace you, and keep you safe too,
Come, be my sweetheart, and I'll be your man,

Darling Bonita, please give me your hand.
Come eat at my table…Come sit by my side,
And say that you love me…For all of time,
Let my love complete you…With me you'll abide,
I love you, Bonita…I'm so glad you're mine.

Aaron put the guitar down and stood to his feet. He took Bonita's hand and pulled her up, then wrapped his arms around her again. "I've waited so long to hold you in my arms."

These words caused a torrent of tears to flow as Bonita clung to the man she loved. He held her until she calmed. She looked up and searched his face. "You are more handsome than I remember. How I have longed to see your face again."

"I feel the same way. You are just as I remember only more beautiful. Why did I ever let you leave the ranch?"

"Let's not think about that now. We did what we had to do, but you are here now and nothing else matters." After a few moments, she asked, "Did you come by yourself? Surely not, not that long way. Who came with you?"

"I brought my cousin, Rand, and a friend of ours, Gabriel. Oh, and a couple of Arapaho. Guess who that might be?"

"Ha! It has not been so long that I have forgotten Little Warrior. Who is the other one?"

"Little Warrior's brother, Fox. I don't remember if you met him or not. They've been good traveling companions and we've felt safe having them with us."

As the two lovers embraced and kissed, the sound of a distant clanging bell could be heard. "Do we have to go down to the house now?" Aaron asked.

"Oh, yes, unless you want the whole family up here. But, we will walk back *very slowly*," Bonita said with a mischievous little smile.

They held hands all the way to the boardinghouse, arriving to find chaotic merriment. Those were the only words to explain the next couple of hours. The large rectangular dining room was filled with cousins, aunts, uncles, and a grandmother, all sitting around four big tables in no particular arrangement. It seemed impossible to keep track of what was going on.

Aaron saw his friends seated with Mr. Berriochoa and Bernardo, along with a few other men. They made their way to that table and Bonita greeted Little Warrior and Fox. Aaron introduced her to Rand and Gabriel, then she quickly called for everyone's attention, waiting for a measure of quietness. "I want you all to meet Aaron Moses Trinity," she beamed. Turning to her uncle, she asked, "Uncle Nicholas, have you introduced Aaron's friends yet?"

"No, Little One, I have not."

She stood behind Little Warrior with her hands on his shoulders. "Please meet our Arapaho friends, Little Warrior and his brother, Fox. This is Rand Trinity, Aaron's cousin, and here is Gabriel Freeman, a good friend."

It was a simple introduction but all that was needed. The people responded with applause and then the room erupted in boisterous conversations at all the tables. Aaron covertly kept an eye on Little Warrior and Fox to make sure they were doing okay. *I wonder what they think of this big family. Surely it's not too different from their own tribal gatherings. The food might be quite different, though.* He smiled at the way Gabriel was deep in conversation with Uncle Nicholas and Bernardo. Some of the younger boys were questioning Little Warrior about what it was like to be an Indian. They wanted to know many things, including how he learned to speak English.

Aaron then noticed that Fox was frowning at something going on across the room. He followed Fox's line of scrutiny and was surprised to see a woman of perhaps twenty, signing to a younger girl. Both had dark complexions, long black hair, and dark eyes. Aaron thought the younger girl was about fifteen or so and quite pretty. He quietly asked Bonita, "Who are those two girls sitting by your Aunt Grace?"

"That's Mary and Lily. Why do you ask?"

"I just noticed they're signing to each other and wondered about them. They don't look like the rest of your family."

"They are Mexican, that's why. My mother and their mother became best of friends when we first arrived in California. When I was born, Mother named me after her new friend, Bonita. One winter, a terrible sickness hit the gold camps where they lived and many died from it. I was a couple years older than Lily and I remember it well. Their whole family got the sickness. No one would take care of them except for Aunt Grace. Their mother and father died along with their baby son. Before the mother passed on, she asked Aunt Grace to promise to take care of the girls, *if* they lived. Lily was *very* sick. Since they had no other family members to take them in, my aunt agreed. They have been with our family ever since. No one realized for quite awhile that Lily had lost her hearing after the fever left her. She's very pretty, don't you think?"

"Yes, she is very pretty. I'm wondering what Fox is thinking."

"Fox? What do you mean?"

"He's been watching them for some time now. I wonder if he understands what they're signing?"

"I hadn't even thought about Fox being deaf. He is so quiet and calm looking. Look, Aaron, he's going over to them. Should we do anything?"

"Your Aunt Grace is there. Let's just see what happens."

Lily didn't see Fox approaching until he tapped her on the shoulder. She startled and turned to find him staring at her. Mary jumped up and pushed Fox's hand away. "What are you doing?" she practically yelled. The room quieted and all eyes turned on them. "Please leave my sister alone."

Little Warrior was immediately at Fox's side. "My brother didn't mean any harm."

Aunt Grace spoke to Mary, "I'm sure he didn't mean to bother Lily. What is it you want, young man?" She smiled at Fox.

"My brother cannot hear," Little Warrior explained. "A sickness took his hearing when he was a baby."

"Oh, we didn't know," Aunt Grace said. "Can you ask him what he wants?"

The brothers signed for a few minutes, then Fox pointed at Lily. He put his index fingers in his ears, asking if her ears were closed, like his. Lily took only a moment to figure out that Fox was deaf. She beamed an incredibly beautiful smile at him and nodded. Fox's eyes lit up and he turned to sign to his brother.

"Fox wants to know if you will teach him the meaning of your signs. He thinks they are very beautiful."

Mary, the older sister, the protector of little sister, was not willing to let just anyone come between them. She stood, unmoving until Little Warrior glared at her. In a firm voice, he said, "Will you please tell her what my brother has said?"

Aunt Grace did her own glaring at Mary until Mary finally signed the request.

Lily's voice sounded somewhat strange, but she signed and spoke very slowly, "I would be very happy to teach you my signs. I have a book that will help."

It was as if no one else was in the room when Fox and Lily began the struggle to communicate. Suddenly, Fox frowned and Lily realized he didn't understand all she said. She signed the word *book* and left the room for a moment. Fox never took his eyes from the hallway into which she had disappeared. She returned with a book in her hands and signed the word *book* again and pointed to the book.

Fox nodded his understanding and excitedly took hold of her hand and led her to a table. The two sat down and began looking at the book.

"I don't like him touching her, Aunt Grace," Mary pouted.

"Hush, Mary. If Lily can help him learn to communicate and have a friend, you should be proud of your sister."

Aaron and Bonita had come over to Aunt Grace's table. "I assure you, Fox won't hurt your sister," Aaron said. "He is a fine young man." Then he turned to Little Warrior. "Do we need to take care of our horses and things?"

Gabriel and Rand had also joined the group. "The horses and everything else is taken care of, Aaron," Rand said. "We're going to go out and help with evening chores. You can stay here and visit with your girl."

Aaron didn't argue since he wanted to be alone with Bonita. "That would be nice. Can we go out on the porch and visit, Bonita?"

She took his arm and smiled up at him. "I would like that very much."

Out on the porch they were finally alone. Aaron pulled Bonita into his arms, but just as his lips touched hers they heard angry shouting and banging from inside the house.

Chapter 29

ARON NEVER GOT TO finish his kiss or spend time with Bonita that night. When they heard the racket they hurried into the house to see what was going on.

"Aunt Grace, is everything all right in here?" Bonita asked, looking around.

Surprisingly, Aunt Grace had a big grin on her face. "Everything is just fine. Our Mary just had a little fit of temper and stormed out of the room."

Fox and Lily were still at the table looking at the book of hand signs. "What happened?" Bonita asked, picking up an overturned chair.

"Mary tried to force Lily to go to bed, that's what happened." An unladylike snort sounded from Aunt Grace. "About time Lily started standing up to Mary. Lily is not a child now since turning sixteen. Her sister has been bossing her around for far too long. It's time Mary started thinking about herself and quit using Lily as an excuse to do nothing about her own life and happiness. She's a nice looking girl and a hard worker. Jacob wanted to marry her but she said she couldn't marry with the responsibility of her sister. Bunch of nonsense! I think she's afraid to love."

"Oh, I never thought of that," Bonita admitted.

"No need for you to bother yourself with it now, either." She glanced at the front door, "Sounds like the men are coming back to the house. I have an idea for you two."

"What kind of idea?" Aaron asked.

"It looks like you two are going to have a hard time spending time together tonight. Why don't you fix a nice picnic lunch, Bonita, and you two sneak off and spend the day together tomorrow."

"That would be wonderful!" Bonita said. "I know just the place. Is that all right with you, Aaron?"

He loved the idea and there was no way he could do anything but agree when he saw her happy face. "Sounds nice. I guess my friends will be all right without me for one day."

Aunt Grace assured him, "Don't you worry about your friends. Leave it to me to see that everyone is taken care of."

The house became noisy with the return of the men. Bonita told Aaron, "You go on with the others. There's a large room with many bunk beds upstairs where the single men sleep. I want to ask Aunt Grace if she will help me plan our wedding. Is Sunday all right with you?"

"I don't even know what day *this* is, Bonita. How far away is Sunday?"

"This is Tuesday so that would be five days from now."

"If that's enough time for you to plan our wedding, then it's fine with me. I'm anxious to start back home."

"Good. I am excited to see Carmen and Maxi again. How is Prince?"

"He's good. The girls love that dog."

"The girls? Oh, the twins! Yes we have much to talk about tomorrow. You must tell me all about them. I don't know if I can sleep, I'm so excited!" Bonita took hold of Aaron's arms and pulled him down so she could kiss him, not minding that the whole room was watching. "Good night, my sweet Aaron."

The boys snickered. Rand let out a big *Whoopee!*

"Way to go, Aaron," they all teased.

Aunt Grace enjoyed their antics but brought the night to an end. "Everyone to bed. Little Warrior, take your brother with you. Lily needs to go to bed."

Aaron and Bonita slipped away early the next morning. The spot Bonita took Aaron to was beautiful. The day was warm with lazy clouds in the sky looking down on a sandy beach along the river bend. Shade trees dropped their branches low, giving them the privacy that they had been waiting for. They sat and talked for several hours. Aaron told about his travels then described where he had chosen to build their house. "It's tucked into the trees but still gets the morning light from the east and a view of the Rocky Mountains to the west.

"You know, those mountain scenes were the pictures that sold the best at the art show. I think I painted three different pictures of the mountains at sunset and one with a storm coming over the mountains into the prairie. They were the ones that sold first."

"It does not surprise me at all. You are wonderful, my Aaron. I love you so much I could…Oh, I don't know what!"

"You love me so much you could come over here and give me a kiss?"

"Yes, I love you that much. But first I must tell you something."

"And what is that, my sweet Bonita?"

"Aunt Grace and the rest of the girls will help with the wedding. It is going to be so much fun, a *real* Basque wedding! We will have a grand time. The only problem is, there is no priest to do the ceremony."

"Oh, I see. Is there *any* kind of clergyman in this area? Maybe where the military is building the new fort?"

"I do not know. What will we do, Aaron?"

"I'm not sure, but I'll go on a search to find someone to do the ceremony, if you and the ladies can do the rest. Does it have to be a priest?"

"That is what my family would like, but they know there is no priest in this area. I do not care as long as we can get married. Just find someone who can perform a good ceremony."

"Then you trust me to find someone?"

"Silly, of course I trust you." Scooting closer to Aaron, she snuggled up under his arm. "Now for that kiss, and then we should eat."

After their lunch, they explored the river for a little while, then rode back to the boarding house.

Everyone was excited about the wedding. Aaron asked his three friends if they would go with him the next day to find a minister to do the ceremony. They all wanted to go, except Little Warrior was hesitant.

"Is there something wrong, Little Warrior?"

"I do not know. Fox is strange."

"What do you mean? Strange *how*?"

"He does not want to go with us anywhere. He wants to stay here with the girl, Lily. He helps her with her work so they can look at the book to learn the signs. It is not how the Arapaho man lives, to do a woman's work."

Aaron wasn't sure what to say. He looked at the others.

Gabriel asked, "Is he doing anything wrong? Looks to me like he treats her real nice and Aunt Grace is watchin' real close. I think it's nice she be willin' to teach him how to talk with his hands."

Rand, not wanting to be left out of the conversation, piped up, "I think it's nice too. I don't see any harm in it. I'd like for him to go with us, but we'll be together all the way home. He'll probably teach me all the new signs he's learned."

"I hope my friends are right. I do not like this strange way of his."

The four men headed out the next morning to visit the military site. It was harder to find a preacher than Aaron had anticipated. They checked with a couple of wagon trains along the river, then made their way up to the area where the new fort was to be built. The construction was in the preliminary stages of cutting timbers, trimming, and dragging logs to the building site.

The workers looked at Aaron like he'd lost his mind when he asked about a preacher. They just shook their heads and went back to work. Then, from the shadows a man stepped out and approached Aaron. He was wearing green clothing with a peculiar looking hat but seemed friendly enough. He told Aaron he knew a man who might be able to do a wedding ceremony, said he was a nice fellow but kept to himself mostly, and he knew his bible; held a bible study on Sunday mornings.

"Where can we find him?" Aaron asked.

"He's back up in the mountains, sawing the trees down. Tall, wiry man, goes by Thomas Tanner. He can cover a lot of ground with those long legs of his. Just head north. You'll be able to tell where he's felling trees."

"Thanks," Aaron said, relieved. "We'll go find him."

"You young men watch yourselves," the stranger warned. "Don't get in the way of the falling trees."

"We'll watch out. Thanks again."

It wasn't hard to find who they were looking for. The warning call of *timber!* the crash of a tree slashing its way downward through the woods, then the jarring slam to the ground took them right to Thomas Tanner.

"Hello," Aaron called as they rode up after the felled tree had settled. "I'm looking for Thomas Tanner."

"That's me," said a man coming toward them. "What do you want with me?"

"I'd like to talk to you a few minutes if you can spare the time."

The man on the other end of the saw, shrugged and said, "I need a break anyway, Tom, I'll be back shortly."

Aaron and company dismounted and introduced themselves to Mr. Tanner. The man looked to be in his late twenties and Aaron immediately felt comfortable with him. "I have a problem, and I was told you might be able to help."

"Well, depends on what kind of problem it is," he answered, amicably.

"I'm going to get married on Sunday and we need someone who can conduct the ceremony. We were told you might be able to do it."

Mr. Tanner seemed bamboozled by that statement. He glanced around the group and rubbed his whiskered chin. "Who in thunder told you I could do a wedding ceremony? No one around here knows my background."

"I didn't get his name, just a man down the hill. He said you were a nice guy and knew your bible and that you have a bible study on Sunday mornings."

"Only a couple of guys show up. I didn't figure the Lord would answer my prayers this way, but yes, I *can* do a wedding ceremony for you. First, I want you to know I've been a preacher of the gospel. Got myself into a mess of trouble and didn't know what to do, so I ran. Wasn't guilty of what the young woman accused me of, but didn't know how to prove otherwise. I feel like a coward now, but what's done is done. I've been asking God what he wants me to do, to show me where I'm needed. Maybe you're an answer to my prayers, Aaron."

"I hope so. I think you're an answer to mine too. Have you performed a wedding before?"

"A few."

"I can't tell you how happy I would be if you would do the ceremony this Sunday. What church did you preach for?"

"Methodist. Is that a problem?"

"Not at all. Do you know where the Basque boarding house is?"

"Sure, we all know where it is. Once in a while we go over there and get a good meal. Nice people."

"Well, can you do the ceremony for me? This Sunday morning?"

"Yes, I'll be there. I'll want to talk to you and your intended bride first. It's important to me that you're both believers."

"We are and we'll be glad to talk to you. Why don't you bring the men who come to your bible study with you? I don't know what all is planned but I've heard them talk about all the food we'll be having."

Thomas Tanner stuck out his hand and Aaron shook it. "All right, I'll see you Sunday morning about ten. How does that sound?"

"That's perfect. Thank you."

As they rode back down the mountain, Aaron wanted to stop and thank the man again for sending him to Thomas Tanner. He looked the workers over but couldn't spot the strange green-clad man. So he asked the workers where he might find him. They didn't know who he was talking about, said no one worked with them like Aaron had described, especially with a strange looking hat. Puzzled, and not sure where the man had come from or where he had gone, they headed back to the boarding house.

Aaron was elated when they rode into the yard. Bonita came out and greeted them. "I'm so glad you're back. Did you find someone to do the ceremony?"

"Yes, I'll be in to tell you all about it when I get my horse taken care of."

"How wonderful! I'm helping in the kitchen, you can find me there."

The men walked their horses to the barn and after storing the saddles, they let the horses into a fenced pasture at the side of the barn. "Thanks, guys for going with me," Aaron said.

"That's what friends are for," Gabriel responded. "And when I get ready for *my* weddin' I may need some help from you."

"Anytime, Gabriel," Aaron chuckled. "Anytime."

As they walked out of the barn, Rand spotted Fox up the hill. "Hey, there's Fox. I think I'll go…." His sentence suddenly dropped off causing the others to follow Rand's line of vision. There was Fox sitting cross-legged on the ground in the shade of a big old tree. Lily was sitting opposite him, also cross-legged, close enough for their knees to touch. The two seemed to be in their own little world and had no idea they had an audience. Lily brought her hand to her mouth then placed it on her cheek. She very slowly leaned forward until her lips touched Fox's, then a second later, she sat back again. Fox repeated the motion, hand on his lips, then his cheek. He then leaned forward and put his lips on Lily's. They repeated the motion together and at the same time met again with a kiss that lasted more than a second.

"Uh-oh," Rand murmured. "I think my friend's in trouble."

"I don't think *he* would call it trouble," Aaron said. "Let's all go to the house. Little Warrior, you and I need to talk to Aunt Grace."

Chapter 30

"I KNOW, I KNOW! I'VE been watching those two for three days now," Aunt Grace fussed. "I've been around too long to not understand what I've been seeing, but I tell you, we can no more stop what's happening between those two than we can stop the sun from rising in the morning. I'll have to admit, you have a nice brother, Little Warrior. He has been real nice to all of us."

"I will talk to my brother and tell him to stay away from Lily. I will leave now with Fox and wait somewhere for my friends. Is this what you want?"

"You know your brother better than I do. If you talked to him or dragged him off somewhere what do you think he would do? Do you think for a minute it would do a bit of good?"

Little Warrior was thoughtful, then answered, "No, he is too much like me. If I found a girl I loved I would let no man tell me what to do."

"There, you have your answer," said Aunt Grace. "Now tell me what would you want your friends to do?"

"I would want them to be happy for me. What would my brother and Lily do? Live here or go back to my people? Could your Lily live like the Arapaho?"

"Lily is young. When you're young and in love, you can do what needs to be done. I don't think Fox would be happy here for very long. From what I've been hearing from you, Aaron, there is a preacher who lives with the Arapaho people and has an Arapaho wife. I'm sure he would give her guidance. That could be a good life for Lily."

"What of her sister?"

"You leave Mary to me. I have taken care of the two girls for years now. Mary's time will come. There are always times in our lives when we have to let our loved ones go for one reason or another. Mary will be fine. She's sulking now, but I think she is slowly starting to understand and accept what might be happening. We've talked a couple of times, but let's not get ahead of ourselves. Nothing may come of it after all." Aunt Grace made her funny little un-lady-like snort again. "But, I wouldn't count on it. I want you all to do something for me and agree not to say anything to them. Don't discourage and don't encourage. I'll be watching but I won't give my blessing to them unless Fox comes to me like a man and asks for Lily himself. I promised their mother I would take care of the girls like they were my own and I won't settle for anything but a man who loves her and will be good to her. Will your brother be that kind of man?"

"Fox is fierce warrior against our enemies. He has a good heart. He has always been gentle with little ones."

"That's good to know. Now we'll just let them be. I'll be watching and you can be sure I know all the tricks that young ones pull to sneak out and be alone. *My* trick is to keep them busy."

"You are a wise woman, Aunt Grace. Thank you." Little Warrior looked around at his friends. "We will do as she says."

They all nodded in agreement. Bonita had been sitting at the table peeling potatoes. "Aaron, tell me about the man who is going to do our ceremony. Where did you find him?"

The next two days were filled with all manner of activity. The women were all in a flurry over food, decorating, what they would wear and many other things that are exciting about weddings. Aaron stayed with Bonita and helped when he could. Little Warrior, Rand, and Gabriel spent a lot of time with Uncle Nicholas and Bernardo watching and learning about the sheep. Bonita's Uncle Robert and his older boy took a day to watch the sheep while Uncle Nicholas took all the men to the trading post down by the new fort site. Fox and Lily spent every moment together that they could find. True to their word, no one bothered Fox and Lily.

Saturday evening, Bonita and Aaron managed some private time on the front porch. As they sat down on the top step the wind started brewing up a spring thunderstorm. Aaron put his arm around Bonita. "You want me to go get you a shawl or coat?"

"No, it feels good. The kitchen has been hot with all the cooking we've done. Your arm around me is all I need." She snuggled closer under his arm.

They were quiet a while before Aaron asked, "Are you ready to become Bonita Trinity?"

She looked up into Aaron's face. "I am ready. I love you so much. My heart is happy just being in the same room with you."

Aaron smiled down at his sweetheart. "Have I ever told you I think you have a cute nose?"

"My nose?"

"Yes, that's one of the first things I noticed about you when we first met."

"What is it about my nose you think is so cute? It is just a nose."

"No, it's not. It's small and turns up a tiny little bit. I love your nose."

"You are funny. Is that all you love about me?"

"No, I love everything about you."

"We will have a good life, my love. I want to make you happy."

"We'll both do all we can to make each other happy. Tell me what is going to happen tomorrow on our wedding day."

"You said the preacher is coming at ten so we will talk to him, then we will leave to get ready for the ceremony. When everything is ready they will call for us. We will come out to the big room where we eat. The preacher will do the ceremony then we will dance and celebrate. There will be a lot of food, beer and wine."

"Beer and wine?"

"Yes, we always have beer and wine to celebrate. Uncle Nicholas is bringing up his best for our wedding. In the cellar he brews his own beer and makes blackberry and elderberry wine from the berries we pick in the fall. Aunt Grace and Aunt Anita take care of the cellar when my Uncles are gone with the sheep. Does it bother you?"

"I really don't know how I feel. But, it's your family giving us the wedding so you decide what is right. I'll be happy with whatever you decide."

"Will we leave Monday morning?"

"I would like to. Would you be all right with that?"

"Yes, I will be ready. It is a long way to our home, but I have made the trip twice now. I know what I should take and I think this third time will be the best trip of all."

"What do you think about Lily? Will she be all right if Fox asks her to become his wife and go with us?"

"Oh, yes. I like Lily, she is a good girl. She can be a lot of fun. I have lived around her long enough to know what signs to use on most things. She always keeps her slate close and I can write notes to her now that you have taught me to read and write. She went with Mary to a special school for a year so they could learn to make the hand signs."

Bonita shivered.

"We should go in now," Aaron said. "It's getting colder. But first tell me where we will be staying tomorrow night. Do you have a room to yourself?"

"No, I share a room with the single girls. It is the same as the one where you are sleeping. I asked Uncle Robert to pull one of the wagons to the place in the trees by the river. It is where Uncle Nicholas sent you the first night you were here. I fixed it up for us." She giggled softly, pressing into Aaron's side.

"Oh, that will be nice," he sighed, relieved.

"Are you nervous to be married?"

"A little."

"Me too," Bonita giggled again. "Let's go in now. If we hurry and go to sleep, our special day will come sooner."

Sunday morning dawned bright and beautiful. As soon as breakfast was over all the tables were moved out to the front yard. Chairs were arranged in the big dining room and in no time the room was filled with wild flowers and lilacs from the two bushes at the corner of the boarding house. The delicate fragrance filled the room, creating a sense of romance that flared in the hearts of all the young women. Giggles erupted from different areas of the house causing a contagious feeling of celebration. The preacher arrived at ten just as he said he would. He brought two other men with him. Bonita and Aaron spent time with the Reverend Tanner and when he was satisfied they were both believers, Aaron went to the men's bedroom and Bonita went to the other end of the house to the young women's bedroom.

"What is this?" Aaron asked Bernardo. He was looking at a white shirt on his bunk and a wide belt of red fabric."

"It is what you will wear. The women made one for you and each of your friends," Bernardo told him. For the first time, Aaron paid attention to the other men. They all had on white shirts with a red belt tied around their waists. Some wore white pants while others had on black pants. "You see, your friends are already wearing theirs," Bernardo beamed.

Aaron had the urge to laugh out loud when he saw Rand, Gabriel, Fox, and Little Warrior with their white shirts and red belts. The two brothers seemed pleased but Aaron couldn't tell for sure how Gabriel and Rand felt. "Well, they sure are bright and festive."

"Wait till you see the women," Bernardo said with a grin.

Aaron took off the shirt he was wearing and with all eyes on him put on the white shirt, tucked it in his pants, and held up the red belt. "I've never worn anything like this."

"Here, let me show you." Bernardo took the belt and tied it in a knot at Aaron's left side. "Doesn't he look handsome?"

Chuckles and laughter filled the room along with cheering and clapping. In the spirit of the day, Rand declared, "We *all* look handsome!"

A knock at the door brought a hush to the room and Bernardo opened it, motioning all the men, except Aaron, out of the room. "I will be back when it is time for you to enter."

Aaron stood nervously waiting. A quick prayer raced through his mind. *Father, bless this day and help me to be a good husband.*

In no time, Bernardo was back and Aaron stepped through the doorway. "Your bride is coming down the hall. You must go to her and take her hand. Walk with her to where the preacher is standing."

Aaron watched Bonita walk toward him and took slow steps to meet her. He was caught up at the sight of this lovely woman who would soon be his wife. She wore a bright red skirt topped with a white blouse, the outfit accented with a black apron and black vest. It was traditional Basque wedding garb. A little tiara sparkled on her head, but dimmed in contrast to her radiant glow. He reached out to her, took her hand and kissed it. "You take my breath away," he murmured. "You are so beautiful!"

She looked deep into his eyes and smiled. Then very slightly, tilted her head toward the sound of giggles coming from two little girls. His eyes swept in that direction and fell on a room full of people watching them, all with big grins plastered on their faces. His own face turned the same shade of his red belt.

"It's all right, Aaron," Bonita said softly. "I love you so much."

He offered her his arm and led her to the waiting preacher.

Thomas Tanner didn't waste the opportunity to preach a little sermon on the meaning and importance of marriage. He led the couple through their vows and when it came time to give Bonita a ring, Aaron pulled a gold band from his pocket and placed it on her finger. Tears pooled in her eyes as she gazed at the shiny gold ring. "Oh, Aaron, it is just *perfect*," she whispered. "Thank you so much!"

Thomas Tanner then concluded the ceremony. "These two young people have said their vows this day before God and all who are here. As of now, they are husband and wife. What God has joined together let no man put asunder." He looked at Aaron. "You may now kiss your bride."

And kiss her he did, while the room erupted with cheering and clapping. The celebration had officially begun. Food was carried out to the tables by women who were dressed like Bonita, but without the tiara. Aaron and Bonita were not allowed to do anything except sit together and talk to those who came to congratulate them. When the food was ready, the preacher said grace and after the newlyweds filled their plates, the others followed.

Aaron stuffed a big bite into his mouth and chewed, savoring the delicious flavor of a food he had never eaten before. "What is this, Bonita? It sure is good."

"It is charizo talos, Sausage. My aunts make their own sausage, the best I have ever eaten. We wrap it in a flat bread made of cornmeal."

"Do you know how to make this?"

"Yes, I have helped many times. I have never made it all by myself but I think I can if Carmen and Maxi will help."

After a while, Thomas Tanner and his two companions came over to Aaron and Bonita's table. "I'm going to leave now," he told them. "I wish you two all the happiness in the world. Thank you for asking me to do the ceremony. And the meal was the best I've ever had."

"Thank you for marrying us," Aaron said. "I'll walk with you to get your horses. I'll be right back, Bonita."

"Hurry, you must not keep your new wife waiting," she teased.

On the way to the horses, Aaron gave Thomas a twenty dollar gold piece and thanked him again. "It was a fine ceremony. I'm glad I found you."

"Glad I could help. These are nice people. Do you think they would let me come back and hold services once in a while?"

Aaron was thoughtful for a moment. "They really are good people, but I can't answer for them. You know they are mostly Catholic."

"Yes, I figured that."

"Well, I guess it wouldn't hurt to ask."

"I'll do that but not today." Thomas looked a little uncertain and Aaron could tell he had something else on his mind. "Uh...."

"What is it, Mr. Tanner?"

"The young lady, I think someone called her Mary. Is she married?"

Aaron smiled. "No, sir. She's a single lady."

"Thank you for that. Now I'll *have* to come back for dinner real soon."

Aaron waved as they rode off then returned to his wedding feast. As he took his place beside Bonita there was a cry of "Topa!" Young and old had a glass or cup that they lifted toward Bonita and Aaron. "Zorta on!" some of them shouted.

"What does that mean, Bonita?"

"Topa means *cheers* and Zorta on, means *good luck*."

She handed Aaron a glass partially filled with dark maroon liquid. "We need to return the salute." He followed her lead and lifted his glass toward the wedding guests. "Topa!" they said together. Then everyone drank.

"Hey, this is good," Aaron said, looking into his glass.

"It is Uncle Nicholas's best blackberry wine. Be careful and don't drink too much, though. You will be sorry."

After their salute, the party got under way with dancing. The bride and groom had the first dance together, then Uncle Nicholas and Aunt Grace took a turn. It was quite surprising how agile the two older ones were. Everyone got in on the act then, with circle dancing and line dancing. Aaron was pleased that his friends were enjoying the festivities. They learned the steps and didn't quit until they were tired and hungry. So back to the food tables everyone went. The accordions started up again and the celebration continued until the sun went down.

"When can we leave?" Aaron whispered to Bonita.

"Any time you want." She smiled at the longing in his eyes. "Are you ready?"

"Yes, I am, but I want to go get my guitar first."

"You are going to sing to me?"

"Well...there might be a song or two in me for tonight. If you want me to, that is."

"Oh, yes, Aaron, I love to hear you sing. I just love *you!*"

"I love you too, my sweet wife. Come in with me and we'll leave out the back door."

Chapter 31

"**A**RE YOU READY TO start for home?" Aaron asked. He and Bonita stood by the river enjoying a few more minutes of privacy before they went back to the boarding house. "Yes, I am ready." She looked around the little clearing where the sheepherder's wagon was sitting. "I will never forget this place."

Aaron hugged her and spoke quietly in her ear. "I will never forget it either. I look forward to when we have our own home."

"So do I. It will be fun to fix it up just like we want."

"Let's get going then. Our home awaits!"

Hand in hand they walked back to the boarding house. At the side pasture, the others were getting ready to saddle the horses in preparation to leave.

"Here comes the old married man," Rand shouted. "We thought you were going to sleep all day. We're almost ready to leave and thought we might have to leave without you."

Bonita and Aaron just laughed at Rand's teasing. "When I get some breakfast I'll be ready to leave, too. How about you guys saddling mine and Bonita's horses while we grab something to eat."

"Oh, no," the red-headed rascal taunted. "Remember the agreement: We all take care of our own horses."

"Fine, I'll do it myself. Give me a few minutes and I'll be right out."

The boarding house was swirling with activity. Aaron couldn't quite put his finger on what he felt from the family. It was almost as if they were holding in their feelings, dreading when Bonita would leave. Aaron ate his breakfast then carried his belongings out to the front yard. Little Warrior and Gabriel were standing alone by the horses when Aaron approached. "Thanks for saddling our horses. How's Fox doing this morning, Little Warrior?"

"He has been very quiet since he found out we are leaving now. He has not shared his thoughts with me."

"Are you going to talk to him?" Aaron asked.

"No, I will keep my word to Aunt Grace. He must speak for himself."

"Here comes Rand and Fox. I'll go get Bonita and her things."

Bonita was tearfully giving the family hugs and saying goodbye. Aaron noticed Lily was quietly standing in the back of the room all by herself. He felt sorry for her as she stood all alone. A tear slid down her face and she looked away. An urge to go talk to her came to him, but he tamped it down when he remembered Little Warrior's words about keeping his promise to Aunt Grace. Bonita drew his attention when she called that she was ready.

Everyone in the family grouped at the front of the house. After loading the last of their things on the pack horse and their own horses, Aaron helped Bonita mount her horse. Sugar was the horse his family had given Bonita when she left the High Meadows with her Uncle and Cousin. Aaron mounted his own horse and turned in time to see Lily push her way to the front of the family. She waved but Fox didn't see her final gesture. Gabriel was already leading off with the pack horse in tow so Aaron waved and nudged his horse to follow. Bonita rode beside him and the others followed with Rand and Fox in the back. His heart broke for the pretty little Lily standing, waving, with tears streaming down her face. No one looked back as they rode up the first hill and disappeared down the other side.

As they started up the next sloping hillside, Aaron heard a shrill whistle. He pulled his horse to a stop and looked back at Rand and Fox. They were stopped and hands were flying in a silent conversation. "What's wrong?" Aaron called to Little Warrior.

"I think my brother has found his courage," Little Warrior said. "I will go back to him and see what is the matter."

The group waited as Little Warrior conversed with his brother. Finally, he told them what the problem was. "Fox says he does not want to leave

Lily. He tells me he must go back and bring her with us to be his wife. I told him I would go back with him."

"We'll all go back," Aaron said. "Did you tell him what he needs to do?"

"No, he will know what to do."

"All right, then. Let's all go get Lily!" The group turned their mounts around, grinning all the way.

Little Warrior told Fox they were all going back, then he handed a small bag to him. Fox seemed to know what was in the bag because he didn't open it or look at the contents. He took a moment to look at each one in the group, nodded firmly, then took the lead back to the boarding house.

Most of the family was standing on the porch watching Lily and Aunt Grace. Lily had apparently collapsed to her knees and had her head bowed to the ground, sobbing uncontrollably. Aunt Grace was kneeling beside her, trying to console the weeping girl. She heard the horses coming back and looked up. A big smile broke out on her face.

The sight of Lily on the ground, weeping, caused Fox to kick his horse and race to where she was. He slipped off in one fluid movement and stopped in front of Lily. Down on his knees, he took hold of her shoulders and gently lifted her head. The pain of rejection was etched in her face and she tried to pull away, not realizing it was Fox who held her. He gave her a little shake and she opened her eyes, gasping at the sight of him.

"Will you go with me and be my wife?" Fox signed.

Lily used her apron to wipe her face and eyes. She hesitated a moment before she signed, "I didn't think you wanted me."

"I do want you. I will be a good husband to you."

Lily finally smiled and signed, "Yes I will go with you. I want to be your wife."

Fox didn't wait any longer. He pulled Lily to her feet and faced Aunt Grace. "I want to take Lily with me to be my wife. Will you give her to me?" He handed her the small bag.

Little Warrior had come to stand by his brother. "Do not refuse the gift if you give Lily to him. It would be an insult. It is the way of our people to give a gift to the parents. Please look at what is in the bag and nod if you accept it."

241

Aunt Grace poured the contents of the bag into her hand. Mary, who had come to stand by her, gasped at the sight of several gold nuggets and a few turquoise stones. Before Aunt Grace nodded to accept the gift, she spoke to Lily. Mary signed her words. "Do you want to go with Fox and be his wife? You need to understand that you will live with his tribe."

"More than anything in this world I want to go with Fox. I will be a good wife to him."

"I know you will, my sweet Lily." She looked at Fox. "Will you be good to my Lily and take care of her?"

"I would die for her," was his simple reply.

Aunt Grace nodded and pointed to the red cloth belt that Fox had chosen to wear that morning. She motioned for him to take it off then put the stones back in the bag and handed it to Mary. Fox took the belt off and handed it to Aunt Grace. No one knew what she was going to do but she called the family to come close. Everyone stood around Aunt Grace, Lily and Fox. She then placed Fox's hand on top of Lily's and wrapped the belt several times around their joined hands.

"I do this to show the joining of Lily and Fox as one. I give her to you, Fox, here in front of all these people. Go with God and be happy."

Lily threw her untied arm around Aunt Grace's neck and hugged her. She turned to Fox and hugged him. He returned the hug and slowly untied the red belt and put it in his shirt close to his heart, never taking his eyes off of Lily.

Aunt Grace said, "Bonita, you and Mary go help Lily pack what she needs. These friends want to go home."

Uncle Nicholas had witnessed all that had happened then suddenly disappeared. He returned about the same time that the girls came out of the house. He led a white horse with large black spots on its body and handed the reins to Fox. Fox tied Lily's bag on the horse and helped her mount. He led it to where his horse was and handed her the reins. Quickly, he jumped astride his own horse. Fox and Rand took the lead, one on each side of Lily and rode away from the boarding house.

Not being used to riding all day, the first two days were hard on Bonita and Lily. They were experienced riders but not to the extent of having to ride all day every day. Lily proved capable of doing her share of the work. The men enjoyed the girls taking the responsibility of preparing the morning and evening meals. On the second day, Aaron could feel tension in the group that he hadn't previously noticed.

"Something's not right, Bonita," he confided when they were alone at evening camp. "Is there some kind of trouble that you know about?"

"You noticed it too? I felt something was not right this morning, but it took me a while to figure it out."

"What is it? What did you figure out?"

"It's Lily and Fox."

"What about them? Fox has been real nice to her and is taking good care of her."

"Yes, I have seen that too. I think it is mostly Lily. We had a long talk earlier today when we stopped to rest the horses. That's why it took me so long to be ready to go. I had to write a lot of things on her slate because I did not know how to sign the words."

"What did you talk about?"

"About the ways of a man and woman after marriage. Aunt Grace talked to me about such things, but poor Lily didn't have anyone tell her how things should be. I think they are both afraid of each other."

"Oh, I didn't even think about that."

"I know but it is all right now, you will see. I told her what she needs to do."

"Oh? What did you tell her?"

"Aha! That is something you do not need to know. We women have our secrets."

"I don't like you having secrets from me."

"Don't worry, you will learn them soon enough."

"I hope you're right about those two. Where are they anyway?"

"Lily wanted to go the river before it got too late. She asked me if I would go with her. I told her no, her husband needed to go and protect her."

"You planned that, didn't you?"

"Well, yes, if you must know. Tomorrow should be better and I think the rest of the men will relax when those two can relax a little. It will all work out."

"You are very wise, my sweet wife."

"Thank you, husband. Bring me the coffee pot please. Gabriel is coming with the water and I want to get the coffee made."

It was amazing, the difference in the mood of the group the next day. Rand was his normal self being funny and teasing everyone. Lily smiled all day and Fox was even more attentive to her.

They left the main wagon road to make their evening camp the next day. Little Warrior brought in a young buck and they ate fresh meat that night. Aaron and Rand played some music on the guitar and harmonica and when Little Warrior and Fox tried to dance, Indian style, to the music everyone had a good laugh. They all were in good spirits when they headed for their beds.

Aaron snuggled up to Bonita and whispered in her ear. "Whatever you told Lily must have worked. The tension is gone and it's more like before. Did Lily say anything to you?"

"No, but when no one was looking, she smiled at me and signed thank you. See, I told you it would be all right."

"You were right and I say thank you too." Aaron kissed his wife and snuggled closer.

The night was peaceful but morning dawned with the sound of gunshots in the distance. Little Warrior was immediately on his feet. "It is not far away, we must be careful. Someone is in trouble and it sounds like it is in the direction of the wagon road."

"That's what I think, too," Rand agreed.

"What should we do?" Aaron asked. "If someone is in trouble maybe we could help."

Little Warrior shook Fox awake. "I will tell Fox what we heard. He will climb the tallest tree and see what is going on."

A few more shots sounded before Fox could get up and back down the tree. He told his brother what he saw. "Fox says there is a wagon train camped in a meadow along the wagon road. There are not very many wagons. He cannot tell what the shooting is about but it is not Indians attacking. He thinks someone is causing trouble for the wagon train."

"I'm going to go see what's going on," Aaron said. "It'll probably be over before I get there but I have to try. If we were in trouble I would hope someone would give us a hand."

"I'm going with you," Rand declared.

"I'll go too," Gabriel said.

Little Warrior looked at his friends. "We will all go. I will ask Fox to help the women pack up camp and follow at a distance. We must not put the women in danger."

"I agree. Let's go!" Aaron was already heading toward the horses.

"Please, be careful," Bonita said as she gave Aaron a hug.

"I will and you stay with Fox. He'll take care of you."

Bonita watched Aaron ride away with the others. Fox climbed the tree again and Lily was tying the last of the supplies on the pack horse. Bonita went to help and Lily hugged her and signed, "He will be all right."

Bonita looked again in the direction the men had gone. She nodded and quickly turned away so Lily wouldn't see the fear in her eyes.

Chapter 32

"**T**HIS IS CLOSE ENOUGH," Aaron said, halting the others. They tied their horses and crept to a thick stand of trees. Careful to stay out of sight, they peered through brush and around trunks at a bewildering sight. "Will you look at that," Aaron hissed. "The wagon train is getting robbed!"

In the center of the circled wagons, a group of men, women, and children, were held at gunpoint. Several bodies lay on the ground, apparently wounded. Women were crying and clutching their children while the wagons were being ransacked.

A gunman leaned out of a wagon, holding a box in his hand. "I found a money box, Ollie! Whoopee! This will make it worth the effort!"

A big man who had his gun trained on the men in the circle, answered, "Get a move on and check the other wagons! You too, Josh. We need to get out of here!"

Another gunman jumped off the back of a wagon. "Oh, all right, but I ain't found nothing worth a hoot."

Aaron motioned for his group to move back so they could talk. "Little Warrior, what do you think we should do?"

"These are bad men. I saw three bodies on the ground. They do not mind killing so we must not hesitate to kill them. Three men guard the group in the middle. We must take them out first. Two men search the wagons. One man is with their horses. Rand, you go that way." He pointed to the right. "Tall Shadow, you go to the other side. Gabriel, stay on this side. I will circle around to see if another man is with the horses. When the two men in the wagons come out, whoever is nearest will take care of them."

"How will we know when to start shooting?" Rand asked.

"I will give the war cry of my people. When you hear me yell, attack."

"How will we know it's you?"

"Do not worry, you will know. Be careful. Do not shoot each other or the people in the circle. We must go now." He retrieved his bow and arrows from his horse and disappeared into the trees.

"Be careful, you two," Aaron warned. "We don't have a doctor with us this time." He moved off toward his designated position. Finding heavy brush by the wheel of one of the wagons, he dropped to his belly and crawled until he had a good view of the outlaw on his side. A wounded man lay beside the wagon facing Aaron, and Aaron realized he wasn't dead. The man spotted Aaron and his eyes widened. Putting his finger to his lips, Aaron warned the man to be quiet. A faint smile played on the man's lips as he closed his eyes and seemed to relax.

Little Warrior's war cry rent the air, followed by several gunshots. Aaron hadn't hesitated. He fired his rifle and the outlaw he had in his sights collapsed in a heap. Simultaneously, Gabriel and Rand shot the other two outlaws who were guards. Chaos ensued. People scattered in all directions, shouting, cursing, and screaming.

Suddenly, the wagon master climbed on one of the wagon seats and shouted, "Quiet, everyone!" He shouted twice before the camp settled down. "Women, see to the wounded. Whoever is out there that helped us, please show yourselves."

Aaron, Rand, and Gabriel walked into the circle of wagons. Little Warrior came in behind them and a girl screamed, "*Indians!*"

"He's a friend!" Aaron called to the crowd. Then to Little Warrior, "Did we get them all?"

"No one was with the horses. The one in this wagon is dead. That is only four."

They glanced around, searching, then heard a horse galloping away. Aaron and Little Warrior realized the danger at the same time. "One of them got away, Little Warrior! Sounds like he's headed toward…."

Little Warrior was already racing toward his horse. Aaron followed, yelling at Rand and Gabriel, "Stay here! We have to get Fox and the girls!"

Rand stared after them for a moment then looked down at the wounded outlaw. "Well, Gabe, looks like we got left behind to guard this piece of trash." The outlaw wasn't hurt very bad but Rand wasn't taking any chances. He kept his rifle trained right on the man's chest. "Looks like we need to get you to practice with that rifle more often."

"Aw, I didn't do so bad," Gabriel protested. "He just twisted when he heard Little Warrior scream and I only put a crease in his ribs."

A young, blond girl approached. She glanced at Gabriel, then very deliberately looked Rand in the eyes. "Should I take care of this man?"

Rand stammered, caught off guard by the pretty girl. "I...I...don't... know. Well, I don't know if it would be safe for you to get close to him." He finally got his tongue to work properly.

Gabriel acknowledged the girl with a nod. "I think maybe I better do the doctorin'. If you can find me something to clean and wrap him up so he don't bleed no more, I'd be appreciatin' it."

"I'll go right away and find what you need," the girl said. "Probably a waste of bandages but maybe it'll stop him from bleeding to death. He needs to think about his bad ways for a while before someone takes him back to Fort Hall to hang."

Rand watched the girl walk away, all the while blowing out a big sigh. "Whew, wonder what's taking Aaron so long. Sure hope Fox and the ladies are safe." He caught Gabriel stifling a chuckle. "What?"

"My, oh my, she's a pretty one! All those blond curls and those pretty blue eyes sparkling just for you. Shore is a shame you goin to stay single. Be kinda nice to have a wife that pretty to look at all the time. Course, I know you ain't interested in no girl."

Rand huffed. "I didn't say I *wasn't* interested. I'm just not ready to get tied down to a wife yet." He glared at the wounded man on the ground.

"Mmm, here she comes with some of the men. Better watch yore self or we be looking for a preacher."

"Aw, shut up, Gabe!" Rand then turned his attention to the approaching men.

"We want to thank you for your help," the wagon master said. He shook their hands. "I'm Warren Thurston. We were in a bad way until you and your friends showed up. Two of our men are dead and one is wounded. He should pull through though."

"Glad we could be of help. I'm Rand Trinity and this is Gabriel Freeman. We were just in the right place at the right time to give you a hand."

"We appreciate it more than words can say. We're in a big jam now. One of the men that was killed was our guide and scout. Is anyone in your group able to guide us to Oregon?"

"I'm afraid not," Rand answered. "We're heading in the other direction."

Gabriel and the girl were wrapping a bandage around the thief's rib cage. She looked up. "Pa, we need to tie this man up. Will we be leaving today? We'll have to take time to bury Mr. Bradshaw and Mr. Simpson."

"No, Caroline, we'll stay here for at least today. I'll get the men together and talk about what we should do now that we lost our guide."

Caroline smiled sweetly at Rand. "Now that it's settling down, the women are starting to cook breakfast. I'd be pleased to cook for you and your friends. That is, if you're hungry."

"I'd surely appreciate it, Miss," Rand said. "I am mighty hungry."

"My stomach don't get along with all this killin, but I'd be glad for some coffee if it's no bother," Gabriel said.

The prisoner was hauled up and tied to a tree so everyone could keep an eye on him. Caroline took Rand and Gabriel to her wagon and introduced them to her younger sister. "This is Doreen, but we call her Dory. You men just sit anywhere and Dory and I will fix you some breakfast."

While the girls worked, Rand and Gabriel talked quietly. "Did you notice that man you shot didn't say a word, just glared at you with those hateful eyes of his."

Gabriel nodded. "Yeah, I seen it. I ain't goin to worry about him. I'm worrying about why it's taking Aaron and Little Warrior so long to get back here."

"I've been thinking the same thing. I haven't heard any gunfire so I hope that's good news. Even though Aaron told us to stay here, we'll stay put a while longer then we better go find them."

"I reckon that's what we should do all right."

Doreen brought them each a cup of coffee. Rand took his first sip and swallowed hard. He whispered behind his cup, "This is the *worst* coffee I ever tasted. I hope they can cook better than they can make coffee."

Gabriel took a sip. "Wouldn't count on that. Look over at the wagon across the way and you see Mr. Thurston eating his breakfast over *there*. Maybe he know something we don't."

Rand groaned. "What'll we do?"

"We eat what the girl be fixing and be grateful. Course, it wouldn't hurt none to be praying we live through whatever she is cooking for us. I seen her put a big slab of ham in that skillet. Can't mess up ham."

Gabriel was *wrong*.

Rand was handed a plate piled high with food. His first bite was proof. The bottom side of the ham was burnt so badly he could hardly swallow it. The scrambled eggs were hard and dry. Without complaint, Rand ate. Gabriel just smiled and drank the bitter coffee.

Caroline came around to check on them. "Are you sure you don't want to eat with your friend?" she asked Gabriel.

"Thank you, Miss Caroline, but I'm doing just fine. Maybe Rand, here, would like another plate of them eggs."

Rand answered quickly, "No, no, this is plenty for me. Besides, here comes Aaron and the others." He sidled up to Gabriel and elbowed him hard in the ribs. "What are you trying to do," he hissed. "See me die a slow death?"

Gabriel chuckled. "From the look on your face while you was eating, it might not be so slow."

"You're probably right. You'd think a girl her age could cook better than that."

"Some women jest don't got the knack for making a tasty meal."

Rand put his plate on the tailgate of the wagon. "Let's go find out what's going on with our bunch. I hope we can leave before too long."

"I take it you don't want to stay and let that pretty little gal fix you another meal?"

"You've got that right." Rand shuddered at the thought.

They hurried over to where Aaron was talking to the wagon master. He was telling Mr. Thurston that they were going to go on. "We're anxious to get past Fort Hall today, so we need to get going."

"Did you get that other no account thief?" someone asked.

"No, he was riding hard and fast," Aaron said. "I don't know if he'll try to come back and find out about his friends or not, but you'd best be on guard in case he does."

"What took you so long to get back here?" Rand asked.

"After Little Warrior and I decided it might take days to track that outlaw we had a hard time finding Fox and the girls. Fox hid their tracks so good even Little Warrior had a hard time finding his brother. Now that we're back are you two ready to go?"

"Yes, we're ready," Rand answered.

"Before you go," said Mr. Thurston, "I have a favor to ask. Your men are young but seem capable of handling themselves. Would you take the outlaw to Fort Hall and hand him over to the military there? You're only about half a day away from the fort by horseback and it would be good to get him away from here. We need to bury our dead today and put our camp in order. Tomorrow, a couple of our men will go back to the fort and see if they can find a guide or check with the wagon train that was just coming in when we left. We're thinking they probably would let us go on with them."

Aaron searched the faces of his friends and saw no negative responses. "I suppose we could handle that for you, Mr. Thurston."

"Good. We'll get their horses and belongings. You might as well take what the outlaws had. You're the ones who saved us from...who knows what."

"All right, Little Warrior's tribe could use the horses so we'll take them."

The lone surviving outlaw was tied on a horse and the group was ready to leave. At the last minute, the pretty Caroline ran up to Rand, handing him a flour sack. "I packed up the food that was left over. I thought maybe you and your friends would like to eat it later."

"Thank you, Caroline." Rand tried to smile convincingly. "That was very thoughtful of you."

Gabriel turned away so fast to hide his amusement, he almost stumbled.

Several miles down the trail, Rand stopped the group. "Everyone wait here. I have something I need to do." He pulled a small shovel off the pack horse, walked away from the hard packed wagon trail and started digging a hole.

"What in thunder are you doing, Rand?" Aaron asked.

"I'm saving your lives."

"What?" the whole group chorused.

"I'm saving your lives," Rand repeated.

Gabriel started laughing so hard, he almost fell off his horse, because he knew what Rand was going to bury. The outlaw who had not uttered a word, chuckled, for he, too, had watched Rand try to eat Caroline's cooking."

"What is he talking about?" Bonita asked. "Does anyone know?"

Rand dropped the sack that Caroline had given him in the hole and scooped dirt over it. He then turned to his friends. "I've decided what I want to do with my life. I want to be a peace officer. I hate seeing innocent people, like my pa, and those people back there on the wagon train, getting robbed and killed. There has to be good, strong men in this country who can make it safe for the decent people coming out here to live in peace. This is my first duty as a peace officer, to bury this sack of food, for it would surely be *murder* if anyone ate what that poor girl cooked. If I die on the way to Fort Hall, go back and hang that girl!"

"He shore be telling the truth," Gabriel said, shaking his head.

Rand tamped the dirt down good before he mounted his horse.

Chapter 33

"**I**'M SURE GLAD TO get rid of him." Rand was fussing about the time they'd spent in the military headquarters at Fort Hall. "I didn't think that General would ever quit asking us questions and let us go."

"He was just doing his job," Aaron said.

"I know, but by the time we answered all his questions and replenished our supplies it was late."

"Why you bein so grumpy, Rand?" Gabriel scolded. "Little Warrior said we'd be at the hot springs when we camp tonight. We can sure enough take us a bath and get all clean."

"Yeah, I'd like that. Maybe that'll cheer me up. I don't know what's bothering me today."

"You're just irritated you had to leave that pretty little blond gal this morning,"

Gabriel teased.

"She was pretty, wasn't she?" Rand was thoughtful a minute. "How old do you think she was?"

"Oh, maybe about fifteen or sixteen. How old are you, Rand? I heard you're about fourteen."

"No, I'm fifteen now."

That got Aaron's attention. "When did you turn fifteen, Rand? I didn't know you had a birthday."

"I almost forgot it myself. I turned fifteen on the day we left the boarding house. That would be June sixteenth."

"We'll have to celebrate at camp tonight," Aaron said.

"How are we going to do that?" Rand asked.

"I don't know right off, but Bonita and I will come up with something."

The rest of the day went by quickly. Aaron and Little Warrior pushed harder than usual to cover some distance. Camp that evening was in a beautiful spot. Everyone ate then took a turn in the hot springs. Relaxed and tired, the group sat around the campfire. Aaron was strumming his guitar when Bonita picked up a container that was covered with a cloth. She walked over to Rand, took off the cloth, and stuck the bowl under his nose. "Happy Birthday! It is not a cake but cookies are a treat. I got these when we were at Fort Hall and thought I would surprise everyone tonight. I did not know then about your birthday but it worked out perfectly."

"Mm, they sure smell good," Rand sniffed. "What kind are they?"

"Applesauce."

Rand took one of the cookies and started to take a big bite, then he stopped. "You sure that a girl named Caroline didn't make these?"

"I am sure. I bought them from a lady named Mrs. Paterson."

"All right, then here goes." He took a huge bite, closed his eyes, and moaned. "Oh, surely an angel just came from heaven made these."

Everyone laughed at his goofiness.

"Are you going to share them or eat the whole bowl by yourself?" Aaron asked.

"I guess if I have to, I'll share." Rand took a hand full of the apple-cinnamon cookies before he passed them to Lily and Fox.

"I have something I want to give you, Rand. It's from all of us. We talked about it and decided to give you this." Aaron pulled out a holster and pistol from a sack. "You're smart enough to figure out that we got these from one of the outlaws. This pistol looked like it was well taken care of. I don't know how much you meant it when you said you wanted to be a peace officer. But a good lawman needs to know how to handle a gun. These were used for evil purposes but I know you will only use them for good. Have you had any experience with a pistol?"

"Some. My pa let me practice a fast draw with his pistols once in a while." A solemn expression settled on his face as he checked out the holster and pistol. "Thanks, all of you. I'll do my best to never shame any of my friends and family with this pistol."

"That's good enough for me," Aaron said. "Gabriel, you can have your choice of the other three pistols. I bought a couple of boxes of shells for you too. They're in my saddle bag. Maybe Rand will teach you how to use a pistol. I'm not very good with one."

"Sure, Gabe, we'll work on it. When I get to be a lawman you can be my deputy."

"No, siree, for sure I ain't going to be no lawman."

"Hey, where are my cookies?" Rand demanded. "Did you all finish them off?"

"Fox and Lily have the bowl," said Bonita. "I am sure they did not eat all of them, there were several dozen cookies in that bowl."

"Someone get their attention and have them hand over the goods or I'll arrest them!" Rand scowled and patted his new holster and pistol backing up his warning.

Little Warrior got Fox's attention and signed Rand's threat. Lily giggled and threw up her hands in surrender. Fox followed her example, but when Rand reached for the bowl, they both grabbed one more cookie and laughed. It was the first time any of them had heard laughter from Fox. Bonita whispered in Aaron's ear, "He is a happy man. It is nice to hear him laugh."

After popping one whole cookie in his mouth, Rand tried on the holster. It was several sizes too large to fit on his slender hips. "Guess I'll have to cut some of the belt off and punch a couple of new holes."

"We can fix it in the morning, Rand. Let's all turn in. I want to get an early start in the morning. I feel like I've been traveling all my life and home is sounding mighty good." Aaron pulled Bonita to her feet and headed toward their bedroll.

Without another word everyone else made their way to their beds.

The next morning, the group decided they could make better time by staying on the wagon road. In the days that followed, friendships grew deeper. The kind of friendships that make life seem a little better no matter what you have to go through. They all were learning enough signs to include Lily and Fox in their conversations. Lily worked with Fox on his reading and writing while Bonita and Aaron helped Gabriel with his. Every chance he got, Rand practiced his fast draw.

One evening after stopping to make camp, Aaron saw Little Warrior sitting on a rock overlooking a meadow down below. He went to sit with him. "How you doing?"

"I am good. Two bull elk just walked through the meadow and into the trees. I was hoping to see them again. It is peaceful here. I like it very much."

"Yes, I love it up here. It makes me feel close to God."

"I have learned much from you, my friend."

"I don't know how you can say that. You have more knowledge about living out here than I'll ever know. There is a lot about you that I admire, Little Warrior."

"I do not speak of the things you talk about. I mean the things in here." Little Warrior touched the middle of his chest. "You are a strong man yet you have a kind, gentle heart. You live like you believe all the words you and Story Teller read from the black book. I think maybe you look a lot like this man Jesus who you say is God's son."

"That's about the nicest compliment you could give me, Little Warrior, but I'm a long way from being as good as Jesus Christ."

"I am not so sure about that. Little Warrior does know that walking with you makes me want to know your Jesus. When I get back to my people I think I will talk to Story Teller and pray like he tells us we need to pray."

"Why don't you pray now, Little Warrior? You don't have to have a preacher to pray and give your life to God. He will hear you wherever you are. Then you can tell Story Teller about it when you get back to your people."

The two friends were quiet for a spell.

"I'm going back now," said Aaron. "But think about what I said. God loves you and He will speak to you. God is spirit and that is how He'll talk to you. It's like a gentle voice speaking to your own spirit." Aaron walked away with a prayer on his lips for his friend.

Two days passed before they saw another person. It was late afternoon when they came to the cut-off to Salt Lake. A huge wagon train was at the intersection and seemed to be in total confusion. Wagons were moving helter-skelter, people were shouting and running hither and yon.

Aaron's group surveyed the activity for a bit then Aaron called to the nearest man passing by. "What's going on?"

"We're just splitting up," the man answered. "About forty wagons are leaving us here and heading to Salt Lake or California. The trail boss is over on the road if you want to talk to him. His name is Jeff Slaughter."

"Thanks, I'll do that." Aaron turned to Little Warrior. "Why don't you go with me and the rest can stay here and keep an eye on our horses."

They all dismounted to stretch their legs. Aaron and Little Warrior walked down the road where the trail boss was giving directions to several wagons. Bonita spotted a woman close by who had a baby in her arms. "Rand, I am going to go talk to that lady and see her baby. Will you hold on to Sugar for me?"

"Sure, but stay where I can see you."

Lily had her back to Bonita and didn't realize Bonita had walked away. She turned and saw that Bonita was talking to a young woman who had a beautiful baby. She tapped Fox on the shoulder and pointed to where Bonita was now holding the baby. Fox nodded his approval and Lily left to join Bonita.

She got about half way when a trio of young men yelled at her, "Hey, pretty girl, come over here and let's talk a minute!" They laughed and jabbed each other, pointing at Lily and acting like fools.

Of course Fox didn't hear them but Rand and Gabriel did and immediately tensed. They stared at the three trouble-makers. Fox couldn't hear what was said, but he *could* read the body language of his friends and knew something was wrong.

Oblivious to anything except Bonita and the baby, Lily kept walking.

The same one yelled again, "I'm talking to *you!* Hey, you stuck up thing! Think you're too good for me?"

Lily kept walking.

She was almost to Bonita when the man dashed over, grabbed her arm, and twisted it behind her back. Totally surprised, Lily screamed and tried to jerk away. In a flash, Fox was there pushing the man away. With a murderous glare he signed that the trouble makers had better leave.

The three agitators stared at Fox. "What's he doing with his hands, Jim? He looks plumb crazy."

"Probably is crazy. But the girl is right pretty. The question is, what's a crazy injun doing with a pretty girl?" The three snickered as they mimicked Fox's hand signs.

Lily huddled behind Fox, fear and confusion on her face. Bonita, Rand and Gabriel moved to stand beside Fox.

"Leave them alone," Rand said. "They're friends of mine and that's how they communicate. You need to leave us alone."

"Well, now, we've got us a red headed fire-cracker here who thinks he's something. I got news for *you*, fire-cracker. You don't tell *me* what to do."

"Listen, we don't want any trouble," Rand said calmly. "Why don't you all just back away and leave us be."

"Slug him, Chad!" The one called Jim said. "You shouldn't let this trash talk to you that way."

Gabriel's ire spilled over. "Who you be calling trash? The only trash I see is *you* and your two friends. *White* trash!"

Chad turned slightly as though to walk away. Instead, he shouted, "Get 'em boys!" and let loose a powerful swing, landing a blow to Rand's face. Bonita grabbed Lily's arm and pulled her away from the fracas.

Rand, taken completely by surprise, was thrown off balance and went down. Chad dropped on top of him landing another blow. He was older and bigger than Rand, but Rand's indignation was a powerful enabler and he managed to roll Chad off him. Total chaos took over as six bodies rolled, punched, and kicked, causing a dust cloud big enough to became the center of attention.

Aaron and Little Warrior heard someone yell, "Fight!"

The trail boss looked frustrated. "That's all I need now. Sorry, but I've got to go see what's going on."

"That's all right, we'll follow you over there," Aaron said.

The crowd made a path for their trail boss with Aaron and Little Warrior right behind him. Aaron stared for a full minute at the struggle on the ground, trying to make sense of it. He understood Rand, Gabriel, and Fox rolling on the ground, fighting three other men. But what was Lily and Bonita doing running around with sticks landing blows on the unsuspecting bullies? Intrigued, Aaron immediately thought to capture the scene on canvas. Well, he would tuck it away in his memory for later, anyway.

No one was attempting to put a stop to the fight. The trail boss waded in and bellowed like a mad bull, "You men help me put a stop to this!"

Aaron and Little Warrior were jarred into action. Aaron grabbed Rand and Little Warrior went for Fox while the trail boss separated Gabriel and his combatant. Just as Aaron managed to pull Rand back, Chad took advantage of the situation and hit Rand again in the face.

"Let go of me, Aaron, I ain't finished with him yet," Rand panted.

"Oh, yes you are!" Aaron said. Chad came at Rand again and Aaron lost his temper. He pushed Rand to the side and decked Chad, landing him on his back with blood spurting from a broken nose. "You get up and you'll be sorry," Aaron warned the now subdued Chad.

"You broke my nose! You...."

Chad tried to get up but the trail boss put his boot on Chad's chest and pushed him back on the ground. "You stay where you're at like the man said. Now, *someone* tell me what this is all about." Several people started talking at once, telling bits and pieces of the fight. The trail boss shouted, "Shut up! Is there anyone here who saw what happened and can tell it sensibly?"

"I can, Mr. Slaughter," said a man. "I saw the whole thing."

"Speak up, Mr. Lester," the trail boss demanded.

Mr. Lester, dressed in buckskins and calm as a sleeping baby down for a nap, spat on the ground and began his eye witness account. "That pretty, little black-headed girl was walking to meet her friend who was talking to Lorrie. Chad and his two friends saw her and were shouting crude remarks at her. She just ignored him and that made Chad mad. He assaulted the girl by grabbing her arm and twisting it behind her back. That young Indian jumped in and pushed Chad away from her. I think he was trying to tell him to go away. The red-headed man and the black man went to help the Indian. I heard the red-headed fellow tell Chad they didn't want any trouble. He told Chad twice to just go away but Chad tricked him and when he wasn't expecting it, hit him in the face, knocking him to the ground. That's what got these strangers all upset and...well...do you want a blow by blow account, or do you get the picture? If you want my opinion, Chad and his friends started it and got what they deserved."

"I didn't really want your opinion but thank you for telling me what happened." The trail boss located Aaron. "Mr. Trinity, are these men and girls with you?"

"Yes, sir, I'm proud to say they are all my friends."

"You seem to be a good man, Mr. Trinity, and I suppose they were just defending themselves and your women, but I don't have time to sort all this out. I'm asking you to take your people and leave."

"We'll be glad to leave, Mr. Slaughter," Aaron assured him.

As his bloody and battered bunch rode away they could hear the trail boss berating the bully. "Chad Banister, if you cause any more trouble we'll have a meeting and dish out some punishment you won't ever forget. I don't care if your father is the richest man here. Now get back to your wagon and don't let me see your face for at least a week."

It was almost dark when the group found a campsite. "Bonita, you and Lily gather up all the firewood you can find. We need to get a fire going for light and heat some water to get our wounded cleaned up."

Fox had a small fire going while the girls scoured the area for more wood. They returned to the fire, each with a stick in their hand. As usual, Rand lightened the mood with his silliness. "They've got sticks men, run for cover!"

Fox was the last to catch on and dove for the cover of a nearby rock. The girls stood by the fire, sticks in their hand and a confused look on their faces. Lily looked at her stick and started to giggle. They played hide and seek for a few minutes, the girls running around trying to find the boys. Finally, Rand called a truce. "Ouch! It hurts too much to laugh. We surrender. Have pity on us, you fearsome women warriors."

Bonita dropped her stick on the fire. "Come on in then, you mighty defenders. We will take care of our wounded."

Chapter 34

USIC FILLED THE CAMP the next morning. Harmonious? No. A chorus of groans and moans, so harsh and discordant it hurt the ears, jarred everyone out of their sleep.

Rand carried the melody. "Oh, no, no! Please have mercy on me! I think I would have been better off to die." That was the first verse.

"There's not a place on my body that doesn't hurt. Just leave me here, I can't move." That was the second verse, vocalized again by Rand.

Gabriel kicked in on the chorus. "I'm in a mess of misery. Bouncing up and down on that road out there shore will do me in."

Fox never made a sound, but moved very slowly as he headed out into the trees.

Aaron chuckled as he crawled out from under the blankets and pulled his boots on. He set about building a fire. Bonita sat up about the same time Rand pushed himself to a sitting position. She gasped, "Rand, your poor face!"

His hand moved unsteadily to touch his face. "Do I still *have* a face? Ow!"

Bonita put her shoes on and went to kneel by Rand. "Both your eyes are so swollen. Can you see me?"

"A little. Does it look like my nose is broken?"

"I don't think so but it bled some more in the night and you need to wash the blood off your face."

"That means I have to stand up and walk to the creek. Unless you want to bring me some water and heat it up for me."

"No you don't," Aaron scolded. "My wife isn't going to haul water for you. You can quit your whining and go to the creek by yourself."

"But, cousin, I can't even see where I'm going. I'll fall and break my neck and it'll be your fault."

Gabriel spoke up. "If you move slow you can hang on to me. Just don't make me talk. This busted lip is sore but the worst is my ribs. Feels like a mule done kicked me."

"That big guy that plowed into you was as big and ugly as a mule," Rand sympathized. "Where are you, Gabe?"

"I'm right here in front of you."

"Oh, yeah, I see you now. Do you suppose it would help if I just laid down in the creek and soaked my whole body? Let's go, Gabe."

Lily sat up and signed to Bonita. Bonita pointed in the direction Fox had gone and Lily left in that direction.

Aaron turned to Little Warrior. "Do you think we should stay here today and let them rest?"

"I do not think it will do much good. Tomorrow they will hurt more than today. Gabriel may have broken ribs. I saw the man he was fighting kick him on his side. It would be good to wrap something tight around his chest. We will let him decide."

"Good idea," Aaron agreed. "We can travel slow and stop early if they think they need to."

Fox came limping back to the fire with Lily holding his hand. He still had nothing to say, but it was obvious he was hurting and didn't want anyone to know just how bad it was. Little Warrior signed something to Fox and Fox signed back with a short gesture.

"What did you say to him?" Aaron asked.

"I told him to remember, Indians feel no pain."

"And what did he say back?"

"He told me to go jump in the creek."

Aaron turned his back so Fox couldn't see him laugh. His attempt to hide his mirth didn't work very well.

Little Warrior said, "Fox told me to tell *you* to go jump in the creek too."

Aaron laughed. "I do need to go wash up. You want to go with me, Bonita?"

"Yes, I will go. Let me get Rand's and Gabriel's bloody shirts. I will wash them out while we are there."

After eating and breaking camp they packed up and started out, taking it slow and easy. They had tended their wounds as best they could and had wrapped Gabriel's ribs. The cold creek water helped the swelling in Rand's eyes but they were still quite puffy. The next day, the three wounded ones felt worse. But by the third day they felt a big improvement. Also, on the third day it was obvious they were lower in elevation. The air was warmer and dryer. Midafternoon found the group on a hill looking in the far distance at a prairie with wide open spaces and blue skies.

"Think we can make it down to the tree line before the sun sets?" Aaron asked. Everyone was enthusiastic and wanted to try.

Fox pointed to an ancient oak and slid off his horse. "Fox will climb the tree and see if any danger is down below," Little Warrior told them.

"Good idea," said Aaron. "Anyone want to get down and stretch your legs?"

They all agreed to stay on their horses and leave as soon as Fox returned. He came back and signed to his brother. "He says there is a group of Indians at the foot of the mountains. They are traveling to the north very fast. We are in no danger."

"Let's go then," Aaron said. "Little Warrior, you take the lead. You can find a trail down better than I can."

"I have been here before," Little Warrior said. "There is a trail that will take us to a good place to camp. I have not been to this place in a long time but there is a spring that makes a pool with cold water."

Aaron, Rand, and Gabriel had some experience following their two Indian friends along trails that most white men wouldn't attempt. Lily was the one who had some misgivings. Fox saw her fear. He pulled her onto his horse, placing her in front of him. His arms around her was a security and seemed to have a calming effect.

Aaron asked Bonita, "Are you going to be all right with this?"

"I will be all right. Sugar doesn't excite very easy. I will follow Fox's horse and with you behind me, I'll be fine."

"Good girl. You stay calm and Sugar will probably be calm."

At a steady pace, Little Warrior wound his way down, what Aaron thought was, an old game trail. There were no problems but everyone heaved a collective sigh of relief when they realized they were at the place Little Warrior told them about.

"What a pretty place," Bonita said, excitedly. "Where shall we tie the horses?"

"The grass is good right here," Aaron said. "Let's tie them here and walk over to that clearing. I'm sure we can see our mountains from there."

Lily was excited and hurried ahead of the others, Fox in her wake. Reaching the opening, Fox put his arm around her and pointed to the distant mountains. They were so engrossed in signing to each other they couldn't hear and didn't see the danger they were in.

Bonita screamed and pointed just as Little Warrior dove between Fox and a huge rattlesnake. The reptile's fangs sank into Little Warrior's right cheek. He rolled away as quick as he could, but not quick enough to escape a second strike. The rattler bit him in the back of the neck. Before it could strike again, Gabriel, with his bare hand, grabbed the snake by the tail and flung it in the air away from everyone. Rand drew his pistol with lightning speed and the snake exploded in mid-air.

Seconds passed. The shock finally wore off and they all turned to Little Warrior. Fox knelt beside his brother as Lily cradled Little Warrior's head in her lap. Her eyes pleaded for someone to do something as she scanned the faces looking on. Then tears started running down her face.

Aaron and Bonita dropped to their knees opposite Fox. "What can we do?" Bonita's voice was frantic. "We need to do something! What can we do?"

Aaron felt desperation creeping into his soul. "God help us," he said aloud. "I've heard that you can make little cuts on the bite marks and suck the venom out, but I've never tried it before. I'll try anything if it will help," he said, pulling his knife from its sheath.

Little Warrior feebly grabbed his wrist. "No, it is too late. I can feel the poison already taking my life. You must leave this place now. There may be a den with many more here…My eyes cannot see good now."

"I've got to try and help you, Little Warrior," Aaron said.

"No, it is all right, my friend." He struggled to focus on Aaron's face. "I talked to your Jesus that night on the mountain. He is my Jesus now.

You were right. He spoke to my spirit and I will go to Him now. Will you see that Fox gets to Black Feather and Story Teller?"

"You know I will, my friend." Aaron felt like he couldn't breathe.

"Fox, Fox." Little Warrior weakly stretched his hand to his brother. Fox grabbed hold as the last of life was fading from the body of Little Warrior. "I am at peace. Tell him, Tall Shadow, I am at peace." He took one last breath, his hand went limp.

Fox signed something and looked at Aaron.

Bonita said, "Fox wants to know what Little Warrior just said."

"Tell him his brother wanted him to know he is at peace."

Right then those words didn't mean a whole lot to Fox. He sat numb for minutes as his friends mourned silently with him. Then Fox lifted his face to the sky and screamed, a cry of raw pain that rose to the heavens and echoed down through the prairie grass. A sound none of them would ever forget. Aaron wept openly. The others forgot their fear of looking weak and wept with him.

No one spoke for long minutes. Aaron thought about Little Warrior's warning that they might be close to a den of rattlesnakes. He got Lily's attention and asked for her slate, quickly wrote the warning and handed it to Fox and Lily. Fox turned his grief inward and nodded his understanding as he stood, pulling Lily up with him.

"Rand, take the women to the horses and get them ready to leave," Aaron said. "Keep that pistol ready in case there are other snakes around. Gabriel, go with him and bring back a blanket to wrap around Little Warrior. We're going to leave this place now. We'll help Fox with the burial in the morning. I don't know their customs, but he can tell us what to do."

Rand carefully watched for rattlers when he took the girls back to the horses. The men quickly secured Little Warrior's body to his horse and the group left without another word. Not really knowing where to go, Aaron rode down to the lower foothills toward the north. Just before night fall, he stopped at a trickle of a stream with a scattering of willows along the banks.

"This will do. Men, check the area before the girls dismount."

A somber bunch made camp, ate very little, all the while feeling gnawing grief at the loss of a good friend. Fox had them place his brother's body a short distance away from where the others planned to sleep.

Lily wrote on her slate to the others, "Fox says he will stay with his brother tonight. At first he didn't want me to stay with him, but now he says I can. I want to be close to my husband. We will build a fire to keep the wild animals away."

They nodded their understanding as Lily left to join Fox. Sleep did not come to any of them for a long time. Sitting around the fire, they quietly talked. Bonita sat by Aaron, leaning against his shoulder. "Why do people have to die?"

"I don't know, sweetheart. I really don't know. I've heard it said, it's because sin is in the world."

"I don't know a lot about such things," Gabriel said. "But I do know that we all got to die and that's just the truth of things. I seen too many die in my life time."

Rand shuddered. "What an awful way to go. I *hate* snakes! And, Gabe, you son-of-a-gun, you picked that snake up by the tail *with your bare hands* and slung it in the air! You've got *guts*, man!"

"What about you?" Gabriel said. "You shot that snake before it could hit the ground. Wish I could of seen you draw that pistol of yours but I was looking the other way. I'm just glad there weren't any more snakes up there."

"Oh, there were more," Rand said. "I saw two disappear in that pile of rocks close to where the big one was."

"Why didn't you shoot them?"

"They were gone too fast, didn't have a chance."

"I saw you draw," Aaron said. "You were *fast*, Rand. I've never seen anything like it. Don't go showing others how fast you are or they'll think they have to challenge you to see if they're faster."

"I'm not a show off, cousin. My pa taught me to understand the danger of using a gun in the wrong way and for the wrong reasons."

"I sure wish I could have known your father, Rand," Aaron said. "I'd dearly love to see my father and your father together. Wouldn't that be something?"

"Yeah, it would."

The camp was quiet for a long time. Bonita broke the silence. "Will we get home tomorrow, Aaron?"

"I don't know. It depends on how long it takes to bury Little Warrior. I don't want to rush Fox. If it doesn't take very long it's possible we could be there tomorrow night."

"Wouldn't that be wonderful?" Bonita sighed.

"Yes, it's going to be more than wonderful. Especially since you'll be there with me in our own little home. Try to sleep and dream of our home, my lovely Bonita. Actually, we all need to try and get some sleep. It will likely be a long day tomorrow."

Even though the mood was somber, Rand couldn't seem to keep himself from saying, "Is it going to be more than wonderful with me there with you, Aaron?"

"Of course, cousin, it will be more than wonderful with you there."

"What about me?" Gabriel sounded offended. "I'm wonderful, too."

"Yes, Gabe, it will be wonderful with you there too. Go to sleep, cousins."

Chapter 35

"WHAT ARE YOU DOING?" Bonita woke up to find that Aaron wasn't next to her. There was light enough that she spotted him sitting on the ground a few feet away.

"Reading Lily's slate. When I woke up, it was on the ground beside me."

"Oh, what does it say?"

"I'll read it to you. 'Fox says we will be back soon. He knows where he will bury his brother and says it is something he must do alone.' It's signed, Lily."

"Does that make you feel bad?" Bonita questioned.

"No, not really. They have their ways of doing things and we need to respect that." He picked up his sketch pad and began drawing.

Bonita, always curious, asked, "What are you doing now? Is that a new picture?"

"It's a sketch I made on our way to find you. I thought I might touch it up and give it to Fox."

"Oh, can I look?"

"In a few minutes. I'll want your opinion about whether I should give it to Fox or not."

"I will be glad to give you my opinion. You are a good man, Aaron Trinity. I love you so much it hurts."

"I love you too, sweetheart."

"All right, that's enough! Cut the mushy stuff," Rand grumbled from under his blanket.

"A husband and wife can be mushy if they want to," Bonita declared. "Someday you will see. You will find a pretty girl to be your wife and she will fix your breakfast of burnt fried ham, bitter coffee, and hard, scrambled eggs. Then you will be mushy and tell her you love her, even if she can't cook."

Gabriel chuckled at Bonita's teasing. "I decided I'm going to go courting that pretty CeCe girl. She's a fine cook. Good cooking is a comfort to a man."

"There, that should do it," Aaron said. "You can come and look now, Bonita."

She studied the sketch a few moments. It was of Fox and Little Warrior on their horses in the deep forests. Fox was in the forefront, Little Warrior was behind but slightly higher, seeming to watch over his younger brother. "It is perfect. I think Fox would be very happy to have this picture."

"All right, but is it too soon to give it to him? Should I wait a while?"

"I don't know about that," Bonita said

"Well, how would you feel if someone you loved died and the next day a friend gave you a drawing of that person?"

Bonita thought a moment. "I would treasure it for the rest of my life. Sometimes I think of my mama and papa and wish I had a picture of them. Their faces are not clear in my mind anymore."

"I'm sorry. I didn't mean to make you feel bad."

"She's right, Aaron," said Rand. "I wish I had a picture of my pa. Especially right after he died and I was in that prison hospital."

"What do you think, Gabe?" Aaron asked.

"I figure it would be a nice thing to do. He can always put it away and look at it later."

"All right, then. I'll give it to him when they get back."

Putting her thoughts and feelings aside, Bonita asked, "Is anyone hungry? No one felt like eating last night, and now I am starting to get hungry."

"I am," Rand and Gabriel said at the same time.

Bonita went for water and put on a pot of coffee. The aroma got everyone moving and helping with morning chores while she cooked.

"Come and eat. It is not fancy but it will fill you up. If we do not get home today we will have to do without coffee in the morning. Our food supplies are really low."

Aaron heard the approach of horses and stood up to investigate. "Fox and Lily are coming. They didn't take very long so we just might make it home today."

"That sounds good to me," Rand said. "I can already taste those hot biscuits Carmen makes. With butter slathered all over and a gob of peach jelly topping them off, a man could feel like he was in heaven."

"You do love your food, Rand," Aaron commented.

"Of course! I'm just a growing boy."

Everyone grew quiet when Fox and Lily joined them at the fire. Lily signed and spoke at the same time, "It is done. We hurried back so we can leave soon. Fox thinks I am getting tired and need to rest a few days. I tried to tell him that I'm all right, but he says he can tell because my eyes are tired."

Bonita signed back to Lily, "Fox is right, Lily. We are all tired and need good food and rest. Our trip is almost over now, we are almost home."

Lily smiled. "That makes me very happy."

"How did things go?" Bonita asked.

"It was hard. Fox saw a small cave yesterday in a pretty spot. It isn't very far from here. I watched the horses and let him have time alone with his brother. He says he is ready now to go on."

"Aaron has something to give to Fox," Bonita said.

"What is it, Aaron?" Lily asked.

Fox had been watching Lily sign and turned his attention to Aaron with a questioning look on his face. Aaron handed his sketch pad to him. Fox took it, quietly studying the picture. He looked up at Aaron.

"Do you want?" was all Aaron knew how to sign.

Without hesitation, Fox nodded. Aaron carefully tore the picture out of the sketch pad and handed it to Fox. He handled it like a valuable treasure and carefully folded and slipped it in his buckskin shirt. He started signing but Aaron couldn't keep up. "What's he saying, Bonita?"

"He is thanking you for the picture. He will keep it always. He hopes to be your friend like his brother was."

"Tell him he already is my friend and more. I think of Lily and Fox as part of my family."

Lily smiled and got plates for her and Fox. Bonita noticed neither one of them ate very much. Nothing went to waste though. Rand and Gabriel finished what was left. "Well, the food is gone. Let's get packed up and go home." Aaron suggested. No one had to be told twice and they were soon headed straight east across the prairie.

By noon, they were on the banks of the Sweetwater River. In the shade of cottonwood trees, they watered and rested the horses. Aaron started digging through his saddle bags. "What are you looking for?" Bonita asked.

"For my bible," he answered, impatient.

"It is in the other side. I saw you put it there last night."

"Thanks. There's a scripture I've been thinking about. I think it's in John." Aaron flipped through the pages of his bible and finally found what he was looking for. "Here it is." He began to read, 'Greater love hath no man than this, that a man lay down his life for his friends.' That's what Jesus did for us. He laid down his life so we could be in heaven with him. I can't seem to get that verse out of my mind. I keep thinking of Little Warrior and how he threw himself in front of that snake so his brother, and really, all of us, would be safe. I want to share that verse with Fox but I'm not sure how."

"Do you want to know what I think?" Bonita asked.

"I always want to know what you think."

"When we have been married many years, I will remind you of that. But, I think you should write a letter to Fox. You will have to print it so he can read it himself. He is learning fast how to read. It will be like the picture, something he can read and look at for a long time. You are smart and will know how to write down good words."

Aaron grabbed Bonita's wrist and pulled her close. "Come here and give me a hug. You are the smart one in the family. I think that's a good idea."

Bonita smiled, knowingly. "I will remind you of that, too."

"There you go again!" Rand interrupted. "Can't you two wait until you're alone for all the hugging and kissing?"

"Well, cousin, we *were* alone until you showed up."

"I think we're ready to move on," Rand said. "The horses seem to know we are close to home and they want some good feed and rest, too."

"I wasn't aware you knew how to read a horse's mind, but I'm sure you're right."

As they trekked across the prairie, they could see cattle dotting the landscape. Aaron called to the others as they passed a large herd grazing on tall grass, "Those are Swanson beef. We're almost home!"

An hour later, Bonita pointed up the hillside. "There is the Double S Ranch."

"We made good time," Aaron said. "We'll have to stop, and at least say hi before we go up the mountain trail."

They pulled up in front of the Swanson ranch as Calli Swanson and Fawn greeted them on the porch. Seth Swanson came around the side of the house. "Man, is it good to see you, Aaron! Hi, Rand, Gabriel. We've all been wondering when you'd get back here. I see you brought your girl back with you."

"I brought my *wife* back with me," Aaron grinned.

"Congratulations! Bonita, we're glad you're here and part of our big family on this mountain."

"Thank you. It is good to be back, and to be home."

"Please, get down off those horses and come inside. I'll fix something to eat or drink," Mrs. Swanson invited them.

"I hope you won't think we're rude," Aaron said. "But we'd really like to go on home. We just wanted to stop and say hello."

"Not rude at all. I understand. But before you go, I think you have a new friend with you?"

"I'm sorry. Yes, we do have a new friend. Her name is Lily. You know Fox, don't you?"

"Why, yes. He's Little Warrior's brother," Seth answered.

"That's right. Lily and Fox are both deaf. We can tell you all about them later, but Fox has taken Lily to be his wife. They make a great couple."

"For sure I want to know all about that. We can visit more tomorrow. Remember, our Independence Day celebration is tomorrow. Everyone is coming here right after lunch. The men have planned races and a rodeo. Then in the evening, we'll go to the High Meadows for a bonfire, music and dancing." Bonita managed to get across to Fox and Lily what was being said. Mrs. Swanson continued, "Bonita, please tell Lily we welcome her and I'll talk more to her tomorrow."

Lily smiled and nodded in Calli's direction.

"I guess we'll see you tomorrow then," Mr. Swanson said.

"You sure will. I've got a lot of stories to tell."

"We'll want to hear every one of them too. Bye, until tomorrow."

The horses seemed slow and tired. Aaron took it easy going up the mountain but excitement built so strong in his heart he thought he might burst before they got to the first meadow. Aaron stopped and drank in the sight of horses in the pastures, the house and barns. The colorful hollyhocks that he'd planted along the fences were blooming. He noticed the tent was still up at the back of the meadow. "Home! Let's go get a biscuit with some peach jelly, Rand!"

Rand kicked his horse into action and raced up the lane yelling, "Yahoo!"

Aaron followed his example while the rest rode in, restrained, but with smiles. Family came from all directions to greet them. Even Prince barked furiously at all the commotion until Maxi made him be quiet. Bonita dismounted and went to kneel in front of Prince. She held out her hand to him. "Come, Prince. Let us get reacquainted." The dog cautiously sniffed her hand, then licked it a couple of times before he joyously pounced on her.

Michael, Cassie, and their kids came running from the back of the house. Paul came out of the barn and grabbed Aaron in a big bear hug. "I'll run and get your dad. They're at their cabin."

"Wait, Paul, I'd like to go and surprise them, myself."

"All right. It'll be a good surprise too. Who do you have with you?"

"Well, you know Rand and Gabriel. The two standing together is Fox, you should know him, and his wife, Lily. This beautiful woman," he said, pulling her up to stand beside him, "is Mrs. Aaron Trinity, my wife. You all know her as Bonita."

Maxi hugged Bonita again. "It's so good to have you back here where you belong. After you surprise Scott and Mama, all of you come on back here. We'll put some food on the table and have a good visit."

"Leave your horses at the fence," Paul said. "I'll take care of them and turn them loose in one of the pastures. Michael can help me until you get back."

"Thanks, Paul. We won't be long. Our horses need some special treatment tonight so I'll be back pretty soon."

Aaron motioned to the others to follow him. Memories flooded his mind as he led them to the cabin. He wondered if Fox was remembering all the times he had spent with his brother in these mountains. He knew they all would sorely miss Little Warrior and his friendship and influence.

Aaron turned and signaled for the others to be quiet as they made their way to the door. Before knocking, they listened to the girls giggling about something. Aaron knocked on the door and waited.

"The door's unlocked, come on in." It was his dad's voice.

Aaron grinned to himself and knocked again. In seconds the door swung open. "Aaron!" His father grabbed him and hugged so tight, Aaron had to fight to breathe.

"Hi, Dad, Mama, I'm home!"

Scott finally released Aaron and turned to Rand and Gabriel, hugging them both.

Carmen ran to the door and pulled Aaron into her arms, then spotted Bonita. Tears started to flow as she grabbed Bonita and held on for a long hug. Both women were crying when she pulled away. "I'm so glad Aaron found you and brought you back home where you belong." She then noticed Lily and Fox standing quietly watching the happy reunion. "Aaron, you've brought me some more children."

"They're not really children, Mama, but they could sure use a mother right now."

Without hesitation, Carmen threw her arms around Lily and gave her a hug that broke a dam of tears in the pretty, little lady. "Are you all right, dear?" she asked, pulling away.

"Mama, this is Fox and his wife, Lily. They are both deaf," Aaron explained.

Carmen looked perplexed. "So what. I don't care if they are deaf or pickled in brine. I have upset her and I want to know why."

Bonita signed to Lily, "She wants to know why you are crying."

Lily tearfully signed and voiced, "You look like my mama. She was beautiful, just like you."

"Her mama died when she was a young girl," Bonita explained.

"Tell her I'm sorry about her mama. And if she ever needs a mother's love to find me. I have a lot of love to give all my children." She hugged Lily again."

All of a sudden, Carmen threw up her hands and exclaimed, "Oh, the biscuits! I'm going to burn the biscuits!" She hurriedly hugged a surprised Fox then Gabriel, then turned to Rand.

"Please don't burn the biscuits," Rand pleaded. "I'll give you all the hugs you want, just take care of the biscuits *first!*"

Chapter 36

HERE WERE ALREADY SEVERAL tables with benches set up in the backyard of the main house, in preparation for the Independence Day Celebration. Rather than try and crowd into the house, the family gathered at one of the tables outside. Everyone was seated and automatically looked at Scott. As the oldest in the family, it was expected that he would take the lead.

"We need to start a tradition of respect for our individual homes," Scott began. "This is Paul's home where we're gathered and he should take the lead. When you come to my house I will take that responsibility. Aaron will be making his own home soon and he'll do the same. Paul, you take over."

Surprise registered on Paul's face, but he stood and gazed around the table. "You have a good idea, Scott, and I agree. We should respect the home we gather in. Before we pray, I want to say I'm glad Aaron and Bonita are back with us. As far as I'm concerned, Rand and Gabriel are part of our family as long as they want to be." He looked down the table at his mother who had made sure she sat beside Lily and Fox. "It looks like my sweet mama has adopted two more and because of that, Fox and Lily are part of our family too." Paul noticed Bonita trying to write on a small slate to let Fox and Lily know what was being said. He quit talking so she could catch up. "Let's pray and eat now."

After the prayer, the family got down to the business of eating. Toward the end of the meal, Scott, who was sitting across from Rand, looked at him thoughtfully. "Rand, you have a lot of nasty looking bruises on your face. I figure from the bluish green color they're several days old. Did your horse throw you on your head?"

Gabriel snickered and Rand elbowed him in the ribs. "Ouch!" he muttered. "I'm still mighty sore there, cousin. You do that again and I'll get Bonita to take a stick after you!"

Aaron and his traveling companions broke out in laughter. Scott said, "All right, I know there's a story here and I want to hear it."

"Go ahead, Rand," said Gabriel. "Tell all these good people how your face got such a purty color and how I came to save you and got busted ribs and a split lip."

"Aw, come on, Gabe," Rand said. "You got bruises on you, too. They just can't see them."

"Out with it, Rand," Scott insisted. "Tell us your story."

"It's really Lily and Fox's story," Rand admitted. "Come on, Lily and Fox. Let's *show* them what happened."

Reluctantly, Lily got up and went to stand by Rand. Fox followed but was uncertain as to what was happening. He watched carefully. Rand set up the scene then took Lily's arm. "There were two other slow-learning men with this one, so it was three against three. One idiot twisted Lily's arm like this." He demonstrated and immediately, Fox understood, playing his part by shoving Rand away from Lily. "Fox was trying to tell the guy to go away, but the guy didn't take the hint. So Gabe and I sashayed over and politely told him to go away and leave us alone. He was kinda hard-headed and didn't take to our suggestion, tricked me and acted like he was leaving but turned back and slugged me in the face, knocking me down. "I don't rightly remember all that happened after that but I do know I was about to get the life choked out of me when a sweet angel came to my rescue." Rand fell to the ground, pretending someone was on top of him choking the life out of him. Fox pretended to be wrestling with a man.

Scott asked, "What were you doing, Gabe?"

"I was down on the ground in a cloud of dust, trying to keep the biggest of them from pounding me in the ground."

Lily took her cue and picked up an imaginary stick and started whaling on the three imaginary men that were fighting Rand, Fox and Gabriel. Bonita jumped up and played her part by picking up an imaginary stick and helping Lily with the whaling.

Maxi laughed with all the others at the role playing, then asked, "Where were Aaron and Little Warrior?"

Rand answered, "They were off talking to the wagon master. Tell them what you did, Aaron, when you saw what was happening."

"When I got to the fight, it took me a minute to realize what was going on, and that I *knew* three of the men in that cloud of dust. The trail boss ordered the men to stop fighting so I pulled Rand off the one who had started the whole fracas."

"Yea, he was holding me back from finishing off that troublemaker when that skunk hit me again and I got this." Rand pointed to his eye which still had visible bruises. "But, he got his due when my cousin here, lost it and slugged the guy. It broke his nose and blood went everywhere!"

"What did Little Warrior do?" someone asked.

"He was having a terrible time keeping Fox from killing his man. The guy had drawn a knife and was going to stick Fox with it."

Somehow, Aaron knew what was coming next. His dad asked the question he dreaded the most. "Where is Little Warrior, anyway?"

Bonita let Fox and Lily know that they were asking about Little Warrior. Fox put his arm around Lily, took her back to the bench and nodded at Aaron, giving his permission to tell about Little Warrior's death.

The group was somber as they listened to the story of how Little Warrior had sacrificed his life by throwing himself between Fox and the snake.

Rosa was asleep on Carmen's lap and Maria was almost asleep on Scott's. Little Michael was getting fussy but Daniel and Katie were listening with wide eyes about the rattlesnake. Katie told everyone, *"Bad snake.* Run away *fast!"*

Paul knew it was time to end the evening. "Yes, Katie, a rattlesnake is a bad snake and you should run away fast."

"We saw a rattlesnake one day when we came here. My dad killed it and told us what to do if we see one again." Daniel looked proud when he told his part of the story.

"Let's hope you never see one again, Daniel." Paul changed the subject. "It's getting late and we need to figure out where everyone is going to sleep."

"I want Lily and Fox to stay at our cabin," Carmen quickly said. "They can have the girls' bed and I'll make a pallet on the floor by the fireplace for them to sleep."

Fox seemed to realize that Carmen was a comfort to his wife and agreed when he was told where they were to sleep. Rand and Gabriel chose the loft in the barn. They were told there was enough hay left to make a comfortable bed. That left the tent for Aaron and Bonita. Michael and Cassie had taken up the spare bedroom in the main house. Katie was sleeping on the couch and Daniel had been sleeping in Aaron's old bed in the loft.

"Can I sleep with my cousin's?" Daniel begged. "Please, can I?"

Cassie and Michael had no problem giving Daniel permission to sleep in the hay loft with Gabriel and Rand. "If you're going to sleep in the barn with us, cousin, you better hurry and get your blanket," Rand encouraged. "Us cousins have a lot of private talking to do."

"Michael had the last word before everyone went in different directions. "Rand, Gabriel, I can't tell you how much Cassie and I have missed you two. Of course, Daniel missed you most of all, and I need to tell you there will be a *wolf* sleeping with you tonight."

Aaron woke up and slipped out of the tent early, letting Bonita sleep. He went to the cabin and found his dad sitting out on the steps drinking a cup of coffee. "Morning, Dad. Is everyone still asleep?"

"No, Carmen is over at the main house talking to Maxi about all the goings-on today. Fox was up early and left for a while. I don't think he's used to sleeping in a house. He came back a short time ago and went back to the room they're sleeping in. Haven't seen him since."

"He's a good man, Dad," Aaron said.

"Stay here and I'll slip in and get you a cup of coffee. It's a little weak since we're having a hard time getting coffee because of the war. Carmen's trying to make it last as long as she can. I'll be back in a minute."

Father and son sat comfortably in silence for a while, drinking their coffee. "I need to make a report to the family about what I've done with the gold you trusted me with."

"That would be good, but we pretty much have it figured out what you've done. You have our whole hearted approval. You're a good representative for the family."

"I'm glad you think so." He was quiet for moments. "Dad?"

"What is it? Is something bothering you?"

"I have one more trip to make and probably should go tomorrow."

"Where is it you need to go?"

"To find Black Feather and the Arapaho tribe. I promised Little Warrior before he died that I would get Fox and Lily back with the tribe."

"Sure was sorry to hear about Little Warrior. I know you liked him."

"Yeah, he was a good man. We got pretty close on the way to find Bonita."

"Do you feel responsible for his death?"

"How did you know?"

"When I was in the military and had to take out the troops, the responsibility for the men was heavy on my shoulders. When one of them got hurt or killed, I'd lay awake at night trying to figure out if I could have done something different to keep them safe. It's hard but you have to learn to put most of it out of your mind and if you did make a mistake in judgment, you'll know not to do it again. No one is perfect and some things you have to give to God. As far as you having to make another trip, you can put that out of your mind right now. Black Feather and the Arapaho people will be here for our Independence Day celebration today."

"All right! That's a relief."

"Were you the one that made the suggestion for Mack to start a ranch?"

"Yes, it was me. Hope it was a good one."

"I think it was a wonderful suggestion. Mack and Black Feather talked to Justin and Seth about the idea. Justin helped them find an ideal place. It's on the other side of the Sweetwater. That will be the boundary between the Swanson ranch and Mack's ranch. It's a beautiful place in the foothills. Close to the head of the Sweetwater is where they will build the ranch. Black Feather chose a place up higher for the tribe's village. It's quite isolated and hard to find. Did you give them the gold to start their own herd?"

"Yes. When the idea came to me about Mack starting the ranch for them, it just seemed the right thing to do."

"You did good, Aaron. I can't tell you how proud I am of you. Carmen has taken a liking to Lily. The tribe will be closer where they are going to build than their old village so she will be able to be a mother to little Lily. She's sure a beautiful girl. Actually, her and Fox make a perfect pair. I've never seen an Indian man pay so much attention to his wife, as he does. He watches her in a protective way all the time."

"I've noticed that too. With his handicap of not being able to hear, I'm sure her safety is heavier on him than what most men feel."

"Oh, by-the-way," Scott said. "Did anyone tell you that Margaret is here?"

"Margaret? Here on the meadow?"

"No, she's down at the Paradise. We left word at the Trading Post that anyone who wanted to come from their ranch was invited. Let me see, there is Brian Chandler, Margaret, and one of the hands, I think his name is Dillon."

"You don't say. Dillon is here with Margaret."

"Yes, I think he's interested in her."

"I know he's in love with her. If she's smart she'll let him catch her too."

"There are a few others with them. I think two other ranch hands and a black girl. I don't remember her name."

Aaron laughed and slapped his leg. "CeCe is here! Wait till I tell Gabe. We may see some sparks fly today for our celebration."

A commotion got Aaron's and his dad's attention. When the object of the commotion came into view they saw Daniel. He had a young wolf pup walking beside him. Rand and Gabriel were right behind the boy and his dog. "Is that what Michael meant last night when he said there would be a wolf sleeping with Gabe and Rand?"

"Yep, that's what he meant."

"Where did he get the wolf pup?"

"From Talker."

"Talker? You mean you saw Talker?"

"I didn't, but Daniel and Michael did. I'll have to tell you about it later. I see Carmen coming up the trail and it sounds like the girls are awake. That means breakfast is about to be prepared. You hungry?"

"Yes, I'm really hungry for the first time in a couple of days. I need to go get Bonita. I left her sleeping."

"All right, but get back here quick. We're going to need all our strength to get through this day. Brian and his hand, Dillon, have brought a couple of horses with them. They say they're going to beat Diablo in the horse races."

"That's a race I don't want to miss."

Chapter 37

*A*T THE SWANSON RANCH the men in charge of the festivities met in the front room of the house. Seth and Marty Swanson, and Justin Myers were responsible for the rodeo. Paul Miles arranged the horse races, and Scott Trinity and Travis Buchannon were to set up the evening bonfire at the High Meadows.

"Our plans are ready for the rodeo," Seth said. "Are you ready for the horse races, Paul?"

"I'm ready."

"Travis, Scott, how are things going with you?"

"Well, there's been a change of plans," Scott said. "Aaron has a surprise for everyone so don't let this out yet. I'm going to have to tell you men because I'll need your help to pull it off. Remember the two crates of Aaron's we picked up in Fort Laramie? The larger one had Aaron's art supplies and his new guitar. The smaller one is fireworks."

"Wow! We've never had fireworks before," Marty said. "That'll be great."

"You're right, it will be a lot of fun, but there could be problems."

Seth asked, "Like what?"

"Like where to set the fireworks off and safety issues. Aaron and I were checking them out last night and they came with warnings about safety inside the boxes. If you don't mind, Seth, we'll keep the celebration here all day. The races and rodeo are here and probably the best place to set the fireworks off is right down in front of your house. We can get them ready while everyone is enjoying the music out back after supper. Almost all of your cattle's off toward the Sweetwater. We'll need to watch the other animals, since the loud noise might upset them. I'll have my boys fill barrels with water and take them down the hill on one of the wagons. We can station them in different places to watch for any cinders that might spark a fire. If we're careful, it can be quite a fun time. Well, what do you think?"

The men talked out all the problems they thought might crop up and agreed they would not tell the women and children about the fireworks. Then they went their separate ways to make sure everything was ready.

In the back yard at the Swanson's home, the women were watching the children and preparing the food. "Do you think we're going to have enough food, Calli?" Judith Buchanan asked.

"Good grief, Judith, we've got more food around here than I've ever seen in one place. I think there will be plenty for the whole day."

"Carmen, how are you making out with all the people up at your place?"

"We are doing great! It's just so good to have Aaron and Bonita back. Maxi and Cassie are like sisters now. And we all love Maxi's brother, Michael. He's a wonderful father to Daniel and Katie. The one that worries me, though, is my new daughter, Lily."

"You adopted another one, huh?" Callie said.

"Yes, and I know you and Judith would do the same. Her mother died when she was young from a sickness in the gold camps where they lived. Not just her mother, but all of her family died, except for Lily and her sister, Mary. That was when Lily lost her hearing. Bonita's aunt took the two girls and raised them. When I first met little Lily, I gave her a hug and she burst out crying. She said I look like her mother. It broke my heart. Lily and Fox fell in love and she left everything and everyone she knew to join his people and be his wife. She's a brave girl. I hope we can all help her adjust to her new life."

"Isn't that what we always do?" Callie said.

"Of course it is. You two started with me when I first came to the Double S Ranch."

Callie reached over and patted Carmen's arm. "I know we are close in age, Carmen, but I have loved you as much as I could have loved my very own daughter."

Suddenly, Justin's voice sounded loud and clear from the corner of the house, "We're starting the games, ladies. Better come on out front, you won't want to miss any of the excitement!"

Paul was just getting the horse races started. He had to add a couple more races because every man and boy there wanted to race. Daniel was put out with his mother when she told him he couldn't race Patches this year, but maybe next year. The winners of the four races were to compete a final time to see who had the fastest horse. A young Arapaho boy called Black Horse, won the race for boys between twelve and eighteen years of age. Brian Chandler won the first race for men. Paul, on Diablo, won the second race, and much to Margaret Chandler's delight, Dillon won the last men's race.

A short intermission gave the horses a short rest before the final race. Finally, Paul called time for the last big race to begin. The four winners, including himself, lined up at the starting line and the cheering began. No one could tell who was cheering for who. The starting gun sounded and the horses took off. All four men rode hard and with skill. They knew their horses and loved a challenge. Paul was behind and it looked like he might lose, but as usual, with a final burst of energy, Diablo pulled ahead and won. He told Maxi, later, that he couldn't let the others win, he had to keep up his reputation for the sake of the High Meadows Horse Ranch.

The competition between the men was almost brutal, but when Paul called that it was time for the ladies to race, everyone was about to see that women could be just as fierce. "All right, ladies, to the starting line!"

Judith gasped when she saw Angel riding down the hill with three others. "I didn't know Angel was going to race. And isn't that Lily, the deaf girl?"

Maxi smiled. "Yes, Angel wanted to race that new horse she's taken a liking to. She's been riding him a lot and thinks she can win. She'll probably start teaching Charity to ride, and put her on Raven. Lily had a hard time convincing Fox to let her race. That girl may be small and look fragile but she's got spunk. She won Fox over when she told him she wanted to ride Little Warrior's horse in the race to honor him. Of course, you recognize Margaret Chandler and the other girl is from the Arapaho tribe. Black Feather wouldn't let Sky Flower race. He told her his children needed a mother who lives another day to take care of them."

"Well, this is going to be one exciting race," Carmen said. "Look at Fox. He's down at the finish line. I wonder if he thinks he'll have to pick Lily up off the ground."

"There they go!" Maxi yelled.

The girls weren't rough riders like the men, but they rode with skill and determination. About halfway through the race, the cheering settled to a dull roar. Mr. Swanson could be heard shouting to Scott, "Would you look at that girl go! They'll never catch her!" His other comments were drowned out by thunderous applause and cheers, as little Lilly flew over the finish line, way ahead of the other girls.

"As I live and breathe," said Judith Meyers. "We'll have to put a rock on Fox's head or he'll float clear off the earth. What a precious sight!"

Lily slowed her horse and rode over to where Fox waited and he helped her down. He looked at all the people cheering for his new wife who had just honored his brother. Without hesitating, he took her in his arms and kissed her, right there in front of everyone.

"I didn't know Indians kissed their women like that," said Calli.

"Oh, Calli, he's a man like any other man," Carmen told her friend, with a gleam in her eye. "Besides, maybe Lily taught him how Mexican girls kiss. We know how to keep our men happy."

The women who heard that had a good laugh, but it didn't last long.

"Goodness, it's time to eat. Help everyone!" Callie said. "There's food in the spring house, the pantry, the kitchen, the front room, and even a couple of pies in my bedroom."

The food was a hit, as it always was and always will be. Much later, the rodeo started and the crowd lined the fences of the corrals. The men were anxious to show off their skills and daring feats. Martin Black Hawk Swanson, who adored his grandpa Swanson, was on his grandpa's shoulders when they let loose the first bull of the day. Marty volunteered to be the first rider. Little Martin cheered with all his might for his father atop the bucking bull. Marty made a good showing but had to wait and see if any other riders stayed on their bull longer than he had. Two ranch hands each rode a bull but no one else was courageous enough to try.

One bull rider was from the Chandler ranch. He gave the crowd a scare when his bull threw him and stomped on his upper leg. A couple of brave cowboys ran in and distracted the enraged bull while the rider was dragged out of harm's way. Michael rushed to check out the cowboy's injury. A collective sigh of relief went through the crowd when Michael gave his report. "Nothing is broken, he'll have a hard time walking and riding for a few days, but no lasting damage was done." Marty was declared the winner of the bull riding event.

Six men volunteered to ride the unbroken horses. The winner of that competition was a Swanson ranch hand called Chigger. Mr. Swanson gave prizes to the winners of all the rodeo and racing contestants. Then he announced a change in plans. "We'll be staying here the rest of the day. After we eat again we'll enjoy what our musicians have planned, and *then* we're having a very special surprise."

During the meal and music time, everyone speculated on what the surprise could be. The women, in particular, were stumped. All the men who knew just smiled and kept the secret.

Aaron found a chance to visit with Michael during a lull in activities. "What do you think of the High Meadows, now that you've been up there for a while?"

"It's a wonderful place, Aaron. Cassie and I have really had a great time and it's going to be hard to leave this fall. We're trying to enjoy it all while we can. God called me to be a doctor and I need to go down to where the people will be."

"If we get any more people up here in these mountains, *we'll* need a doctor."

"For your sake, I hope you don't get any more people up here. It's perfect the way it is."

"You're probably right. I don't figure Rand will stay when he gets a few years older. He said he wants to be a lawman."

"You don't say! Well, that's got to be a dangerous life, but we need good, honest lawmen out here."

"He may change his mind, who knows. It's Gabriel I'm wondering about."

"Oh? What do you mean?"

"I don't know. I love Gabriel like a brother, but what's he going to do? It's hard for a black person who's been a slave all his life. I want him to have a *good* life."

"Thanks to you, Gabriel is learning and has a decent chance at a good life. Let me tell you my plans. I'm going to talk to Gabe about being my partner. Cassie's father is building a house for us as a wedding present. It will be a few miles from the store he built and where the town will hopefully be. I want to start a ranch so I don't have to count on what I'll make as a doctor to support my family. Since I'll need a partner to do that, I want it to be Gabriel. Maybe he'll have a wife by this fall." Michael chuckled. "Every time I've seen him today he's been with CeCe."

"There's a good chance that will happen," Aaron said. "Gabe told us he had decided to court her and it doesn't look like she's running away. Dad told me about your ride to save Daniel's life. That must have been quite an ordeal."

"It was scary, but that's when I found out that CeCe would make a wonderful nurse. She helped me with the operation and did a good job. I've ordered some books for her and will start training her as soon as I can. That is, if she marries Gabe and we get a house built for them that is close to ours. That's something I need to talk to you about. Since Mr. Chandler is building our house, I don't think I'll need the gold you gave me. I've spent a little but there's a lot left. I really should give it back to you."

"No way am I taking that money back. God gave it to you. You use it however you want. Maybe you can help Gabe and CeCe if they get married. Maybe build them a house for *their* wedding present."

"Thanks, Aaron. Somehow I figured you would feel that way. God blessed me the day I found you and saw that picture you painted of the Frontier Soldier and Princess Warrior."

"I was blessed too. Helping you to get back to Maxi has been one of the best things I've done in my life. Well, except for finding Bonita and bringing her back as my wife. Angel is going to do a mini concert on her violin in a few minutes. Have you ever heard her play?"

"Yes, a few times at the church services. I'm anxious to hear her play again."

"Well, you go on and listen. I've got some things to do. See you later."

On his way to the front of the Swanson house Aaron ran into Mack going the same direction. "Hey, you going to help with the fireworks?"

"Yes, I'm on the water patrol."

"I hope everything goes well. I didn't think about a prairie fire when I bought the fireworks."

"If we're careful it should be a lot of fun."

Aaron changed the subject. "You seem to be really happy to have Willow as your wife. Are you happy you went with her tribe?"

"Yes, I love Willow and because it's where God wants me I'm at peace with her people. By the way, Aaron, I want to tell you that since we are with her tribe she decided not say anything to Justin about being his sister. She thinks it might just cause trouble, so if you can keep her secret we would appreciate it."

"Of course, I'm glad you both are happy."

While music entertained the crowd, the appointed men carried out their preparations for the fireworks. Scott had suggested they start out with the smaller stuff so the children could get used to the noise and not be scared when the larger rockets were set off. It worked like a charm. As the sun dipped below the western mountains, Scott set off a small whirly-gig that made a soft whirring sound while the rotation sent sparks of red, white and blue in all directions. A collective gasp of surprise rustled through the crowd. Cheers followed as Scot set off more of the smaller fireworks. A loud boom sounded and a single white spot of light lifted high above the ranch. Everyone watched in silent anticipation, until a burst of sound and streams of all colors arched in the sky then slowly drifted toward the earth. Murmurs of approval and laughter mingled with applause.

When the second rocket went off in the same manner, only white and blue streamers shot through the sky instead of the multicolored ones. Katie excitedly asked her mother, "Mama, can I go catch some of the blue stars? I like blue. My dress is blue." Michael answered as he pulled Cassie closer to himself. "We can only *look* at the pretty stars, Katie. If you caught one in your hand it would burn you."

Another burst of light with multi colors lit up the sky. Cassie looked up into Michael's face. "This is wonderful, Michael. I've never seen anything so beautiful. We'll have to thank Aaron for doing this. Do you realize how much he has touched our lives?"

"Yes, and I thank God for our friendship all the time. If it hadn't been for him, I never would have found Maxi…Or *you*."

Epilogue

"THIS IS WONDERFUL, BONITA," Angel said. "Thanks for inviting us to your house."

"You are welcome, but it was not my idea. The mothers suggested it. They said we had all been working so hard to finish putting up our food supplies for the winter that we needed to take a break before we start making soap and candles."

"The grandmothers aren't going to get a break taking care of the children," Angel said, chuckling.

"Yes, but now that we all have our own homes they can just pick up and go home to get away from all the activity," Maxi said. "Well, except for Mama Carmen. I'll make it up to her and take care of Rosa and Maria so she can have a day to herself or a day with Scott."

"That would be a sweet thing to do. If you need any help, Maxi, let me know. I would be glad to come up and help you," Bonita offered.

Maxi noticed that Fawn had been unusually quiet all day. "Are you all right, Fawn? You're not being yourself today. Don't you feel good?"

"Oh, yes, I am fine," Fawn replied. "It's just that...." She hesitated then smiled. "My stomach is a little upset in the mornings, but it will pass."

"You mean you're pregnant?" Maxi asked. The other girls looked at Fawn, waiting for her answer.

"Yes, but you must not say anything. I have not told Marty, yet.

"We won't say anything until you tell us we can, right girls?"

They all pledged their silence, and Fawn changed the subject. "I really love how you've fixed up your house, Bonita. It's so bright and cheerful. Aaron's pictures make it look so nice. Do you think he would paint a picture for me to give to Marty for Christmas?"

"I am sure he would be very happy to paint you a picture. What would you ask him to paint?"

"I would like a picture of Martin to hang on our wall. I'm not sure what we are going to do with another baby. If I have a boy, it will not matter so much, since they can share a room. But if I have a girl we will need another room."

"I'm sure the Swanson's will help build a new place or add on a room," Maxi said.

"Yes, you are right," Fawn agreed. "They are very good to me."

"How are things at your place, Angel?" Maxi asked.

"Busy. Justin is pleased that we've almost doubled the size of the herd in the last few years. There's still sadness about the place, though. We all miss Bill, but the new hand Scott sent down is working out fine. Charity and I went to put flowers on Bill's grave the other day and it broke my heart the way Charity cried. I think she misses him more than any of us. How about you, Maxi? I bet you miss Michael and Cassie?"

"Yes, I miss them and the kids, but they're not so far away that we can't see each other once in a while. When Gabriel and CeCe get married, Aaron and Rand say they *have* to go for the wedding. I've been thinking that maybe Bonita and I will go with them. That way I can see Michael's new house and visit with Cassie. I understand why Michael fell in love with her. She is one special lady."

As the morning quickly slipped away, the four girls laughed together, shared stories about their children, and ate a special lunch that Bonita had prepared. When they decided it was time to go, Maxi and Angel rode to the Swanson ranch with Fawn.

"Thank you for riding home with me," Fawn said. "I hope you aren't going to ride back to the Meadows by yourself, Maxi. Since the men had that run-in with the Sioux a couple of weeks ago, they don't want us off by ourselves."

"Paul said he would meet me at the Paradise and ride home with me."

"That is good, I had a wonderful time," Fawn said. "Thank you for being such good friends to me."

"That goes both ways, Fawn," Angel said. "You are a sister and a friend to all of us girls. Bye, see you in a couple of days."

Maxi and Angel rode side by side, comfortable with the silence between them. Finally, Maxi asked, "Remember after we first met and we were in the trading post where you told the owner your father was somewhere watching over you? I thought you had told him a big, fat, lie."

"I will *never*, as long as I live, forget those days, Maxi."

"I won't either and I realize now you were right. Our Heavenly Father has been watching over us all along. It's like we were *always* in the palm of His hand and He put us right here, where we belong."

THE END

Printed in the United States
By Bookmasters